The Battlefield Recruits

R. B. Gibbons

Kwitch Books

THE BATTLEFIELD RECRUITS
First Edition

ISBN-13: 978-0-9949572-2-1

DEDICATION

To Jessica, who let me do it.

CHAPTER ONE

"Lois kidnapped twenty-four kids, killed at least three of them, and turned Jen catatonic," Ian whispered, his mouth nestled against Erica's ear. "And Renee might be physically fine, but she has those memory issues."

Erica squeezed her eyes shut. Waking up in Ian's arms in her white room was thrilling, but she hadn't been able to savor the moment. All too quickly, the conversation had turned to the Gauntlet.

"I'm not trying to say what she did was right. I'm furious at her for doing it, betraying us in that way. Everything Lois did, pretending she didn't know what was going on…" Erica realized her voice was getting louder just from thinking about what her mother had done. Shaking her head, she took a deep breath, leveling herself. "All I'm saying is she had a reason for locking us in there with all those traps. The Gauntlet was intended to elicit strong emotions, to ensure we'd discover our abilities in a controlled setting. And she might have saved lives by doing it. She certainly saved yours."

"She did. But that doesn't excuse it. Lois confined us in there for days." Ian's voice became rough. "She killed Denise and made me kill Vince."

Erica flinched. That was one way of putting it. Another way was that Erica had tricked Ian into killing Vince. It was the only time Ian had used his ability, ripping magnesium particles from the cement floor onto his hands and igniting them. The white-hot fire enabled him to defeat Vince, but it had left Ian severely burned. Only Lois'

1

cutting-edge medical printer—which could print living cells, healing any wound in seconds—had saved him.

Erica didn't regret Vince's death, but she did regret the pain it was causing Ian.

"I'm not saying that saving your life excuses anything. It's just…" Erica sighed, trying to untangle her twisting emotions. "Lois is my mother. She did all those horrible things, and, while I don't agree with any of them, I understand why she did them.

"If I were in her position, I wouldn't have created the Gauntlet or kidnapped high school students. But I'm not sure what I would have done, either. And I keep coming back to you. If you had materialized those flaming gloves at school rather than in the Gauntlet, you'd be dead. And one thing I know for sure is that I'd rather have you alive than dead."

"Hey, that's unfair," Ian said, adopting an over-the-top, deeply wounded tone. "You've never even known me when I'm dead. At least give poor dead me a chance. I'd be a good listener, and we'd never argue…"

Erica smiled, swatting him on the hip. "Stop it. I'm serious."

Ian's grin faded. "I know. It isn't straightforward. But even so, I'll never forgive your mom for what she did."

"And I'll never ask you to. I don't think I'll ever forgive her either."

"Yeah." Ian squeezed Erica's shoulder. "I wonder how your dad is involved. Did Lois say anything about him?"

"No. He wasn't in the room when Lois' soldiers abducted me." She grimaced. "He must know about the things she's been doing, though. They've been married for decades, and how could she hide something like this from him?"

"I think for now, we should assume all our parents are in on it. Everyone is untrustworthy. And this might not be the Gauntlet, but we're not safe, either. We're still locked in here. We're still prisoners."

"Do you think we should try to escape?"

"Of course. These people kidnapped and tortured us. Who knows what they'll try next?"

"I agree," Erica said. "And they still believe my ability is luck. No need to correct them, right?" Erica had visions of what would happen five seconds into the future—both whenever she desired and spontaneously when something was about to go drastically wrong—

allowing her to change the outcome of events. But, uncertain who they could trust, they had told everyone that Erica was just lucky.

"Yeah. The less they know—the better. And we should maintain this facade."

"This facade?"

Ian's tone was matter of fact. "Pretending I'm your boyfriend so we have an excuse to whisper to each other. I'm sure every room is bugged."

A facade. Erica's stomach clenched. She never would have phrased it that way. The description was so empty, as if there were no real emotion behind their relationship.

Perhaps for him, there wasn't.

Why had she allowed her adolescent crush to grow into so much more? She'd promised Renee, Ian's sister, that she wouldn't let anything develop between her and Ian, yet she'd failed completely.

But for Ian, their relationship was nothing but a facade.

Why didn't he love her? Was she not smart enough? Not pretty enough? Why wasn't she good enough for him?

A facade.

"Yes," Erica said. Her voice sounded hollow, like somebody else was speaking. "Until we figure it out."

"What's wrong?"

Ian didn't even understand how his words hurt her. She felt like running away, telling Lois everything, and never seeing Ian again. Tears brimmed in Erica's eyes, but she blinked them back. "It's everything. I thought you were dead. I thought we had escaped, but we're still trapped. And I thought I could trust my mother. It's so hard."

"Oh, Erica." Ian wrapped his arms around her. "It'll be fine. You have me and Ren."

She didn't have him.

"We'll take care of you," Ian continued. "And who knows? After the Gauntlet, maybe we've just become paranoid. Your mother assured us it will all work out. She could be telling the truth."

"Do you believe that?"

Ian snorted. "No. She's hiding something." His mouth twisted. "Probably many somethings. But what I do believe is that with you, me, and Renee working together, we'll be fine."

After all they'd been through, it was the same old Ian. Optimistic, reassuring, and still completely oblivious to how crazy she was about him.

Enough self-pity. She'd been happy without Ian her whole life, and she'd be happy without him today. "I suppose we're better off than we were a few days ago." Erica rubbed her eyes and pushed back her hair. "Heck, there aren't even any biting ants in this room."

Ian grinned. "Yeah, no animals at all. After the Gauntlet, I was wondering if they'd let me get a cougar. Or let Renee get a moose."

Erica gave a slight smile. Ian's sister mistaking a moose for an ugly horse had been a recurring joke for years.

There was a hesitant knock on the door. "Erica, you in there?"

The room was smaller than Erica's bedroom at home, little more than a bed and a curtained doorway hiding a small bathroom. It took only three steps for Erica to reach the door and open it. Renee, a book in her hand, was waiting there, smiling.

"Hey, Ren," Erica said.

"Hi." Renee raised her eyebrows. "Have you seen—" Renee craned her neck to peer past Erica. Her eyes darkened. "Oh, there he is." She pushed by Erica to talk to Ian. "I went to your room, and you weren't there."

"Yeah. How are you doing?"

"I'm doing great," Renee said flatly. "Though, apparently, not as great as you two." Her eyes fixed upon the messed-up sheets.

Erica wasn't sure if Ian's confused look was sincere or feigned. "We're a couple, you know," he said.

"I thought that was just in the Gauntlet," Renee said pointedly. "Or did I forget something?"

Erica's stomach dropped. After all their planning, was Renee going to blow their cover out of pique? "Well, it started there, but kept going," Erica said. She let her eyes wander away from Renee's face to the ceiling where they were convinced the spy cameras were located. "I want to talk to you about it. But alone." She glanced at Ian. "No offense."

"Why would I be offended at being shunted aside the minute your best friend shows up? No offense at all." Ian's smile was broad and his eyes bright.

"Excellent," Erica said cheerily. "I love a boy who knows his place."

Renee looked as though she had stepped on something squishy.

4

"We can talk later. Lois said I need to show you around. Let's go."

Erica ran her hands over her wrinkled clothes. "I need to get changed first. I slept in this." She selected yoga pants and a T-shirt from the clean pile of clothes in the corner and walked behind the curtain covering the door to the bathroom.

"I'll do that too. Be back in a second…" Ian said. His room was beside hers.

Erica heard the door close. She pushed back the curtain and beckoned to her friend to join her in the bathroom.

"How are you doing, Renee? Really?" Erica asked, mostly to get a better read on how annoyed Renee was to learn that Ian and Erica had spent the night together.

Renee stared at Erica, her body rigid. "Perfect. You?"

That well, huh? "Renee, it's not my fault."

"Not your fault?"

Erica couldn't say what she needed to with the hidden microphones listening. "It's hard to explain…" She turned on the tap, and then paused as if she had just had a thought. As the water continued to run, she turned to pull Renee into a hug. It was like squeezing a cardboard cutout.

"I know I promised, but I couldn't do it," Erica whispered. "I couldn't pretend to love him while feeling nothing. I'm not built that way."

"So what, you're back in seventh grade with a stupid crush on my brother?" Renee said sarcastically.

Erica couldn't lie to her best friend. And she didn't want to. Surely, Renee would understand if she just chose the right words. "Renee, it's not a crush. It's so much more. That time in the Gauntlet was horrible, but also wonderful, because I was with him. Everything he does fills me with joy. It's the most amazing thing ever, like nothing else." Erica couldn't keep the excitement out of her voice.

If anything, Renee got even more rigid. "But you promised. Why are you even telling me this?"

"Because you're my best friend and I want you to understand. It's too big not to share." Her face fell. "And it doesn't matter anyway."

"It doesn't matter? You're composing rancid poetry in his honor. How can it not matter?"

Renee's tone was biting, but Erica ignored it, still trying to explain. "Ian doesn't care at all. He just sees our relationship as a way to talk in private. He told me that this morning."

"Good. At least I can trust one of you."

Erica winced. "You can trust me, Renee. I'm sorry. I couldn't stop myself. But Ian's been clear. Nothing will happen."

"Yeah, right. So you're going to stop pretending to be dating?"

"No. We need to be able to talk privately. At least until we understand what's going on here."

"Of course *you* think that. Well, don't expect me to stand here, listening to your woeful tale of unrequited love. You enjoy your fake boyfriend because you don't have a best friend." Renee pushed Erica away, whipped aside the curtain, and strode out.

Erica stood frozen for a few seconds. She swallowed, and then mechanically continued to change. How could Renee not understand how important this was to her? She had broken her promise to not get emotionally involved with Ian, but how could she not? It wasn't possible to decide not to fall in love.

Someone knocked on the door.

"Just a second." Erica took one last glance in the mirror before opening the door. Ian and his sister were waiting there, Renee hugging her book against her chest like armor. She barely glanced at Erica.

"Let's go," Renee said crisply, spinning around and marching down the corridor.

Ian shot Erica a curious glance, evidently wondering why Renee was suddenly so abrupt, but Erica ignored it. She raced to follow.

"There's not much to see," Renee said in a flat voice as they walked along the white concrete corridor. About every fifteen feet on both sides were steel doors, each with its own hand scanner and keypad. "They call this place the bunker. It's an old repurposed mineshaft. The lowest floors have the Gauntlet, but I've remained on this floor. It's almost entirely bedrooms. You know where I am, and, clearly, both of you already know Erica's room. Cam's in 1306."

Renee walked by the elevator and turned right at a T intersection. Ian, lagging behind slightly, pressed the elevator's call button. It lit up, and Ian and Erica stopped.

Renee turned. "You can call the elevator. But it won't do much good."

The door opened, and Ian pulled Erica inside. He scanned the buttons, his eyes narrowing as he realized that there were forty-five floors.

"Why's that?" Ian asked. He pressed several buttons, but none seemed to register.

Renee shuffled in, pointing to a panel with the outline of a palm print. "It's the same as the doors. Everything's restricted. Only nine, the medical floor, will work. We could go there if you like."

Erica shook her head. "No. We saw it yesterday."

"Suit yourself." Exiting the elevator, Renee continued around the corner, still walking rapidly. "There are a couple of bathrooms. The mess hall is through here. It's always unlocked." She pushed a door open.

To Erica, "mess hall" seemed like a misnomer for the classroom-sized room. Four wooden tables with maroon plastic chairs were near a panel on the wall that—after her time in the Gauntlet—Erica associated with the delivery of food. But the other half of the room was more like a recreation room.

It had several couches and two television sets, each with three different video game consoles attached. Bookshelves holding thousands of books lined two of the walls. Another holding various board games was on the third. In the corner was a wooden craft table, covered with all manner of paint, pens, pencils, pastels, paper, canvases, and glue. In the center of the room, there was even a ping-pong table.

"Wow," Ian said, walking toward the lounge area. "After how bare the rest of this place is, I never would have guessed this was here." Ian bounced one of the table tennis balls. "This is one ugly pool table."

Renee grinned. "We should play a game of H-O-R-S-E. Or M-O-O-S-E," she said, continuing Ian's inside joke about the time she had mistaken a moose for an ugly horse. It was the first time Erica had seen her smile since their conversation in the bathroom. Renee caught her watching, and her face grew grim again. "I'd prefer a pool table. Cam's awful at ping-pong. Maybe he'd put up more of a fight at pool."

Erica wandered over to the bookshelf. She recognized many of the titles, even if she hadn't read them. "The library seems good."

Renee nodded, rolling her eyes. "It's horrible." Perhaps in response to Ian and Erica's confused looks, she added, "Remember my ability? If a bunch of people know something, I know it too."

And it extended beyond knowledge. Renee could also do anything that a bunch of people knew how to do. Erica had seen Renee pick locks, perform astonishing gymnastic feats, and even disable a man twice her weight, all without any training. But her ability came with an unfortunate side effect. Renee's memory had become unreliable. In the Gauntlet, she'd even forgotten her allergy to bean sprouts.

"I know what happens in almost every novel here," Renee continued. "Everything except the obscure stuff, and I'm working my way through those." She held up the book she'd been carrying. "I just finished *A Dissolution of Mind*. There's a reason it's obscure." She ran her finger along the books' spines, and, when she found the right spot, pushed the novel into place.

"Brutal," Ian said. "What about TV?"

"Even worse. Everyone on the East Coast sees everything two hours before us. Sports programs are delayed seven seconds. Local broadcasts are the only thing I haven't seen already. It's like I'm stuck in the 1960s, but without the cool clothes."

Ian walked over to the craft table. "At least there's other stuff to do."

"Yeah." She smirked. "I hate to say it, but I paint better than you now."

Ian grinned wryly.

"Why did they put a light under—" Erica said. She flinched, eyes widening. "Get back. Now." She shuffled back three feet, pulling Ian behind her.

Renee stared at them in bemusement. "What?"

"Renee." Erica stared at her. "Listen to me when I tell you to do something."

Renee sneered. "Whatever."

Erica gestured toward Renee's feet. She looked down and hopped back.

Peeking out from beneath the table was a teenage girl, her dark hair a mess, like she had just woken up from a feverish nightmare.

Ian's mouth dropped. "Wait. Is that…?"

Erica nodded. "I think so." She cautiously stepped toward the girl. "Hi. I'm Erica. Are you Jen?"

CHAPTER TWO

Jen was about five foot six and dressed in the same blue T-shirt and black yoga pants that the rest of them wore. Erica smiled, but Jen's eyes drifted over them like they weren't even there.

She pulled herself out from under the table, stood, and looked to the wall on her left. A brown smudge on it began to glow.

"Hello?" Ian said.

Jen didn't respond.

The glimmer danced over to the bookshelf, alighting on a knot in the wood. Jen walked to it, running her fingers over the whorls. The wood continued to glow beneath her hand.

"Are you able to speak to us?" Erica said hesitantly.

Jen turned to face Erica's direction, her eyes focusing on Erica's left foot. A mole on it began to glow, feeling pleasantly warm. In contrast, the exposed skin on Erica's ankle seemed cold, like she had stepped outside on a chilly morning. Jen knelt, crawled all the way over to Erica, and stroked the spot with her index finger.

Erica remained rigid. She was tempted to pull her foot away, but it seemed mean-spirited. Clearly, something wasn't right with Jen—if that was even who she was. But she seemed fascinated by the spot and wasn't doing any harm.

"Yes, that's my foot," Erica said in a tone used to soothe animals.

Jen pressed down harder, and the skin shifted under her finger, sliding over the bones. She giggled. Then her head turned, and the light hopped over to a screw in the metal leg of the ping-pong table. Jen pulled herself along the floor with her hands until she reached it.

She caressed the glowing screw lovingly.

"That girl is nuts," Renee said. "I can't believe you let her touch your foot like that."

"Don't say that. She can hear you," Erica whispered, staring at her friend disapprovingly.

Renee shook her head. "She's not hearing anything. She doesn't even know we're here."

Erica couldn't disagree. The girl had moved from beneath the table and was now playing with one of the video game controllers, turning it over in her hands, pressing buttons, and flicking the joysticks. The light continued to follow her gaze, jumping around like a manic butterfly.

Erica frowned. "Still. It seems rude."

"Whatever."

"Has she been here long?" Ian said.

"No," Renee said, the ice in her tone melting when she addressed Ian. "First time I've seen her."

"Are you sure she's Jen? I thought Jen was catatonic, locked up in some old folks' home," Ian said.

Renee nodded. "I recognize her from school."

Hearing the door open, Erica finally tore her gaze away from Jen.

"Cam!" Erica and Ian said in unison.

"Hi guys," Cam said, his lips twitching.

Erica ran over and hugged him. "We were so worried when you vanished from the Gauntlet. I'm so glad you're okay."

Cam looked at his feet. His face was fiery, but he was grinning. "Me too."

Ian slapped Cam on the shoulder. "What happened? Tell us everything."

Cam's forehead furrowed. "I woke up here two days ago. That Lois woman said a bunch of stuff. She pretends to be nice, but she made the Gauntlet."

"Yeah," Erica said, keeping her voice carefully neutral. "She's my mother, you know."

"Oh." If it was possible, Cam turned even redder. He looked away from Erica, and then flinched when he saw Jen. She was licking a glowing spot on the floor. "Who's that?"

Ian looked over his shoulder and sighed. "We think it's Jen. She's having some issues."

Cam studied her like she might transform at any moment into a dangerous animal. "Oh." He stepped back.

Two high-pitched beeps came from the dining area.

"Breakfast is here," Renee said. She walked toward the panel on the wall and pulled out a tray holding a pancake breakfast. A few seconds later, after another two beeps, Cam did the same. Eventually, they collected a tray for each of them, assembling at the table.

"It's such a relief to get food," Erica said as she devoured the meal. She glanced at Jen. "I wonder if she'll eat?"

Renee shrugged. "I'm not sure she knows how."

Erica nodded. "I wonder…" She stabbed a fork into a piece of pancake, mopped up some syrup, and walked over to the girl.

Jen ignored her until Erica waved the pancake under her face. Jen's nose glowed, and she touched it with one finger. She opened her mouth, and Erica shoved in the pancake. The light shifted down and disappeared into Jen's mouth. She chewed reflexively before swallowing. Her eyes widened.

The light jumped over to Cam's plate with Jen only a second behind it. Cam had already cut his whole meal into mouth-sized rectangles. She poked at several, seized one, and shoved it in her mouth.

"That's mine," Cam said, and then frowned. "I mean, um… you can have it." He pushed the tray closer to Jen, leaning away from her. "What's that glowing thing?"

Ian shrugged. "We don't know. It seems to go wherever she looks."

"It went in her mouth," Cam said.

"Well, maybe not where she looks. But something like that."

"It's where her attention is focused."

Erica turned to see her mother standing in the doorway. Her stomach tightened.

"Jen creates light and heat on whatever she's thinking about," Lois said, pulling up a chair from the other table. Cam glowered at her, but Lois ignored him.

Erica realized that she was gritting her teeth. She deliberately exhaled. This wasn't the time to fight with her mother, not with everyone else around.

"What's she doing here? I thought she was brain damaged or something." Erica tried to keep the question conversational, but it came out accusatory. She resolved to stay silent until she could better control her voice.

Lois nodded, seemingly not even noticing Erica's tone. "She was. It wasn't our fault. Something happened in the Gauntlet. Her brain was injured, and she became unresponsive to stimuli. She wouldn't have survived an operation to fix the damage, so we placed her in a care facility."

"You did not. You ditched her. Someone found her standing all alone in the street," retorted Ian, making no effort to hide his anger. "She could've died."

Lois' expression grew chilly. "We didn't ditch her, and we didn't leave her in town."

"How did she get there, then?" Ian said.

"That's classified. All you need to know is that we didn't abandon her. On the contrary. When we recovered her, we ensured she had the best care possible from professionals who specialize in supporting people with these kinds of challenges. And even that was temporary, just until we had the means to heal her. Our acquisition of the medical printer provided those means. The wounds were too old for it to address the problems directly, but the printer allowed us to keep her alive while we performed the surgery to fix the worst of her brain injuries. She still has problems, but she's mostly fine."

"She doesn't seem fine." Renee's eyes strained as she tried to look at Jen without making it obvious by turning her head. "She was licking the floor a few minutes ago."

Lois waved her hand dismissively. "I meant physically. Most parts of her brain are intact and functioning. But the brain's more than a collection of cells, and she went through an extreme trauma. We think she'll recover—neurons are amazing at rewiring when needed—but it doesn't happen overnight. It takes time and experiences."

"Experiences like licking the floor," Ian said, sneering. He clearly wasn't buying Lois' explanation.

Lois shrugged. "A seven-month-old baby might do that, and you wouldn't consider it unusual."

Erica's jaw felt warm. She glanced over at Jen and saw her staring back. Erica smiled. The warmth moved up her face, the light momentarily blinding her as it crossed her eyes. Jen's mouth opened in a wondrous smile. She reached down, grabbed a handful of pancake, syrup, and butter, and tried to stuff the glowing mess into Erica's mouth.

Erica nudged Jen's arm away. "No, thank you. I'm full."

Jen tilted her head, smiled, and opened her hand, allowing the mess to fall to the floor, barely missing Erica's lap. Jen wiped her hands on the table, sucked the remaining syrup off her fingers, and hopped out of the room.

Renee grimaced. "Shouldn't she be somewhere else? Why does she have to be here with us?"

"This is where people recover from the Gauntlet, so this is the best place for her," Lois said. "Jen needs to adjust to her experiences, just like you. She isn't dangerous, and interacting with her peers should help her. Besides, this floor is under constant surveillance. If anything goes wrong, we'll know right away."

"That's fine for you to say, but what's the point of this?" Ian growled. "What are we adjusting to?"

Lois' eyes narrowed. "You needn't raise your voice. I'm not the enemy, and you should recognize that better than anyone. After all, I saved you after you nearly died from your ability." She stared at Ian, but he was unmoved, his arms crossed over his chest. "That's why you need to adjust. To learn to control your abilities. If you create those magnesium gloves again when we're not nearby, you will die. My job is to make sure that doesn't happen."

"After all you put us through, that's hard to believe." Ian's voice dripped contempt.

"I understand, and that's another reason you're here. To give you time to process what's happened to you. So you don't do anything reckless."

"And what about afterward?" Erica said. In her ears, her voice sounded shrill, but at least she'd managed to rein in her earlier anger.

"Well, afterward, we're hoping you'll join the Jeemoh team."

"Jeemoh?"

"Yes, we're a government organization created to deal with problems that no other agency can handle. We work with the National Security Agency to take the actions needed to address long-term threats. If the NSA is the brain, Jeemoh is the hand."

Erica chewed on her lower lip. As if they'd ever join Jeemoh after what her mother did to them. Still, this was an opportunity to gather information. "What sort of things have you done?"

"I can't discuss the details of our covert operations. But we cleaned up an oil spill off the coast of California that would have poisoned the beaches for decades. In Washington D.C., we stopped a doomsday cult from infecting four elementary schools with a highly contagious, antibiotic-resistant strain of bubonic plague. That would've had worst-case casualties of over a million. And, we retook a nuclear power plant terrorists had captured and threatened to melt down. Without us, half of Chicago would've been radioactive for generations."

"I don't remember an oil spill," Ian said.

"No, you wouldn't," Lois said breezily. "The effort I'm most proud of—though it isn't as flashy—is super wheat: wheat genetically engineered to handle the temperature and moisture extremes in Eastern Africa. It seems boring, but it could be the best thing we've done. The NSA projects that, over the next fifteen years, it will cause median incomes in Somalia to quintuple, reducing by ninety-three percent terrorist threats of Somali origin. And that's only Somalia."

Ian sneered. "So what, you're just a big Boy Scouts organization, out to make the world a better place? Torturing teenagers is just a side gig?"

Leaning forward, Lois looked at him levelly, her tone no longer conversational. "Ian, let me be clear. Jeemoh is the most influential organization ever created. On any day, the things I do are probably more important than anything any other person on earth is doing— including the President of the United States. I am saving lives and improving the world. Sometimes, as a side effect, innocent people get hurt. I try to minimize casualties, but they are unavoidable.

"Vince's loss was tragic, but it's a cost we have to bear for the greater good. You did what you had to do, and now you have to get over it. What we're doing is too important.

"I want you to see the bigger picture. I want you to join us. But I won't sugarcoat it. If terrorists attack, and the only way I can save New York City is by sacrificing you, I'll do so in a heartbeat and never look back."

"And Erica?" Ian said sullenly. "Would you sacrifice her?"

Lois' face softened as she looked at her daughter. "I'm sorry, Erica. Even you."

"That's horrible," Erica said, recoiling. "I wouldn't do that."

Lois nodded. "I know. I wouldn't expect you to—not today. It *is* horrible. But it's the world I live in. A world where, with the right technology, a handful of people can kill millions. Or even billions. In this world, someone needs to make the tough choices, and that falls on me.

"All that said, I don't want to over-dramatize it. Those situations are uncommon. We take care of our own, prepare well, and rarely lose anyone. I only mention the worst-case scenarios because I want to be completely up-front. You need to understand and accept what could happen if you join Jeemoh."

"And if we don't join you?" Ian said, a clear challenge in his voice.

"You can leave. After we determine that you're not a threat."

"Of course. After *you* determine it."

Lois' eyes narrowed. "Grow up, Ian. I'm in the business of making the world a better place, not creating new threats."

Ian sneered. "Yeah."

Lois looked back at the others, and her tone brightened. "Regardless, you don't need to decide today. There is one small thing we have to deal with, but your primary goal should be to acclimatize to your new abilities and recover from the Gauntlet. Just hang out and enjoy yourself. Treat it like summer vacation before school starts in the fall. Most of the stuff in this room is obvious." She gestured vaguely toward the ping-pong table and television. "On channel three hundred, you can view your experiences in the Gauntlet. Not everyone watches it, but it helps some people.

"Also, we discourage romantic relationships. They cause friction and often escalate into bigger problems. So I expect everyone to sleep in their own bedrooms from here on." She looked pointedly at Erica. Renee's mouth twitched, as if she were holding back a smirk.

"What?" Erica said, her anger rising again. "You don't have·a problem imprisoning us together in the same room for days, but now that we're out, you suddenly become the concerned parent?"

"It's nothing to do with my being your mother. It's a rule we have to ensure everything functions smoothly. And I expect you to abide by it."

Erica rolled her eyes in exasperation.

"So that's it then? The 'one small thing to deal with'?" Ian spat out. "Breaking us up?"

"No." Lois looked at Renee. "Do you remember a girl called Elizabeth Kingly? Our intelligence indicates that you were Elizabeth's babysitter whenever her mom was out of town and her stepfather had to work the evening shift."

Renee paused, and then nodded. "Yes, of course. I babysat her many times." She abruptly jumped to her feet, beginning to pace beside the tables. "What about her?"

"Elizabeth's one of you. She has the same genetic modifications. We expected her to be ready for the Gauntlet in about a decade."

Renee's eyes widened. "Really?"

"Yes. Except something's gone wrong. We don't have accurate information, but she has realized her ability early. It's unprecedented, having an ability manifest at her age. She surprised us all."

"Okay. So why tell me? Is she coming here?"

"Hopefully, yes. But the situation is more complicated than that. We tried to retrieve her, but things went badly, and we lost a squad of soldiers."

Renee stopped walking to stare at Lois. "She killed them? By herself?"

Lois nodded. "Yes. And now we need your help to capture her."

CHAPTER THREE

"What?" Renee said. "You just bragged for twenty minutes about how wonderful your super-secret agency is. And now you want to send me to pick up a girl who killed your toughest soldiers? I don't even work for Jeemoh." She began pacing again, even faster.

Lois smiled wryly. "I appreciate how strange it sounds. But when a problem arises, I will use whatever resources give me the best chance of a positive resolution. I care only about results. Today, that means you."

"Why me?"

"Three reasons. First, she knows you. It's not surprising she reacted poorly to having a bunch of strangers trying to grab her. It's safer using someone she knows. Second, you know her. You've spent enough time with her to understand her personality and quirks better than anyone else available." Renee's brow furrowed, and Lois added, "In a dangerous negotiation, things like that matter.

"Finally, you're adaptable. Your ability enables you to do almost anything. If you need to negotiate, you can. If you need to incapacitate her, you can do that too. When we have poor intelligence, that adaptability is a big advantage."

Renee shook her head, her lips forming a narrow line. "I won't help you abduct someone else. You're dressing it up, but it's still kidnapping an eight-year-old. It's not right."

Erica nodded. Put another kid into Lois' hands? After what Lois did to them? Why on earth would Renee even consider doing that?

"She's an eight-year-old who—in all likelihood—accidentally

killed her stepfather and all the adults who tried to help her," Lois said. "Her ability may not even be under her control. This isn't about us. It's about doing what's right for Elizabeth. She's alone and terrified. And we're the only ones who can help. Are you going to abandon her when she needs you? An innocent child?"

Renee's face fell. "I want to help her. It's just..." She looked at her brother. "What do you think?"

Ian's eyes narrowed. "I think we should do it. All of us. You, me, Erica, and Cam."

Erica's protest died on her lips. Ian was as annoyed at Lois as anyone, yet he wanted to help her with this? What did he see that Erica didn't?

Lois shook her head. "No. We only need Renee. She's the one who knows Elizabeth."

"Fine." Ian's casual shrug made it clear it didn't matter to him either way. He scraped some syrup off his plate with his index finger, popping it in his mouth. "The four of us are a team. If that's your decision, send more soldiers instead."

Lois' eyes bored into Ian, but he didn't even seem to notice.

"We don't need Erica," Renee said, her voice cold. "We can do this without her."

Erica flinched. Her best friend was acting as if she were the enemy.

No. A traitor.

"We do need her." The tiniest bit of obstinacy crept into Ian's tone. "Erica's luck might keep us alive. In the Gauntlet, she saved me more than once."

"Fine." Renee spat out the word. She turned to Lois, her jaw set. "It's all of us, or none of us."

Lois frowned. "Ian can't go. If he uses his ability out there, he'll die. Do you want to be responsible for your brother's death?"

Renee swallowed, pursing her lips.

"I'm going," Ian said firmly to his sister. "I won't use my ability. And if something goes wrong, it's on me, not you." Seeing Renee's dubious expression, he added, "Renee, I don't want to be separated from you again, even for a day."

Renee's features smoothed. "I agree." She looked at Lois. "All of us, or none of us."

Lois scanned their faces and shrugged. "If that's what you want, we can do it that way this time." Touching the face of her watch, she gestured toward the TV. "We know little about what happened. This call from Elizabeth's house came in on our emergency number four hours ago."

The TV screen remained dark, but there was the click of a phone being connected. "Hello?" said a woman crisply. There was no response. "Hello?" the voice asked again. There was some bumping. In the distance, the haunting weeping of a child could be heard. It went on for about a minute until the sound of a door closing came through.

Lois touched her watch again, and the barely noticeable static ceased. "Nobody hung up the phone, but we can't hear anything else. We believe that Elizabeth's stepfather dialed our number, but was killed before he could say anything. That's why we sent in the soldiers. This broadcast is from their camera." Lois looked toward the TV screen again.

The camera jiggled as it approached the wooden door of a two-story white house. Reaching the porch, it spun around momentarily, revealing four male soldiers, each dressed in high-collared black military uniforms with miniature microphones taped to their cheeks. On the side of each of their helmets was a tiny camera lens. In their gloved hands, they held Javelins, the Taser-like weapons that had knocked out Ian in the Gauntlet.

The camera swung back around, bouncing as a heavy black boot kicked the door open.

Clearly valuing speed over stealth, the soldiers rushed inside, their weapons pointed. The camera swept around, revealing a hallway with a closet door on one side, an archway on the other, and the banister of a stairway near the end. Family pictures lined the walls. Arranged on a mat were adult-sized running shoes, polished leather wing tips, and a pair of tiny pink sneakers. Above them, several coats hung on hooks shaped like smiling ducks.

The soldiers inched forward.

"Three o'clock." It wasn't clear to Erica who said the words, but the camera spun to the right, looking through the archway. That room was split into a formal dining room and a living room. A TV was mounted on the wall over a brick fireplace with two couches and a chair arranged in a U, facing it. Sitting on a couch, peering back toward them, was a young blonde girl. Her face was red and her eyes wide.

"Aargh!" The camera swung down and focused on the soldier's feet. Translucent, spaghetti-like strands were rapidly climbing up his legs. In less than a second, they covered everything below his knees, the individual strands seeming to melt together until they looked like plastic wrap. A fraction of a second later, the tendrils were at his waist. The soldier struggled to push the strands away, but his hands slid off. "Help me!"

The image spun around wildly. There were several thuds, and the screen went dark brown.

"He fell over," Lois said clinically. "The camera is pointed at the hardwood floor."

"What is that stuff?" Erica said, trying to remain equally detached, though her heart was pounding. "Those webs?"

"We don't know. It covered the entire bodies of the soldiers in a few seconds. Based on biometrics, the soldiers suffocated. We surmise the substance is impermeable to oxygen."

Erica's eyes widened. "So how do we escape if the same thing happens to us?"

Lois shook her head. "You don't. In all likelihood, if that happens, you die. But we believe Elizabeth won't attack Renee."

"You said that the power might not be under Elizabeth's control. It's insane even to try this," Erica protested.

"So don't." Lois' lips thinned. "Renee has the best chance of stopping Elizabeth. There's no need for the rest of you to risk yourselves."

Ian stood up. "Yes, there is. We're a team. It's all of us or none of us."

Erica shook her head. Ian and Cam didn't need to be involved. Her ability to see the future might make a difference, but Ian couldn't use his ability, and Cam had neither the judgment nor the people skills to negotiate with a dangerous girl. One misstep could ruin everything. "It should just be Renee and me. Nobody else needs to be there."

Ian's face hardened. "Erica, we're a team. We're all going."

Erica knew that look. He would insist, they'd argue, and she doubted she'd win. "Fine. We're a team. What's the plan?"

Lois nodded, businesslike. "We'll outfit you in the best equipment we have available—bulletproof armor, video cameras, Javelins, radio communicators. Everything you need. We'll have three squads. One will enter the house with you through the front door, one through the back, and we'll hold one in reserve. You will enter and—"

"This is a stupid plan," Erica said, no longer caring if her anger was clear in her voice and on her face. "We're not doing it that way."

Lois flinched. "What?"

Inwardly, Erica smiled. Two weeks ago, she never would have used such a tone with her mother. She thought she saw the hint of a grin dance across Ian's lips. "That's a dumb plan, Mother. You told me last night that these abilities are often triggered by strong emotions. How did you expect a kid would react to a bunch of strangers kicking down her door? And now you want us to barge in there, looking like more soldiers, doing the exact thing that got your first team killed? No way. That's just dumb."

Erica turned toward Renee. "We'll dress casually. Like we would on a normal day. Jeans and T-shirts or whatever. We're not taking the cameras or Javelins. We don't want to arouse suspicion. If we have to incapacitate Lizzy, Cam can use his Javelin."

Cam's ability enabled him to absorb electronics into his body. In the Gauntlet, he had absorbed a Javelin into his right arm, and it remained there since.

"Renee will act like Lizzy's babysitter, and we'll be Renee's friends," Erica continued. "We'll persuade Lizzy to come here with us. She won't get excited, and nobody will get hurt."

Ian and Renee were nodding. Cam, huddled up and nervously rubbing his legs, didn't appear as convinced, but he had seemed skeptical of the entire affair. In any case, he kept his mouth shut.

Lois rested her chin on her fist and thought for a few seconds. "Fine. But the driver of the van will be one of ours."

"No," Erica said. "Ian will drive. If Elizabeth sees a soldier, she might freak out."

"That's non-negotiable. We need someone there in case something goes wrong. But she'll stay in the van and won't be in uniform."

"Fine," Erica said, her tone saying the opposite. "But she'd better realize that if Lizzy sees her, it could all be over."

Lois nodded. "She won't mess up. Lauren is disciplined." She tapped on the face of her watch, and then spoke. "Sergeant Irenic, come to the mess hall on thirteen immediately. Dress like a mother."

A tinny voice emanated from the watch. "Rog—like what?"

"You heard me right. Dress like a mother."

"Okay. Roger."

Lois tapped the watch again, breaking the connection.

They discussed the plan in more detail, agreeing that Renee, as the one talking to Elizabeth, would lead the encounter. The key priority was to get the girl into the van without upsetting her. Nevertheless, Lois emphasized with a hard look that—if the circumstances required it—they should use any means to defend themselves and eliminate Elizabeth as a threat.

Ian had nodded blandly at that, perhaps not realizing the implications of what Lois was suggesting. Erica wanted to roll her eyes at his naiveté. Perhaps Ian still viewed Lizzy as an innocent girl, but Erica had seen those soldiers die. After the threads began their attack, it had taken only a few seconds to engulf the men. Though it might seem monstrous, Cam might need to use his Javelin to incapacitate Lizzy. Shocking the eight-year-old into unconsciousness might be necessary. Maybe Ian didn't recognize that possibility, but Erica certainly did.

After a few minutes, a soldier arrived, carrying civilian clothes. Erica had to hold back a fatalistic smile. It was the same jeans and T-shirt she had been wearing the night she was abducted from her house and dropped into the Gauntlet.

They changed in the bathrooms and regrouped in the mess hall. Waiting there was an angular woman with cropped dark hair who must have been easily over six feet tall. She had paired a fluffy pink sweater with a knee-length brown skirt and sensible black flats. Despite the informality of her dress, she stood rigidly, as if each vertebra in her spine were glued to an invisible wall. She reminded Erica of a plastic action figure dressed by a fashion-challenged three-year-old.

Lois gestured to the newcomer with an open palm. "This is Sergeant Irenic. She might look like a mother, but don't be fooled. She's one of our best. Listen to what she says, because she may save your life."

Lois introduced the others. "On this mission, you can call the Sergeant 'Mom', Cam. The rest of you can call her 'Mrs. Fletcher'. Understand?" Everyone nodded. "Any questions before we get going?"

Cam hesitatingly put up his hand. Lois nodded at him. "Yes?"

"If Elizabeth's hungry, what should we do?"

She blinked at him. "Get her a snack before coming out."

"What if there's no food? Should we go shopping or to a corner store or something?"

"What? No."

"But if she's hungry, then—"

"Cam, just listen to what Renee and the others say. They'll figure it out," interrupted Irenic. "Now, are there any other *important* questions?" she asked loudly, glaring at each of them in turn, almost daring them to open their mouths.

"Nope. Thanks, Mom." Cam's grin was like that of a golden retriever.

Irenic sighed.

She walked them to the elevator, scanned her hand, and pressed a button near the top. The elevator opened onto a large concrete garage with all manner of vehicles, from sedans and sports cars to vans and military jeeps. There was even a tank.

Irenic guided them to the side door of a windowless black van. Ian entered first with Renee shoving past Erica to sit beside him, leaving Erica and Cam to take the seats in the next row. A steel wall separated the driver from the passengers, though Irenic warned them if they had any concerns just to speak.

Even with the air conditioning on, Erica felt warm and claustrophobic in the dimly lit vehicle. After Irenic's no-nonsense gruffness, it felt odd to make small talk. So, Erica was left gazing at the back of Ian's head, wondering if he found the situation as uncomfortable as she did. She wished she had been able to sit beside him.

Erica sighed and rapped her knuckles on the wall. She wondered how many people the soldiers had abducted in this vehicle.

The ride seemed to last for hours, but the van eventually stopped. As she hopped out, Erica looked at the sky, shading her face. She hadn't seen daylight for days. After the dimness of the van, the sun hurt her eyes.

It was disorienting. She'd had no real sense of time for so long. "Is it late?" Erica asked Irenic through the passenger window.

Irenic was holding the handset of what looked like a CB radio. "Irenic here. Mission's a go. Over." She turned to Erica. "What?"

"I asked what time it was."

"1624," Irenic said without glancing at the watch on her wrist.

"Oh," Erica said, squinting as she tried to orient herself. They were parked in front of a large house with a brown door, the one the soldiers had opened only seconds before they perished.

Were they walking into their deaths? Trembling, Erica bit her lip. This was what they had agreed to. She couldn't back out now.

"We'll take it from here," she said with a confidence she didn't feel.

"Yes. Renee and I will go check on Elizabeth now, Mom," Cam said loudly and woodenly.

Huddled together, they walked toward the front steps like death-row prisoners taking their last stroll. They paused in front of the door.

"Are you ready, Renee?" Ian whispered. "Have you planned out what you'll say?"

"No," Renee said, her voice shaky. "I'm not sure." Her face was pale.

Ian squeezed her hand reassuringly. "Don't worry, you'll be fine. Start by talking about things she likes. Games you've played together. That sort of thing. She needs to understand that you're her friend."

Renee swallowed, looking back at the van. "That's the problem. I was faking it when I told Lois I knew her. I don't remember her at all."

CHAPTER FOUR

"You used to take care of Lizzy almost every week, Ren," Ian murmured.

"Did I? I don't remember any of it."

"What do you mean?" Ian hissed. "It was years. Just try harder."

Renee glowered at him. "I don't remember her, okay? It's not a question of trying. It's like it never happened."

Ian shook his head in frustration. "But—"

"Give Renee a break, Ian," Erica said. She rested her hand on her friend's arm, but Renee shook it off. "We'll work around it. You don't remember Lizzy, but she'll recognize you. Pretend to know her. Just don't mention any specifics."

Renee's mouth twisted. "No problem. Ignorance I can do."

Erica's smile was rueful. "Perfect. Let's give this a try." She rang the doorbell.

They waited a minute, but nobody came to the door, and the house was silent.

"I guess nobody's home," Cam said. "Oh well. We can try again later." He stepped back.

Erica gripped his arm. "Try the door, Ren."

Cautiously, Renee turned the knob, and the door swung open. She froze.

Inside were the still bodies of the soldiers, four prone, one staring sightlessly at the ceiling. There was no trace of the strands that had overcome them.

Erica scanned the hallway, but there was no sign of the girl. Erica carefully stepped inside, knelt, and touched her fingers to the neck of the closest man. He was cold and had no pulse. "Dead," she murmured. She didn't bother checking the others.

Ian, Renee, and Cam stood rooted outside, craning their necks to spot any threats in the corridor without entering the building.

"Say something, Ren," Erica whispered. She gestured to the archway a few yards down the hall. "She's probably in there."

Renee swallowed. She poked her head inside and said loudly, "Elizabeth? It's Renee. Your mom sent me to check on you."

The words seemed to echo in the stillness. After a few seconds, a thin voice replied from the living room. "I'm in here, Renee."

Renee glanced at the others. She inched inside the house and through the arch with the others behind her.

As they had seen on the video, the living room had two ragged couches and an armchair arranged around a fireplace. A skinny blonde girl wearing a dress covered in bright yellow sunflowers sat on a couch, clutching her knees to her chest as though she were trying to squeeze herself into a box. Tears had streaked her cheeks. Though it wasn't cold, the girl was shivering.

"Hi, Lizzy. How are you doing?" Renee asked. The hardwood floor squeaked as she slowly approached the girl.

"I want Mommy. When is she coming home?" Elizabeth said. Her voice sounded hollow.

"She sent us to pick you up," Renee said, sitting down on the far end of the couch from Lizzy. "See? That's Ian, my brother, and two of my friends, Cam and Erica."

The frail girl glanced at them, and then looked back to Renee. "You'll take me to my mom?"

"Yes. It's a bit of a drive. But we can take you there."

Lizzy looked down, squeezing her legs even tighter. "Does she know?"

Renee swallowed. "Does she know what?"

"That I was bad? That the police want to take me away?"

Renee's brow furrowed. She put a reassuring hand upon the girl's knee. "You don't have to worry about that, Lizzy."

Tears slid down Lizzy's cheeks. "I do. Everything's wrong now. Daddy said that if I were bad, the police would come. They'd put me in jail, and Mommy wouldn't love me anymore. Does Mommy know what happened?" She crossed her arms, her hands leaving white prints on her legs.

Renee shook her head. "No, I don't think so."

The girl looked up, hope shining in her eyes. "Don't tell her, Renee." Her voice was insistent, the words coming out in a flood. "I'll go with the police. I don't care if it's a day or even longer. You can tell Mommy I ran away. And when the police are done with me, I'll come back. And Mommy won't hate me."

Renee slid over on the couch, putting her arm around the girl. "It's fine, Lizzy. Your mom loves you, and no matter what happens, she'll always love you."

"She won't. She won't! Please don't tell her, Renee. You can't tell her."

"Shh, it's fine, Lizzy. I won't tell her. I promise." Renee hugged the girl, rocking her gently until the tears subsided. "Are you ready to go now?"

"To Mommy?"

Renee shook her head. "I think maybe to the police. We can talk with them, clear up everything. Afterward, you can see your mommy again. How does that sound?"

Elizabeth swallowed, her face sagging. She nodded once, a quick motion, like a pigeon retrieving a seed.

Erica felt the tension leak out of her body. They weren't dealing with a monster. Lizzy was just a frightened girl. She must have done something wrong. Maybe she broke a lamp or spilled some milk, and then assumed that the soldiers were policemen coming to arrest her. But Renee had been perfect, using Lizzy's own words to convince her to come with them.

Renee smiled reassuringly. "Is there anything you'd like to take with you? A toy or something?"

The girl pondered the question, her face serious. "Nettles."

"Nettles?" Renee said.

A confused look flashed across Lizzy's face. "Nettles the donkey. My stuffy."

"Of course. Where is he?"

"Upstairs. In Mommy's bedroom."

Ian nodded. "I'll go up—"

Ian turning to leave. Two steps. Lizzy's eyes widening. "No!"

Ian clawing at tendrils, climbing up his legs, covering his face.

The vision almost staggered Erica with its intensity. "Wait. Stop,

Ian," she hissed.

Lizzy's eyes grew large, and she blanched. "No!" she shouted, leaping to her feet.

Ian stared down at his legs. Translucent threads were climbing up his body, like a fast-motion video of vines scaling the side of a building.

"Erica," Ian said, the panic clear in his voice.

Erica turned to Cam. "Cam—"

Cam raising his hand. His Javelin hitting Lizzy's chest. Lizzy bending unnaturally backward. Her head smashing the hearth.

"No, wait," Erica said as Cam lifted his arm, preparing to fire.

None of the others had twisted so violently when hit with the Javelin. Had Lizzy's spine snapped? Her head had hit the brick fireplace so hard. What was going on?

Renee shook the girl. "Stop it, Lizzy." Then her hands slid away, her palms coated in threads.

"Erica, help me," Ian screamed. And then, his cries stopped.

Though it killed her, Erica ignored him. She needed time to think. The Javelin's jolt was so intense. Had it killed Lizzy? Would hitting the fireplace? Why did Lizzy react so differently? The Javelins had just knocked out everyone else.

Lizzy was short and skinny. Those Javelins took down Vince, and he was bigger than most men.

Cam's weapon wasn't calibrated for a child. A jolt could kill her.

But Lizzy was an innocent kid. She was frightened, nothing more. They couldn't murder her. They needed to stop her, not kill her.

Erica heard a thump behind her and glanced back. Ian writhed on the floor. The threads covering him had melted together like plastic wrap. He clawed at his mouth, struggling futilely to punch a hole in the substance.

Renee was thrashing on the couch, her head entombed.

Erica had thought for too long. She should have let Cam fire, and now Ian and Renee would die. "Elizabeth, stop it!"

Running. Webs on her feet, her arms. Her mouth.

She sprinted toward the girl. But the tendrils were climbing up her legs, caressing her, pulling at her. They felt snug and welcoming, a warm bed on a rainy day.

If she could only reach Lizzy, she could…

But she knew she wouldn't. The threads already gripped her chest.

She had no time left. She leaped forward. Lizzy dodged, diving back onto the couch.

"Fire, Cam!"

As the tendrils tickled her chin, Erica saw the cable fly past her right arm, the dart embedding itself in Lizzy's stomach. The jolt of electricity caused the girl's upper body to wrench to the side and then whip back.

The webbing vanished. Erica shook her arms and legs. She spun toward Ian. He lay on the floor, gasping as the cable retracted into Cam's arm. The burnt photocopier smell of the Javelin was heavy upon the air.

Panting, Renee raised her body, shaking her head as if flicking off the last remnants of the threads. She looked at Erica, her eyes wide, and then at the girl lying beside her.

Cautiously, Renee grasped Lizzy's wrist. "There's no pulse," she said, licking her lips. "Should we do something?"

Erica's tone did nothing to hide her disgust that Renee thought it was even a question. "Of course. She's a kid."

Renee nodded. Kneeling, she lifted Lizzy down to the floor. With both hands, she pushed down on her chest and then blew air into her mouth. Lizzy didn't stir.

Her face grim, Renee pumped Elizabeth's chest again, hard. Erica heard a crack.

"Don't worry about that," Renee said robotically. "It's her ribs breaking. It happens."

Erica's knees shook. She dropped down on the couch.

Renee continued to pump, but shook her head. "Her heart's stopped. We need a defibrillator. To shock her."

Erica winced. She turned to Cam. "Can you do that?"

"Yes." Cam clawed at his wrist. Somehow, he dug the Javelin's dart out from under his skin, its cable tugging at his flesh as if it were sinew ripped from his arm. Renee seized the dart and stabbed it into Lizzy's chest.

"Is it possible to ease up on the voltage?" Erica said.

Cam nodded.

"Then do it. Shock her," Renee said. She leaned back from the body. "Now."

Lizzy's tiny body spasmed at the surge of electricity. Erica had to look away.

"Stop." Renee touched Lizzy's wrist, and then put her cheek near Lizzy's mouth. "She has a pulse. She's breathing."

Erica finally exhaled. "Way to go, Ren." She wiped her forehead with the back of her wrist.

Ian had caught his breath and risen to his feet. He walked by Renee and Lizzy, picked up a poker from the hearth, and turned around, pulling on Erica's hand. "Follow me," he whispered. "Before Lizzy wakes up. Hurry."

Erica's brow furrowed. "What are you going to do with that?"

Ian put a finger to his lips and crept through the archway. Confused, Erica and the others followed.

"I think Renee's convinced Lizzy to come with us," Ian said loudly. "But we need to do something with these bodies. If Lizzy sees them, she might freak out again."

Walking to the closest body, Ian smashed the camera on the front of the soldier's helmet against the floor, and then struck the headset with the poker. Moving deliberately to avoid the sightline of any of the cameras, he destroyed the rest of the surveillance equipment.

When Ian finished, he turned to the others. "I doubt we have much time, but this is our chance to escape. That's why I wanted everyone on this mission."

Ian wanted to leave now? Erica felt slightly queasy. "What about Lizzy?"

"We've done what we said we would. She's no longer a threat. We can't take her with us, but Lois can deal with her now. She's set up to handle her. We aren't."

"I agree with that. But—" Erica squeezed her eyes shut. Why was she hesitating? She was furious at Lois. Every night since the abduction, she'd dreamed of escaping. "I mean, Jeemoh doesn't sound that bad." Even to herself, her objection sounded weak.

Ian turned on her, his eyes wide in disbelief. "They locked us up, starved us, and tortured us for days." He took a deep breath, speaking more calmly. "Your mom has a good story, but we can't trust her. She might be telling the truth about Jeemoh, but maybe it's all another lie. And we'll never again get such a good chance to get away."

Erica nodded, finally figuring out her indecision. It was just instinct. Even after all that had happened, she still wanted to believe Lois, trust that her mother would take care of her.

But that was stupid. Ian was right. She wouldn't even consider staying if Jeemoh were led by a stranger.

And really, Lois might as well be a stranger. She acted like her mom, but how could Erica be certain what was real and what was fake? Erica's whole life was a huge lie constructed by Lois. Until yesterday, Lois hadn't even told her she was adopted. She couldn't believe anything Lois said.

But what about Ian? "Wouldn't we be risking your life?" Erica said. "Lois said that if you use your ability without access to their medical printer, you'll die."

"I'm not worried about that." Ian gestured toward the room behind them. "Lizzy encased me in unbreakable webbing. If my ability doesn't surface in a situation like that, I imagine I'm safe. It's worth the risk." He stared at her. "What is it? Don't you want to escape?"

Erica shook her head. "No, it's not that. I'm confused, that's all. Everything's happening so fast." She looked at the others. "Do you think we should run?"

Cam nodded vigorously, and Renee said, "Absolutely. After what they did to us, I don't know why you're even thinking about it."

The others found it an easy decision, and Erica certainly wouldn't return on her own. "Okay. Grab anything useful off these soldiers. I'm going upstairs."

Ian raised one eyebrow. "Didn't I tell you to go to the bathroom before we left?"

Erica grinned manically. "No, it's not that. Lizzy freaked out when you took two steps toward the stairs. Before we leave her alone, I want to make sure there's nothing dangerous up there."

"We don't have time. They have to be suspicious about the broken cameras. How long will they wait before they decide we aren't bringing her out?"

"She's a little girl. I'll be fast." She strode down the hallway.

"I'm coming with you," Ian said, catching up to her.

Together, they raced up the stairs, knocking a family picture off the wall in their haste. At the top was a short hallway with three doors, two on either side and one at the end. By unspoken agreement, they split up to search faster.

Lizzy's room had a single bed with a pink bedspread and cartoon characters painted on the walls. A toy house and some dolls lay in one corner, and an even larger basket filled with stuffed animals rested in another. A neat shelf of children's books was against a wall.

Nothing seemed out of place, so after a quick scan of the room, Erica kept moving. "Lizzy's room looks normal," she reported to Ian.

"I got a bathroom. If you like, they have a bottle of bubble bath we could try out."

Erica flushed. Then she felt a pain in her stomach and sobered instantly. "Nobody's watching us. You don't have to pretend," she said flatly.

Ian turned red. "I'm sorry... I was just joking. I didn't mean anything by it." He looked away.

"I know," Erica said. She knew all too well he'd never say something like that to her and mean it.

Ian swallowed. "I'm sorry."

Erica nodded. "We have to hurry." She strode forward and turned the handle of the last door. It opened into the master bedroom, dim with the curtains drawn.

Glancing around, Erica flicked on the lights. A king-sized bed with a plain cream bedspread took up much of the space. Against one wall was a meticulously arranged cherry-colored vanity with a large mirror and a dresser.

On the floor beside the bed lay a middle-aged man dressed in casual clothes. Beside him lay a phone and a stuffed donkey.

"Lizzy's stepdad," Ian said solemnly. He knelt, lifted the man's wrist for a few seconds, and gently placed it back down. "He's dead."

"Nothing seems dangerous," Erica said in a slightly confused tone. She picked up the stuffed animal. "I guess Lizzy was scared of the body."

Ian nodded. "We need to go."

Together, they returned downstairs. While Ian shared their discoveries with the others, Erica laid Nettles down beside the unconscious girl.

"Find anything good?" Erica asked as she entered the hallway.

"A bunch of neat stuff," Renee said. "Javelins, flashlights, knives, handcuffs, rope, a first aid kit, and some syringes."

Erica grimaced. "That's what they used when they abducted me."

Cam waved a metallic device in the air. "I found a smartphone. It's an Android device, but kind of strange." He held it up to his ear as if to listen for a dial tone.

The moment the phone touched his head, the flesh swelled up and enveloped it.

"Ah!" Cam shouted, struggling against the skin that had engulfed his hand. "It's got me. I mean, I've got me." Finally, he tore his hand free. "That's better." He shook his head. "Actually, no. Not really."

A distinct bulging rectangle remained on the side of Cam's head where the phone had disappeared.

"Does it hurt?" Ian asked hesitatingly. He stepped forward, raising his hand to touch the swollen area.

Flesh stretched and rippled. The phone slid beneath Cam's skin to the back of his skull.

"It feels very…" Cam's eyes widened. "Oh." He froze, and his body went rigid. He pitched forward.

Thanks to a vision, Erica was there in time to cushion Cam's fall and ease him onto the floor. She was about to check for a pulse when a second vision struck.

"Hold it," she said, jerking up her hand.

Ian froze. Renee, rolling her eyes, knelt beside Cam.

The door opened. Sergeant Irenic peered in.

CHAPTER FIVE

"Where's Elizabeth?" Irenic said. Her eyes stopped upon Cam, lying on the floor. "He dead?"

"I don't think so." Ian somehow kept his tone casual. "Lizzy's in there. Unconscious. She freaked out when we tried to leave, and Cam had to stun her." He gestured toward the living room. Irenic strode off in that direction.

"We've got to go," hissed Ian the instant Irenic disappeared through the archway.

"But what about Cam?" Renee said. She flipped him over. It was like rotating a rigid mannequin. Renee waved her hand in front of his staring eyes. He didn't respond.

"There's no time. We need to leave him," Ian whispered.

"No," Erica said.

"We can't carry him, and, even if we could, they can probably track that phone in his head. Besides, he's seriously hurt. He needs medical attention. If anyone can help him, Jeemoh can."

Erica bit her lip, nodding reluctantly. She felt terrible leaving him, but she'd figure out a way to free him later. Or was she fooling herself?

Erica was about to reach for the door handle when Irenic stepped back into the hall. "What did you say you did to Lizzy?" Irenic said, her eyes narrow.

"Cam used his Javelin. She'll be fine," Erica said confidently, though she had no idea whether that was true.

Irenic gave a curt nod and slid her left foot forward, bending her knees slightly. "I will escort you to the van now."

Ian speaking. Irenic moving. Ian falling.

Before Ian could say anything, Erica jumped in. "Yes. Of course." She cast about for something to say, visions twisting through her mind. Any indication that they didn't want to go to the van seemed to result in a fight. But what other choice did they have? Meekly returning to their prison? That wasn't an option.

Though Erica's visions didn't extend far enough to be certain, she was confident that between her and Renee, they ought to be able to win a confrontation with Irenic. Heck, Renee had the knowledge and skills of the top fighters in the world. In the Gauntlet, she'd defeated Vince with ease. She could probably handle Irenic on her own.

But Ian might be hard-pressed to defend himself. Her vision showed her how quickly he'd go down if he wasn't prepared for an attack, and more than half the scenarios had Irenic targeting him first. She should warn him.

In the Gauntlet yesterday, she'd used the word "ready" to indicate a potential threat.

"Is everyone *ready* to go?" Erica said, her tone dripping with significance. Ian's eyes narrowed. He repositioned his legs to lower his center of gravity slightly.

Erica turned to Irenic. "We're leaving. You can't stop—"

Though Ian was five feet from Irenic, she closed the distance almost faster than Erica's eyes could track her. Ian tried to raise his arms to defend himself, but, even after Erica's warning, he was too slow. Irenic's fist struck his chin, and he crumpled to the ground.

Renee jumped to her feet, barely dodging as Irenic pounced. She scampered back a few paces down the hall. Irenic followed, ignoring Erica.

Irenic's explosive speed seemed impossible. "You have an ability?" Erica said, her eyes wide. "Super speed?"

Sergeant Irenic smirked. "No." She leaped at Renee, grabbed her about the waist, lifted her from the ground, and threw her to the floor. Renee landed heavily, with Irenic on top of her.

Renee wrapped her legs around Irenic's torso and clutched at her upper body. Irenic casually blocked Renee's hands and elbowed her in the chin. Renee pushed aside the next elbow, but Irenic began striking the side of her head. When Renee tried to block that, Irenic targeted her neck and torso. No matter what Renee tried, Irenic seemed to have an answer.

Irenic clearly wasn't Vince. Renee was outmatched, already bleeding from a cut over her eye. She was mounting a desperate defense, but it was only a matter of time.

It hadn't even occurred to Erica that Sergeant Irenic might be as good a fighter as Renee, and that Irenic's huge weight and strength advantage would turn the fight into a slaughter. And if Renee couldn't defeat her, what hope did Erica have? She hesitated, unsure of how to help.

Finally, Renee twisted her way out from under Irenic. She turned her back for an instant to push away and scamper down the hall, but Irenic was too quick. Her forearm encircled Renee's throat and her hands locked near her ear.

It was Erica's opportunity. Irenic was facing away, focusing on maintaining the choke against Renee's grasping hands.

Erica picked up the poker that Ian had discarded after destroying the cameras. It took five light footsteps to close the distance between her and Irenic and twelve visions to find the right place to strike.

With all her strength, Erica smashed the poker into the back of Irenic's head.

Irenic was out instantly. Her grasp weakened, allowing Renee, gasping, to tear Irenic's hands from her neck. Renee spun around to attack, pausing only when she saw Irenic's prone form on the floor.

"Are you okay, Ren?" Erica said.

Renee shook her head. "No." She wiped away the blood on her face with the bottom of her shirt and crawled over to the first aid kit they had found earlier. She rifled through it, taking out bandages and a small pair of scissors, and then tossed a small, plastic tube over to Erica. "Give Ian a whiff of that," she said.

Erica caught the tube and knelt beside Ian. She opened the cap and waved it under Ian's nose. He shook his head, his eyes opening.

"Where are we? What happened?" Ian's chin seemed misshapen.

"We're still in Lizzy's house. Irenic knocked you out, but Renee and I beat her," Erica said quickly, unsure how much time they had until Irenic recovered. "Can you stand?"

"I don't know. Maybe."

Erica helped him to his feet. Ian was pale and winced whenever his head moved, but he didn't complain. He looked over at Renee, who was bandaging the cut on her brow. "Looks like you got it worse than me, Renee."

Renee nodded.

Ian looked back at Erica. "Is this really how you planned it?"

Erica winced. What else could she have done? Her visions showed a fight was inevitable if they didn't obey Irenic's order to go to the van.

Or was it? Maybe she simply didn't come up with the right response, the magic phrase to say to Irenic to allow them to escape without a confrontation. She hadn't even tried that hard because she'd taken it for granted that Renee could steamroll anyone in their path. She'd misjudged the situation completely.

And that was only minutes after messing up with Lizzy. She should have ordered Cam to shoot Lizzy the second her tendrils ensnared Ian. Because she delayed the shot, Lizzy's threads had nearly killed all of them. She kept making the wrong decisions.

Erica looked at the floor, her lower lip quivering. "No. I thought we'd... Never mind. It doesn't matter."

Ian put his arm around her shoulders. "Are you okay, Erica?"

Erica's mouth twisted. "Better than Renee." She looked at Cam, still lying supine on the floor, and then turned to her battered friend. Renee seemed to have stopped the worst of the bleeding. "Ready to go?"

"Yeah," Renee said tersely, shoving everything back into the first aid kid. "They'll be here soon."

They each took a Javelin, handcuffs, and a knife, and Ian borrowed a bag near the door to carry some rope and the first aid kit. After Erica cracked open the door, they peered outside. Nothing seemed amiss. It looked like the typical quiet suburban Saturday. Even some children were playing on a lawn several houses down, oblivious to what had transpired in Lizzy's house.

"Let's go. Calmly," Erica said, though her heart was still beating furiously.

Taking one last glance at Cam, they shuffled out of the house, walking in the direction of their school. Few people were on the sidewalk, but whenever someone passed Renee looked away to hide the worst of the bruises on her face. If anyone spared them a second glance, Erica didn't notice.

After about ten blocks, Renee turned to Ian and said angrily. "Why do you do everything Erica says? Why can't you think for yourself?"

"What?" Ian said, astonishment on his face. "Where did that come from?"

"I know I'm not imagining it. You're not even her real boyfriend. So why do you keep sucking up to her?"

"Auditioning for the role?" Ian said brightly.

Erica's heart leaped.

"No, I'm kidding." Ian's smile felt like a dagger in Erica's side. "It's because we lied about her ability. Not to fool you, just the others. We didn't get the chance to tell you until now. You see, Erica can see the future. When she tells you to do something, do it."

"What?"

Ian explained Erica's visions, going all the way back to their time in the Gauntlet. "We told everyone that Erica's just lucky because if Jeemoh knew the truth, they'd be able to find ways to attack her outside her five-second view into the future. Like spiking her meal with a poison whose effects aren't noticeable until a few minutes after she's eaten."

Renee shook her head, frustration clear upon her face. "I don't get it. If these visions tell you what's about to happen, why is this going so badly? Why didn't Cam shoot Lizzy before she wrapped Ian in her web? Why did you let Irenic beat me up? You could have shot her with a Javelin the instant she opened the door."

Erica looked at the ground. "It didn't occur to me. It all happened so fast. There wasn't enough time to think."

"Well, think faster, because you nearly got me killed back there. My right zygomatic bone is broken, and I bet I have a concussion." At Ian's look, she spat out. "My cheekbone." She quickened her pace.

Erica sighed, rubbing her forehead. Renee was only saying what they all knew—how utterly ineffective Erica had been. Even with the visions, she couldn't make the right decisions. She'd all but killed Ian yesterday in the Gauntlet and, after Irenic's punch, he was probably concussed too.

Ian glanced over at her. "Renee's just frustrated." He snagged Erica's elbow, swinging her into a hug.

She pushed her face into his shoulder. He caressed her hair and stroked her back.

"Don't worry about it. You're doing great," Ian murmured.

The solid warmth of Ian's embrace reminded her of their time alone in the Gauntlet, when their relationship had seemed so real. But it wasn't. He didn't like her that way. He'd all but said so to her face.

So why couldn't she get over him? It hurt so much.

It didn't matter. She would take what she could get. They had no future, but she had this moment at least. She was lying to herself, but the blissful lie was better than the painful truth.

Erica relaxed in Ian's arms and exhaled, releasing the tension. "You're good at this," she whispered. She leaned back to look at his face, and her mouth twisted. "You'll be a great boyfriend for someone."

He smiled, continuing to hold her. "I hope so. I've been practicing hard." He bent his face down slightly toward hers, frowned, and turned to look at his sister. Renee had walked about fifty feet ahead of them and was lying on the grass, staring up at the sky. "We should keep going."

Erica nodded.

They hurried to catch up to Renee. She sighed dramatically as they approached.

Ian ignored it. "We should figure out what to do next. We don't have any money, and it will be dark in a few hours."

"Money isn't difficult," Renee said. "I can pick a lock on a house or we can pickpocket someone."

Erica shook her head. "I'd rather not commit felonies unless we're desperate."

Renee shrugged. "With your ability, we won't get caught."

"It's not about whether we get caught. It's not right."

Renee rolled her eyes. "It's nothing compared to what they did to us in the Gauntlet."

"Still." Erica pursed her lips. "Money's a secondary issue, anyway. Lois will try to recapture us. We need to figure out how to evade her."

"That's tricky," Ian said. "At minimum, all our parents were in on this, but it might be half the people in Battlefield. I'd say we should go to the police, but they're probably involved too."

"And who knows Jeemoh's other capabilities?" Renee said. "I wonder if they've hacked into government surveillance."

Erica's brow furrowed. "They don't need to hack. Lois made a big deal of claiming they work with the National Security Agency. They are the government."

Renee swallowed. "Yeah. I forgot." Her head tilted. "So if that's the case, can they view footage from traffic cameras? What about other cameras, like storefront cameras or the security cameras in banks? Can they access people's private cell phones?" She grimaced. "It's so hard to know what to do without understanding their capabilities."

Ian's lips twisted in a fatalistic grin. "And that's before you factor in abilities. Maybe someone on their team has the ability to pinpoint instantly where any person is."

Erica frowned. "If they have someone like that, we'll never escape." She gnawed on her lip. "The problem is that we don't know enough about Jeemoh. What they can do, their limitations, or their goals. Heck, maybe everything Lois said was true, and we're making a huge mistake by fleeing."

"It's never a mistake to run away from someone trying to imprison you," Renee said.

Ian nodded. "Even if Jeemoh is everything they claim, they can't kidnap and torture us, and then expect us to forget about it because they're the 'good guys'."

An idea had been percolating through Erica's head. She was reluctant to suggest it, both because her recent decisions had been abysmal and because it sounded insane. But there didn't seem to be many reasonable options, so perhaps it was time to consider the unreasonable ones.

"I've been thinking about what you said, Ren." Erica spoke slowly, trying to lay out her logic as clearly as possible. "That if we understood Jeemoh's limitations, we could figure out how to get them off our tails. So how about this? We go to my house and ask my dad about them."

Ian looked at Erica as if she had suggested they shave their heads and join a traveling circus.

"Are you nuts?" Renee said.

"I wouldn't rule it out," Erica said, smiling. "Because it kind of makes sense to me. We need information about Jeemoh. After being married to Lois for decades, my dad must know something."

"He'll call her the second he lays eyes on us," Renee said.

"We can prevent that."

"Lois will know. There will be security systems and cameras."

Erica shook her head. "I don't think so. Lois wouldn't install surveillance equipment in her own home. Spying on other people is cool. Being spied on? Not so much."

"Even if that's true, I don't see how it helps us," Renee said. "If Lois is lying to us, why wouldn't your dad lie too?"

"I'm not sure he's involved in this to the same degree as Lois. He wasn't there when they abducted me, and Lois didn't mention him. And shouldn't your ability allow you to tell if someone's lying? Like, by reading body language?" The more she spoke, the more confident Erica became.

Renee nodded. "It's not that clear cut, but yeah, I can recognize the signs. Except with people trained to hide them."

"Interesting." Ian's eyes lit up. "So was Lois lying to us earlier about what Jeemoh does?"

Renee turned pink. She stared down at a bright green caterpillar inching its way across the sidewalk. "I... I'm sorry. I can't remember that conversation at all."

"What?" Ian exclaimed. "That was only a few hours ago."

Renee sighed. "Yeah. Some stays, some goes. It's bad. Please don't tell anyone. You're my brother and my best friend, so I can trust you guys, right?"

Best friend? Had Renee forgotten the earlier conversation where she'd disavowed her friendship with Erica? And if so, did Erica have a responsibility to remind her?

"Of course," Erica said quickly.

"The truth is," Renee continued, "I've been faking it, pretending I know what people are talking about, going with the flow." She giggled, but it sounded forced. "I imagine I can improvise as well as any actor. I'm practicing constantly. Or maybe that doesn't matter because I won't remember it. Is it possible for me to learn new skills if I forget everything I do?" She flinched as she saw the expression on Erica's face. "What? Did we discuss this already?"

Erica sat down beside Renee and put her arm around her shoulders. "No, it's not that. I just didn't realize this was so hard for you. You're doing great at hiding it. We won't tell anyone, and we'll do our best to help. Let us handle conversations when you struggle."

Renee rubbed her eyes with the back of her hand. "Thanks, Erica. I'll do that." Her mouth curled. "Or maybe I won't because I'll forget that was my plan." She stared down the street into the distance for a few seconds before turning back to Erica. "But anyway, it still seems risky confronting your dad."

Erica nodded. "It is risky, but we need to take risks. If we 'play it safe' and do nothing, it's only a matter of time before Jeemoh finds us. We need to find out what we can before my mom starts searching for us. Besides, I have money at home. Even if we learn nothing, we'll at least get some cash."

"It's certainly the last place they'd expect us to go," Ian said. "I agree with Renee that it's nuts, but I trust you even when you're nuts." He grinned at Erica. "Maybe even more when you're nuts. I think we should try it."

Renee shrugged. "Fine. If you both want to."

Ian reached down and helped pull the two girls up to standing positions. "Great. Let's go talk to the father of my new girlfriend. I hope he doesn't own a shotgun."

CHAPTER SIX

The walk to Erica's house took twenty minutes. They remained alert, scanning the streets for any suspicious vehicles or any other sign that Jeemoh had spotted them, but saw nothing. Erica wasn't surprised. They were dealing with a covert agency. If Jeemoh found them, it was unlikely they'd realize it until black-uniformed soldiers surrounded them.

Erica's dad's car was in the driveway.

"So how should we do this?" Ian said. "Just walk in there and say 'hi'?"

Erica nodded. She hadn't thought through the details of confronting her dad.

"No," Renee said firmly. "We're here because he's either part of Jeemoh, or co-operating with Jeemoh, which is basically the same thing. We can't give him a chance to call anyone."

"What do you think we should do?" Erica said.

"Is there a key under the doormat?"

"Under the big rock near that tree."

"I'll handle it. Wait near the front door. I'll call out when I'm done." She raised both eyebrows mischievously and glided toward the rock.

"Wait," Erica hissed. "What are you doing?"

Renee returned a languid smile while palming the key. "Don't worry. I won't kill him." She brandished the knife she'd taken from a soldier. "There are more elegant ways to use a knife than stabbing someone in the eyes, neck, or gut…" She crept to the front door.

Suddenly concerned, Erica tried to follow, but Ian hooked her arm. "We shouldn't interfere. She knows what she's doing."

"It's my dad."

"And it's Renee. She won't hurt him."

Erica wasn't so sure, but it was too late anyway. Renee had already unlocked the door and slipped inside. "Well, let's at least go over there, like she said."

Ian nodded. Together, they walked to the door. After seeing Renee's casual stealth, Erica felt clumsy, but at least she didn't trip on anything. They only had to wait a few seconds before Renee called out. They entered the house.

"We're in the office."

With the front door closed, they no longer had to worry about someone finding their actions suspicious. They sprinted upstairs to the office beside Erica's bedroom.

Philip, Erica's dad, lay prone on the floor beside his desk, his hands cuffed behind him. Renee perched on his back, holding the knife to his throat. Otherwise, the room was undisturbed, legal books neatly arranged on the bookshelf and diplomas on the wall. Philip's laptop still displayed the legal brief he had been reviewing.

"Easy-peasey," Renee said, grinning. "Help me tie him to the chair."

"This is the biggest mistake you've ever made, young woman," Philip said in a matter-of-fact tone as Ian hauled him to his knees. "But it's not too late to— What? Renee?" He quickly looked toward Ian and Erica.

Philip's face collapsed. "Erica. It's you."

Erica could see tears in his eyes. She wanted nothing more than to hug him, but she pushed the emotion aside. Philip might be faking his reaction—he'd fooled her for her entire life. She had to be hard.

"Sit down," Erica said firmly.

Renee shoved him into the office chair and tied his hands, still cuffed, to it. "Yes. It's your darling daughter. And us."

Renee's tone implied unspoken threats, but Philip didn't seem to notice. "After you disappeared, I thought I'd never see you again. I can't believe you're here."

"Yeah, we made it," Erica said, keeping her voice neutral. "And now we want to know why we were taken."

Philip pursed his lips, his eyes darting to the open door. "Oh.

But… what do you know so far? How did you get away?"

Renee stood up, spun Philip's chair around, and bent down so her face was inches from his. "What's your name?"

"What?" Philip said weakly. "You know me, Renee."

In a single quick motion, Renee stabbed the knife into the back of the chair behind Philip's right shoulder. He blanched, looking at Erica. "I'm Philip. Erica's dad."

Renee smiled. "That's better. It's like this. We've been through a lot the past week, and we're here to get answers. Not give answers. Understand?"

Philip nodded, trembling.

They had to be ruthless, but this was a bit too much. Erica stepped forward to tug at Renee's shoulder. "Maybe we should tone things down, Ren."

Renee shrugged. "Sure. No harm in trying your way first." She stepped a few paces back, smiling sweetly. "We can always do other things later if it seems more productive." She flipped the knife in the air and caught it by the handle.

"Perfect." Erica pulled out the second office chair and sat facing her father. "Dad, we're looking for information about Jeemoh. We want to understand what you know about it, and what you do for them."

"What I do?" Philip shook his head. "I do nothing. That's your mom's thing." At Erica's warning look, he sighed. "Look, I'm glad you've found out about Jeemoh. If I'd told you about it before, I'm not sure what Lois would've done. But now that you know, it's different. I'll share everything. I *want* to share everything." If Philip was anything but earnest, Erica didn't see it.

"So tell me, then."

"It all started twenty years ago. We moved to Battlefield when Lois got a government research job. That work transformed into Jeemoh. Your mom pretends to be an oncologist—well, she is an oncologist—but that's mostly a cover. She works with cancer patients for a few hours a day and spends the rest of her time on Jeemoh.

"I'm not privy to the details. The only time I asked her about it was about fifteen years ago when the organization began using the 'Jeemoh' moniker. Lois didn't want to discuss it at all. When I pressed her, she resorted to threats. Horrible threats. If I spoke about Jeemoh to anyone, she'd make my worst nightmares come true. My only role was to shut up and be your dad."

Philip's head hung low. "That's what I did."

Erica looked to Renee. "Is he telling the truth?"

"Probably."

Philip nodded. "Of course I am. Despite your mother's threats, I've kept thinking about it over the years, and I've figured a few things out. And I'll note that these are speculations. But they are educated speculations, based on what I've seen.

"Jeemoh has something to do with genetic engineering of humans—something that is highly restricted but technically legal in the USA. I think Jeemoh's responsible for the disappearances of all those kids over the last few years." His eyes grew dark. "I suspect that Lois is using them as human test subjects."

"You believed Lois was taking kids to use as guinea pigs, but did nothing?" Erica cried indignantly.

Philip shook his head. "I wanted to do something, but I had no choice. Her threats were unthinkable. There was no way to fight back. I just closed my eyes to what was happening."

Erica looked at her father contemptuously, her voice growing louder as she spoke. "How could you ignore it? I don't care if she said she'd kill you. These were innocent kids, and it's not like you don't know how to navigate the legal system."

"She didn't threaten to kill me."

"You said she did."

Philip swallowed. "No, she didn't threaten *me*. She threatened *you*. She said she'd take you away." His voice was low, barely above a whisper. "And she didn't put it in so many words, but it was clear what she meant. She'd use you in her experiments."

He stared at an invisible spot on the floor in front of him. "I had no choice. I did as she said. Kept quiet. As long I was here, I figured I could at least protect you." Philip shook his head, wilting even further. "But it didn't matter. She took you anyway. And since then, I've been playing dumb, trying to figure out the best way to confront her." He looked up at Erica. "Are you hurt? What did they do to you? After Jennifer and Alexander, I've been going insane, thinking about what might have happened."

Erica ignored the questions. She swiveled her chair toward her friends. "I believe him. Do you?"

Renee gave a slight nod.

Ian raised an eyebrow. "Well, he's a lawyer, the closest thing to a professional liar. But he seems sincere."

Erica considered her options. She probably couldn't read him as well as Renee, but all of her dad's body language seemed consistent with his story. And if he wasn't working with Lois, perhaps he could help them. *Could he truly be the dad she knew?* In that case, she should tell him everything.

Yet, it was hard to be certain. Her dad had hidden the truth for years. Maybe he was lying to her right now. Maybe he'd report everything they said to Lois.

But it couldn't hurt to share information Jeemoh already had. Even if Philip turned out to be a Jeemoh collaborator, he wouldn't learn anything new. That was the place to start.

"Let me tell you what happened. Some parts might seem unbelievable." Erica smiled ruefully. "Though maybe not. You've already seen what Renee can do."

Erica described their experiences, both in the Gauntlet and afterward, implying her sham relationship with Ian was real and her ability was luck. Philip listened silently.

After she concluded, Philip turned to Renee. "What happened on September 13, 1974?"

Renee looked bored, as if the question were beneath her. "The USSR tested a nuclear bomb. A French ambassador was abducted. *The Rockford Files* was broadcast for the first time."

Philip nodded. "It's also the day I was born. Why's Buckley versus Valeo significant?"

"The Supreme Court decided to limit contributions from individuals to political campaigns. But, as part of free speech, corporations could spend as much as they wanted to promote a candidate as long as they didn't directly tell anyone to vote for them."

Philip looked back to Erica. "This story is difficult to believe, but Renee's ability is convincing evidence." He shook his head. "So, what do you propose to do now?"

Erica scratched the back of one leg with her other foot. "I'm not sure. We came here hoping to get information about Jeemoh, but you know less than we do. Lois made it sound like this great organization that worked for humanity. But from what you say, there's no way we should join her." She leaned forward. "I'm leaning toward fleeing."

Ian nodded.

"I don't think we should have this conversation in front of your dad," Renee said.

Philip didn't look the least bit upset at her statement, but just nodded, in full lawyer mode. "You're wise to be wary. I'm on Erica's side, but I have no way of proving that to you. Similarly, though I trust Erica, I have no evidence this isn't a trap for me set by Lois.

"Nevertheless, it makes sense for us to work together. If Jeemoh is as you describe, it's irrelevant whether I work for them. If they have the resources you claim they do, you have almost no hope of escape. There's little to lose by trusting me." Despite the handcuffs, he seemed unruffled as he made his case, pivoting to face his daughter. "The same goes for me. I only stayed with Lois to protect you, Erica. If you are working with her to trick me, I've lost regardless of what I do." His mouth twisted. "In that scenario, I can't imagine how trusting you now would make things any worse."

Renee stared at him, her eyebrows upraised. "You really are a lawyer."

Philip nodded. "I am. So how about releasing me, and we'll figure out what I can do to help?"

Both Renee and Ian turned to Erica. She rubbed her chin. Everything her dad said seemed reasonable, and she didn't get a lying vibe. Yet, Lois had lied to her for years without her being the least bit suspicious, so perhaps she shouldn't be too quick to trust her gut feelings. Maybe she just wanted to believe that something in her life was real, that one of her parents still loved her.

But, even putting her emotions aside, her dad had a good argument. If Jeemoh was as Lois described, they were naive to think they could escape so easily. Jeemoh would track them down regardless of what they did with Philip. But if he were trustworthy, having his support might make a difference. He'd been married to Lois for decades. Surely, he understood her better than anyone.

If her dad was a potential ally, then she was the one who needed to take the first step.

"I believe him," she said firmly. "Release him."

Philip blinked several times, and his cheeks turned pink. "Thank you, honey."

Renee unlocked the handcuffs and slashed through his bonds with her knife. The instant the rope fell, Philip stood.

"May I?" he said to Erica, holding his arms wide.

"You're not even my real dad."

"I never wanted to hide that from you. But believe me; I love you as much as any father ever loved a daughter. For the last seventeen years, you've been the only thing that mattered to me."

Erica nodded, her emotions churning.

Philip hugged her like she'd been away for years. "I truly thought I'd lost you, Erica. I've been imagining so many horrible things, trying to decide how and when to confront your mother. Thank God you're safe."

Could she trust him? He'd lived with Lois for so long, yet he sounded so sincere. She relaxed into the hug. It felt like home.

"I don't want to interrupt," Ian interjected, "but we need to decide what to do. Philip could be right about the difficulty in running. In that case, we've got to fight." Ian's uncertainty was reflected in his eyes. "Right?"

Philip broke the hug, returning to his chair. "I'm not sure. Why do you want to fight her?"

"You told us that Lois is evil."

Philip shook his head. "It's not that simple. Lois isn't evil at all. At least, I don't think she is."

"But you said that she threatened to take away Erica, to do all sorts of sick experiments on her," Renee protested. "To me, that doesn't scream 'goodness and light'."

"Yes. She did. But that wasn't because she's evil. That was because she's like a pit bull. Once she gets her teeth into something, she never lets go."

Renee drummed on the desk with the eraser on a pencil. "I don't get what you're saying."

"Let me tell you about our third date. We went to the movies and were on our way back to her house to drop her off. We were driving through this neighborhood, and a Labrador jumped in front of the car. The memory of the thud as it hit the bumper still makes me cringe.

"We stopped and ran back to the poor animal. But this dog was in terrible shape. It was covered in blood, its leg broken, two of its ribs sticking out through its fur. And it looked at us with these big brown eyes that said, 'I know I'm done for. Please. Just make the pain stop.'

"Well, your mother took off her coat, wrapped up the dog in it, and picked it up. It bit her, but Lois didn't even try to get free. She carried it to the car with its teeth still embedded in her wrist. She laid it down in the backseat, and only then pried its jaws open. 'We're finding a vet,' she said.

"By this point, it was after midnight, and this was before the days of twenty-four-hour animal hospitals. But your mom cross-referenced the ads for veterinarians in the yellow pages to the addresses in the white pages. So, at one in the morning, covered in the animal's blood, we pounded on doors, looking for a vet to help us.

"The first two told her they could give the dog a fast death. The third, still in his pajamas, worked on that animal for hours.

"The dog didn't have a collar. The next day, after getting no sleep the night before, Lois knocked on all the doors in the neighborhood, trying to find the owner. Eventually, we concluded it was a stray. We took it in ourselves, and it passed away five years later.

"That animal shouldn't have survived. With anyone else, it wouldn't have. But this was Lois. It wasn't even her dog, but she did what she believed was right, regardless of the consequences to her or anyone else."

Philip shook his head. "Lois isn't evil. She's relentless. Only someone like Lois could have kept Jeemoh hidden for so long, with so many people involved. She'll do whatever it takes to achieve her goal. She doesn't care about compromise or human frailties. Temporary pain is nothing if it's necessary to accomplish her plan."

"So do you think what's she's doing is right?" Erica said, her tone conveying her astonishment. "She's done horrible things."

"Frankly, her judgment is usually correct. If she believes something is for the greater good, it probably is. And I admire her persistence. It's why I fell in love with her. But I disagree with her methods. You can't just wave a 'greater good' flag and claim that's all that matters. What's more—"

The phone rang.

"Should I get that?" Philip said. Erica nodded.

"Hello?" Philip's eyes widened, and his face froze. "Just a sec." He held out the phone to Erica. "It's your mother."

CHAPTER SEVEN

Erica pressed the mute button on the phone's keypad. "Should we run?" She kept her voice steady, but her arms were trembling.

"She knows we're here. We need to leave now," Ian said breathlessly.

Philip shook his head dubiously. "If she's calling, it's already too late. Lois wouldn't give up the advantage of surprise unless she didn't need it."

Renee crawled to the window, lifting one eye above the sill. "The street's blocked off for construction. Three windowless vans on the street. Four people in civilian clothes sitting on lawn chairs in front of the house. The neighborhood looks busy. Lots of people on the sidewalk." She squinted. "And I see two... no, make that three, snipers." Carefully, without raising her head, she tugged the curtains closed, and then turned back to Erica. "Your mom is thorough."

"I wonder if any of them have abilities or if they're just soldiers," Ian said, his eyes darting from face to face.

"Doesn't matter for now. We have to talk." Steeling herself, Erica unmuted the phone and lifted it to her ear. "Hello?"

"Hi, Erica. So I take it you've decided not to join us?" Lois sounded calm.

It was too early to tip her hand. "No, not at all. We haven't decided yet."

"Really? For someone still considering it, you seem rather uncooperative."

"Didn't you say that people coming out of the Gauntlet often have emotional issues? Consider this an emotional outburst."

"You gave Sergeant Irenic a concussion."

"No worse than what she did to Ian and Renee. We wanted to leave, and she was trying to stop us."

"You injured Lizzy's spine and broke her ribs. We suspect her heart stopped."

"What is it you said? Any means to eliminate a threat?"

Lois sighed. "Yes, but killing her was supposed to be a last resort. I thought I could trust your judgment, Erica. She's a little girl."

Her mother was right. She should have handled the situation better. By delaying Cam's shot, she had nearly allowed Lizzy to kill them all. Even then, despite Erica's efforts, Lizzy had almost died. If Renee and Cam hadn't been there, she would have.

She had messed up, big time. "I know. It was my fault. It didn't go the way I planned."

"At least your dad is alive. You didn't hurt him, did you? He's not as tough as Irenic."

Erica looked at her father. He was rubbing his right wrist where the ropes had cut into his skin, and his face seemed lopsided. Was his cheek swollen? What did Renee do to take him down, anyway?

"Well... Dad's not badly hurt." Erica bit her lip. "As far as I can tell..."

"What? What are you doing, Erica? He's your dad. He's not involved with Jeemoh at all."

"I'm sorry. You're right. We were only—"

Ian tore the phone from Erica's hand, his earlier trepidation gone. "Lois, cut the crap. You have no moral high ground. You sent us to capture a girl who'd already killed your elite team, and we took her alive. We decided not to return right away to the people who abducted us, and, when your goon tried to force us to, we defended ourselves. And now we're having a pleasant conversation with our kidnapper's spouse. We did nothing wrong, and Erica's been great. If anything, we deserve praise for our restraint."

Ian paused to breathe, shook his head, and said, "I'm not done talking. It will work like this. We will spend an hour discussing whether we want to go back to your headquarters with you. At the end of that hour, you will call us, and we will tell you our decision. If you try to come in this house, there will be fatalities."

Ian stared at the phone for a few seconds before pushing a button to end the call. "Stupid wireless phone. After that tirade, I should be slamming it into its cradle to emphasize my point."

Erica grinned. "It was quite the outburst."

Ian shook his head. "Sorry. She annoyed me. I can't believe that she was trying to make you feel bad about what happened. You've been awesome." He looked at Renee. "We've all been awesome."

Renee smiled. "I agree."

Erica gave a wan smile. "Yeah. Renee's been great." Erica appreciated Ian's enthusiasm, but she wasn't going to pretend she'd done well. Maybe without her ability, she would've been satisfied with how things turned out. But now she could see her mistakes and correct them before they happened. Everything she did ought to be perfect. But it was so far from that.

In the Gauntlet, her failure had killed Denise, and today was the second time she'd nearly killed Ian. She hadn't even been able to stop Irenic—a normal human—from beating up Renee. They trusted her to look out for them, and she let them down, over and over again.

Philip had been watching Erica's face. "If there are snipers, we should close all the curtains." He turned to Ian and Renee. "You do downstairs, and we'll do up here."

Renee nodded. "And we'll barricade the doors. It won't keep them out, but might slow them down." She and Ian scrambled downstairs while Erica and her dad crawled to Erica's bedroom.

Crouching to avoid the window's sightline, Erica tugged at the curtains.

Her dad just watched, concern etched on his face. "What's wrong, Erica? You look upset."

The window blocked, Erica sat with her legs outstretched and her back against the wall. "It's nothing, Dad." She kicked at a pen on the floor, nudging it toward her desk.

"It's not nothing. Tell me."

Erica sighed. "It's... I don't know. I feel so useless. Like I can't do anything right." She shook her head. "Renee's amazing. Almost anything you can think of, she can do perfectly. Ian can't even use his ability, but even so, he's great. He stands up for Renee and me. You saw how he wouldn't back down from Lois. He's always like that, fighting for what he believes is right.

"And then I look at myself, and everything I do is *wrong*." Erica's stomach clenched. It hurt to admit the truth. "This luck ability is providing me with a huge advantage, yet I still manage to ruin everything. Even the small stuff, like that phone call. I should have stood firm, but I didn't. I crumbled. Ian had to take over so I didn't mess it up.

"I'm terrified of what will happen. I feel like the next time I make a mistake, someone will get killed." Erica couldn't keep the desperation out of her voice, and she gave up trying. "And I'm not making a big deal out of nothing. If I had been better, a tiny bit smarter, Denise wouldn't have died." Erica folded at the waist, putting her face in her hands. "Next time it will probably be Ian or Renee."

Her dad put his hand on her shoulder. It was warm and steady.

"Erica, you went through a lot in the Gauntlet. More than anyone should ever have to go through. You survived, and that wasn't just luck. It was because of the choices you made. And they weren't easy decisions. They were tough choices, and you chose a path that kept you, Renee, and Ian alive."

Philip's eyes grew distant. "You know, the thing that impressed me the most about your mom wasn't her persistence. It was her willingness to make the tough decisions. Even when she didn't have enough information, she'd make the call. More often than not, she was right. If she made a mistake, she'd learn from it, but wouldn't spend a single second regretting it.

"You're like her, Erica. You're smart, and your decisions are almost always correct. But you're still young and haven't figured that out. And in this situation, you need to.

"Trust yourself. You don't need to be perfect. Leave your regrets behind. Don't agonize over past mistakes and don't apologize for doing what you think is best. Not even to your mother."

Was her dad just saying that to make her feel better? She'd made so many blunders, and her friends always seemed to suffer the consequences.

On the other hand, Ian and Renee were alive. Even Lizzy had survived, which might not have been true if Erica hadn't delayed Cam's shot.

And her dad was right about Lois. She had abducted high school students, locked them in the Gauntlet, and even killed them, indirectly. Yet, Lois seemed to regret nothing. She was confident in her decisions. That confidence let her do what needed to be done.

Erica wasn't like that though. Whenever she was alone, she saw in her mind every mistake she'd made, like a TV commercial played over and over until it was etched in her consciousness. It was maddening.

Erica sighed. She was home, and now all she wanted was to curl up in her bed, pull the sheets over her head, and let the others deal with the world.

But she couldn't. She had made mistakes, but regardless of that, she couldn't keep on like this, crippled by doubts. She needed to be decisive and quick to act, not fearful that anything she did would result in someone's death.

Erica's lip curled. With her ability, she had the potential to make a difference in the world, to save countless lives, either working with Lois or against her. She had no room for self-pity or remorse. The stakes were too high.

Her judgment *was* good, and her visions only improved her ability to make correct decisions. She wouldn't be perfect. She knew that by now. But she would do the best she could, without regrets.

She sat up, her eyes clear. "Yeah. I can't dwell on the past. Regret is useless. It doesn't help me at all."

Philip nodded, smiling wistfully. "It's a hard lesson to learn, but it's part of growing up. Either you allow the regrets to overwhelm you, or you recognize that you did the best you could, learn from the situation, and leave the self-condemnation behind."

Erica stood. She wouldn't dwell on things she couldn't change. She would be resolute, decisive.

But first, she would close some curtains.

Erica and Philip secured the master bedroom and went downstairs. Renee and Ian had already dealt with the windows and the front door and were jamming an armchair into the space between the back door and the wall. Erica and her dad helped them with the final positioning, and then they all gathered around the dining room table to discuss what to do.

To Erica, it felt surreal. The last time she sat in that chair was only hours before Jeemoh's soldiers abducted her. Back then, her parents had called her paranoid for claiming there was some sort of conspiracy behind her schoolmates' disappearances. Turned out her wildest theories had grossly underestimated the truth.

"So there's fifty minutes left to figure out if we want to join Lois, or try to fight our way out of here. Does anyone see any other options?" Erica said decisively.

Heads shook around the table.

"The problem is we came here to get the information to help us make that decision, but we've learned nothing." Renee glanced at Philip. "No offense."

He shrugged. "I'm glad you came, regardless."

Ian looked at Erica, his expression sober. "We should fight. Even if we're surrounded, our chances of escaping now must be better than if we're locked up in the bunker. And who knows what Lois will do if we surrender after what we did to Irenic."

Erica gnawed on her lip. "I'm not sure if we can turn our backs on Lois and forget about her, even if we escape this house."

"Yes, we can," Ian said. "We're not children. Between Renee's abilities and your luck, it ought to be easy to get money. We can leave the state or even the country."

Erica nodded. "I didn't mean from a practical perspective. I meant ethically." In response to Ian's confused expression, she added, "I see two possibilities. Either Lois is doing what she says, trying to improve the world. Or that's a cover, and she's got a larger plan that she doesn't want to share with us—probably because it's horrible. If we're in the first scenario, do we really want to be standing on the sidelines when we could be saving lives? If we're in the second, can we ignore it and let her do whatever she wants?"

"Heck, yes," Renee said, as if it were the most obvious decision ever. "It's not our job to fix everything that's wrong with the world. We have our own problems to deal with."

Ian's dissatisfaction with Renee's response was clear on his face. "No. We're talking about someone who kidnapped and tortured teenagers. If she's doing things even worse than that, we can't ignore it. We need to figure out what she's doing and stop her."

Erica nodded. Ian always saw where she was coming from. "That's my point," she said to Renee. "Remember how you felt before they grabbed us? That everyone who could prevent these abductions was ignoring them? Do you really want to be one of those people who looks the other way?"

"But..." Renee closed her eyes briefly, and then groaned, shaking her head. "Fine. We can't leave. What should we do?"

"We can't discover the truth from the outside." Erica folded her hands on the table, her gaze unwavering. "We need to join Jeemoh."

#

Erica opened the door, raised her hands, and strolled onto the grass. The men and women sitting on the lawn chairs leaped to their feet.

"Don't move," said the man in the red golf shirt.

"You guys are all about giving orders, aren't you?" Erica said, her tone mocking. Her mother had bullied her on the phone, but only because Erica had allowed her to. She would not repeat that mistake.

She continued to walk forward. They wouldn't shoot her, and even if they tried, she'd see it well before it happened. "Does anyone actually listen to you?"

The man blinked. "Yes." He paused for two seconds, and his eyes grew distant. "You still have twenty-one minutes."

Erica shrugged. "We decided to join Jeemoh. We debated whether we should come out right away, or play a couple of video games to use up our time. But we figured you'd be bored, so we decided not to leave you waiting."

"That's a good decision." The man slipped his hand into a pocket above his right knee. When he pulled it out, Erica could see a glint of metal in his hand. "Keeping your hands at your sides, you're going to walk to the closest van, open the side door, and sit in the middle row. I will place these handcuffs on the floor and close the door. Then, you'll lock one of the cuffs on your right wrist and the other on the metal loop hanging from the ceiling of the van. Start moving now."

Erica was now within five feet of the man. "Yeah, I don't think so. We're part of the same team now. If you want prisoners," she said firmly, gesturing to the south, "Battlefield High is over there. Kidnap some of them because we're not those teenagers anymore."

The man's eyes bulged. He swallowed deeply.

A black wireless microphone was clipped to his collar. "Maybe it would be faster if I talk to Lois directly," Erica said. Slowly, she reached for the microphone, detaching it from his shirt. "Earphone?" she said, holding out her palm.

Numbly, the man pulled an earplug from his ear and placed it on her hand.

"Eww. Gross." She held it up to her ear.

"Hi, Erica. Decided to join us after all?" Erica could hear the smile in Lois' voice.

"Yes. But we won't be carted away like convicts."

"I understand. Go to the first van. It's the same one as before. Cam and Sergeant Irenic are inside."

"Irenic's still in the field?"

Lois chucked mirthlessly. "She wouldn't have it any other way. She obeys orders perfectly, but you can't tell her to do anything. You'll see..."

She'd have to think about that later. Erica looked to Ian and Renee, standing on the stoop behind her, and gestured at the vehicle. "We're going in that."

Together, they sauntered across the grass to the van.

An idea spontaneously occurred to Erica. "One other thing. I want to see Dad regularly and call him whenever I like," she said into the microphone.

Lois took a few seconds to respond. "That's not a good idea. So far, I've kept him out of all this. Do you really want to drag him in?"

"Yes." Erica wasn't sure if her dad was trustworthy, but he had been helpful so far. And if Lois disapproved, it was probably a good thing. "I'm not willing to cut him out of my life."

Lois sighed. "Fine. See you back at the bunker."

Erica slid open the van and peered inside. Cam was in one of the backseats, comatose, held in a sitting position only by the seatbelt crossing his chest. At the front and back sat two new men dressed in police uniforms.

Curious, Erica peered through the passenger window. Irenic sat in the driver's seat, with yet another man beside her. He wore a T-shirt and jeans, but from his posture and clipped hair, Erica pegged him as another soldier. "Hi, Sergeant," Erica said through the open window.

Irenic looked at her with pursed lips. "Hello, Erica. Get in." She smiled slightly before turning back to the road.

What was with that look? Irenic didn't seem mad, although she had to realize Erica was the one who had knocked her out.

Erica shrugged and slid into the seat beside Cam. Ian and Renee clambered in and sat in front of her.

Half an hour into their journey, Cam raised his head.

"You don't need Einstein's mass-energy equivalence to explain Jen's ability," Cam said as if he were responding to a comment from Erica. "The first law of thermodynamics is sufficient. She's just redirecting energy from one location to another."

Erica stared at him. "What the heck?"

CHAPTER EIGHT

Erica entered the mess hall. Cam and Renee sat in the lounge area playing Trivia, as they had so often since they returned three weeks ago. The rectangular bulge of skin and hair on the back of Cam's head marking the position of the smartphone no longer seemed creepy, just part of Cam himself.

It was Renee's turn. "What is the temperature in Hope, British Columbia?"

"Sunny. Ninety-two degrees Fahrenheit," Cam said. The weather questions had worked in the first few days, but it had been two weeks since Erica had seen Cam stumped by even the most obscure town.

"How many pages are in Wikipedia?" Cam asked.

Renee shook her head. "I don't know. About thirty-five million."

"36,193,358," Cam said blandly.

Crossing her arms, Renee rose abruptly. "Have I ever won this game of yours? It seems pointless."

"You've won thirty-one percent of the time."

"But I just lost, like, twenty-five times in a row." Shaking her head, she walked to the bookshelf.

"Fourteen, not twenty-five. You've only won twice this week." Cam trailed her like a puppy.

"You're not disproving my point. Why even play if it isn't competitive? So boring." Renee scanned the books' spines. "Even these are boring. I swear, the only thing here I don't know by heart is this." Renee flipped through *A Dissolution of Mind* and carried it back to the couch.

Cam looked down at the floor as he followed her, his hands quivering. He swallowed, sat down opposite Renee, and said, "How about we reverse the game then? I'll be you and you be me. Instead of trying to stymie me, come up with a question that will stump you, but you think I know the answer to."

"I don't think that even makes sense."

Cam turned pink. "I'm sorry."

"I just don't want to play stupid games." Renee emphatically opened the book and scrutinized the first page as if she were alone in the room.

"Oh." Cam pulled his knees up toward his chest, staring blankly at the coffee table.

Erica sat beside him. The smartphone affixed to Cam's skull enabled him to access the Internet, making him a monster at any trivia game. He also seemed smarter, although Erica wasn't sure if she was simply mistaking knowledge for intelligence.

She patted him on the knee. "Don't fret, Cam. It's a compliment. You're too good at that game now."

Cam glanced up at her, and then back at the table, giving a tight nod.

Ian strode in. He had been taking too long in the bathroom, so Erica had gone on ahead without him. He looked toward the food panel, and then wandered over to sit beside his sister on the couch, peering at the book in her hands.

"Haven't you already—" He frowned, shaking his head. "Never mind."

Renee flinched, turning her head to stare at the bookshelf on the wall.

"No lunch yet?" Ian said. "What time is it?"

"11:39," Cam and Renee said simultaneously.

"Hmm." Ian looked at Cam, and his brow furrowed. "What is that? An earring?"

Cam shook his head.

"Let me see," Erica said. She gently turned his head. Embedded in Cam's earlobe was a tiny, shiny black dot. Erica ran her finger over it, causing Cam to flinch.

"Sorry," she said. "What is that thing?"

"A camera."

"Where did you get a camera?" She shook her head. "No, stupid question." Cameras were all over the bunker. "Why do you have a camera on your ear? You're into jewelry now?"

Cam shrugged.

"Can you record stuff?"

He nodded.

"That's creepy. How about you don't activate it when we're around?"

Cam turned pink and nodded.

Renee pursed her lips. "You can record me. Provided you can play it back for me when I ask," she said, her voice excessively casual.

Cam stared at her, his eyes unfocused for a few seconds. "I think I can." He scampered to the TV, turning it on and playing with the connections on the back.

Jen danced into the room, her light jumping from one hand to another, to her feet and back. She pirouetted twice, ran on her toes to where they were sitting, and settled on the floor beside the coffee table.

"The butterfly is empty," she said. The food panel glowed.

"Lunch shouldn't be long," Erica said.

Jen smiled as if Erica had given her the world. "Ooh." The light bounced over to Erica's face, and then onto the TV.

Standing with one hand behind the TV, Cam had to stretch to view the picture of Renee on the screen. After a few frozen seconds, it began to play. "Provided you can play it back for me when I ask," the larger-than-life Renee head said.

"Yeah," Erica said, cringing. "I definitely don't want you recording me."

Renee nodded. "My face is so skinny. I look like a rat and sound like I have a cold. It's embarrassing." She scratched her cheek and added, "But I guess it's fine."

Cam nodded, pulling his hand away from the TV. Then he froze, staring at the door.

Everyone turned. Lois was standing there.

"Oh, good, everyone's here," she chirped.

Lois had been true to her word. While she refused to allow the teenagers to leave their floor unaccompanied and complained about Erica and Ian's living arrangements, she'd started to bring them into the organization. She had given each of them a tablet connected to Jeemoh's internal network, claiming the first step in joining any organization was learning its history, goals, and culture.

Erica had spent hours browsing Jeemoh's electronic archives. Everything Lois had said appeared to be true. While Erica only had the lowest level of access, she could still read about many of Jeemoh's missions, from rescuing hostages to fighting wildfires. She was convinced Jeemoh censored the accounts—there was no mention of people with abilities. But unless the information was outright lies, Jeemoh seemed to be living up to its goals of helping people and making the world a better place. It made Erica wonder if all of their fears were unfounded.

As she had promised, Lois allowed Erica contact with her father. He had visited weekly, and they spoke almost nightly. Philip was impressed but not surprised by all that Lois had accomplished with Jeemoh. Nevertheless, he cautioned his daughter to stay alert since Lois' goals might not always align with Erica's.

Ian had wanted to contact his parents too, but, according to Lois, they weren't even in Battlefield anymore. "For most people, raising Jeemoh's kids is just a job. They move on after they're done," she'd said. Ian had taken in the information stoically. He had been quiet for a few days and hadn't mentioned it since.

Lois pushed two tables together. "I decided to have lunch with you so we can talk about your progress."

The panel beeped. Lois retrieved the pizza from it and brought it to the table. Jen lightly jumped onto the tabletop, sitting down cross-legged, but, by now, that sort of behavior didn't merit a second glance. The others decided the chairs were a better option, even Renee, who rarely sat if she had a choice. But today, she seemed content to sit quietly, not even fidgeting.

Lois looked from face to face until she had their full attention. "Other than that first hiccup and minor tampering with the surveillance equipment"—she looked at Cam—"you've been doing well. That leaves one ongoing issue of certain people not sleeping in their own rooms." Her eyes seemed to bore into Erica. "I expect that will cease at this instant. Relationships between team members are forbidden."

Erica blushed, looking down.

Ian stared at Lois for a few seconds. Then, with a theatrical motion, he swept Erica into his arms, bent her over backward, kissed her firmly, and then lifted her upright again.

Ian had been like that the whole time—willing to express his fake feelings for her, anytime, anywhere, regardless of anyone's disapproval. And Erica loved it, in the moment. He made her feel like she filled his thoughts as he did hers. That to him, she was irresistible. Was that what it was like to have a boyfriend who loved you?

The problem was the moment always passed, and then she felt empty. She was a junkie, searching for that hit of artificial bliss, knowing it wasn't real. She was using Ian, using this fake relationship, all because he made her feel good for an instant. And she was doing it despite her commitment to Renee not to get involved with her brother. The instant Renee had forgotten Erica's promise, so had she.

She wasn't a very good friend, to Renee or Ian. Yet, for all the relationship's falseness, she couldn't give it up.

Lois glared at Ian. "We will talk about this. But not right now." She scanned the others, the severe expression vanishing. "Because your decompression period from the Gauntlet is over, it's time for the next step."

"What next step?" Erica said, leaning forward. "We go out and save people?"

Lois shook her head. "Not so soon. Elizabeth was an anomaly."

Erica had heard nothing of Lizzy since their return. Lois had confined her in her own quarters rather than with the rest of them. Erica didn't disagree with that decision—while Jen was unbalanced, she couldn't kill them in seconds the way Lizzy could. Even so, Erica wondered how the girl was doing.

"Under normal circumstances," Lois continued, "we wouldn't deploy you without training. Over the next three months, you'll learn the basics, the bare minimum required of our field agents. Even after that, your training will continue. That never ends.

"Within a year, I'd expect any of you will be able to subdue anyone who doesn't have extensive combat training. You'll handle most common weapons confidently and will know how to interrogate someone and resist interrogation. You'll understand the basics of flying a plane, parachuting, lock picking, computer hacking, game theory, and surviving in hostile environments."

Renee sniffed. "I already know all that. I could probably teach your courses."

"And who knows? Maybe you will," Lois said pleasantly. "But

you'll have your own coursework. And you can help the others get up to speed and figure out if you have any gaps in your knowledge."

Renee frowned. Erica could tell what she was thinking—of course there were gaps in her knowledge. Just not things that were taught in a classroom.

"We also expect you to master your abilities." Seeing Ian shake his head, Lois added, "Even you, Ian. Especially you. We have the medical equipment to keep you alive, and until you learn to harness your ability, there will always be a chance of you incinerating yourself. You must learn control."

"Easy for you to say," Ian said sullenly. "You're not the one burning."

Lois' eyes narrowed. "Deal with it. You're a member of Jeemoh now." She turned her attention back to the others. "Our teams work in squads of six to eight. We have two additional team members who lost their squad. Now that your depressurization is over, they will join you."

Erica frowned. "What happened to their old squad?"

"Do I have to spell it out? They died."

"How?"

"On a mission. The details of which are above your security grade," Lois said firmly. "Each squad is led by an unenhanced human. You've already met your team lead. Sergeant Irenic will manage your training and ensure you maximize your potential."

Erica blanched. Irenic would surely have it in for Renee and her after their earlier fight. Or maybe just her because she was the one who whacked Irenic with the poker.

"Irenic isn't just any leader," Lois continued. "She's also the best unarmed fighter in this facility, and that's saying a lot."

Renee shook her head, smiling. "No, I'm pretty sure I'm the best fighter in this facility."

Lois didn't even look at her. "Irenic will dispel that illusion. Again."

Renee's eyes widened, and then her face crumbled. Even in the Gauntlet, Erica didn't think she'd ever seen her friend look so lost.

"In addition, you will now have access to the four training floors—fifteen, sixteen, seventeen, and eighteen. Fifteen has the armory, target ranges, and maze. Sixteen has the dojo, classical weapons like knives, bows, staves, and swords, and the weight room.

Seventeen and eighteen have classrooms and computer, electronics, chemistry and biology labs. In two days, you'll resume your high school education, but we will customize your curriculum to your skills and abilities.

"Each one of these floors is available to you twenty-four hours a day unless it's otherwise in use. There are no babysitters, so please try not to blow yourself up. The cleaning bills can be horrendous.

"You will encounter people from other squads in the labs and—after you finish the basics—in your classes. Socializing with other squads is discouraged. It reduces compartmentalization and weakens security. Treat people from other squads like colleagues, but you should neither volunteer nor ask for information. It's dangerous to share. If you want to talk, talk to your own squad.

"Now, everyone seems to be finished eating. Any questions before we go see Sergeant Irenic?"

Cam cautiously raised his hand. At Lois' nod, he asked, "Why can't we go to the other floors? If we're part of the team."

"Please don't waste everyone's time asking stupid questions, Cam. This is a high-security military base."

Blushing, Cam looked down at his hands. He gripped his chair on either side of his knees, his knuckles white.

Jen slowly raised one shining hand.

"Yes, Jen?" Lois said.

Jen brought her arm down while raising her other hand. Her fingernails glowed. She stared at them for a few seconds, wriggling her fingers.

Lois sighed. "Let's get going."

They walked to the elevator. Erica, after using her handprint for identification, pressed the button for the sixteenth floor as her mother directed.

The elevator opened onto a white hallway like all the others. Waiting there was a teenager. His brow was bleeding, and he was cradling his left arm from which a splinter of bone protruded. He stepped aside to give them space to exit.

"That's one ugly horse," murmured Ian, staring at the wound.

Renee's mouth quirked ironically. "No, it's one beautiful compound fracture of the left ulna."

Lois ignored their comments. "Tough day, Assiz?"

Assiz frowned. "I've had worse. She may have gone easy on me."

Jen's light danced across the wound on Assiz's arm. "Do you mind not doing that?" The light shifted up to the blood on his face.

He shook his head as if to flick off a fly, took their place in the elevator, and pressed the button for the medical floor. "Good luck," Assiz said with a fatalistic grin.

Lois gestured to the left. "The dojo's at the end."

She led them into a large, open room smelling of sawdust, sweat, and blood. The dojo's floor was divided into three equal parts—each finished in a different way—padded wrestling mats, wood, and concrete. On the walls hung staves, spears, knives, and gloves.

In the center of it all stood Irenic. After seeing her in her bulky "mother" clothes, Erica had assumed Irenic was slightly overweight. That misunderstanding was instantly dispelled now.

Irenic looked like the chiseled statue of a Greek god, her tight-fitting shirt and pants only emphasizing her extraordinary physique. Irenic's muscular biceps seemed larger than Cam's thighs, while her legs looked like a speed skater's. The clinging shirt highlighted her washboard abdomen as if it were selected to do so, except Erica didn't think Irenic was the type to choose clothing for any reason except sheer utility.

"Here they are," Lois said. "I'll send down the others."

Irenic nodded curtly. Lois surveyed the scene one last time and strode out the door.

"Sit," Irenic said.

They cautiously gathered in a circle around her. Erica felt tiny and frail beside the huge woman. It was as if she were back in kindergarten, waiting for story time. It didn't help that Jen was languidly waving her arms in the air like seaweed twisting in a current.

Irenic ignored Jen as she looked them over for several seconds, her gaze steely. "You're here to learn combat. We have one rule. No killing. We can fix anything but death. So, do anything except instant kills. If you kill someone, I will beat you with a stick."

Ian and Cam laughed nervously.

Irenic's eyes narrowed. She marched over to the wall and picked up a staff an inch in diameter and seven feet long. "This is the stick." The boys instantly grew sober. She walked back to them while gesturing at a corner with three hospital stretchers. "The first aid equipment is over there for when you need it."

She stomped. They all jumped as the sound echoed through the room. "In my class, we train on wood and cement. Life does not have padded floors."

The teenagers sat there motionless, eyes wide. To Erica, it felt like she was having a vision of a disaster about to happen. Only, there was no vision.

"I will evaluate you. Renee first. Stand up." Irenic gestured at the padded floor. "Everyone else, sit there."

The instant Erica, Cam, and Ian stepped off the wooden floor onto the mat, Irenic attacked. She threw three punches in rapid succession. Renee scooted back and to the side, avoiding all Irenic's jabs.

Irenic continued advancing and attacking. Other than a low roundhouse to her thigh and a punch to the abdomen, Renee dodged or deflected all strikes. When she saw an opening, Renee tried to fight back, but, hindered by Irenic's longer reach and superior speed, didn't come close to landing any solid blows.

After a few minutes, Irenic changed tactics. She dove for Renee's legs, lifted them off the ground, and slammed her onto her back. Renee seemed stunned, but Irenic didn't hesitate. She grasped Renee's arm, bending it backward at the elbow. Renee's face contorted in pain. Erica was certain the arm was about to snap.

Renee tapped furiously on her leg.

"Life does not have tap outs," Irenic said. She didn't even appear to be exerting herself.

Renee contorted her small body and somehow tore her arm from Irenic's grasp. Irenic didn't pause. She placed her arm across Renee's neck and pressed down.

Renee struggled, trying to push Irenic to the side, gouge her eyes, anything to clear her airway. It was futile. After a few seconds, her body went limp.

"See?" Irenic said, gesturing at Renee's throat as if pointing out an interesting bug to a child. "I didn't crush her windpipe. No kills."

She walked to a red cupboard in the corner near the stretchers, retrieved smelling salts, and waved them under Renee's nose. After a few seconds, Renee regained consciousness.

"You did well," Irenic said. "Go to medical later. Avoid brain damage." She turned her gaze to Erica as if Renee no longer existed. "Erica."

Renee crawled over to where the rest of them were sitting while

Erica cautiously got to her feet. Was there any way to get out of this?

"Excuse us," a male voice said. "Lois said we should come here to meet our new team."

Ian gaped as he saw who was standing in the doorway. "Morrison! You're alive. They said you committed suicide." He leaped to his feet and took a few steps toward his friend

The dark-haired, slightly overweight boy standing in the doorway shook his head. His eyes were dark. "They lied."

CHAPTER NINE

"Sit down there," Irenic commanded, pointing to the mat.

Morrison silently walked into the room. He had been Ian's best friend before he had supposedly killed himself six months earlier.

A teenage girl with short, blonde hair and brown eyes trailed Morrison. An hourglass tattoo took up much of the right side of her neck. When she got closer, Erica could see a head imprisoned in the bottom half of the hourglass, its mouth open in a silent scream as the chamber filled with sand.

Erica had never met the girl, but she recognized her from school. The teachers at Battlefield High had claimed her family had moved away in the middle of the night last year. What was her name? Eve?

After his initial shock, Ian's grin was as big as the sky. "I can't believe you're here. What happened?" He opened his arms wide to give Morrison a hug.

Morrison trudged by him and sat down. "Later."

Ian's hands dropped to his sides. "Come on. What have you been doing all this time? What happened to you?"

Morrison looked from Ian to Irenic.

As Ian followed his gaze, Irenic grasped his left arm and right hip. She swung her body around, lifted Ian off the ground over her hip, and slammed him onto the wooden floor.

"Pay attention," Irenic said. "Talk later." She strode away, gesturing for Erica to follow.

Ian, gasping for air and clutching his stomach, crawled back to the mat. Erica was concerned he would say something, but, apparently, he was smarter than that. Or perhaps he was unable to.

Shivering, Erica inched toward her opponent. What was the best strategy? Use her visions to dodge Irenic until she gave up? Take a quick fall? Even with her ability, trying to win the fight seemed futile. Irenic was a monster. Even if Irenic stood there and let Erica hit her with her hardest punch, she'd just shrug it off like a fleabite.

Irenic would know if she didn't try, and probably make her suffer for it. Dodging seemed like the safest plan. Certainly, it would be less painful.

Irenic swung at her. Erica's vision let her see it coming. She moved out of the way.

The sergeant attacked more seriously. She was much faster than Vince had been in the Gauntlet. Erica avoided Irenic's blows, but was soon panting from the exertion.

"Like Vince," Irenic said. She started moving her body more, shifting and following Erica, forcing her back. Soon, they were on the concrete floor with Erica continuing to retreat, conscious of the wall getting ever closer. She was within twenty feet, and then ten. Realizing the risk of being confined, she tried to shift to the side, to circle away, but Irenic was there almost the instant she considered it. If she tried, she'd be hit in the head. The only safe alternative was stepping back.

And then, there was nowhere to go. She was in the corner. The visions cascaded through her mind, but there was no good option. A hard blow landed on her shoulder, making her stagger back into the wall.

Take a punch to the head or allow Irenic to grab her arm? Her arm was surely the better choice.

Irenic spun as she grasped Erica's right arm. She pulled it over her head and used her shoulder as a fulcrum to snap Erica's arm backward at the elbow. Pain exploded, as if a sword had sliced off her forearm.

Irenic continued to twist, lowering her body, pulling on the broken arm, using its leverage to lift Erica's body over her hip.

She was going to be thrown. The only question was how much more her arm would be mangled in the process. Erica leaped into the throw, doing everything she could to minimize the damage. She flipped over Irenic's back and landed hard on the concrete floor. It was as if she had jumped from a second-story window.

Erica lay on the ground, gasping. She didn't think she could move if she tried. The pain across her back, stomach—her entire body—was more intense than anything she'd ever felt before. And that was like a minor bruise compared to the knifing torment of her elbow.

She needed to get away from this psychotic woman. She needed the pain to stop.

Irenic towered over her. "Good dodging. You need to fight, too." She reached down and grasped Erica's left arm, hauling her to her feet. "Sit. Go to medical later."

Erica didn't think it was possible, but she was somehow standing, walking. Apparently, her legs were the one unbroken part of her body. She staggered to the mat and fell beside Ian.

Her pulse was like acid running through her right arm. "I think it's broken. I need to get it fixed now."

Irenic shook her head. "Of course it's broken. You won't die. Learn to cope with pain." She looked to Erica's right. "Ian."

Ian lasted for a few minutes. Through the haze of pain, Erica couldn't really concentrate on the fight. Irenic seemed slower than she had been with her and Renee, but she eventually sped up and broke Ian's ribs.

Even the concept of fighting seemed alien to Jen. She spun around like a carousel, her arms wide. Irenic jabbed lightly, and Jen didn't even try to defend. She sat down on the floor and sobbed, her cheek glowing like a spotlight where Irenic's gentle blow had landed. Irenic frowned.

Cam's fight was over even faster. The second the match began, he pointed his right arm at his opponent. The prong from the Javelin in his forearm shot out, but Irenic twisted to the side, allowing it to sail past her. She stepped forward, casually broke his wrist, and smashed him onto the wooden floor. Cam howled as the wire from the Javelin retracted.

"Use your weapons. Don't depend on them," Irenic said, not at all upset that Cam had used his Javelin in the martial arts class. "Eve, demonstrate."

The blonde girl's lips thinned. "Can't Morrison do it instead?"

Irenic shook her head. "Why bother asking?"

With a sigh, Eve stood up and walked onto the wooden floor. She stood a respectful distance away from Irenic, raising her hands in front of her face.

This time, Sergeant Irenic was more cautious. She and Eve circled for at least half a minute before closing the gap between them. Eve moved her head out of the way of the first blow, but blocked the second, deflecting the left jab to the side. As she did, she winced.

When Irenic pulled away, Erica saw something white protruding an inch from Eve's wrist. A red line running the length of Irenic's forearm dripped blood on the wooden floor. Irenic ignored it.

Eve fought back, white spikes that looked like bones springing from her knuckles, but Irenic danced away. She landed a kick on Eve's side. When she pulled her foot back, a crack echoed through the room. A growing red spot appeared on Eve's shirt where the kick had landed, but a white spike remained impaled in Irenic's leg, just above her ankle.

Despite the damage she did to Irenic's leg, the force of the kick had made Eve double over. Irenic followed up her advantage with an uppercut that landed perfectly on Eve's jaw. Eve fell to the ground, unconscious, but again, Irenic didn't escape unscathed. A four-inch spike had appeared on Eve's chin, impaling Irenic's fist and cutting into her arm.

Erica glanced at Ian. His face pale, he seemed transfixed by the blood dripping from Irenic's arm, splattering the floor.

Erica gently touched his shoulder. "How are you doing?"

"I... I don't do well with blood."

"I remember."

Irenic snorted. "You'll get over that." She walked once more to the first aid cupboard—barely limping despite the bone embedded in her leg—and retrieved the smelling salts to revive her opponent. Then, she pulled the bone spike out, tossed it into a garbage bin in the corner, and slapped a sticky bandage onto the hole that was now gushing blood.

Erica frowned. If she'd entered the room now, she would have a hard time determining who had won. Several bloody spikes of bone protruded through Eve's skin, and she had what looked like a knife wound in her side, but she otherwise seemed unscathed. Irenic, on the other hand, had crippling cuts on both arms and a temporary bandage on her leg, already soaked with blood.

Irenic loomed over Cam. He shivered, staring at the floor. "Eve integrates her weapons into attack and defense. She doesn't rely on them." She paused and then added, "Don't grapple with Eve. Hit her, but never head-butt her."

Eve wiped away the blood that was dripping down the bone spike on her chin. "Gee, thanks."

Irenic's expression didn't change. She gestured to a stack of towels beside the door. "Clean up the blood."

That job took several minutes, made even longer by the occasional red drop from Eve's bone spikes.

Eventually, Irenic gave a satisfied nod. "We will go to medical now. Jen, go back to your floor."

Jen smiled, looked around, and then lay on her back. "I'm here on my floor."

Irenic looked pained. "Just follow us."

When she walked to the elevator, Erica's wounds didn't seem to hurt so much anymore, just dull aches accompanied by a slight queasiness in her stomach. The others were in worse shape. Limping, wounds gaping, blood still dripping, they looked more like casualties of war than casualties of a single lunatic martial arts teacher. As if that weren't enough, Jen's light bounced around the corridor highlighting injuries, a spotlight on misery. Erica had to hold back a manic giggle.

She looked over at her fake boyfriend to see if he saw the same dark humor in the situation. Each of Ian's breaths looked painful, and he still seemed pale. He stared at Morrison, although his gaze occasionally darted to Irenic. Maybe he was unsure whether he was allowed to talk to Morrison or if Irenic would smash him again.

But Erica didn't have that problem. If Irenic tried anything, she'd see it well before it happened.

Irenic helped Jen onto an elevator destined for the floor where they lived and called another for the rest of them. As they crowded in, Erica said, "So, Morrison... How did you survive your apparent suicide?"

He looked at her with heavily lidded eyes. "Your mom didn't tell you?"

Erica shook her head.

"It's a pretty boring story. I fell and couldn't get up. Your mom took me here, and I joined the team." Morrison's cheek twitched. "They never told me the explanation back home was that I committed suicide. But it makes sense, I guess."

Erica looked at him in confusion. "What do you mean, you fell? I don't get it."

"Maybe I should demonstrate."

"Don't." The single word from Irenic's lips left Erica with the distinct impression that disobeying would have dire consequences.

Morrison's face remained neutral, but Erica thought she detected a hint of a smile. "I eliminate friction. I can make it feel like you're standing on ice coated in oil. Heck, if you don't have an elastic waistband, I can even drop your pants."

"You better not. She's my girlfriend," Ian said, his threatening tone at odds with his amused expression. Morrison couldn't hold back a smirk.

Doctor Rahal, the doctor who had treated Ian after the Gauntlet, nodded as they entered medical. Though Erica hadn't been there since that first night, the room appeared unchanged. Glass-doored cabinets holding a wide variety of medical supplies lined the walls of the room. An operating table and several chairs were positioned at one end. In contrast, the other end of the room looked conspicuously empty, with only a solid, six-inch-high platform jutting eight feet out from the wall. But Erica knew the space wasn't wasted. The platform was the medical printer, an almost miraculous machine capable of healing wounds in an instant.

"There you are. Assiz mentioned you were on your way here." Looking at Eve, Dr. Rahal sighed. "I'll plug in the bone saw. The rest of you can use the printer."

Irenic pressed a button on the wall, and red light bathed the platform. "Renee," she said, raising her voice to be heard over the regular metallic thumps of the warming-up machine.

Renee hopped onto the platform. After a second, the bruises on her neck vanished.

One by one, they stood in the red light and were healed. Irenic went last.

Hearing a grinding sound, Erica glanced behind her. While Eve sat on the operating table, Rahal was using a circular saw to carve through the bone sticking out of Eve's chin. Eve looked like she was about to weep. Seeing Erica watching, Eve glowered and pivoted away. Rahal glanced up, muttered something, and pulled a curtain attached to ceiling tracks around the table, hiding them from view.

"Why are they doing that to her?" Erica murmured to Morrison, suppressing a shiver.

Morrison frowned. "Eve can make her bone spurs grow instantly in any direction. But she can't shrink them. They have to cut them off."

"Can't she just use the medical printer?"

Morrison shook his head. "They tried. Her wounds closed, but the bone remained. So they need to remove it before she uses it." Morrison winced as the saw shrieked, hitting a bone at the wrong angle. "It's bad, but it was far worse before they got the printer."

"Gossip is for the insipid. Life isn't watching others. It's raising yourself," Irenic said flatly. "You're dismissed. Thirteen hundred tomorrow in the dojo."

Erica didn't even want to think about it. "Shall we go to the mess?"

"Yeah," Ian said. "I'm dying to find out about all the things Morrison has been doing."

They left Eve behind and returned to the elevator.

"How have you been?" Ian said to Morrison the instant the door closed, his voice giddy. Irenic's presence had clearly restrained his enthusiasm, but now that she was gone, it bubbled over. "How was your training? Was it hard?"

"Not too hard." Morrison didn't even look at Ian, but just stared at the door.

Ian cocked his head. "Have you been on any missions?" he asked, still smiling.

"Yes."

"What were they like?"

"Bad."

"Dude, you're not giving me much information here," Ian said, the reproach in his words diluted by his grin.

Morrison shrugged. The elevator opened on their floor. "How about you and I talk in your room?"

Ian's brow furrowed. "Okay." He squeezed Erica's hand. "I'll see you in a bit."

Erica nodded. Ian and Morrison vanished down the corridor.

Cam's eyes swung from the two women to down the corridor. "I'm going too," he mumbled, leaving at a half-sprint.

"See ya," Erica said to Cam's back. She turned to Renee. "I guess it's just you and me. Though it's great to see Morrison again, isn't it?"

"He seems all right," Renee said, her tone excessively casual. "Who is he again?"

Erica's eyes widened. How much had Renee forgotten?

"He's not related to me, is he? Ian's my only sibling?" Renee said haltingly, her face pink.

Erica nodded. "Let's chat."

They sat down on the bed in Renee's room. Like Erica's room, it was mostly taken up by the single bed. Carelessly discarded clothes, a book, and a tablet covered much of the floor space. But Renee had done some decorating since the last time Erica was there. On the longest wall was a paper floor plan. Beside it were labeled photos of her, Ian, Cam, Jen, and Lois.

"Tell me about Morrison," Renee said.

"He was Ian's best friend. You've known him almost as long as you've known me. He hung out with Ian every day until he killed himself six months ago. Or so the adults said."

"I never knew he existed," Renee murmured. She closed her eyes, leaning her head against the wall. "Did I know Eve?"

"I don't think so." Erica bit her lip and stood, studying the pictures on the wall.

After a few seconds of silence, Renee opened her eyes, saw Erica examining the photos, and swallowed. "They're there so I don't forget. I look at them every morning."

"It's not getting any better?" Erica asked sympathetically, trying to keep her own fears from her voice. Renee had enough on her plate without Erica piling on more. "Lois said that it would stabilize eventually."

"Not yet. Not as far as I can tell."

"Oh." How was she even supposed to support her friend? Anything she could think of to say seemed inadequate. Erica traced a finger along a hall on the floor plan. "Give it a few more days, I guess."

Renee's lips twisted. "Yeah."

Perhaps Renee recognized how uncomfortable Erica was with the discussion, or maybe she found discussing her memory issues too painful, because, as if by unspoken agreement, they moved on to topics that were more neutral. Even so, the rest of the conversation felt forced, burdened by the weight of Renee's decline. Erica was pleased when the lights flashed to indicate bedtime was approaching.

When she returned to her room, her false lover was waiting.

"Did you have a good conversation with Renee?" Ian asked.

"Yep." The truth was too bleak. Erica didn't want to dwell.

Ian pulled her into a hug. "Good. Because I'm ready for bed."

"You're always ready for bed."

"Not always. Only since you," he whispered, feigning a bad Spanish accent.

Erica smiled. Even with his ridiculous, over-the-top flirtations, Ian always made her feel special, like she was the most captivating woman in the world. It was reason #362 why he always got to her, why she couldn't get away. Other than his heart, he was her perfect boyfriend.

They got ready for bed, and the lights dimmed. Erica snuggled up to Ian. By now, it was a familiar ritual, but it still made her pulse race. Her head seemed to fit into the curve of his shoulder as if they were designed to fit together.

"So, how does it feel knowing Morrison is alive?" Erica whispered. After Renee, she needed to distract her brain with a happier topic.

"I'm still stunned. I mean, I saw his coffin lowered into the ground. This is like a second chance." Erica could hear the awe still in Ian's voice.

"I can imagine. Was he glad to see you? He seemed... subdued."

"Yeah. I think he was happy, but something seemed off. We used to joke around so much. Now, he's quiet. It's like he doesn't want to be friends anymore." Ian spoke as if the conversation was inconsequential, but the pitch of his voice was unusually low.

So much for Morrison being a lighter topic.

Erica frowned. "Seeing you again could be as shocking for him as it is for you. Maybe he needs time to get used to it."

"It seems like more than that. I told him about what you and I went through in the Gauntlet, and he got quiet, not really asking anything. And then we talked about missions, and he said he did one, but he won't tell me anything about it, claiming it's classified. So I asked about day-to-day life in the bunker and he shared a bit about that, but at a really high level. Whenever I tried to get more details, he just clammed up, giving these two-word answers. Almost like he was angry."

"But he didn't even go through the Gauntlet. Why would he be angry?"

"I don't know. Maybe Jeemoh did something? Threatened him?"

Ian's tone made it clear he was baffled.

Erica grimaced. "Possibly. I don't know why they would though." And that was the crux of the problem. They still didn't have reliable information about Jeemoh's goals. Both Lois' explanations and the tablets implied that Jeemoh was trying to improve the world. But did that mean that Jeemoh was benevolent, or simply skilled at telling a consistent lie?

Erica needed to be certain that the information she was getting was accurate. But anyone with enough knowledge of Jeemoh to help her untangle the web would be untrustworthy for the same reason.

She clenched her fist. "It's so frustrating. Everything always comes back to whether we can trust Jeemoh. We've been here for weeks, and I feel no closer to knowing the truth than when we started."

"Have you seen anything that makes you think your mom is lying?"

"No. Irenic beating us up doesn't seem like something a 'good guy' would do. Beyond that, I have nothing. But how can we really know?"

"Yeah," Ian said. They lay there, staring at the ceiling for a few minutes. Then, Ian flinched.

"What is it?"

Ian pulled her close, so his lips were right beside her ear. "I know what we can try." Erica could feel his pulse racing where his temple touched hers.

"What?"

"Renee can do almost anything, right? She's, like, an expert in everything."

"Of course."

"So how about we don't listen to Jeemoh, but go to the source?"

Erica shook her head. "What source?"

"Jeemoh's computers. Let's get Renee to hack into Jeemoh."

CHAPTER TEN

The corridor outside was only lit by a few dim lights, but even total darkness wouldn't have deterred Erica and Ian. They tapped on Renee's door, waited half a minute, and then tried again.

Eventually, the door opened a crack. "What's going on?" Renee whispered.

"We want to talk to you about something," Erica said. "Can we come in?"

Renee gestured to them to enter and sit on her rumpled bed.

In a barely audible voice, Erica said, "We were talking about Jeemoh, and Ian suggested that the best way to find out the truth is to break into their computers. You probably know how to do it, so we thought we'd come to you."

Renee nodded slowly, squeezing her eyes shut. "Interesting idea," she murmured. "We're already on the network, so firewalls aren't a problem." She picked up the tablet that was lying on the floor beside her bed. She took the top layer of the covers on the bed, stretched it out, and pulled it over their heads.

"Why are you—" Ian said. "Oh, the cameras."

Renee nodded. She began typing on the on-screen keyboard.

"Can you do it?" Erica said eagerly.

"I'm not sure yet. It depends on the hardware and software they're using, what patches they've installed. Basically, how paranoid they are about security."

Erica grimaced. "Pretty paranoid, I imagine."

"Maybe. We'll see." Renee's fingers continued to dart across the tablet's screen, her tongue flicking between her lips. After a few minutes, she held down the power button on the tablet to turn it off and on again.

"You failed?" Ian said.

"Nope," Renee replied, turning the screen of the tablet in Ian's direction. It was black except for some white text and a flashing cursor at the bottom. "I succeeded. In hacking the tablet, anyway."

"So what does it say?" Erica leaned forward, trying to decipher the words on the screen.

"The tablet doesn't have any information," Renee said. "It's just a display. We need to get into the server it's talking to. That's where the actual data is stored."

"Oh," Erica said. "Let's do that then."

"Yeah," Renee said in a dry tone that perfectly conveyed how unhelpful she considered Erica's suggestions. "There are actually two problems, not one. The first problem is getting into the server. The second problem is hiding that we've been there. There's software on the web that solves both issues."

Renee lapsed into silence while continuing her machinations. Erica became warm, so poked her head outside the covers for a few minutes.

"There," Renee said.

Erica popped her head back under the sheets. Unintelligible symbols covered the screen. Renee stared at them intently.

"You're in?" Erica asked.

After a few seconds, Renee shook her head, "No. It didn't work."

Erica exhaled. "Darn. I guess we should have expected that. Thanks for trying, Ren."

"We're not done. This was just my first try."

"Oh. There's something else you can do?"

Renee nodded.

The process repeated itself into the night until Erica lost track of how many attempts Renee had made. Every time she resurfaced for cool air, she glanced at the door, wondering if soldiers were about to charge through and grab them in response to some alarm Renee had set off. Finally, she lay back against the wall, closing her eyes.

"Erica."

Ian was gently shaking her arm. Erica yawned, looking around the darkened room.

"She did it. Renee got in."

Erica ducked her head below the covers. Renee's eyes were riveted to the screen, but it still was unreadable to Erica.

"How do you know?" Erica said.

"Trust me, I'm in. What do you want to look at?"

"I don't know. What is there?" Ian said.

"Lots of stuff. Let's see… Facilities, Equipment, Missions, Personnel, Cameras and Security—"

"Cameras?" Erica said. In her eagerness, the question came out louder than she intended. "We can see the videos from the cameras?"

"In theory," Renee said. "But it might take me a while to figure out the mechanics of streaming it to this tablet."

"What about missions?" Ian said. "If anything's incriminating, it would be there."

"Let's see," Renee said. She touched the screen a few times and began reading. "*San Clemente Oil Spill*; *Kandakrass Instability*, *Blue Canyon Dam Attack*; *Baker Assassination Attempt*; *California Brushfires*; *New York Dirty Bomb*; *Narakonsk Genocide*… There are, like, fifty-eight missions here."

"This is what we want," Erica said, her excitement growing. "There were only eighteen on the 'official' list."

Ian grinned. "So let's look at the ones that sound suspicious. What about that assassination? Can you bring that up?"

Renee nodded. "I'll get the overview." She placed the tablet on Ian's lap so they could all read it.

```
NSA intelligence indicated a potential
assassination attempt on Secretary of State
Candice Baker during her energy negotiations
in Alphina. Hunter intercepted a plate
containing aconite destined for Baker's
hotel room. The perpetrator was determined
to be a busboy working in the kitchen. He
identified a cell of four other hostiles.
All hostiles eliminated by Haddy, Inoue,
Grimes, Hunter, and Jones. Jeemoh's
involvement went unnoted.
```

"Aconite?" Ian said.

"It's a poison," Renee said.

Erica nodded, her voice thoughtful. "So Jeemoh saved Baker's life. No smoking gun there. Try another. What about that 'K' one?"

"The Kandakrass Instability," Renee said, bringing up the summary.

```
Protests following the fraudulent fifth-term
election of Moroso Karmai led to a potential
massacre as President Karmai ordered the
military's weapons turned upon
demonstrators. Merta and Smith protected all
but six of the civilians, while Wu, Skerrit,
and Ray infiltrated the presidential palace
and convinced Karmai to resign peacefully.
Stability was restored within three months.
Jeemoh's involvement went unnoted outside
Karmai's inner circle, all of whom are now
dead.
```

"That might be bad," Erica said, her stomach clenching. "It sounds like Jeemoh overthrew an elected government."

"It says the election was fixed," Ian said.

"Well, maybe it *says* that." Erica's voice dripped with implication. "But look at the source. Jeemoh isn't exactly unbiased in this matter. And how did the guy's inner circle die?"

Renee shook her head. "Karmai was an evil guy. His thugs would grab people in the middle of the night, stuff bags over their heads, and make them disappear. Political opponents, teachers, priests, business owners. They all were taken and never returned. Almost one percent of the population of the country disappeared. None of them has been found to this day. If anything, Jeemoh waited too long to overthrow him. As for his cronies, well, after what journalists reported to be fair trials, they were hung for a variety of treason and corruption charges."

"So Jeemoh's fine there too," Ian said.

"Yep."

They spent over an hour clicking through the missions, reading the summaries for over half of them and delving into the details of a few. Erica tried to keep a rough count of how many people Jeemoh had saved, but gave up after Renee pointed out that Jeemoh had saved more people by preventing the dirty bomb detonation in New York City than all the other missions combined.

Not once was there any indication that Jeemoh was doing anything but good. In a few cases, Ian complained about their methods, arguing some terrorists should have been tried in court rather than killed outright. But Erica disagreed. Arresting someone who was in the process of killing people seemed too much to ask even of Jeemoh agents.

The detailed mission logs also provided insight into some agents' abilities. One seemed capable of disabling missile weapons while another could knock people unconscious with a touch. A third could access the senses of anyone nearby, seeing and hearing everything they did.

Eventually, Erica yawned.

Renee noticed and checked the time on the tablet. "Two thirty AM. Maybe we should get some sleep."

"Yeah," Erica said, stretching. "I think we got what we were looking for. Nothing in there screams 'malevolent organization bent on evil'. But let's come back to it tomorrow. I'm curious if we can access the cameras."

Renee nodded. "Sounds good."

#

"Every single mission seemed legit," Erica said in a low voice to the faces around the breakfast table. Everyone was staring at her in rapt attention except Jen, who was attempting to stuff scrambled eggs into a ping-pong ball. "And really, there wasn't anything even close to the line."

Ian paused with his fork halfway to his mouth. "They killed a lot of the terrorists rather than arresting them."

"In the heat of combat," Erica clarified. "There weren't any missions where the sole goal was to murder someone."

Eve smirked. "I can't believe you did that. You guys have balls."

"It was all Renee," Erica said. "My role was cheerleader."

"Still. Very impressive." Eve nodded approvingly at Renee.

Renee shrugged.

Cam leaned forward. "Did you look at every mission? And are you certain they weren't hiding anything?"

"Not every mission. We skimmed about half of the forty new missions, focusing on the ones that seemed the most worrisome."

"So there could have been something you missed?" Morrison said sharply.

Erica frowned. "Anything's possible. But—"

"Did you read about our mission? With the dam? The one that's classified?"

"No. I remember one about a dam, but we didn't look into the details." Erica scrutinized Morrison's face. "Did Jeemoh try to get you to do something questionable?"

"No. Not questionable." When Erica raised her eyebrows to get him to elaborate, Morrison added, "I'm just saying you might have missed something. You *claim* they're fine, but you could be mistaken." Squeezing his lips together, he looked away.

"Okay…"

"So, leaving aside certain people's paranoia," Eve said breezily, "we're the good guys. Nice to know."

"I'm a bit upset, actually," Ian said. "I had these big plans for world domination. Black leather costume, high-tech lair, rocket car…" He looked at Eve earnestly. "I had you pencilled in on my organizational chart for the chief lackey position. Now all that's gone." He shook his head mournfully.

"Probably for the best," Eve said. "I can't imagine I'd be a lackey for long before I felt the need to depose or seduce you." Her mouth quirked into a wicked grin.

"Hey!" Erica said. "That's my boyfriend."

"Don't worry. I'd just want to beguile him into fulfilling my every command. Nothing personal." Her eyes drifted over Ian's body. "At least at first."

Erica glared at Eve, but Eve just smirked. For once, Ian didn't have a comeback.

Over breakfast and in the hallways, they furtively discussed the details of the missions they had reviewed. By the time their class with Irenic rolled around that afternoon, everyone but Morrison seemed to be convinced that Jeemoh—though sometimes extreme in its methods—generally had good intentions.

Irenic's second class proved even more challenging than the first as the teenagers began learning martial arts techniques. Once again, they left with contusions and protruding bones. The medical printer addressed those issues, but not Erica's exhaustion after the lack of sleep the night before. Thus, soon after dinner, Erica and Ian retired to her room.

"You know, we did good work yesterday," Erica whispered to Ian as they lay on her bed relaxing. "It's put my biggest fears to rest. I think everyone's convinced Jeemoh's fine."

Ian nodded. "Except maybe Morrison."

"Yeah. What's his deal? How could he still be skeptical after everything we found?" Erica's tone conveyed her frustration.

Ian said nothing, just rubbed his chin.

Erica turned to examine his face. "What?"

Ian glanced at her, pursing his lips. After several seconds, he said. "I don't know if I should say this, but I talked to him again today, trying to find out why he was acting so weird." Ian took in a big breath. "It's like this. He doesn't trust Jeemoh. I think he hates your mother and, well… he doesn't like you either. It's not your fault. He was fine with you back in school. But now you're Lois' daughter. He thinks you'll report to her on everything we do."

Erica rolled her eyes. "As if I need to report on anything. There are cameras everywhere."

"Yeah."

"Does he know what we've been through? What Lois did to us all? She hasn't treated me better than anyone else." Despite her attempt to remain calm, the words came out louder than Erica intended.

"I know. I tried to tell him. It didn't help. He just stopped talking to me. The more I said, the quieter he got. I don't think it's necessarily a logical reaction."

"Then what can I do? We're on the same squad. I have to see him every day."

"There's not much you can do." Ian's voice took on a raw edge. "In fact, I don't think he trusts me now, either. Because you and I are together."

"Everyone seems to hate us going out. It's so unfair." Erica shook her head in frustration. "You know, if pretending to have a relationship is causing all these problems with Morrison and Lois, I kind of wonder if it would be better if we ended it." The moment she said it, she regretted the flippant remark.

"What are you suggesting? That we 'break up'?" Ian's voice was flat.

Erica bit her lip. "I don't know. It makes sense, doesn't it?" She didn't mean what she was saying, but the words kept careening out of her mouth. "I mean, we've accomplished our goal. We know Jeemoh's sincere. We don't need to talk privately anymore." It was like she was speeding toward a cliff, but couldn't find the brakes.

Ian was silent, his body stiff. The seconds seemed like minutes.

What was he thinking? Erica couldn't handle the dead air between them. "It's all just pretend, anyway. Renee doesn't like it, Lois nags us constantly, and your best friend's scared of you. If our act is hurting us rather than helping us, we should drop it, shouldn't we?"

Why was she talking? Was she *trying* to convince him to end this, to stop these nighttime conversations that she eagerly awaited every single day? She needed to shut her mouth now.

So quickly, Ian had become such a big part of her life. Every second they were apart, she missed him, even if he was only a few doors away. His embraces, false though they were, felt as life sustaining as the food she ate. She had only the shadow of his love, but even that was a million times better than nothing at all.

Why was Ian so quiet? What was he thinking? Surely, he'd pull her back from the precipice now, as he always did.

Erica knew what he would say five seconds before he said it, but could do nothing.

Ian nodded. "You're right."

What had she done?

CHAPTER ELEVEN

"I guess we should use your mom as an excuse?" Ian said. His voice was low, but firm.

Erica nodded, numb. "When?" In a few days?

"Now. No reason to wait. One last performance," Ian whispered. He sat upright, turning his back to Erica like a wall.

"It's not you. It's just that it's not working," he said, loud enough for any microphones in the room.

Erica couldn't keep her voice steady, but maybe that didn't matter. "I know. I don't want to admit it, but I'm beginning to think Lois is right. In the Gauntlet, it was simple. Here, it's so complicated. Renee hates us. Lois hates us. Even Morrison hates us. If everyone we care about thinks this relationship is a bad idea, well..."

Ian nodded, standing up, still with his back to her. "Yeah. We've got these abilities and the potential to do so much good. We need to focus on our training, not each other."

Erica had always known this was how Ian truly felt. It was no surprise. What he was saying—what they both were saying—made sense. But no matter what she told herself, her stomach still felt as if it were made of lead.

She stared at the floor. "So we should end it?"

Ian turned to her, his eyes still tender. "We should end it," he murmured.

"I..." Erica swallowed. "I'm sorry it didn't work out."

Ian nodded. "Me too." He reached down, clasped her hand, and gently pulled her up into a hug. It was tender, warm, and over far too soon.

Ian walked to the door and opened it. He glanced back over his shoulder. "Goodbye." The door closed behind him.

"Bye."

It was inevitable. Their relationship had always been a sham. She was so stupid to get emotionally involved. She should have known better.

Erica sat on her bed, put her head in her hands, and sobbed.

She could still smell him in the air, and now they'd be what? Friends? There was too much pain. How could they be friends when even thinking of him was like a knife in her side?

How could he throw away their relationship so abruptly? In minutes. Did the last month mean nothing to him? She loved him so much. How could he not love her? Why wasn't she good enough for him?

Her stomach roiled. She ran to the bathroom and vomited.

#

In its way, that night was worse than any in the Gauntlet. She didn't sleep, but turned over in her mind everything that had happened, again and again.

One moment, she could accept it, knowing the relationship was never real and it was best to rip the band-aid off quickly. The next, she was nothing but tears, certain even a fake relationship with Ian was a hundred times better than something real with anyone else. Nobody else made her feel so alive. Nobody else challenged her, supported her, and cared about her the way he did. Even when it was fake.

She'd lost all that forever.

Erica rose the next day and went through the morning routine. She felt disconnected from it all, like she was outside her body, watching herself go through the motions.

She ran into Renee in the mess.

"Erica, what's wrong?" Renee said. "You look... I mean, your eyes are red and..."

Erica's mouth twisted. At least she was putting on a good show for the cameras. "Yeah. Ian and I broke up."

"Oh. That's good. I mean..." Renee shook her head, cleared her throat, and looked at the door.

"No, it's fine," Erica said, struggling to maintain her composure.

"It was a mutual decision. But I'm still sad."

Renee wrapped her arms around Erica. "I understand."

Erica relaxed in the hug. It wasn't Ian, but it was something. This was how things were meant to be. She just wished it didn't hurt so much.

They separated when Cam entered the room. He had a pronounced limp.

"Are you hurt, Cam?" Erica said, wiping her eyes, happy for any distraction from her tumbling thoughts. "Didn't you get fixed after Irenic?" She knew the question didn't make sense. Irenic hadn't gone anywhere near Cam's leg yesterday.

Cam shook his head. "No. Something else." He sat down and rolled the right leg of his pants up to his knee. Just above Cam's ankle, the skin bulged.

"You absorbed something into your leg?" Erica said.

"No. My leg was aching yesterday. I woke up with this."

"What do you think it is?" She wouldn't expect a sensible answer from anyone else, but this was the new Cam.

"Bone cancer," he said, his voice bland.

"Let me see," Renee said. She knelt down, pressing the tips of her fingers against the lump. After half a minute, she looked up, concern in her eyes. "It could be. How long have you had symptoms?"

"Since yesterday."

"That's too fast."

Cam shrugged.

"It's probably something else, then," Erica said quickly. "I wouldn't worry about it until you know more. But you should show Lois. She's an oncologist." Her forehead smoothed as a thought occurred to her. "I imagine they can fix it in five seconds with the medical printer."

Cam nodded, and they began eating breakfast.

After a few minutes, Ian arrived. He looked as composed as ever, not a hair out of place. But then again, he had no reason to look flustered—it wasn't like the breakup meant anything to him. He nodded to Erica as he went to get his meal. She wanted to cry. Instead, she kept her expression neutral as she nodded back.

Eve, Morrison, and Jen soon followed. Though Ian and Erica shared the news of their breakup—leading to a small, satisfied smile from Morrison—most of the breakfast conversation revolved around

Cam's leg. As a group, they concluded that even if it were cancer, the medical printer should take care of it.

Jen seemed particularly intrigued with the distended skin. Her light shone on it for a few seconds, then on the ping-pong ball, and then back to the bulge. It bounced to a round eraser on the arts desk, one of the lightbulbs, and back to the leg. Finally, it flip-flopped between the bump and the yolk of Erica's egg several times.

"You ate too many eggs," Jen said authoritatively.

"I don't think that's it," Cam said. Although he had only eaten half the meal, he pushed his plate away. "I'm going to medical." The others continued to eat in silence.

A few minutes after they finished, Irenic strode into the room. "Renee, Erica, and Ian. To the dojo."

The three looked at each other.

"It's still four hours until class," Ian said.

"Yes." Irenic turned and walked away, not even glancing back to see if they were obeying her command.

Ignoring Eve and Morrison's questioning glances, they followed Irenic, trotting to catch up. The elevator ride was silent, with Irenic maintaining her usual stony expression and the three students afraid to even speak. Was it a coincidence that Irenic had requested the three of them? Or was this related to them hacking Jeemoh's servers?

They shuffled into the dojo, waiting anxiously in the center of the floor for Irenic's instruction.

Irenic's face gave away nothing. "You three against me. The usual rules. Go."

Renee instantly stepped to the side, away from the others, raising her arms into a guard position. Irenic pivoted to face the other two. When she got close, she feinted toward Erica, and then did a side kick into Ian's kneecap. The crack echoed through the room. As Ian fell, Irenic followed up with a hard uppercut. His head snapped back, and he collapsed on the ground.

Trying to take advantage of Irenic's distraction, Renee approached from the side. But Irenic spun to face her, and Renee retreated once more. This time, Irenic pursued, circling cautiously.

"You have to attack, Erica," Renee said. "We can win this."

Erica nodded. Despite her skepticism, she inched forward.

Faster than it seemed possible, Irenic dove for Renee's waist, tackling her to the ground. Renee wrapped her legs around Irenic's waist, trying to hold her close.

Recognizing that this would be the best chance she would get, Erica charged forward. Before she reached them, Irenic raised her upper body, her overwhelming size and strength enabling her to break Renee's grasp. Irenic slammed her elbow down, her full body weight behind it. Renee tried to interpose her hands, but she wasn't strong enough. The blow landed impossibly hard on her cheek. Renee's eyes rolled back in her head.

Irenic didn't follow up with another blow, but instead touched the side of Renee's neck just under her jaw. For an instant, Erica was behind Irenic. She quickly evaluated the different options. All her punches and kicks seemed to cause no real damage, not enough to stop Irenic. But there was one thing that seemed to work.

Erica reached both arms around Irenic's head. Irenic batted away her left hand, but was too slow with the right. Erica dug her fingers into Irenic's eye.

Irenic spun away on the floor and stood up. Even with her right eye closed, blood trickled down her cheek. But she seemed unfazed. Her only concession to the injury was to turn her head slightly to the right as she strode forward to attack.

Irenic's wound didn't seem to slow her down. From then on, the fight was much like their first. This time, Erica ended up with two broken arms and a disturbing bulge on the right side of her abdomen she suspected was a broken rib.

Irenic revived the others with smelling salts, and then stood in front of them, holding a gauze square over her eye.

"Hacking Jeemoh's computers is forbidden."

Erica flinched. That was a mistake. Spikes of pain shot through her arms and torso. She resolved to keep her upper body as motionless as possible.

"If you do it again, I won't be as gentle," Irenic continued.

Erica wanted to glance at the others to see their reactions, but was afraid to take her eyes off Irenic.

"Understood?"

The three nodded.

"Let's get fixed. It's not long before your martial arts class."

Erica groaned. Irenic ignored her, marching from the room.

Lois looked up from a tablet as the group limped into medical. Her lips thinned as she saw them, but she didn't comment on their condition. "You dealt with the issue?" she asked.

"Yes," Irenic said.

"Excellent." She went back to perusing an X-ray on the tablet as, one by one, the medical printer healed them.

"You're dismissed," Irenic finally said as she wiped away the dried blood around her now-healed eye. "Thirteen hundred hours, remember."

"As if we could forget," Ian muttered as he turned toward the door.

Lois looked up. "If you have a moment, Erica?"

Erica sighed. After Irenic's beating, she now had to sit through a lecture from her mother as well? She stood rigidly as the others left.

Lois gazed at her calmly. "That wasn't your brightest idea, but you've always needed to find out stuff yourself."

Erica's eyes blazed. "It was worth it."

Lois chuckled. "I imagine it was. Just don't do it again." She looked back to the image on the tablet.

Erica frowned. "Is that all? I can go?"

"No," Lois said. Holding two opposite corners, she spun the tablet in her hands several times. "There's one other thing. What do you make of Cam?"

"You're the doctor, not me," Erica said acerbically.

"I don't mean his medical condition. I mean, how is he coping? He and Renee have abilities that impact their mental facilities, and that can be difficult. How's he doing with that?"

Erica bit her lip. What the heck was her mother looking for? "You know how he is. He never really says much of anything. I guess he's smarter and knows more. He rarely loses playing that trivia game with Ren. But he doesn't talk about emotions and stuff. He's Cam, right?"

"Yes." Lois shrugged. "It's not that big a deal. I just want to be sure he's okay. Maybe I'll talk with him."

"So he's fine, then? I mean, his leg's fine?"

Lois passed the tablet to Erica. It felt hot in her hands. On the screen was an X-ray of a lower leg. The bone was mostly well defined, but near the ankle was a blurry bulge.

Lois moved a few steps toward the cabinets. "That's his leg. Most of it's normal, but near the lower tibia, you can see—"

Flames erupting from the tablet's screen. Skin blackening in the fire. Shrieking.

Reflexively, Erica hurled the tablet away. It hit the concrete wall, shattering the screen.

Lois stared back at her in astonishment. "What on earth are—"

Flames burst from the tablet, rising a foot into the air. Almost instantly, sprinklers came on.

"Mom, watch out!" Erica shouted. She leaped forward, pushing her mother to the floor, away from the flaming device. Erica barely had time to shift her body before the tablet exploded.

She staggered as the heated air and tiny pieces of glass impacted her back and legs. Thanks to her adjustments, the biggest shards missed, but several smaller pieces sliced into her like darts. Erica fell to her knees, covering her head with her hands, cowering as the heat washed over her. The sour burning smell made her want to retch.

Her mother turned her head toward her, eyes wide. "Are you okay?" To Erica's ringing ears, she sounded like she was on the other side of a window.

Erica nodded. The water drenched her clothes and made the wounds sting, but that was nothing compared to what could have happened. She stared back at the blaze. The fire was halfway to the ceiling.

"Let security take care of it," Lois said.

Even twenty feet away, Erica could feel the heat. She crouched lower, ignoring the pain as the shards of glass shifted in her back.

Lois seemed almost unharmed. She'd been shielded by Erica's body.

Had her mother just tried to murder her? Erica's eyes widened as the thought occurred to her. Lois had passed her the tablet only seconds before it exploded. She'd stepped away the instant the device left her hands.

Erica trembled. Only her vision had saved her. If she hadn't thrown the tablet, the explosion would have killed her. It might have hurt Lois, too, but they were in medical—anything short of a fatal wound could be healed.

The sprinklers stopped as two soldiers burst in carrying fire extinguishers. The fire hadn't spread, so it only took seconds to extinguish it.

Erica slowly rose. With every movement, her wounds sent spikes of pain through her back.

Seeing Erica wince, Lois spun her around to examine the injuries, and then guided her to the operating table. "Lie on your stomach." She turned to the soldiers. "Both of you, go find Dr. Rahal. She was in Imaging."

The soldiers nodded, scampering from the room.

Lois eyed Erica's back critically. "None of this looks too bad. We just need to get the glass out before we fix you."

"Okay," Erica said quietly, her thoughts spinning. Should she just lie there? If Lois had planned the attack, she could grab a knife, complete the job, and claim Erica had been killed by the flying glass. Had she sent the soldiers away for that exact reason? Why send two soldiers to get one person?

But if Lois was guilty, this could be her best opportunity to get proof. Her visions ought to warn her before her mother struck, allowing her to catch her in the act.

Erica deliberately relaxed, trying to appear calm and confident.

Lois slid open a glass-doored cupboard.

That was where Dr. Rahal kept the surgical tools. It took all of Erica's willpower to just lie there as her mother surveyed the implements.

Finally, Lois decided. She picked up a scalpel.

CHAPTER TWELVE

To appear unconcerned, Erica looked away. Lois rummaged for a few more seconds before turning. Her steps echoed on the concrete floor as she returned to Erica's side.

Erica's muscles tensed. She waited for the vision, ready to move the instant before Lois struck, listening for any sign of what her mother was doing. Would she go for the throat? Or stab her in the back?

Were the fans on the ventilation system always that loud?

A heartbeat passed. And then another.

The blow didn't come. Erica turned her head, unable to resist the temptation to see what her mother was up to. Lois was meticulously lining up medical instruments on a tray beside the table.

"I could do it," Lois said. "But Dr. Rahal's better."

Erica shook her head in confusion. "Better at what?" Murder?

"At extracting glass. Do you remember me saying that?" Lois' concern was clear in her eyes. "Do you feel disoriented?"

"No, I'm fine. I misheard you earlier. But the ringing's gone now." Erica relaxed. Maybe Lois wasn't responsible. "What could make the tablet catch fire like that?"

Lois shook her head. "I don't know. I've heard of lithium batteries exploding when they overheat, but it's rare." Her eyes narrowed. "Why did you throw it?"

Erica thought quickly. "It was scorching. Nearly burned my hands."

"That's probably what it was then. A defect. I'll have someone look at it to be sure."

Dr. Rahal entered at a run. She surveyed the twisted remnants of the tablet, wrinkling her nose. "What's the situation?"

"The batteries in a tablet exploded," Lois said dispassionately. "Erica has glass in her back, but nothing too concerning."

"Let's see what I can do about that." Dr. Rahal's manner got more businesslike. After putting on a surgical gown, she snapped on latex gloves.

Selecting a pair of scissors from the tray of tools Lois had assembled, Rahal cut away Erica's shirt. "It doesn't look too bad. We'll have you fixed in no time. Any idea of the cause of the explosion?"

"A random defect in the hardware, we think," Lois said.

"Hmm," Dr. Rahal said, her tone distracted. "I didn't think those could happen around Erica."

Lois frowned. "It is surprising. But her wounds are superficial. Maybe something worse would have happened to her if this hadn't occurred. The apparent bad luck could actually be good luck."

The explosion still seemed too well timed to be an accident, but Erica kept her voice bland, hiding her suspicions. "That's probably true. It would explain why the failure happened at that exact moment."

"Mmm," Lois said.

Dr. Rahal didn't apply anesthetic when extracting the shards, but she mostly didn't need the scalpel and the pain was almost insignificant compared to what Irenic had inflicted. After the glass was removed and the medical printer had closed the wounds, Lois dismissed Erica.

She went to her room for a shirt to replace the temporary hospital gown, and then met up with the others in the mess. They were sitting on the couch playing video games.

Ian raised his eyebrows, grinning as she approached. "That took a while. Your mom had a lot to say."

Erica shook her head. "A tablet exploded. You didn't hear anything?"

Ian's jaw dropped. "No. Are you hurt?" Putting down the video game controller, he scanned her for any sign of injury.

"I got hit by some glass, but I'm fine now."

"What happened exactly?" Morrison said, his voice suspicious.

"I was talking with Lois in medical. She passed me a tablet to show me something and stepped away. The tablet got hot, so I threw it. A few seconds later, it exploded. It was all really fast."

Morrison's face darkened. "It sounds like your mom was trying to kill you."

"I don't think so," Erica said, shaking her head. She didn't intend to defend Lois, but she wouldn't lie, either. "Lois seemed as surprised as me."

"She lied to you for your entire life without you realizing it, so excuse me if I don't consider you the most reliable witness," Morrison said sarcastically. "Tablets don't just blow up."

"They do," Renee said, and Cam nodded. "It's rare, but it can happen if the batteries overheat."

"It's too big a coincidence," Eve said, her tone definitive. "I swear, I would've stabbed your mother on the spot."

Erica shook her head. She'd had ample time to think it through. "If Lois wanted me dead, she's had many opportunities to do it. She could just tell Irenic to have a training accident."

"Someone else, then," Morrison said. "Dr. Rahal."

Erica's frowned. "She wasn't there when it happened, but the tablet was hers. I suppose she could have set it up beforehand."

"It could be someone in security, if they're watching us all the time," Ian said, glancing at the ceiling. "Or one of the computer guys."

"But why?" Erica said, her tone far more dubious than she felt. "Why would they want me dead?" That was the piece she was missing. The explosion had been too perfectly timed to be a random malfunction. But without a motive, how could she make any sense of it?

"Who knows why?" Morrison's face was red, his voice bitter. "We don't know why Jeemoh does anything. Just what they tell us."

Ian grimaced. "Medical's open to everyone. Anyone could have gone in there and sabotaged it. Anyone with a grudge."

That wasn't a scenario Erica had considered. "A single disgruntled individual seems far more likely than a Jeemoh plot," she said thoughtfully. "Realistically, Jeemoh can kill us almost any time they want. Blowing up a tablet seems far too convoluted. Someone acting alone makes much more sense. But even then, I can't think of anyone who hates me enough to kill me." She flinched as a thought crossed her mind. "Though I guess Vince's dad works for Jeemoh."

Ian blanched. "I didn't even consider that. Do you think he would go after you?"

Erica nodded slowly. "If he's anything like Vince. I've never met him, but we did kill his son. We had no choice, but he might blame us anyway."

"Do you really think it's him?" Ian rubbed his forehead with both hands.

"I don't know."

"What about Irenic?" Renee asked. "You smashed her in the head with that poker."

Erica winced. "I forgot about that." She chewed on her lip as she considered the possibility. "She's certainly psycho. But I wonder if she'd know how to do it. Isn't she just muscle?"

"She's a Jeemoh agent." Ian said. "She couldn't kill you in class without everyone knowing exactly what happened."

Erica nodded. "It could be her." But there was no evidence, and everyone here was a Jeemoh agent, capable of rigging a tablet to explode. She sighed. "It could be anyone. If it wasn't an accident."

"It was no accident," Morrison said emphatically.

"Then we need to figure out who it was," Erica said firmly. "And do it fast, before they strike again." Everyone nodded. "And we should all be careful. If there is a killer, we don't know their motives. Any of us could be the next target."

Irenic entered the room, clutching a stack of papers. Instantly, everyone went quiet.

She stared at them suspiciously, her eyes moving from face to face. Finally, she said, "I have your schedules. You'll start this morning."

"What?" Ian said. "After what happened to Erica?"

"She's unharmed," Irenic said as if that settled everything. "Your schedules are customized." She held out a piece of paper. "Erica."

Erica took it hesitantly. It was a grid of days and times, with course titles in bold. Half of them looked like classes from high school, albeit with an emphasis on math and statistics rather than the humanities. The other half was more intriguing. *Covert Operations. Applied Modern Weaponry. Basic Survival. Practical Persuasion.*

They compared schedules. Ian, Cam, Morrison, and Eve's classes overlapped a lot with Erica's, though they each seemed to specialize—Ian on chemistry, Cam on electronics, Morrison on physics, and Eve on anatomy.

Renee and Jen's schedules, completely different, looked like the self-help section of a bookstore—*Creative Thought*, *Decision Theory*, and *Improvisation* for Renee, and *Social Interactions*, *Prioritization*, and *Life Skills* for Jen.

Irenic escorted Ian, Morrison, Eve, Cam, and Erica to a classroom on the seventeenth floor. They peered around warily as they entered, as if Erica's attacker might be lurking there, ready to try it again. But the room seemed safe.

As with most other areas within Jeemoh, the classroom made no concessions to adornment or beauty, but was strictly functional, a classroom without a soul. Several heavy tables, each with two notebooks and two pens, faced a wall covered in whiteboards. At the front of the room, a middle-aged man with grey hair and a stringy moustache sat at a desk. He nodded to Irenic. She nodded back and departed.

The man waited for them to find seats. When everyone was ready, he stood, adjusting the front of his ill-fitting black military uniform.

"Hello. I am Senior Special Agent Hackett. If you have something stuck up your ass, you can call me 'Sir' or 'Agent Hackett'. If you don't, 'Hack' is fine. You're here to learn about covert operations.

"We'll start with what I call the 'shoot-yourself-in-the-head-boring' material: history and theory of covert operations, information gathering and analysis, mission planning, and project management. From there, we'll move on to more interesting topics such as observation and surveillance, information technology and encryption, weapons of mass destruction, money laundering, terrorism, sleight of hand, and disguises.

"Any questions before we get started?"

Perhaps this was an opportunity to find out more about what Jeemoh expected of them. Erica put up her hand.

"Don't bother raising your hand," Hack said. "Just talk when you get an opening."

"Are we actually going to use what we learn?" Erica shrugged, looking around at the others. "I mean, aren't there experienced agents who will be able to do this stuff way better than we can?"

"You'll definitely use some of it. Whether you will use everything you learn will depend on your assigned missions. But one thing to remember—and this will be a constant theme in this class—even if you don't use all these skills, you will meet people who do. Your life will be easier if you can identify and nullify such individuals before they put a knife in your back. Figuratively and literally."

Eve's hand twitched upward a few inches before she put it back. With a slight, lopsided grin, she asked, "Will we learn how to use a tablet to assassinate someone?"

Erica barely held back a gasp.

Hack's eyes narrowed, but, otherwise, he didn't react. "That's a surprisingly specific question. As a defensive measure, you will learn general assassination techniques related to electronic devices. More detailed discussions would be reserved for future courses or on a case-by-case basis."

Ignoring Eve's smirk, Hack asked, "Now, can anyone name the primary goal of all covert operations at Jeemoh?"

Everyone in the class suddenly seemed to have a reason not to make eye contact with Hack. He looked at them flatly, standing there with his arms crossed. After about thirty seconds, he sat on his desk. Another minute passed, and the class started to get uncomfortable, but Hack just sat there, watching them.

Finally, Ian said nervously, "Accomplishing the assigned mission?"

"No. That's always a secondary goal, though."

Morrison's mouth twisted. "Not getting killed?"

"Another good try. But no."

"Figures," Morrison muttered.

Erica, frowning, actually started thinking about the question. Covert operations? Was everyone missing the obvious? "Not to get caught?"

Hack smiled. "Close enough. The primary goal of every covert operation is *deniability*. Not all operations will be covert, but on a covert operation, the top priority is to conceal Jeemoh's involvement and enable plausible deniability." He reached into a drawer, drew out a black ballpoint pen, and tossed it to Erica. "Good work. Here's your reward. You can keep it, but see if you can figure it out."

Figure it out? Erica half-listened to Hack as she played with the pen. It seemed completely normal. She clicked the button at the end and the tip retracted, reappearing when she clicked it again. She scribbled on a sheet of paper. A smooth black line appeared.

Like most retractable pens, it had a line in the center where the upper half connected with the lower half. She tried to unscrew the two halves, but it wouldn't turn.

Erica glanced over at Ian to her left. He was watching her. He raised his eyebrows as if to ask if she was having any luck with the pen. She was about to smile at him and roll her eyes, but then she remembered their breakup and felt like crying, so she didn't. She looked back down.

Nothing had changed for him. He wasn't the one in love. But how could she pretend life was normal when everything he did reminded her that he didn't want her? It hurt constantly.

She gripped the pen, pushing down on the button at the end, squeezing it so hard that the pocket clip cut into her hand. The physical pain was a relief, a sign she could still feel something other than the pain in her heart.

Erica jumped as an inch-long needle popped out of the pen's tip. She glanced around to see if anyone had noticed, and then pressed the button on the end again, causing the needle to retract. After a few minutes of fiddling around, she figured out how it worked. One short click would bring out the regular ballpoint head, but holding the button down for several seconds would result in the needle.

"Good job, Erica," Hack said. "That was quick."

"I got lucky."

Hack smiled at her. "Yeah, I guess there's that. The pen is easily hidden and won't show up on most security scans. The needle is used to deliver a poison, but that one isn't primed. I'd estimate that in the past forty years, one hundred and twenty American agents have fallen victim to pens like that. If you have an occasion to use one, swing by and we can talk about the best substance for your job. Sarin's good if you're in a rush. Polonium, if you'd prefer it to take months."

This time, Erica did gasp. Was Hack saying what she thought he was saying?

CHAPTER THIRTEEN

Jeemoh did murder people. And Hack wasn't even trying to hide it.

Erica glanced around at the others. They were frozen, their eyes glued on Hack.

She swallowed, rubbing her mouth. If Jeemoh considered murder to be just another way to accomplish a goal, then the tablet explosion seemed even less likely to be a random accident. She shivered.

Ian was the first to voice his concerns. "You are saying we might want to murder someone?"

Ian's tone was flat, but Erica could see a vein on the side of his neck pulsing. He'd killed Vince in self-defense and was still upset about it. How would he react if Lois ordered them to kill?

"Not today, but it could come up," Hack said, his tone casual. "A strategic assassination can be optimal in many situations."

Eve raised an eyebrow, grinning. "Now we're talking." Hack ignored her.

Ian leaned back in his chair, crossing his arms. "I won't do it."

Hack nodded. "And that's your choice. Those missions are only done by volunteers." He shrugged. "Let me tell you a bit about the world. In Lacundi, Hovati Lato has been organizing an army of children between the ages of seven and twelve. To recruit 'soldiers', he sends roving gangs into villages at night. He tears kids from the arms of their screaming parents, killing any who resist. He beats the children until they comply, teaches them to hold a Kalashnikov, and sends them out to grab more kids. And that's the boys. It's worse for the girls.

"Lato's goal is to build a big enough child army to overthrow the ruling party of Lacundi. Which, I admit, is corrupt.

"Over the last three years, we estimate Lato's recruited or murdered approximately fourteen thousand children. Even if that ended today, every one of these children will be scarred, unlikely to ever integrate back into Lacundian society. They are permanently broken. Even their families don't want them anymore. At best, those kids can look forward to becoming mercenaries, criminals, and prostitutes. Almost all will die of drugs, starvation, disease, or violence before their thirtieth birthdays. And every week that passes, Lato's conscripting hundreds of new kids.

"If we quietly eliminate Lato, we estimate an eighty-percent chance that his whole organization collapses. The kids he's taken won't recover, but at least they won't be kidnapping anyone else. I think that's the best outcome we have available right now. And to me, one carefully planned assassination is low cost and low risk.

"But I'll mark you down in the 'murder is wrong' column, Ian."

Ian was silent, his eyes troubled.

Hack scanned the faces of his students. "Jeemoh is about getting results in the most efficient way possible. Black-and-white thinking is a luxury.

"Besides, even if you don't use these tools yourself, you should expect our enemies to use them. So, if you suspect you are ever in contact with a dangerous substance, go to medical, even if symptoms don't appear immediately. You aren't immune to polonium."

Erica swallowed. First an attempt on her life, and now a lecture about the moral justification for murder. What the heck had she got herself into?

#

Most of the rest of the classes were structured similarly. The only exception was *Statistics* where Erica was the only student and had one-on-one tutoring.

The day went by quickly, but Erica was a terrible student, sleepwalking through her courses, her mind on Ian and the explosion. She knew intellectually that she needed to absorb the material, but it just didn't seem that important.

What was it Ian said? They should end their relationship so they could focus on training? Yeah, right. Even with all the other distractions, she still got queasy whenever he crossed her mind.

After the first class, Cam had limped away, claiming he needed to get the diagnosis on his leg from Lois. When Erica went to the mess hall for dinner—hoping that, unlike lunch, she'd be able to keep it down—she found him waiting with the others.

Erica adopted a pleasant expression she didn't feel. "How's it going, Cam? All better?"

Cam shook his head. The others were silent.

"What is it?"

Cam looked down. "Bone cancer."

Erica frowned. Why was everyone so quiet? She must be missing something. "Have you tried the medical printer?"

"They say it only repairs trauma. It prints cells. It doesn't remove them. It would probably make it worse. They won't let me near it," he said in a monotone.

"What about traditional treatments? Chemotherapy?"

"Lois is looking into it. But she's never seen a tumor develop so quickly and is worried that it might be related to my ability. She's scared to rush into anything."

Erica's eyes widened. "So what are they doing?"

"They're looking at the biopsy and discussing it. They're doing nothing." Cam stared down at the lump near his ankle. It was larger than it had been that morning.

Erica stared at him in shock. At home, Lois had seemed a miracle worker, telling story after story of people she had cured. But now, when Erica's friend was sick, she was helpless.

"I'm sorry, Cam," she said sympathetically. "Don't worry though. I'm sure they'll figure it out."

Cam just sat there, his shoulders slumped. "Yeah."

The conversation over dinner was muted. Afterward, Renee selected *A Dissolution of Mind* from the bookshelf and returned to her room to read it for what Erica thought must have been the tenth time. Cam similarly vanished while the others gathered around the TV.

Erica didn't feel like spending the evening trying to avoid eye contact with Ian, so she retreated to her own room. The temporary phone her mother had given her was ringing as she arrived. Amid all the distractions, she'd forgotten her regular call with her father.

"Hi, Dad."

"Hi, honey. How's it going?"

"It's going." The phone was probably tapped, but it didn't matter. By now, her self-censorship was instinctive. "Had a slight problem with a tablet today."

"What sort of problem?"

"The explosive kind." Not wanting to upset her father, Erica kept her tone light.

"What?"

"Yeah, it got hot and blew up."

"Are you hurt?" The concern in Philip's tone was clear.

"I only got some minor cuts from the glass. I'm fine."

"What caused it?"

"Lois thought it was an accident. That it was defective."

After a short pause, Philip said cautiously. "You know that it could be something else, right? Something deliberate."

"I'm aware of that." Erica said crisply. She didn't want to get into a big discussion about it, sharing all her fears over the phone with her dad. He couldn't help, and the perpetrator might be listening.

Her dad seemed to understand her reticence. "Well, as long as you're fine."

"I'm great. It was no big deal. Irenic hurt me more."

"Irenic?"

"Our martial arts instructor. She snapped my elbow. Twice, in fact. It hurt way more than the glass."

"Good grief. She actually broke your arm?"

"Yes. And Ian's ribs and Cam's wrist, all in the span of about half an hour. Her fight with this new girl, Eve, was worse. Blood was everywhere." Erica kept her tone matter of fact because if she did anything else, she was pretty sure she'd be overcome with either manic giggling or uncontrollable weeping. Was this what it came to when she tried to explain her life to an outsider?

"She sounds like a psycho."

Erica grunted, an ironic smile on her face. "You think?"

"When you recover, you should find someone else to train with. It's too risky. She might kill you."

"Then she'd have to beat herself with a stick."

"What?"

"Never mind. I don't think she'd go that far."

"It sounds like she would. I'm worried about you."

"Don't be. Irenic's completely nuts, but she's disciplined and precise. I don't think she'd kill someone without orders, and she's not the type to get sloppy and kill accidentally." Erica realized how silly the words were as she said them. Even if Irenic wasn't behind the tablet attack, after Hack's lecture, how could she be certain that someone wouldn't order Irenic to murder her?

Erica could hear her dad's frown over the phone. "I can't not worry, Erica. First, you tell me about an explosion. And now it sounds like even the training could kill you, let alone a mission. This is extreme, even for your mother. You know you don't need to stay there. You have a choice. You can leave."

Could she? Not really. She couldn't abandon all her friends just because of the possibility that someone had it in for her. In fact, it was better if the attacker targeted her rather than the others. With her visions, she'd be able to thwart most attacks.

And she could cope with the martial arts classes. Irenic's training methods were unorthodox. But perhaps that was no more than she should expect considering the easy availability of the medical printer. They would learn more from real fighting than sparring. How it felt to hit someone. How it felt to be hit. How to continue fighting when your arm was broken. Why hold back if they didn't need to? Going all out now might save their lives later.

Erica could almost hear Irenic's voice echoing in her head. *Life does not have padded floors...*

Besides, despite the threats, her original reason for joining Jeemoh still seemed valid. They'd investigated Jeemoh for weeks and had discovered nothing incriminating. Jeemoh was a force for good as her mother claimed. And if that was the case, could she abandon it out of fear, when she had the potential to do so much, to save innocent lives?

"No," Erica said, trying to sound certain. "I won't give up just because the path's a bit bumpy."

Philip sighed. "Yeah, I figured. Still, if you change your mind, I'm always here."

"Thanks, Dad. I love you."

"I love you too."

Erica hung up the phone and sighed. Her dad supported her, as always, but he had sounded so worried. She wished she could dismiss his concerns as normal parental paranoia. The problem was that the tablet had proven he was right.

It was early. Erica didn't mean to fall asleep, just read in bed for a half hour. But, after the exhausting day, she was asleep minutes after her head touched the pillow.

When Erica awoke, the lights were out. She squeezed her eyes shut and tried to sleep again, but couldn't. The breakup conversation. The explosion. Her mother holding the scalpel. It all mixed together in her swirling thoughts until she wanted to pound the bed in frustration.

Finally, she arose. She needed to do something, find a distraction from the images in her brain. Lois had said the labs were available twenty-four-hours a day, and this seemed like as good a time as any to verify that assertion. It was probably safe—a potential murderer wouldn't expect Erica to be prowling around so late at night.

She took the elevator to the seventeenth floor and was surprised to find the lights already on in the chemistry lab. Erica peered in to see Renee pouring one beaker of transparent liquid into another. As she did, the fluid turned pink.

Renee looked up as Erica approached. "You too? This is Grand Central Station tonight."

Erica raised her eyebrows. "Oh?"

"Cam came by earlier. Why are you here?"

"Couldn't sleep. You?"

"Same." Renee crouched, lowering her eyes to the level of the liquid in the container. "Is it weird I find this soothing?"

"What? Chemistry?"

"Yep. Following a recipe, mixing the chemicals, building something new. It's like gardening, but with the added excitement of flames and toxic gas when you mess up."

Erica grinned. "Yeah, that's weird."

Renee nodded, turning back to the beaker. "I thought so."

Erica sat on a stool, watching her friend, for ten minutes. Renee didn't seem to be in a chatty mood. Finally, deciding Renee might not want her staring over her shoulder, Erica departed.

She continued down the hallway, past the other labs. Near the end, light shone through the crack beneath a door. Like a moth drawn to flame, Erica walked toward it.

As she approached the door, she heard a methodical grinding sound, like someone rubbing a rock over rough cement. The sign on the door indicated it was the electronics lab, although Erica couldn't imagine what electronic equipment would make that sound.

Erica smelled a faint, familiar odor in the air, like iron. In an instant, her mind shot back to the Gauntlet, to the room where she and Ian had found Vince's severed hand.

That smell was blood.

Erica tried the door handle, but it was locked. She rapped twice.

The noise stopped, and then she heard Cam's voice, faint, behind the door.

"Go away."

CHAPTER FOURTEEN

The grinding noise resumed.

"It's Erica, Cam. Let me in. The labs are supposed to be open all the time." Erica tried to sound confident, not concerned.

Cam didn't respond. The methodical grinding continued.

Had her attacker targeted Cam this time? He hadn't sounded scared, but there *was* that distinctive odor. Why wasn't Cam answering?

Erica shook the door handle and pressed her hand against the scanner, but the door didn't budge.

What was happening? Was Cam hurt? She needed the door open now.

Renee could help. She could do anything. Erica raced down the hall to the chemistry lab. Her friend was still there, stirring a beaker.

"Renee, I need you. Cam is…" What could she say? She didn't even know what was going on. "Just follow me."

Erica ran back toward the electronics lab, not even glancing back to see if Renee was behind her. She arrived well before her friend.

The grinding noise had stopped, but the door still wouldn't budge.

"Cam's in there, and I can smell blood. Can you open the door?" Erica asked breathlessly.

Renee jiggled the handle and touched the panel beside the door as Erica had earlier. "Not quickly. In a couple of hours, maybe."

"I don't think we have that much time."

Renee knocked on the door. "Cam, it's Renee. Can you let us in?"

"I will. Just a sec. I'm cleaning up."

Renee paced back and forth while they waited. After several minutes, the door finally swung open, Cam peering out from behind it.

Erica pushed by him into the room. She hadn't seen the lab earlier, and she couldn't tell if anything was out of place. Computers, soldering irons, and half-assembled electronics were in bins, on countertops, and even on the floor.

The smell of blood was more noticeable than ever, but Cam was the only person in the room. Erica turned to him, her eyes intense. "What were you doing?"

"Surgery," Cam said.

Erica glanced toward the garbage can and realized it was filled with bloody rags. She looked back at the rest of the room. Her mouth fell open. A hacksaw rested on one of the tables.

"What did you do?" Almost unwillingly, Erica's eyes were drawn to Cam's right leg. The bottom half of his leg was completely gone. In its place was a futuristic-looking prosthetic, all springs, wires, and steel.

"Wha— Why?" Erica said. Her knees felt weak. She collapsed on a chair.

"To maximize my chances of survival."

Erica was close to hyperventilating. "Cam, Lois is one of the best oncologists in the country. She's an expert on cancer. Why didn't you let her treat you? You didn't have to do this." A trickle of blood from the stump found a path down the shiny shin, finally coming to rest on the metallic foot.

Cam looked away. "There was no time." Leaning heavily on wooden crutches, he hobbled to the nearest chair, the metal making a disconcerting tapping sound on the concrete floor.

"Of course you had time. Lois just needed to figure it out. This is appalling."

Cam shook his head. He shivered, though Erica didn't know whether it was from loss of blood or just being the focus of the conversation. "It isn't so bad. I would have died."

"You don't know that," Erica said, trying to keep her eyes from drifting down to where gleaming metal met ragged flesh.

"I do. I've... I've read stuff. Every study on bone cancer. Every scrap of data I could find. I've crunched it all, and this is my best option. Thirty-two percent long-term survival rate and eighty-nine percent medium-term survival rate."

"It's been, like, sixteen hours since you found out."

"I read fast."

Had Cam gone mad? That didn't even make any sense.

Renee knelt down beside Cam, peering at the prosthetic and stump. "It's not bleeding much, considering."

"My ability helps. Though the hacksaw was stupid. I should have absorbed the bone saw from medical. Would've been neater, but after I started, I couldn't stop to go get it." He looked at Erica earnestly. "Will you get it for me?"

"No!" Erica said. She felt dizzy. She closed her eyes and rested her head in her hands. How was this even possible? How could Cam cut off his own leg without passing out from pain or blood loss?

When Erica opened her eyes again, she caught Cam watching her. He quickly turned away, lifted a beaker with a sand-colored liquid in it, and gulped down several mouthfuls.

"Is that anesthetic?" Erica said. It was a banal question at a time like this, but the whole conversation seemed surreal.

"No."

"How did you deal with the pain?" Renee said, sounding almost like Dr. Rahal quizzing a patient.

"I control electricity in my body." Perhaps in response to Erica's blank look, Cam added, "Like nerve impulses. I shut them off."

Cam's ability was clearly much more than Erica had realized.

"And that's what, then?" Renee said, gesturing at the beaker. "Methotrexate?"

"Yes. And some other experimental chemotherapy drugs I made in the lab."

Cam was going to kill himself. A month ago, he probably couldn't even spell cancer. Now, he was performing surgery on himself and mixing chemotherapy cocktails. He was taking his life into his own hands instead of leaving it to Lois, the expert. Cam's stupidity was legendary, but this was a new low. What a horrible decision.

"It was a good decision," Renee said dispassionately. "Both the leg and the drugs."

Apparently, everyone had gone insane.

Cam smiled faintly at Renee, nodded, and looked away, blushing.

"We should get you down to medical," Erica said. "The printer can fix it."

"Lois says I can't use the printer until she's sure there's no cancer anywhere in my body."

"At least have them look at it."

Cam shook his head. "No need. It's fine."

"I insist."

Cam's brow furrowed. "Insist away. I'm going to bed." He chugged the rest of the liquid from the beaker, stood up, and limped toward the doorway. His gait was awkward—clearly he was still relying heavily on the crutches—but his confidence with the prosthetic seemed to have improved even over the short time they had been talking.

She thought about trying to stop him, but realized how ridiculous it would be. As the door closed behind Cam, Erica shook her head and turned to Renee. "A good decision?"

"He's much smarter than you realize."

"It's Cam," Erica said, aware her voice was getting louder, but not caring. "With a phone in his head. The 'smart' in smartphone isn't meant to be taken literally. And how bright could he be, sawing off his own leg?"

Renee crossed her arms. "I don't say I understand it. I never would have guessed a phone would have this huge impact on him. But he's brilliant. Sawing his leg was the correct decision. It gives him the best chance of survival."

Erica wanted to deny it, but how could she even argue with someone who had the knowledge of the best doctors in the world? She felt inferior and contrary. "Still, he's Cam. He might not be stupid anymore, sure. But he's definitely not that smart."

Renee looked at her flatly. "In less than twenty-four hours, he synthesized Methotrexate in the equivalent of a university chemistry lab and still had time to build a prosthetic limb out of scrap metal and salvaged microchips. Trust me, he's smart."

Erica sighed. It still didn't make sense to her. In biology, the teacher had said that even the biggest computers weren't a match for the human brain in terms of computational power. So how could a tiny phone make that big a difference? Renee must be mistaken. "Maybe you're right. I don't know." She stood up. "I need to sleep."

Erica walked out of the room, trying not to think about what might be in the garbage can underneath all those rags.

It all seemed so impossible, so bewildering. Maybe Ian would…

Ian would nothing. She was all alone.

Erica returned to her room and wept.

#

"What were you doing last night with Cam? Did you have any role in that?"

Lois' voice roused Erica from sleep. Shaking her head to clear the cobwebs, she sat up to see her mother glaring at her.

"Did you know he was planning to do that? Did you help?" Lois demanded.

"No. Renee and I found him after he finished." Erica rubbed her eyes. "Wait, don't you know all this? From security footage?"

Lois shook her head. "We don't record everything, Erica. Particularly not trusted members of Jeemoh. We shouldn't *have* to."

Even in her foggy, half-asleep state, Erica found that hard to believe. Her mother, borderline obsessive about everything, had shut off the cameras simply because they were Jeemoh members?

"So what happened?" Lois said.

"I couldn't sleep, so I went upstairs and found him in the electronics lab. He'd already cut off his leg by the time I saw him."

"He shouldn't have done that," Lois said, her features finally softening. "I could've helped him. Amputation should only be considered in extreme circumstances."

Erica nodded. "I know. I think it was the dumbest thing Cam's ever done, and that's saying a lot."

Lois shrugged. "I'm not even sure if it will make a difference. The chance of metastasis for this particular cancer is high. It may have already spread."

Erica felt ill. After all that, it might not even matter? "How long until we know?"

"Days or weeks. Probably not months."

"That's fast."

"It's an aggressive cancer. The most aggressive I know of."

Erica frowned. If the cancer was so aggressive, maybe amputating the leg was a reasonable strategy. How could she tell the difference between idiocy and brilliance when they both looked the same?

"How smart do you think Cam is right now? Renee and I talked about it, and he seems pretty bright," Erica said hesitatingly, waiting for her mother to contradict her.

"Much smarter than before. Certainly above average," Lois said crisply.

"But I don't get it. How could a phone make such a big difference?"

"We have a theory, but it's just a theory. Suppose his weaknesses were logical reasoning and information retention. If his brain delegates the logical reasoning to the phone and uses its wireless Internet to get any information he's missing, then the phone might perfectly address the major gaps in his intellect. Like the final piece of a puzzle."

Was that enough to catapult Cam from idiocy to genius? It didn't seem possible. "How much data is he getting?"

"A fair amount, a few hundred megabytes a day. But it plateaued a few weeks ago. It's all web pages, mostly related to conversations he's having. Hence our theory that he's using the phone to fill in missing information."

Erica gnawed on her lip as she thought through the implications. "You can see what he's thinking?"

Lois nodded. "In a way. We can see anything that goes through our routers. Anything on our network."

Erica wondered how Cam would feel about that if he knew. But then again, if he was as smart as Renee claimed, he probably already knew, and he didn't seem to care. And who could blame him? Considering what he got out of it, the loss of privacy seemed like a small concession. And it wasn't as if they had any privacy anyway.

"Pretty amazing, the difference in him," Erica said.

Lois nodded. "Yes. He's full of surprises." She glanced at her watch. "I have to go." She turned toward the door, but then looked back. "Thanks Erica. And I never got the chance to say it the other day, but thanks for doing the right thing with Ian. I know it was hard."

The emotions came flooding back, instantly at full force. Erica wanted to yell at her mother, tell her she'd ruined everything, that Ian was worth more to her than all this Jeemoh garbage, that she'd trade it all for him in an instant.

But that would accomplish nothing. In the end, she'd still be lying in her bed, alone and miserable.

Erica gave a tight nod. Her mother left the room.

Erica lay back down, willing herself to fall asleep, but it was futile. She'd gain no relief there.

Eventually she arose to begin her second day without Ian. She took her time getting ready. So, when she arrived, everyone was already in the mess hall except Renee and Jen. Most of them had already finished eating and were embroiled in a discussion. Erica picked up a tray of eggs and toast and joined them.

"I'm still debating if sawing off your own leg is badass or asinine," Eve said, sounding almost like she admired him for it.

"It was—" Cam began quietly.

"Both, most definitely," Ian said. "I mean, what if you chopped it off, and then realized the prosthetic didn't fit?"

Cam's forehead wrinkled. "It had to—"

"It'd be so gross." Eve's face split in a broad grin. "You'd have to hop around on one leg, blood spraying everywhere, trying to get down to medical before you bled out."

"I—" Cam said.

"It wouldn't be that bad. He could have bandaged it before going for help," Morrison said imperiously.

Erica pictured the garbage can the night before and felt ill. "Cam didn't have any bandages. Just towels."

Cam nodded.

"Was the room covered in blood?" Morrison asked enthusiastically.

Erica shook her head. "No. Cam cleaned everything up. You could smell it though. And I didn't look at the garbage can too closely."

"Eww!" Eve wrinkled her nose. She grinned mischievously, her eyes shining. "I wonder if it's still there."

"Let's go check," Morrison said. Pushing aside his empty plate, he raced from the room with Eve following.

That left just Ian and Cam. Erica shifted uncomfortably in her chair.

"You don't want to see it?" Erica said to Ian, keeping her tone light.

"Nah. I don't need to go up there to see Cam's leg." He made a show of looking under the table. "There's another one right here."

Cam blushed. "Two, actually."

Erica and Ian stared at him blankly.

He grew redder. "I mean, my original leg and the new one. I still have two legs."

"Oh," Ian said, peering down at his empty plate. "Yeah."

Erica focused on the eggs in front of her. Cam was never the best conversationalist, and it felt odd talking with Ian now. It would be much easier if Renee were around.

She shoveled up the food in record time. "I think I'll check on Ren. It's not like her to be so late."

Erica paused as she realized what she had said. It really *wasn't* like Renee to be so late. Had Erica's attacker targeted Renee next? Was Renee lying dead in her room?

No, surely she was just being paranoid.

Ian didn't seem to notice Erica's reaction, but stood too. "Good idea." He moved forward a half step as if to follow her, and then abruptly stopped. He looked back at the couch. "I think I'll play some video games before classes start."

"Okay, bye." Erica scampered away, not waiting for a response.

Renee opened the door a few seconds after Erica knocked, but then immediately returned to her bed.

"How's it going?" Erica said, finally exhaling. She sat cross-legged on the floor across from her friend. "We missed you at breakfast."

"I didn't really feel like getting up." Renee sounded exhausted.

"Thinking about the explosion? Or Cam?"

"Cam?" Renee's eyes flicked upward.

"About his leg? It was *the* topic of conversation this morning. Eve thought it was cool."

Renee crossed her arms over her chest as if she were chilly. "No, just things."

To Erica, something felt wrong. Renee was facing her direction, but looking beyond her. Following Renee's gaze, Erica turned her head to look up. Above her were all the pictures Renee had hung.

"Oh," Erica murmured. Something in her tone made Renee look her way. Erica swallowed.

Renee blinked several times, turning her head to the right to stare at the blank wall. "You know why those pictures are there?"

Erica said nothing. She knew the reason for the pictures, but saying so might make Renee feel worse.

Renee looked back at Erica, her lower lip trembling. "It's so that when I wake up in the morning, I'll know who everyone is. I haven't forgotten you and Ian yet. But I will. I know I will."

Erica rose and moved to the bed, putting her arm around her

friend. "It must be horrible."

"It is. I don't even remember some of the most basic…" She shook her head. "Erica, do you know… I know there's a world outside this place. That I've been there with you and Ian before, when we were young. But do I have parents? Not Lois. Real parents. My own parents. Or have we lived here our entire lives?"

"Yes, you have parents who loved… who you loved. You grew up in a normal subdivision, two blocks from my place. You used to play in the park behind your house, enjoying the swings the most. That's where we met. You played softball on two different teams. You took drama at school and were brilliant, but hated it and quit. You had your own room, with a white bed, posters on the wall, and a beanbag chair in the corner. You dated four different boys, but didn't get serious with anyone. You had an entire life before you entered here."

Renee's face was bleak. "I've lost all of that. How could I forget so much?"

"Don't worry. It will come back to you. And until it does, Ian and I will take care of you."

"I'm terrified, Erica. What if it doesn't come back? What if I lose everything? Will I even be myself anymore? People are formed by experiences. I'm losing that, and nothing's taking its place except mindless facts. So what will happen to me? Will I cease to exist? Will I be a robot, blindly obeying Lois' orders?" The desperation in Renee's eyes felt like a kick in the gut. "The worst part is, until someone mentions something, I don't know what I'm missing. I don't even know my own *mother*. Everything slips away. There's nothing I can hold on to."

"Then hold on to me." Erica hugged her friend. "I don't blame you for being frightened. It is scary. But we'll manage. We'll get through it. This is just a rough patch. You know that, right? That things will get better?"

"Yes." Renee smiled bitterly. "Even now, there's one thing I'm looking forward to."

"That's good. What?"

"The day I forget everything I've lost."

Erica's eyes widened. "Oh, Renee," She squeezed her friend. "It won't come to that. We'll figure out something. I promise."

Renee nodded, but she didn't say anything, just clung to Erica like she was the only life preserver in a vast ocean.

Finally, Renee released her. "You know that I'm going to forget this conversation."

Erica squeezed her hand. "Then we'll have it again."

Renee nodded. "Thanks, Erica. I wish—"

She was interrupted by her tablet beeping loudly. Frowning, Renee lifted it. "There's a message from Cam."

"I didn't know we could instant message on those things," Erica said.

"Neither did I." Renee touched the screen and gasped. "We have to go." She dropped the tablet on her mattress, leaping to her feet, pulling Erica behind her.

Erica glanced back at the tablet. She barely had time to read what was written there.

They're trying to get Ian to use his ability in medical.

CHAPTER FIFTEEN

Two soldiers stood on either side of the door to the medical room, each with a javelin holstered in his belt.

"No entry except medical emergencies," the man on the right said, crossing his arms.

"Our friend is in that room. This is your one chance to move." Erica stared at him, her jaw set.

He shook his head, standing taller. "We have orders. Go away."

Five weeks ago, Erica would have sighed, complained to Renee, and slunk away. But that was before Jeemoh put her through the Gauntlet. Only yesterday, Irenic had broken bones Erica didn't even know existed. Clearly, Jeemoh believed that the end justified the means, and they had no qualms about using violence to achieve their goals. But she could play that game too.

Erica examined the guard. He seemed relaxed, even dismissive. Sure, he was a foot taller than she was and built like a truck, but was he stupid enough to think that in here, when confronted by two teenage girls, size mattered?

She took two seconds to evaluate eleven unsuccessful strategies for dealing with the soldiers. Her twelfth vision showed her what would work.

"Fine. We'll go then." Erica pivoted around as if to leave while simultaneously reaching toward the soldier. Behind her back, she seized the Javelin from the man's belt, continuing to turn until she faced him once more.

"Disable him," she said to Renee.

119

Renee spun her body in a circle. One of her legs went high over her head, her foot connecting with the cheek of the soldier closest to her. Erica pushed the tip of the javelin under the chin of the other and pressed the trigger. Two bodies fell to the floor. She and Renee stepped over them and into the room.

Lois, Dr. Rahal, and Ian were seated together, talking.

Lois rose. "How did you get in? We weren't to be disturbed." Her face grew hard as she looked past Renee and saw the two unconscious soldiers. "Erica, you can't just beat people up to get whatever you want."

Erica's eyes narrowed. "Lois, you can't just grab Ian and do whatever you want."

A vein pulsed in Lois' temple, and her voice was cold. "I run Jeemoh. I make the decisions, and you're on my team. If you keep attacking our people, we will have a problem."

"And if you keep trying to keep me from my friend, we will have a problem as well." Erica's gaze was unwavering. "I understand that you care about security. But I won't allow you to use that as an excuse to separate me from my friends."

Renee nodded. "You can't keep us away when my brother's in danger."

Lois gazed at Erica and Renee darkly, considering her options. "Go check on the guards, please," she said to Dr. Rahal. When she turned back to Erica, she seemed calmer. "I wasn't trying to keep you away. I was trying to protect you. The strength of people's abilities often fluctuates. I didn't want you to die if Ian accidentally fills this room with burning magnesium."

"That's why you should want us here," Erica said. "My luck is the one way to be certain that something like that won't happen." It was a lie, but not far from the truth.

"It doesn't matter anyway," Ian said, folding his arms. "I'm not doing it. There's no need. What's the point, if I can't use my ability without dying?"

Lois shook her head, clearly exasperated but doing her best to stay cool. "As I've been saying, not learning to control it literally means you won't control it at all. Your ability will surface once again at an unpredictable time. And when it does, it will kill you. Your choice is to master it now, or die at some random time in the next few months."

"It hasn't happened since the Gauntlet, so maybe it'll never happen."

"It will, and you *will* die."

Ian shook his head. His eyes looked haunted.

He was afraid, Erica realized. The last time he'd used his ability—used it to save her—he'd lost both his arms to the flaming metal. Only the medical printer had saved him. It was understandable that he was terrified.

But on this, Lois was right. Ian needed to learn to control his ability... or it could kill him. There was no other option.

Could she ask him to do such a thing? To burn for her again?

Decide and have no regrets.

She looked Ian in the eyes. "Ian, you know, the worst moment of my life wasn't getting abducted by soldiers. It wasn't those biting ants. It wasn't dangling on that cliff. It wasn't even having my arm snapped by Irenic.

"The worst moment of my life was sitting alone in that room, knowing you were dying, that you burned to save me, and I couldn't help you. That, in a way, I'd caused your death." In every way, actually. She'd used her visions to determine how to provoke him into using his ability. He'd be dead if Lois hadn't saved him.

"You didn't—"

"I can't handle seeing you burn again," Erica continued, as if he hadn't spoken. She grasped his hand. After two days without his touch, Ian's hand felt strange, warm, and new. Swallowing, she suppressed a shiver, trying to focus on her words rather than her feelings. "But I will. For you. Will you please try this? You need to be able to control your ability. I'll stay here. Between my ability and the medical printer, we'll make it through."

Ian squeezed his eyes shut, sighing. When he opened them again, his gaze was clear. "Okay. I will. I trust you."

He still trusted her. After she'd already burnt him once.

No regrets.

Erica smiled at him. "Thank you."

Ian released her hand.

Erica glanced at Renee. She had been quiet through the whole exchange. A few weeks ago, Renee would have recognized how she reacted to Ian's touch and said something, but, today, her face was simply stoic disapproval.

No. It wasn't disapproval. It was a mask. Renee wasn't tolerating Erica's reaction. Rather, she didn't know how she was supposed to react and was trying to hide that fact. Erica was almost sure of it.

How often had Renee been faking it over the last few weeks? Erica's heart hurt.

Ian took a deep breath, looking at the platform of the medical printer. "Let's get this over with. If anyone wants to grab marshmallows to roast, this is your last chance." He turned to Lois. "What do I have to do?"

"Stand on the printer," Lois said, every bit the scientist now that Erica had convinced Ian. "We'll turn it on as a preventative measure. If anything goes wrong, you'll be healed instantly." He did, while Erica, Renee, and the doctor—who had returned after reviving the soldiers—trailed him.

"The mechanics of triggering abilities vary greatly," Lois continued, "but after you've triggered your ability once, it's typically far easier the second time. Take your mind back to the Gauntlet. Feel what you felt then. If you felt the wind in your hair, feel the wind in your hair. If there was an ache in your bones, feel the ache in your bones. It's the feelings that matter. But think small. Like only one glove. Or even better, a half-inch spot on your palm. Do it now."

Ian closed his eyes and stretched out his hand. He breathed deeply.

Ian focusing. A shiny sphere blinking into existence.

Erica smiled as the sphere appeared. There was no flame and no heat, just a perfect metal ball nestled in Ian's palm.

"I did it," Ian said. His radiant smile made Erica's knees weak. "And I didn't burn. It was so much easier than I expected."

"Well done." Lois selected a Petri dish from a cupboard and held it out to him. "Can you pass it to me?"

"Sure." Ian tilted his hand, and the sphere rolled off, but as soon as it was more than a few inches away from his hand, it disintegrated into black dust.

Lois inspected the remnants. "I don't think this is magnesium. It's too dark."

"It smells like iron," Dr. Rahal said.

Lois nodded. "We can analyze it later to be sure. Now, wait a minute, Ian." She put the Petri dish aside, walked to a tablet resting on a counter, and tapped on the screen. Erica followed, peering over her shoulder. Lois was watching a replay of the creation of the sphere, flipping between twelve different cameras, zooming in and out, and examining it frame by frame.

"Look there," she said, raising the tablet and pointing at the zoomed-in ground near Ian's foot. "See that little puff? It's hard to see, but the iron came from the floor. Is there iron in cement, Renee?"

"Yes. Iron oxide."

Ian, bored with waiting on the platform, had walked over to join them. "So I'm ripping particles out of the ground and shaping them somehow. I wonder why I made iron this time rather than magnesium, and why it didn't burn." He smiled at Erica. "Not that I'm complaining or anything."

"Clearly your ability lets you pull different elements," Lois said. "Let's try it again."

Ian returned to the platform and produced another shiny iron marble. By the fifth and sixth tests, he was shaping his creations, making pyramids, cubes, and a three-dimensional heart that he passed to Erica. Erica couldn't resist a bitter smile at the irony of Ian giving her a fake heart that disintegrated in her hands the moment she tried to touch it.

Eventually, Ian even constructed iron gauntlets for his hands, eerily reminiscent of the flaming magnesium gloves he'd used against Vince.

After that, Lois instructed Ian to conjure other elements, starting with aluminum, another component of concrete. After several failed attempts, he finally materialized an aluminum sphere by focusing on creating something light and bendable. From there, it didn't take long before he was materializing knickknacks made of copper, nickel, and zinc.

"Great," Lois said after Ian yawned. "That's enough for today. Isha, can you and Renee take the samples to the materials lab?"

"Certainly." Dr. Rahal turned off the medical printer and stacked the Petri dishes into two towers. She gave one stack to Renee. Together, they left the room.

Ian hopped off the podium to join Erica and Lois. Though he was clearly trying to hide it, he seemed giddy.

"Good work," Lois said, patting Ian on the shoulder. "Few people realize their abilities so easily."

"Didn't seem so easy when I was burning." Ian's smirk took all the bite out of the statement.

Lois chuckled. "Well, yes. But you know what I mean. How do you feel about creating different metals? Are you sure you won't create magnesium again?"

"Yeah. Each metal is distinct. It's like they taste different, and by remembering the taste, I can ensure I get that metal."

"In that case, it's fine to experiment outside this room."

"Are you sure that's safe?" Erica said, rubbing her bottom lip.

"Of course not. But if Ian's smart, it probably is." Lois looked back to Ian. "Only materialize substances that won't hurt you or the people around you. Don't rush things. I suspect you can create several different elements simultaneously and possibly even compounds that are more complex. Magnesium doesn't ignite spontaneously, so, when you materialized those flaming gloves, you probably used a different chemical to light them.

"You need to be careful though. I imagine you can isolate arsenic, mercury, or uranium, all of which can kill you. So take tiny steps. Only create substances you are certain are safe. And, if you create something you're unsure about, come to medical immediately.

"Also, from now on, you'll have an extra hour of chemistry every day. You will focus on learning the properties of different substances and materializing them at will."

"Oh, boy," Ian said unenthusiastically. "Back to school."

"Don't knock it," Erica said. "You're the only one in our whole chemistry class who might actually use something we learned."

"That's not true." Ian's lips quirked. "Holtby sold those homemade fireworks last year. He'll probably profit more from chemistry than me. If he doesn't get brain damage from the fumes first."

"Yes, but I wouldn't underestimate the chance of brain damage. It would explain Ambrose's Tevas and his peculiar enthusiasm for the periodic table," Erica replied, thinking of her chemistry teacher.

Lois gave them a weary look. "Don't you two ever get tired of talking?"

Ian tilted his head, looking at Erica. "No. Not really. You?"

Erica stared back with an innocent expression. "No, not at all."

Lois sighed. "Fine. We're done. You can go." She shelved the unused Petri dishes.

As they turned to leave, Erica paused. Ian gave her a questioning look, but Erica waved him away. It was better not to involve him.

"I had a question about Renee," Erica said after the door had closed behind Ian.

"Yes?"

"She's forgetting a lot. I know you said it's because her brain can only handle so much information, and it would take time to adjust, but it's getting bad."

"How bad?"

"Really bad. She's forgotten some big things. How long will it take for her to recover?"

Lois turned back to the Petri dishes, wiping one with a towel. "I don't know. It's all just a guess."

"Can you do something to help?"

"Like what?"

How the heck would I know? Erica longed to voice the thought and had to struggle to keep her irritation from showing. "Drugs? Or surgery? That worked on Jen, right?"

Lois lowered the towel, her face solemn as she pivoted to face her daughter. "Erica, it's totally different. Jen's damage was physical. Renee's isn't. And we don't understand enough even to experiment. Anything we try is more likely to hurt than help."

"Surely, there's something we can do."

"There's not much. Be her friend. Help her feel comfortable. And wait for her to reach an equilibrium."

And what if that equilibrium only happened when Renee lost her memories completely? Lois' response was entirely inadequate.

Erica sighed. "And did you learn any more about the exploding tablet?"

"It was a defective battery. As we thought."

Erica still didn't believe it. Lois was useless.

"I see. Thanks." Without waiting for a response, Erica stomped from the room.

She considered returning to Renee's room, but was worried that Renee would pick up on her frustration. She didn't want to explain it, so she went to the mess hall instead.

Cam was alone there, sitting on the couch, staring off into space. Though Erica wasn't being particularly stealthy, he jumped as Erica sat opposite him.

"Sorry," she said. "Didn't mean to surprise you."

"Oh." Blushing, Cam looked away.

"What are you doing?"

Cam turned redder. "Nothing."

Man, it was hard to get a word out of the guy. "Thanks for the message about Ian." Erica paused to give Cam a chance to acknowledge her gratitude. He didn't, so Erica added, "Lois got Ian to use his ability, but it turned out fine."

"Oh. Wasn't he scared?"

"Yes. But he was kind of forced to use it. Otherwise, he couldn't control it."

Cam's lips thinned and his nostrils flared slightly. "Oh."

Erica crossed her legs at the ankles. "It was good though. He can create other substances. Not just magnesium. He didn't burn at all."

Cam just sat there, staring at her.

She turned her body toward the bookshelf. "And he can shape them. He made a marble and some gloves out of iron."

"Neat." Cam's voice was devoid of emotion.

She'd had better conversations with her stuffed rabbit when she was six. "Well, I guess I'll head to my room. I only came in here for a book." Erica walked to the bookshelf. Grabbing the first thing she saw, she strolled toward the exit.

"Erica?" Cam said hesitatingly.

Erica stopped, looking back at him. "Yeah?"

"Does it bother you that they forced Ian to do it? He could have burnt."

Erica shook her head. "No. Lois said if he didn't learn, it'd come out at some other time. The only safe option was to use it then. Why?"

"I don't know. Just thinking." Cam glanced in her direction before quickly looking away. "It seems like your mom will do almost anything to get what she wants. You know. The Gauntlet and stuff. I wonder if we should—"

"I don't think she's that bad. They did it in medical so that, if there was a fire, she could heal him right away. She was very concerned about safety."

Cam's cheek twitched. "Oh."

Erica's eyes narrowed. "You were wondering what?"

Cam rubbed the back of his neck as he stared at the legs of the

ping-pong table. "Um, if she's always been like that. So...
determined?"

"Pretty much, yeah. But as a kid, it seemed normal. I thought all
parents were like that."

Cam nodded. Erica expected him to say something else, but he
just sat there.

"Okay. Bye," she said.

"Bye."

#

The next morning passed like a meandering dream. The action of the
previous day had at least provided a distraction. Today, there was
nothing to drive the thoughts of Ian and the explosion from Erica's
brain.

Even Irenic noticed. "Get out of your head," she said, looking
down at Erica. With Jen in life-skills training and Cam consulting
with Lois about his illness, it was Erica's turn to be partnered with
the instructor.

"What?" Erica said, staring up from the floor, her arm broken yet
again.

"Luck is fleeting. To be a great fighter, you need to put aside your
worries and focus on the moment."

It seemed easiest to just nod. Erica wanted nothing more than to
lie there for a few seconds, to gaze at the pinhole lights in the ceiling,
but it wasn't to be. Irenic pulled her up using the arm from which the
bone wasn't protruding. The coppery blood trickling into Erica's
mouth made her feel queasy, but it seemed like too much of an effort
to wipe it away.

Irenic turned from Erica, clapping her hands. "We're done."

"Thank goodness," Ian said. After sparring with Eve, he had tiny
puncture wounds clustered over the vulnerable areas of his body.
Eve's answer to the "no-kill" rule seemed to be to execute the fatal
strike, but only use a bone needle rather than a bone spike.

Ian had managed to get one of his own attacks through though.
Eve's right arm dangled at her side, her shoulder dislocated.

Irenic frowned when she saw it. "You let him get your arm?"
While the rest of them mopped up the blood, she tugged on Eve's
arm, maneuvering it in a circle.

"It was a suicidal attack," Eve said through gritted teeth. "I killed
him four different ways as he came in. But none of them were real."

Irenic nodded, mollified. She jerked on the limb, popping the shoulder back into place. Eve shrieked.

"So do disabling attacks too," Irenic said. "You don't always need to kill." She scanned the others, noted that nobody needed urgent medical care, and strode out of the room.

There was less blood than usual, so the others left the dojo just as the elevator arrived for Irenic. Erica called out, and Irenic held the door long enough for them to hobble inside.

A few seconds after the elevator started moving, the vision flashed through Erica's mind.

Hissing. Yellow-green gas billowing from holes in the ceiling.

CHAPTER SIXTEEN

Erica looked at the ceiling. It had hundreds of holes. She'd assumed they were for ventilation.

The elevator stopped abruptly, but the door didn't open. The others looked at each other in confusion.

"Did someone press—" Ian began.

"Irenic!" Erica said. "What gas is used to secure the elevators?"

Irenic eyed her suspiciously. "Why do you—"

"There's no time!" Erica yelled. "What gas?"

Irenic blinked. "Chlorine. If this some joke—"

"Renee, how do you counteract chlorine? What's in gas masks?"

"Activated charcoal."

Erica ripped off her shirt, jerking at the jolt of pain as it caught against the protruding bone in her left arm. Ignoring the others' looks, she held it out to Ian. "I need charcoal. Now."

Ian held his hand over the shirt. Nothing happened.

Yellow gas began to hiss from the nozzles.

Morrison dropped to the floor. "They're trying to kill us! Get down."

"No," shouted Eve, pushing against the door. "We need to get out of here."

Renee tugged at Morrison's arm. "It's chlorine. Heavier than air."

A black charcoal block appeared on the shirt beneath Ian's hand. It disintegrated into dust as Ian released it. "It breaks up when I'm not touching it."

"Doesn't matter. We need the dust," Renee said.

"Make more," Erica shouted. "Everyone, your shirts." Her eyes were starting to sting.

Morrison grasped Irenic's arm. "Do something!" he screamed.

Irenic shook him off, pushed Eve aside, and tried to force the door open. It didn't move.

"Close your eyes," Renee said, tearing off her shirt. "The chlorine burns."

Erica folded her shirt over to keep the dust inside and pressed it against her mouth and nose. It was awkward to breathe through, but she was getting oxygen. She hoped it was enough. She squinted. Through her blurry vision, she could make out Ian filling up someone else's shirt. She squeezed her eyes shut once more.

Was Ian holding his breath? Erica quickly passed the makeshift filter over to him. He held it over his nose for a few seconds and then returned it.

"Eve," Irenic said. "Open these doors." She coughed.

Erica's skin felt like it was on fire, and the wound on her arm felt like someone had inserted a jagged knife. Ignoring the pain, she used the bicep of her broken arm to hold the filter over her nose and mouth. Still without looking, she grasped at Ian's shirt with the other hand and was somehow able to tear it off him. She felt her way along his arm to his hands and held the shirt out flat.

"Eve, we need this door," Irenic shouted.

Erica opened her eyes enough to see Irenic grab Eve's hands from where she was holding her shirt out for Ian. Irenic forced them against the crack in the elevator door, nearly pulling Eve off her feet.

"Bones now!" Irenic yelled, her voice harsh and rasping.

Coughing, tears streaming down her face, Eve shot bone slivers from her hands into the crack in the door. The bones thickened.

Ian's shirt felt heavy. Erica folded it over and passed it to him, and then fell to her knees, groping for the shirt Eve had dropped. It took several long seconds to find it. She held it before Ian.

Eve collapsed, writhing and mewing, her bones still caught in the crack between the doors.

Irenic still didn't have anything covering her mouth. Her face red as she tried to keep from coughing, she reached down and grasped Eve's arms. Using the bones, she levered the doors open two inches. Just as Eve's wrist snapped, Irenic jammed one hand between the doors. Pulling mightily, she tore them open.

The elevator was between floors, with only a two-foot gap at the top of the door.

Erica stumbled toward it, but Morrison pushed her aside. He grasped at the floor above, trying to heave himself up.

She was burning alive in a pool of fire. Someone was trying to snuff out blowtorches in her eye sockets.

She couldn't do it. The gap was too far away. Her knees began to buckle.

Erica felt a firm grip on her shoulder and crotch. She lost all sense of direction as she was hoisted up and thrown through the air. She didn't fall, but rolled. A few seconds later, another body hit her.

Erica had lost the shirt, but she needed a breath. She tried to hold out, just a few more seconds, but couldn't. Gasping, she inhaled, sandpaper on cement.

It was oxygen. Screaming, she writhed for an eternity. Pain was her entire existence.

She was moving. Hands held her as she thrashed.

And then, she was fine. She stared up at red lights as beautiful as a sunrise.

"Out of the way," Dr. Rahal said, nudging Erica with a toe.

Erica looked around wildly. Renee was crying. Eve and Morrison were there, too, all whole.

Ian wasn't. Erica lurched to her feet and off the platform of the medical printer, sprinting toward the door. Before she reached it, a soldier entered with Ian draped over his back.

Ian's arms and legs hung limply. His skin was bright red. Foam bubbled from his mouth, the only sign he was still alive.

The soldier dropped him on the platform, and the wounds vanished. Ian opened his eyes. He looked to Erica and smiled.

Eve gasped. Erica followed her gaze to the door.

Irenic was standing there. If anything, her skin was brighter than Ian's. Blisters rose on her cheeks and arms, every inch of exposed flesh. She blinked her red eyes constantly, as if doing so would eventually restore her sight. Her breath rasped. As she coughed, white foam dribbled down her chin.

Nevertheless, guided only by a soldier's hand, Irenic managed to stagger to the platform herself. She stood there, ramrod straight, as her wounds healed.

Vision restored, Irenic's gaze lit upon one of the soldiers, indistinguishable to Erica's eyes from all the others. She strode over to him. "What happened?" she said, her tone sounding like death itself.

"Malfunction, we think," the soldier replied. He stood frozen, petrified by Irenic's stare.

"Don't think. Know," Irenic said. "Figure it out, *now!*"

"Yes, sir." The soldier fled from the room.

Erica blinked. Her eyes still stung.

Dr. Rahal put her hand upon Irenic's arm. Irenic spun around, glaring.

The doctor didn't flinch. "You all need to have showers. You'll still have chlorine on your skin."

Irenic waved her hand toward the teenagers. "Go shower. Now."

Erica nodded, wheeling toward the exit. As she reached the door, Irenic yelled after them, "And take the stairs."

By the time Erica got to her room, she was already feeling itchy. In a frantic effort to remove any residue, she scrubbed her body for half an hour until her skin grew pink.

Consequently, when Erica arrived in the mess, she found the others already there, huddled together on the couches, as if numbers and closeness provided a measure of protection. Even Cam looked distressed, even though he hadn't been in the elevator.

"Is everyone fine?" Erica said as she approached.

"We're great," Ian said. "We've already finished the 'Aaahhh! Someone's trying to kill us' freak-out, and we're onto the 'wild speculation about who was responsible' phase."

Eve smiled wryly. "After considerable debate, we've agreed that Irenic is out."

Erica sat down in the only free spot, beside Ian. "So you don't think it was an accident?"

Morrison jerked forward. "You think it was an accident? Really?"

Erica turned pink. "No. I mean, that's what they were saying. I was curious if anyone believed them."

"Of course not," Eve said, her lip curling. "Not after what happened with the tablet. Someone's targeting us." She stared at Erica. "Or maybe they're just after you and don't care about collateral damage. Any ideas who it could be?"

Erica shook her head. "I can't think of anyone who hates me that much. But we've been under surveillance for weeks, in the Gauntlet and here. Maybe someone saw something they didn't like."

"What have you done that would annoy someone enough to kill you?" Morrison said, not making any effort at all to make his tone sound anything but accusing.

"Nothing," Erica exclaimed. "I've just been me." She blushed and looked away. "Well, I guess Renee and I beat up those guards who were keeping us out of medical yesterday. But that was after the tablet. And that wouldn't justify them trying to kill us."

Ian contemplated Erica's face thoughtfully. "I think our standards in that respect differ from many people here." At the others' confused expressions, he added, "Jeemoh tortured us in the Gauntlet, Irenic pummels us every day, and, in our first day of classes, Hack said that murder was a good way to get things done. Violence isn't an exception here. It's an accepted way of life. And if that's the case, someone here might consider a minor offense to be enough to justify murder."

Erica lowered her gaze, rubbing her forehead. "But if that's the case, it could be almost anyone."

Ian nodded.

"I doubt that," Morrison said. "It's got to be someone you've seen a lot. I still think it's your mom. She handed you the tablet."

Erica turned to Cam. "You were with her this time, right? Talking about your illness?"

Cam blushed, looking at his knees. "Yes."

"Did she do anything suspicious?"

"I don't know. We talked for an hour. She poked at her tablet a few times. And then a soldier came in and said what happened."

"She could have done it with the tablet. Or set it up beforehand," Morrison said.

Cam nodded. "She did seem distracted."

"There you go," Morrison said, as if the evidence were irrefutable.

"I don't believe it," Erica said, her voice firm. "If she wanted me dead, there would be so many easier ways to do it. Why would she bother with all the training if she were just going to kill us? Besides, if she were really trying to gas us in the elevator, the attack would have succeeded."

"It nearly did," Eve said.

"But it didn't," Erica said. "The elevator doors could have been locked. The elevator could have been sent to a different floor, far from medical. The medical printer could have been disabled for maintenance. Anything like that and we would've died. If Lois wanted to kill us, she would've ensured something like that happened."

Erica glanced at Cam, Eve, and Morrison, who were sitting across from her. Their faces were frozen as they looked over Erica's shoulder.

"What?" Erica said. She pivoted to look behind her.

Lois was standing in the doorway. "That's exactly true," she said. "I wasn't trying to kill you, but if I were, you'd be dead now." Renee and Eve's jaws dropped.

"What?" Lois marched over to them. "Of course I expect you to wonder whether this was a deliberate attack and to put me near the top of your list of suspects. As Jeemoh agents, it's your job to consider such possibilities. You'd be terrible agents if you didn't."

She sat on the arm of the couch. "Let me say this, though. Hack's 'shock-jock' tendencies aside, it would be unusual for Jeemoh to decide that murder is an optimal solution. But if—hypothetically—we decided it was, let me assure you, you'd be dead."

"So what, this was just an accident?" Morrison said, sarcasm dripping.

Lois nodded. "Everything seems to indicate that. We've done a full scan of our systems and identified an odd intersection of several low-probability scenarios that resulted in the error that occurred."

"What?" Erica said, utterly confused by her mother's explanation.

"Basically, we've tracked it down to a bug in the system. Or rather, how several systems interact."

"You've got to be kidding," Morrison said. "You expect us to believe that?"

Lois shook her head. "Not really. I don't believe it myself. That's what it is, but it's too big an anomaly. I think it was an attack. A subtle one, disguised as a computer malfunction."

"An attack by whom?" Erica said, exchanging nervous glances with the others.

Lois' face gave nothing away. "I don't know. It could be someone inside or outside. One possibility is that it was a time bomb planted in our system when it was installed that just happened to go off today. Or it could have been more targeted.

"Because Irenic was with you, I believe the most likely scenario is that the perpetrator wasn't targeting you, as individuals, at all. Rather, they were attacking you as Jeemoh's resources, attempting to eliminate you before you reach your full potential."

Ian stared at her, fear and consternation playing out across his face. "Who would do something like that?"

"That's confidential."

"What?" Morrison said, jerking upright, his face red.

Lois nodded blandly. "Secrecy is in place to protect everyone. Need to know, only. We wouldn't violate those rules just because of an attack. In fact, that's when these rules are most important."

"That's ridiculous," Morrison yelled. "Someone tried to kill us, and you're not even going to tell us what you know?"

Lois just shrugged. Morrison stared at Lois for several seconds, fire in his eyes. When she didn't waver, he threw up his hands and stomped to the crafts table, turning his back on all of them.

"This won't be the last attack," Erica murmured, not making eye contact with her mother. "How can we defend ourselves?"

Lois pursed her lips. "Pay attention to what's going on around you. Alert us to anything suspicious. Apply everything you're learning in Hack's class. This is why we teach these things. And listen to Irenic. She saved your lives."

"That seems incredibly vague and not at all useful," Ian said.

Lois shrugged once more, standing up. "Welcome to the world of covert operations. Those who aren't adaptable, observant, and quick of mind need not apply."

"Bit late now." Ian sounded like he was trying to be flippant, but bitterness leaked into his tone. "We've already applied. Or, were applied."

Lois smiled. "So you were." She half turned toward the door. "I need to get back to things. I just thought you deserved an update." She looked from face to face expectantly

What was she expecting? A thank you? Erica and the others just stared at her.

"Okay, then. I'll see you later." Lois left the room.

"So to summarize," Ian said with cheery sarcasm, "we were attacked by someone who could be anyone in the entire world, through a mechanism that Jeemoh hasn't properly identified. And, if we want to survive, we should try to avoid being killed. Very helpful."

Erica raised her eyebrows at him. "Hey, we specialize in that. Random deadly threats from unknown parties? It's the Gauntlet, only with ping-pong tables. And ping-pong's fun."

Ian nodded. "Yeah, that's what I like, dealing with daily lethal attacks. Life would be so boring, otherwise."

"If Lois is right, it will be almost impossible to defend ourselves," Eve said, her eyes darting from face to face. "Before that gas started hissing, was there any possible way to see that the elevator was a trap?"

Erica's expression grew sober. "No. There were no signs at all." Except for the vision, but that hadn't been early enough to help.

"So what are we supposed to do?" Eve said, desperation coloring her tone.

"I don't know," Ian said, his earlier black humor absent. "If they're targeting us because we're in Jeemoh, then maybe try to find and address vulnerabilities in Jeemoh?"

Erica shook her head, gnawing on her lip. There was no possible way that she could have identified the elevator as a vulnerability, and the next attack could come from an equally obscure direction.

"And we're going to identify problems better than Jeemoh's experts?" Morrison said scornfully. "This is their problem, not ours. And they need to figure it out before it gets us killed."

"Yeah, but I'd like to do whatever we can. Maybe we can avoid dangerous places and objects," Ian said.

"Like elevators and tablets? Everything's dangerous," Morrison replied.

Ian gritted his teeth. He turned to Erica. "What do you think? How can we protect ourselves?"

Erica squeezed her eyes shut. There must be a million different potential threats, coming from a million different potential directions.

She grimaced. "I don't know if we can."

CHAPTER SEVENTEEN

Erica paused in front of her door. The other two attacks had happened in common areas, but that didn't meant she wouldn't be targeted in her room.

They'd spent the rest of the day talking about the attacks. Everyone seemed reluctant to set out on their own from the mess hall. But finally, when people started yawning, the group had broken up.

Ian had left at the same time as Erica. He, too, stood at his door, his hand raised in front of the scanner. He moved his hand forward, but then stopped.

Ian glanced at Erica, rubbing his chin. "It might trigger a bomb when I touch it."

Erica bit her lip. Even with her ability, it was nerve-wracking, constantly watching for potential threats. She couldn't imagine how stressful it must be for Ian. "Open it now. There's less chance of something happening if I'm here."

Ian nodded. "Yeah." He touched the panel. When his door opened uneventfully, he exhaled. He looked toward her once more. "Goodnight."

"Goodnight." For the thousandth time, Erica wished she didn't have to say that to him, that things were back as they were before, if only to be sure he was safe. Quickly, she tapped her own scanner, opened the door, and slid through, leaning back against the door as soon as it shut.

Forget Ian. There were issues that were more important. She

surveyed the room.

The tablet. If the enemy could detonate the medical tablet, they could do the same to hers. She couldn't get rid of it, but she could minimize the damage. She moved it to the corner and heaped clothes on top of it. That should block the shards of glass if it exploded.

The bathroom. Could they attack her there? They could crank up the hot water in the shower to burn her, but she'd be able to get out before that happened. Maybe poison the toothpaste? Attacks using poison were a problem since they might not fall into the five-second window provided by her visions.

She could brush her teeth without it. But no, they could poison the toothbrush, too. Better to not brush at all.

Same with contact poison on the soap. She'd have to risk the water though. Drinking was unavoidable.

The bed. Contact poison was a possibility there, too. Or they could insert a venomous spider beneath the sheets. But she needed to sleep. Stripping and inspecting the bed every day was about the best she could do there. She had the same issues with her clothes.

Erica looked at the ceiling. Ventilation holes dotted it, just like the elevator. Were canisters of chlorine gas hidden there? Erica chewed on her lip. Jeemoh designed these rooms not just to house agents, but also teenagers with random abilities who had just escaped the Gauntlet. Teenagers furious at Jeemoh. If there was gas protecting the elevator, it was here as well.

Erica felt like crying. There was no way to deal with the chlorine. The attacker could activate it while she slept, and she'd be dead before she awoke.

It was hopeless. She couldn't guard against every threat. It was like the Gauntlet all over again, but this time, there were no rules, and she was all alone.

Erica curled up in her bed, squeezing her eyes shut, trying to not think of all the different ways she could die.

#

The next attack didn't happen the next day or the day after that. Though Lois pronounced the elevators safe, Erica and the others took to using the stairs. Luckily, most of the classrooms and labs were within five floors.

Over meals, they discussed potential attacks and defensive strategies. But to Erica that only showed just how helpless they were.

For every attack vector they could safeguard themselves against, five others remained. And, if someone in security was targeting them, they might be listening to every conversation, searching for the method that would be hardest to thwart.

As each day passed without a new attempt, Erica began to relax her guard. One night, she accidentally left the tablet beside her bed while she slept, while the next, she used the elevator without even thinking about it.

She forgave herself for such mistakes. It would be difficult enough to sustain the paranoia if she believed doing so would keep her alive. Knowing that her actions could only guard against a fraction of potential threats made it near impossible.

Erica found her attention drifting. She meandered through life in a daze, walking from classroom to classroom, doing everything expected of her. She occasionally encountered members of other squads in the labs and the dojo, but they seemed to take Lois' proscription against inter-squad socializing seriously. They didn't talk with her beyond meaningless inanities, and that suited Erica fine. Never in her life had she felt less like talking.

Sometimes, she'd experience a moment of excitement—team paintball, Javelin training, sharpshooting—and feel alive, but afterward, her melancholy would descend once more. Though death was a constant fear in the Gauntlet, this new paranoid life felt worse, to a large degree because she had to deal with it on her own.

Each day, Erica swore to herself that she'd stop thinking about Ian, stop hurting, and each day, she found it wasn't true. She couldn't help how her heart accelerated whenever she saw him. She even joked with him, just like the old days. But afterward, she felt horrible, like she was offering the best of herself to Ian, and he was rejecting her all over again.

Erica found herself looking forward to the sessions with Irenic. Physical pain seemed to be the only thing that would block out her mental anguish.

The practice seemed to pay off. Ian mostly got over his light-headedness at the sight of blood—a necessity, considering the dojo's floor was often drenched by the end of training.

Though Irenic cautioned the others not to do any serious damage to Cam—his cancer-induced inability to use the medical printer made him uniquely vulnerable—she had no problem with people using their abilities while sparring. Consequently, Morrison fought infrequently.

His first match against Ian was how they all went. The instant the fight started, Ian's feet lost traction. While Ian scrambled around on the ground like an upside-down turtle, Morrison casually walked over and knocked him unconscious with a single blow. After a few such encounters, Irenic reluctantly changed the rules for Morrison to disallow the use of his ability so he could experience real combat situations.

Thus, except for Renee, everyone's fighting skills improved. Even Jen was getting better. She seemed less addled than when they'd first met, and, after Irenic suggested she float like a butterfly, she began dodging the others' attacks.

Despite everyone's advancement, only Irenic could hit Erica. So Erica was pleased to step onto the floor with her. Once, she even egged Irenic on, daring her to hit harder. Though Irenic admonished her, she seemed to respect Erica's work ethic. Eventually, Erica became skilled enough to land the occasional solid blow, but she never came close to defeating her instructor.

Others had some success against the huge woman. Irenic lost to Cam twice, which shocked Erica considering Cam's history in fights. The first time, as Cam jabbed with his right hand, a spike flew out of his prosthetic leg, embedding itself in Irenic's gut. The second time, Cam somehow overpowered Irenic, produced a serrated knife from his forearm, and pinned her to the ground through her right shoulder. When Erica asked him later about his victory, he mumbled something about enhancing his muscles.

Ian also beat Irenic occasionally, typically by breaking Irenic's hands on steel plates which coalesced an instant before her punch landed or—more rarely—with a successful head strike with brass knuckles.

After each defeat, Irenic would smile. Then, the next day, she would adapt her style and thoroughly thrash all of them.

Outside of Irenic's class, an even more significant war was being waged. Lois' prediction about Cam's cancer proved prescient. Every few days, he was diagnosed with a new tumor.

Cam took the news calmly, and—over Lois' strong objections—refused all her treatments. Instead, he split his free time between the chemistry and electronics labs, concocting new and ever more potent drug and technology combinations to hold the disease at bay.

That battle raged back and forth. Cam sawed off one of his arms, extracted an eye, and replaced several of the muscles in his body with electro-mechanical equivalents. Erica wasn't even sure if Cam viewed these amputations as defeats. Seeing the relish with which he added the prosthetic hand, she wondered whether the cancer was just a convenient excuse to do what he might have done anyway.

In a way, Erica understood it. Cam's ability to integrate anything electrical into his central nervous system made him more capable with the prosthetics than he had ever been when he was only flesh and blood. His eye could telescope or magnify, and Erica suspected the spikes she had seen pop out of Cam's prosthetic leg were only the start of his integrated weaponry.

Though the toxic cocktail of anti-cancer drugs he constantly imbibed caused his hair to fall out—making the smartphone's bulge on the back of his head even more prominent—Cam didn't seem to care. And Erica couldn't blame him. According to Renee, he was fighting several of the most deadly cancers simultaneously, and he was winning.

Erica had never seen her mother so perplexed by a patient. One day, she'd express doubt over whether Cam could even get out of bed, only to be utterly baffled the next, seeing Cam march down the hall, his steel heel clicking against the cement floor, as robust as ever. Lois tried to get the formula for the drug concoctions Cam was using, but Cam wrote down nothing, claiming he memorized everything. The impact of the Android device had been remarkable.

In contrast, Renee's decline continued. She no longer paced, but just sat lethargically, as though her energy were being sapped along with her memories. Almost every night, she visited Erica—a distraction from her thoughts that Erica welcomed, though it made Renee's deterioration even more clear. Renee never forgot Erica or Ian, and she could usually remember much of what had happened the day before. But she seemed to lose almost everything else within a week. And when she wasn't with Erica, Renee was in the chemistry lab, aimlessly mixing chemicals. The only improvement in Renee seemed to be her ability to hide her failing capabilities, a skill she practiced constantly.

Though Erica and Ian didn't discuss it, Morrison seemed more comfortable with Ian after the breakup. But he still avoided Erica.

When he was forced to interact with her, he was terse and uncooperative. Frustrated, Erica called him out on it one day. Morrison said it wasn't personal, but he didn't want to spend any more time than he had to with her and her family. Erica didn't know how to respond to that.

Eve, on the other hand, was quite willing to talk about anything with anyone. She was quick to answer questions in class, but Erica got the impression that she wasn't trying to impress the teachers or anyone else, but rather to get through training as fast as possible.

As they got to know each other better, Eve's mischievous side flourished. She enjoyed playing practical jokes on the others. Setting an hourly alarm on a digital watch and pushing it into Cam's back to see if she could make him absorb it—he didn't—trying to convince Renee to call Morrison by his 'real name' Scooter—she did—and growing a bone spike shaped like a miniature skull, snapping it off, and leaving it on Jen's pillow—Jen added a body using a rolled-up shirt and cherished it like a younger sister.

After a lunch like any other, Irenic approached the group in the mess hall.

"Follow me," she said. Glancing at Jen, she added, "You can stay here and... do whatever it is you do."

"What's up?" Erica said. "We still have half an hour before class."

"Just follow."

Erica licked her lips nervously. Deviating from their schedules like this was unusual. The only reassuring thing was that, if Irenic was involved, this couldn't be a third murder attempt. Irenic was relentlessly brutal, but she was the only person they all agreed couldn't be behind the attacks.

Aware of their discomfort with the elevator, Irenic marched them up ten flights to the third floor, down a corridor, before finally stopping in front of a steel door. She opened it and gestured for them to go inside. Still panting from the climb, they did.

The concrete room was about as large as a classroom, but empty other than a single tablet computer on the floor, and a familiar, curtained-off doorway in the corner. Memories of the Gauntlet came flooding back. Erica flinched and nearly turned around.

"If you're throwing us back in the Gauntlet," Ian said, vocalizing Erica's concerns, "how about springing for an interior designer? This spartan white theme does nothing for me."

"What's this about?" Erica demanded, the reminder of the Gauntlet overcoming her natural reticence to demand anything of Irenic.

"Midterm," Irenic said. "To demonstrate the skills you've learned in class."

"A midterm? For what course?"

Irenic's eyes narrowed, but she otherwise remained impassive. "*Practical Persuasion.*"

Erica froze. "Really? But that's…"

"Torture," Ian said grimly.

CHAPTER EIGHTEEN

"Maybe," Irenic said, smiling faintly. Erica was pretty sure she was enjoying this. "*Practical Persuasion* means what you choose it to mean."

Irenic's eyes moved from face to face. "Each of you has something you don't want the others to know. Your goal is to convince the others to tell you. You will only leave this room when you succeed or when you need urgent medical attention.

"There are two rules. First, don't kill each other. Second, using the tablet, you can ask for anything you need to achieve your goal. I imagine Ian will request an iron maiden."

Was that a joke? If so, it was the first joke Erica had heard from Irenic's mouth.

"That's all." Irenic closed the door before any of them could say anything.

Morrison scooted back, looking at the others nervously. Erica scanned faces. Nobody looked like they were about to do anything drastic, and she knew her ability would prevent her from being surprised. Nevertheless, she felt uneasy. Her rivals would reveal their strategies in the next few minutes.

Would any of them actually try torture? Ian and Renee wouldn't. She was less sure about Cam. A few weeks ago, she wouldn't have thought so, but he'd been so erratic lately. A guy who would saw off his own leg might not be squeamish about doing the same to someone else.

She was even more uncertain about Eve and Morrison. Eve was a complete wild card, while Morrison had to be considered a threat considering the hostility he still harbored for her.

If things got nasty, her ability would enable her to avoid Eve and Cam. Morrison was a problem though. He could eliminate the friction beneath her and leave her helpless on the floor as he'd done in the dojo. If she saw he was about to try something, she'd need to incapacitate him before he could bring his ability into play. She wished she had a weapon.

"Who wants to share?" Eve said with an impish smile. "Anyone want to confess to having impure thoughts? Stealing a cookie from someone else's lunch tray?"

Morrison just stared at her, barely reacting, but Ian's eyes lit up. "No need to rush, Eve," he said. "I need to order a rack. This might be the only opportunity I'll have to use one, and I don't intend to squander it."

Apparently, it wouldn't be an instant bloodbath. That suited Erica fine.

"Forget that," Erica said, her tone haughty. "We can get anything, and the rack is so 15th century. In India, they used elephants for torture. We should ask for an elephant."

Ian nodded. "Interesting idea. Asian or African?"

"What's bigger, Ren?" Erica said.

"African."

"African, then. I'm not accepting an inferior elephant for my torturing needs."

Eve sighed. "Though I admire a massive, well-trained torture elephant as much as the next girl, you guys are missing the whole point of this exercise. Did you forget everything they've been teaching in *Practical Persuasion*? They spent a couple of days on torture, but said it's mostly ineffective for interrogation. The best way to get accurate information is by making friends."

"Oh, yeah," Ian said. "For some reason, the torture part sticks in my head."

"It's understandable," Eve said, grinning slyly. "I, too, am seriously considering poking you until you agree to my every whim. But remember, Hack told that story about the guy who needed information from a terrorist. So, for a month or two, they hung out, playing video games and watching TV. And in the end, the terrorist told him everything."

Ian made a big deal of considering the suggestion. "I suppose there would be less to clean up afterward."

Erica gave him a distraught look, spoiled by the twinkle in her eye. "Does this mean no elephant?"

Ian somberly shook his head. "No elephant. I'm sorry."

Erica pouted.

"So, what?" Morrison said, his posture finally loosening. "We order a TV, video games, and recliners?"

"I think we should," With a mischievous smile, Eve grabbed the tablet and began typing.

"Ooh, get hot wings, chips, and soda, too," Erica said.

"Good call." Eve typed a few more words. "Done. We will extract information using the comfy chair."

"Um," Cam said, raising his hand.

"What is it?" Erica said, shaking her head. For all his alleged intelligence, Cam still hadn't figured out even the basics of human interaction.

"Game theory says we should collaborate. There is no conflict. We all gain by getting out of here and lose nothing by sharing."

"That's silly," Ian said. "If we all want to hide something, then sharing is losing something."

Did she even have something she wouldn't want to reveal? The fact she liked Ian? Maybe, but she kind of wanted to share it, too. It would be embarrassing, but at least it would be out in the open. But there was the bigger picture to think about. She didn't want to tip off Jeemoh that they had been faking their earlier relationship. Even if Jeemoh wasn't a threat, it could become awkward.

Actually, now that she thought about it, she had something worse she didn't want to divulge, an opinion that had been forming ever since she escaped the Gauntlet. None of them would like it. They might hate her, or shun her as Morrison did.

Maybe she did have something to hide.

"If you eventually have to reveal it to get out of here," Cam said, shivering, "there's no loss from sharing it sooner rather than later."

"The cyborg has a point," Eve said. "We could get out of here in half an hour and never give Hack and Irenic the satisfaction of seeing us break."

"What's your secret, then?" Ian said.

Eve smiled at him sweetly. "I'd tell you, but then I'd have to skewer your heart."

The door opened, and Irenic entered carrying a TV and extension cord, followed by soldiers lugging the two couches from the mess hall. She placed the TV in the corner and plugged it in while the soldiers positioned the couch.

"You forgot the wings," Erica said helpfully.

Irenic looked as though she were going to say something, or maybe break Erica's arm, but then just shook her head. She left the room for about a minute, returning just long enough to drop off sodas, a few bags of chips, and a platter of chicken wings.

"Wow," Ian said. "These guys take their interrogations seriously."

They sat to begin some intensive TV watching.

Halfway through their second terrible daytime talk show, Ian stretched and said, "This is boring. I wonder how long it takes for the comfy chair to kick in. Anyone feel like confessing?"

Erica giggled. "No, but I'm right there with you on the boredom. I regret we didn't ask for the elephant."

"Not so fast. We have elephants." Cam waved his hand, and the TV flicked to a documentary about orphaned baby elephants.

"So cute," Renee said.

"No way," her brother replied. "That's one ugly-looking horse."

Renee tilted her head. "Horse? It doesn't even look a bit like a horse."

"No, I mean—*it's one ugly-looking horse*," Ian said, his voice deep with meaning.

Renee's expression was blank.

"The moose? With the horses?" Ian said.

Renee shook her head, turning back to the TV.

"Oh," Ian said. He looked like his dog had just died.

Renee glanced quickly toward him. She frowned. "It's fine, Ian. I just forgot."

Ian nodded, but his expression didn't change.

"Don't look like that. I'm doing my best." Renee paused, and then punched her knee. "Oh, what the hell. My great 'secret', for all the good it will do getting us out of here…" She jabbed her finger toward Morrison. "I don't know you." Then Eve. "Or you." Finally, Cam. "I don't know what you are, let alone who you are. Ian and Erica are the only ones I've met. The rest of you act like I'm your friend, but I've never seen you before in my life. I don't know if I've been drugged, or if maybe I hit my head. I don't even know where the hell we are.

"I've been hiding it, just pretending. But why?" Renee looked Erica with a desperate anger in her eyes. "I don't even know the point of it. Screw this!" Renee hurled the empty bottle she was holding. It missed the TV by inches, shattering on the wall.

"It's okay, Renee," Erica said, putting her hand on her friend's knee. "We know."

"You don't know crap." She stood up and strode to bathroom, viciously pulling the curtain closed behind her.

Everyone was silent for a few seconds.

Ian took a deep breath. "It felt good to kill Vince," he said, looking at the floor in front of the TV.

"What?" Erica said, her eyes as wide as saucers.

"It was wrong. I know that. I never should have done it, and I'll never do something like that again." Ian shook his head. "But, in the moment, I loved it. I barely even felt the fire; I just wanted him to burn so much. I was delighted as he died."

He looked at Erica, his chin quivering. "I'm a monster."

She shook her head. "You aren't." She shifted on the couch, cradling Ian's head against her shoulder. "You aren't."

She never would have guessed. As with a rabid dog, Erica had been willing to use any degree of force necessary to defend herself against Vince. She had numerous regrets, but Vince's death wasn't one of them.

But Ian was idealistic. He was always urging reconciliation and was upset for weeks after killing Vince. He wasn't faking that. But now he admitted he enjoyed watching Vince burn? How could he even begin to resolve that in his head?

Did Ian's confession make her own secret better, or worse?

"This is such a fun game," Eve said flippantly. "I think it's my turn."

Erica nodded. Apparently, they were going with Cam's idea—giving in to the inevitable to avoid potential nastiness. It seemed to be the smartest strategy.

Eve took a deep breath. "I'm not real. I'm just a construct of my imagination."

Morrison stared at her darkly. "What are you talking about? This is supposed to be confession, not philosophy."

Eve's face twisted. "Shut the hell up, or I'll stab you," she said as if she actually meant it. Erica jerked back.

"You don't get it," Eve continued, slightly quieter. "Nobody does. Inside, I'm dead. I don't even know who I am. I just keep doing stuff. Smile. Talk. Joke. Keep moving, play the game, and nobody will notice that there's nothing deeper than my skin.

"I want to be real. I want to care about something. I want to *want* to change the world. But I'm just an empty puppet, swinging this way and that. I dance on the ends of strings to amuse others. But I feel nothing. I'm passionate about nothing.

"Do you know it hurts when I use my ability?" Eve's voice was rough. "It's like shoving a knife through my own skin, slicing tendons and muscles and veins. And then leaving it there for a bit to rattle around.

"It's horrible. But even so, it tempts me. Because I know that when that bone slides through my flesh, I'll at least feel something. For those few minutes, I'll be real."

Erica could empathize. She squeezed Ian tighter.

"So that's me." Eve looked levelly at Cam. "Got anything, Stumpy?"

Cam blinked at her. "My ability doesn't hurt. It feels like tendrils and leaves unfurling."

"Lucky you," Eve said, rolling her eyes. "What's your confession?"

"You know, when we're in a group, you guys rarely listen to me. When I say something, forty-one percent of the time, you don't hear it. Thirty-two percent of the time, you ignore me. Seven percent of the time, you acknowledge but ignore me, and ten percent of the time, you deride me. Only nine percent of the time do you actually listen."

Erica frowned. She didn't ignore Cam. She remembered vividly the conversation they had after he cut off his leg. He must be referring to the others.

"Boo-hoo." Eve rubbed her eyes mockingly. "So speak louder. This isn't therapy, and that's not a secret."

Cam shrugged and looked at the floor. "I know. I just thought it was interesting. Because people listen to you ninety-four percent of the time. Anyway, my deal is that I'm recording everything."

Erica's jaw dropped. "What? You said you wouldn't."

"I said I wouldn't activate the camera. But I'm not using the camera. I'm using my eyes."

"I don't want you to have a video of me whenever I'm with you," Erica said, louder than she intended.

"Me neither," Ian said, releasing Erica.

Cam smiled ironically. "Hence, the secret." He shook his head. "It's not anything you'd recognize as a video anyway. It's like memories. Digitized brainwaves I can play back in my head. You don't have to worry about anyone else watching it. I don't think it's possible. Nobody's invented a way to convert brain waves to video, and it's encrypted with security routines I'm confident are unbreakable."

He shrugged. "Besides, it's a part of me now. No different, really, from you using synaptic connections to remember what you had for breakfast yesterday. At this point, I don't think I could stop it any more than you could turn off your kidneys. So it's not a big deal."

It seemed like a big deal, but Erica couldn't put together an argument for why it mattered. None of the others appeared comfortable with the idea, either, but nobody seemed to understand what Cam was saying well enough to challenge him.

Renee returned to the room, her face solemn. "What'd I miss?"

"The usual. I'm a monster, Eve's fake, and Cam's recording," Ian said. He turned a contemplative eye toward his best friend. "And we were just about to get to Morrison..."

Erica stared at Ian. Was he deliberately avoiding her? Maybe it was just a coincidence.

"I have nothing to share," Morrison said tersely.

"Come on," Ian said. "Irenic said that you do. Just tell us."

"No." Morrison's jaw was set. It looked like he was going to stop talking, but Ian continued to stare at him silently until he relented. "Irenic doesn't know anything. Do you think Jeemoh knows how you felt when you killed Vince or about Eve's teenage angst? They're just messing with us. They put us in here to discover our secrets. To find something to exploit. Well, I'm not playing that game."

"So what if they overhear your great secret?" Ian said. "What does it matter? Ever since you came back, you've been so uptight. Paranoid that the world is out to get you. And I'm not saying that's unjustified. But I know you. You're not that guy, scared to open a door for fear it will hit you in the nose. Just tell us. Trust me, you'll feel better after you do. Who cares what Jeemoh hears?"

"Whatever." Morrison shook his head. "Fine. I'm afraid of spiders." He rolled his eyes.

"Come on, man," Ian said.

"My mother never loved me."

"It has to be real."

Morrison's face was red as he glared at Ian. "You're pissing me off. You know that, dude?"

"I know." Ian looked at Morrison expectantly.

"Okay, fine! You know my last mission? The one that's classified?"

Everyone nodded.

"My team died because I killed them. All of them."

CHAPTER NINETEEN

"What?" Ian said, his eyes wide. "You killed everyone?"

Morrison's nodded curtly. "Except Eve."

Ian looked at Eve for confirmation, and she nodded as well.

"Deliberately?" Ian asked.

Morrison's face screwed up in disgust. "Of course not. It was an accident. Who do you think I am?"

"I know. I didn't mean to imply anything. It's just..." Ian pursed his lips. "How did it happen?"

"It shouldn't have. It was Jeemoh's fault. I was so new. Just six or eight weeks into my time here." He shook his head, sighing.

"Lois told me it's unusual for someone's ability to appear near the end of the year, rather than close to the summer solstice. So I don't think Jeemoh was ready for me. When my ability surfaced, they took me and threw me into isolation for a couple of weeks, claiming it was for everyone's protection. At that point, my ability was triggering randomly. I probably fell out of bed twenty times, just trying to roll over, but finding there was no friction to stop my momentum. After the first night, I put my mattress on the floor. Even so, I still got pretty banged up.

"Lois and her soldiers visited a few times to talk and deliver food. They treated me well, but didn't stay for long. Soon, after a couple tumbles to the concrete floor and a broken arm, the soldiers started avoiding me.

"It was rough, and I didn't ask for any of it. All these strange things were happening, and the 'experts'—the ones who messed with my DNA, who gave me my ability—were afraid to visit. I was lucky if someone came by to talk every third day. The point is that my power wasn't one of those 'magical rainbows and unicorns' kinds that everyone imagines. It was terrifying, uncontrollable, and painful. And the people responsible didn't give a crap."

Ian nodded. "Yep. Unicorns and rainbows. Exactly my experience."

Eve's lips curled sardonically. "Yeah."

Renee sat there silently, her face frozen.

Morrison chuckled without mirth. "Yeah, I guess I have nothing on you guys." He took a long swig from the bottle he was holding. "Eventually—no thanks to them—I figured out enough to turn it on and off. I had no real control, but at least I wasn't breaking everything. So Lois decided I was ready to move in with the rest of my team. My first team. Eve, Hunter, Maurice, Nami, and Kiara. I'm sure you guys remember them from school."

"Though I was joining them late, they made me feel welcome. Hunter had an incredible sense of smell. Like, better than any dog. They said he could detect one particle in a million, and, using gradients, track down the source. Maurice could knock people out with a touch. Nami had flexible joints and muscle control. Every joint could bend in every direction. It was odd and kind of disturbing. Kiara was a fluid telekinetic. She could make the wind blow in whatever direction she wanted or produce a current in still water. They even hoped she'd learn to pull the air from someone's lungs, but she hadn't figured that out yet.

"The others had already been training for six months, led by Sergeant Haddy, our Irenic equivalent. Lois didn't ask me what I wanted. She just made me join the team.

"I didn't protest because it was better than isolation, and I knew they wouldn't care even if I did complain. You know what it's like. A lot of coursework and training during the day, but a decent amount of free time and socializing at night. Before long, it even felt normal.

"One day, we were in *Survival* class when Lois came in. She made the teacher leave and announced that we were going on a mission.

"At that point, I wasn't even sure what to make of Jeemoh. Lois didn't hide that they were doing genetic-engineering experiments on people, and Nami told me about her experiences in the Gauntlet. I had no idea whether Jeemoh was the 'good guys'." Morrison's tone made it clear that even now he wasn't convinced the organization was on the side of the angels. "So I didn't know if I wanted to go on a mission for Jeemoh at all.

"And I wasn't ready. My power was still flaky—I'd only been training for a few weeks. Lois should have known better than to put me in the field. I didn't want to go. But everyone else was excited about the mission, and I didn't want to let my team down. So I didn't argue.

"The mission itself seemed worthwhile, and we were the right team to do it. Terrorists had seized a dam in Washington State. Before the authorities even knew there was a threat, the terrorists had full control of the dam, planting explosives all over. They threatened to blow it up unless the president released twenty domestic terrorists.

"Obviously, he couldn't do what they asked. But if the terrorists had demolished the dam, it would have been terrible. Towns and bridges along the river would have been wiped out, not to mention a significant chunk of the power-generating capacity in the northwest. Basically, we were screwed.

"The problem with dams is that there aren't many ways to get inside. Even a handful of people with guns can hold out against a much larger and better-armed force, certainly long enough to detonate explosives. That's why Jeemoh had to intervene."

Erica nodded—yet another piece of evidence that Jeemoh's missions were about making the world a better place.

"They came up with a plan," Morrison continued. "A stupid, deranged plan. You see, in a hydroelectric dam, huge tubes called penstocks carry the water from the lake down through the turbines to generate electricity. But in this dam, just before the turbines, the penstocks are open to the powerhouse, the main room inside the dam where the terrorists planted the explosives.

"If someone was insane, they could, in theory, swim in through the water intake and down through the penstocks. Just before they hit the turbines, they could hoist themselves onto a ledge a few feet out of the water, climb up this wide, rubberized ramp, and find themselves in the powerhouse.

"But nobody would actually try this. The dam holds back so much water that the current in the penstock is far too strong. If you get sucked through the intake, you're not stopping to get out. You're going through the turbine.

"So, of course, we decided to try it."

Erica found herself holding her breath. If that was their plan, it seemed like a miracle—not that most of the team had died, but that Morrison and Eve survived.

"That's nuts," she said.

Morrison nodded. "I agree. But try telling that to your mother. She said it was perfectly safe. That it was the only way to deactivate the bombs. And I believed her."

"But how was that even possible?" Ian said, shaking his head in confusion. "Wouldn't you be chopped up?"

"The key was Kiara," Morrison said. "Her fluid telekinetic ability could negate the current. So, instead of the penstock feeling like a raging river, she could surround us with calm water, like swimming in a pool.

"So, late at night, we put on scuba gear, and they dropped us into the lake a few hundred yards from the dam. I'd never even dived before. But in the pitch dark, they expected me to swim underwater to the intake pipe, guided only by a tiny light on Sergeant Haddy's belt.

"Somehow, we all made it. With Kiara counteracting the current, Haddy cut a hole in the grill blocking the intake, one big enough for us to swim through.

"The silent swim in the dark lake was spooky, but diving down through the penstock was far worse. We could use flashlights then, but I would have preferred at that point not to have their dim light. Really, it wasn't that narrow. You could've fit a small car in there. But there's something terrible about swimming down, down, down in an enclosed space.

"The water rushes by. The shadows dance on the walls. You know that if your tank fails, there's nowhere to go. You could try to surface, but that smooth pipe is above you. You'll rip off your fingernails clawing at it in the darkness in a futile effort to get one more gasp of oxygen."

Erica shuddered, imagining the scene.

"It seemed like hours, but we reached the powerhouse. Haddy grabbed the ledge above and pulled us out of the water. Together, we crept up the rubber ramp.

"Only two terrorists were there—the others were guarding the entrances and 'knew' that nobody could get by them. The inside of a dam is loud, so it was easy to sneak up and incapacitate them." He glanced at Eve, who was rubbing a spot in the center of her hand. She shrugged.

"It took about half an hour for Hunter and Haddy to sniff out and disarm all the explosives. Until that point, the operation was going perfectly."

"The plan was to sneak out the same way we got in and allow the authorities to take it from there. Without the explosives, it would just be a matter of time before the terrorists would be forced to surrender.

"We were about to leave, all gathered at the top of the ramp down to the pool, preparing to put on our tanks and flippers again, when everything fell apart.

"One of the terrorists came downstairs. We still don't know why. Maybe his pals didn't check in. Maybe he was just looking in on them. But it didn't matter. He came and spotted us before we saw him."

"He was a long way away and shot wildly with an automatic weapon. Even so, he hit Kiara twice. We fled down the ramp toward the penstock, but Kiara was bleeding pretty badly. She was awake, but Haddy didn't think field bandages would hold up in the water. If we swam, she'd be unconscious from blood loss long before we got out of the penstock. And without her stopping the current, well...

"We had a contingency plan in case something like that happened—taking out the terrorists ourselves.

"Near the bottom of the ramp was this big bulge from the turbine casing. We hid behind it while working out the details of our counterattack. Meanwhile, five or six other men came down and opened fire. We shot back, but you can't carry big weapons while diving. Soon, we ran low on ammo."

Ian looked at Erica, eyes wide.

"The turbine casing was big enough for all of us to hide behind and solid enough that their bullets barely scratched it. So they couldn't hit us, but they figured out that we weren't firing back anymore either. So, with two guys covering, they sent four guys down the ramp to flush us out.

"That's when I saw the opportunity to use my ability. I eliminated all the friction on the ramp. It worked. The terrorists fell and slid into the water

156

"But I was still new. Nobody had taught me targeting. And Lois knew that, but sent me on the mission anyway. What happened was her fault.

"Instead of just hitting the terrorists, I eliminated friction everywhere on the ramp except under my feet. And that was the problem. Kiara, Nami, and the rest of our team fell too. Only Eve was able to avoid sliding into the water. She shot bone spikes out of her hands and legs deep into the rubber, nailing herself to the ramp.

"Kiara held the current at bay while the others scrambled around, trying to fight the terrorists in the water, climb out, and avoid the gunfire from those above, all at the same time. I wanted to help, to reach out to grab Nami. But I knew if I tried, the two remaining terrorists would shoot me. I could only huddle behind the turbine casing and watch.

"Kiara fought to stay awake. She did. She tried so hard. But the bleeding was too much. And the instant she succumbed, her ability stopped, and the current resumed. And that was it."

Morrison stared down at an empty bottle on the floor in front of him. "I used my ability to put the other two terrorists on the floor." His eyes grew hard. "I disarmed them and nudged them into the water. No less than what they deserved."

He paused. Then, blinking several times as if rising from a dream, Morrison looked around and swallowed. "Eve was bleeding pretty badly, both from the spikes and from a couple of bullet wounds in her legs. So I carried her outside where Jeemoh picked us up."

Morrison turned to Ian. "I never should have been there. Lois hadn't taught me enough." Morrison's eyes were riveted to Ian's face, like the two of them were alone in the room. "And I was really pissed off at her for sending me out there.

"When we got back to Battlefield, I wanted to quit. When the van stopped at a traffic light, I held it there and told them I was never coming back.

"I walked to my parent's house, certain they'd take me in. But they turned me away. They said they weren't really my parents. Nothing in my life was real. For them, I was just a job, and that job was done.

His eyes were bitter. "So I wasn't lying. My parents don't love me."

Ian shook his head. "I'm sorry, man."

Morrison shrugged. "Whatever. I'd rather know the truth than live a lie. After that, I wandered the streets for a night. I couldn't do anything. I had nowhere to go."

"You could have come to me," Ian said.

Morrison frowned. "You're my friend. I couldn't draw you into this. So I returned here. I went over to Erica's house, found Lois, and she took me back." He placed his empty bottle on the floor. "So there's my secret. Satisfied?"

Ian nodded. "I'm sorry."

Morrison's voice sounded frail. "Doesn't matter now. It's done. They've destroyed my old life. Everyone thinks I'm dead." He looked to Erica. "So, can you match that?" His tone was derisive.

Erica bit her lip. "No. It makes my secret seem trivial."

"Great," Morrison said sarcastically. "So what is it?"

Would they hate her when she said it? Would they think she was a Jeemoh collaborator, as Morrison seemed to believe?

It didn't matter. After what the others had said, she owed them the truth.

"Lois was right to put us in the Gauntlet and to lock us up afterward," Erica said, staring at the TV.

Ian pulled away from her to look at her face. "You're joking."

Erica shook her head. "I'm not."

Eve smiled knowingly. "Ah, Erica finally reveals her true allegiance."

"It's nothing like that," Erica snapped at her. "It just makes sense."

"Denise and Vince died there," Ian said. "We nearly did too."

"There was no other way. Jeemoh's brutal, but it's because there are no alternatives."

Morrison's face was dark. "How can you say that? Six people have died while in Jeemoh's tender-loving care. And that's not even counting what happened to Jen."

Erica nodded. "I know." She fought to keep her voice calm while laying out her case as clearly as she could. "It's appalling. That's why I didn't want to share it. But look at it this way. You accidentally killed five people because you didn't have full control over your ability. Lizzy killed another handful for the same reason. Ian would have died conjuring his magnesium if Jeemoh hadn't been there to heal him. So, because of uncontrolled abilities, we have, like, ten people dead and one almost dead. And that's just what we've seen with our own eyes.

"The Gauntlet is an atrocity, but it's also the only safe way to elicit these abilities. Similarly, locking us up afterward is unfortunate, but until we master our abilities, there's no alternative. How bad would you feel if you were taking an exam at school, and, because of the stress, your ability surfaced, accidentally killing someone? Or everyone?"

Erica scanned the faces of her teammates, looking for reactions. Morrison's jaw was set. Clearly, he wasn't buying her argument, and he hadn't even been in the Gauntlet. Eve had a small grin, as if she found the conversation amusing, but not at all important.

Ian and Cam seemed more thoughtful. Renee looked like she was pretending to consider the question, but actually had no clue what they were talking about.

Finally, Ian spoke. "I'm not saying I agree with you, but I also can't say you're wrong. And that surprises me."

Cam shook his head. "The end doesn't justify the means. Not when the means is the torture of innocents."

"It's not a question of ends and means," Erica insisted. "It's a question of the lesser of two evils. Of risking everyone in Battlefield by allowing these abilities to come out on their own or limiting the impact using the Gauntlet. I think it was the right thing to do."

"I don't," Cam said unemotionally, staring at the TV. "If they—"

Erica jerked up her palm to stop the conversation, her breath catching in her throat. Heavy footfalls sounded in the corridor, stopping outside their room. Erica shifted on the couch to look at the door an instant before it was flung open.

Irenic stood there, her gaze penetrating.

"Did we pass?" Ian asked.

"Focus on the learning, not the pass or fail." Irenic's face softened slightly. "Your strategy was effective. You got the information quickly."

"We definitely passed," Ian said smugly.

Irenic looked at him flatly. "It's not important now."

"Why?" Erica said.

"Something's come up. We're going on a mission."

CHAPTER TWENTY

"But we barely finished the midterm," Ian said.

"Life doesn't wait upon your convenience," Irenic said.

"I knew she would say that," Erica said, smiling at Ian.

Ian nodded knowingly. "That's because life speaks in platitudes."

"And then life snaps your arm like a twig."

"Life's kind of a jerk like that."

Erica shook her head. She was about to respond, "No, jerks are like life,"—a statement without substance that nevertheless made her want to giggle—when she saw Irenic's eyes narrow and her lips thin. She decided that it was perhaps unwise to mock her insane martial arts instructor.

"Yeah." Erica stared at Irenic with manic attentiveness. She really shouldn't giggle. "You were saying?"

Irenic's stare was uncompromising. "Follow me."

She escorted them to a large but austere office on the sixth floor, containing little more than a desk, a single bookshelf, a conference table, and chairs. The walls were bare, without even a picture to break the stark whiteness.

Lois sat at the desk, but rose as they entered. She led them to the table, gesturing toward the chairs.

"You're here because something has come up and you're the only team available," Lois said, nothing but business.

"Where are the others?" Ian said.

"Do you think I'm going to answer that?"

Ian shrugged. "We just came from our *Practical Persuasion* midterm.

160

Give us a few hours and an African elephant, and you might."

"Unlikely. And irrelevant. Because someone attacked Battlefield High this afternoon. Your old school."

Everyone went still, their eyes glued to Lois.

"So that's what it takes to get your attention," she said.

"What happened?" Erica said, leaning forward. "Is everyone okay? Is it the same person who sabotaged the elevators?"

Lois shook her head. "We don't know. We suspect that the same group might be involved in the attack here, but we have no evidence yet." She touched her tablet, and a projector dropped from the ceiling, shining on the white wall. "At about thirteen hundred hours, twelve men entered the school through each of the four main entrances."

The projector displayed a pair of double doors that Erica recognized from her school. Three men in street clothes, each in reflective sunglasses and carrying a backpack, entered. The instant the door closed behind them, the men opened the bags, pulling out handguns that they stuffed in their pants. Then, one boosted another up until his face was right in the camera. Erica could see the whiskers sprouting on his chin. He moved a pair of pliers toward the camera, and the screen went dark. After a few seconds, a similar scene repeated at another door.

"Nice shades," Ian said. "So fashionable."

Lois ignored the comment. "This was perfectly timed and executed, with all the door cameras nullified within five seconds of each other. These people had scouted the building already. They knew the locations of our surveillance equipment. What's more, we suspect they haven't turned off the equipment, but rather taken it over."

"Why do you think that?" Cam said.

"Because they could've just smashed the cameras rather than disabling them with pliers. And because of what happened when we sent in our team. Nine hostiles intercepted them within seconds of them entering the school. Either the enemy was lucky, or their surveillance abilities are excellent." The video flickered to a new scene, a bobbing head-cam view. The wearer of the camera was staring through a glass cutout in a metal shield. When the camera reached the school doors, a gloved hand reached out and shoved them open, revealing the familiar stairway up to the main floor of the school.

The camera swung down, showing the bottom of the shield. It was on wheels and looked heavy. Though there was no discussion, the soldier was clearly trying to decide whether he should try to carry the bulky anti-ballistics shield up the stairway, or leave it behind.

After a few seconds, he abandoned the shield and began creeping along the wall up the stairs. The camera mostly pointed up the stairs, but jogged to the left occasionally. There, Erica could see three more soldiers hugging the wall as they climbed.

Finally, they reached the top. Several teachers' desks were lying in the hall, tipped onto their sides. Without warning, guns poked out from behind the desks. Bullets flew.

Within thirty seconds, the cameraman was hit. The camera spun wildly and ended up pointed at a wall. Soon afterward, the sound of the gunfire ceased.

"Your soldiers aren't that good, are they?" Ian said flippantly. "Any time you send them anywhere, they get beat up."

Lois' glare felt as hot as the sun. "Show some respect. This isn't a video game. Those people died doing their duty."

Ian swallowed. "I'm sorry."

"The fact is, they're extremely proficient. You only see the places they lose because we rarely send in our special teams unless conventional measures fail. They are Plan A. You are Plan B." Lois turned her attention away from Ian. "Now, you should have spotted something wrong with that scene. What was it?" She scanned the faces at the table.

Erica gnawed on her lip. She had seen nothing strange. The enemy was hiding behind desks, but it was expected. They'd want cover in the wide-open halls. And it worked. She'd barely seen them. It had been a one-sided massacre.

"The hostiles weren't looking when they fired," Renee said. "You never even catch the slightest glimpse of their heads. Just their weapons."

"Exactly," Lois said. "How did they shoot all our people without looking?"

This time, Renee didn't have an answer. Even Irenic seemed baffled.

Cam raised his hand. When Lois raised her eyebrows at him, he said, "They... they probably used the cameras. I'd guess they are projecting images from the cameras onto their sunglasses. Or maybe they have cameras mounted on their guns. It would be hard to aim. They must have spent a fair amount of time practicing."

Lois smiled, though her eyes remained cold. "Good work, Cam." He blushed and looked down. "We agree."

"What about the students? Has anyone else been killed?" Erica said. All her friends—well, at least the ones who weren't at Jeemoh—went to that school.

"We don't know for sure. Most of the students got out. According to the people who escaped, the attackers were primarily targeting the teachers, but we know at least three students are still in there." She looked at her tablet. "Kelly Kim, Jacob Silverstein, and Alice Wood. But there could be others."

Alice had been in several of Erica's classes, though Erica wouldn't consider her more than an acquaintance. The others she didn't know.

"Do they have any special abilities?" Eve asked.

Lois shook her head. "None has shown anything so far, or they wouldn't still be at Battlefield High. But all three of them do have the gene."

"You genetically modified them?" Morrison said, his lips thinning.

Lois nodded. "All of them are candidates."

"With abilities that often manifest during stressful situations?" Ian said.

Lois nodded again.

"In situations like, I don't know… *being taken hostage?*" Ian said, starting mildly and ending loudly. Erica couldn't help but smile.

Lois rolled her eyes. "Yes, that is an implication. Kelly and Jacob are young, so they are unlikely to be activated. Alice is on the schedule for the Gauntlet next year. So she's a slight risk. Say, a twenty percent chance. To the best of our knowledge, no abilities have been triggered yet."

"Um," Cam said.

"Yes?" Lois said.

"How many people at Battlefield High have these genetic modifications?"

"That's classified."

"Yeah." Cam looked at the table. "But…"

"What is it, Cam?" Lois said, her exasperation showing in her tone. "Just ask your question."

"Could it have been just luck that they captured three candidates? Like, if half the students at the school have been modified, they might have just got lucky grabbing them. A one in eight chance."

"Far fewer than fifty percent of the students are candidates. If they chose randomly, there would be an extremely low chance of getting three candidates."

"Oh," Cam said.

"Along with those three, five teachers are unaccounted for," Lois looked at Erica, "including your old chemistry teacher, Mr. Ambrose. So, our best estimate is that they have eight hostages."

"What are their demands?" Erica said, glancing at Ian. He'd been in the same chemistry class.

"They haven't asked for anything."

"But then why take hostages?" Ian said.

"We don't know," Lois said. "It's possible they are just delaying before communicating what they want, maybe to consolidate their position."

Cam raised his head, stared at Lois for a few seconds, and then asked, "Do any of the teachers work for Jeemoh?"

"That's also classified."

"What happened to the whole 'on the same team' thing?" Morrison said, leaning over the table. "Why is all this stuff confidential? We're supposed to work together."

Lois shook her head. "This is a covert agency. We stay covert by compartmentalizing information and communicating on a need-to-know basis. If one person is compromised, they can reveal only what they know. You should have already learned all this from Hack."

Erica nodded. She had. Her mother was running things by the book.

Morrison seemed unsatisfied, his voice growing louder. "We *do* need to know. They killed your guys in a few seconds, and now you want us to go in there. We need all the information we can get."

Lois shook her head. "I decide what you need to know, not you."

Morrison didn't even try to hide his glare.

"Um," Cam said. When everyone looked at him, he trembled, turning his body, directing his attention and remarks at Erica, Ian, and the other team members. "This is what's happening. This isn't the typical hostage taking. Rather, it's an attack on Jeemoh, though your mother is uncertain whether it's the same people responsible for the elevator. All the teachers remaining in the school are part of Jeemoh, or active collaborators. The attackers probably want information from the teachers, and to capture or eliminate genetically modified candidates. Lois strongly suspects this is the case, but she doesn't want to share it. The attackers are as well funded as Jeemoh, and may even be more technologically advanced."

Everyone was silent, looking at Cam, waiting for him to say more.

Cam shook his head. "That's all I wanted to say." He looked at his hands, which were resting on the table.

Erica glanced at her mother. She was staring at Cam, her face flushed and her lips pressed together.

The expression lasted no more than a second. Lois flipped back her hair and smiled. "That's an interesting hypothesis, Cam." Her tone was patronizing. "But I'd caution about going into a volatile situation like this with ill-formed assumptions. You don't want to depend on anything you don't know for sure because bad information costs lives."

Cam didn't look up. "I do know—"

"In any case," Lois said loudly, "this mission has a single goal—to rescue the hostages. Lethal force is authorized. We expect you to use the ballistic shields to get close enough to enter the building, locate the hostages, and extract them."

"Wow," Eve said, her eyes alight.

Ian frowned. "And why won't we be mowed down just like the last squad?"

"Because you will be the least threat. We will enter from four directions simultaneously. The other three groups will be body-armored soldiers carrying assault rifles.

"Though you'll have bulletproof vests under your clothes, you will be dressed as civilians and will be carrying Javelins, an easily hidden weapon. Helped by Erica's luck, we expect the hostage-takers to misjudge the situation. They will perceive you as far less worrisome than the soldiers and will focus their limited personnel elsewhere, enabling you to enter the building with little resistance. From there, Erica's ability will help you locate the hostages quickly. Even if you don't disable all the hostiles, once the hostages are free, we'll have more flexibility to mop up the pieces."

Erica bit her lip. This was the downside of claiming that her ability was luck. She was unlikely to find the hostages faster than anyone else, but she couldn't say that now. Still, her ability should at least enable her to avoid being shot.

"This is a bad idea," Morrison said, crossing his arms. "It's too dangerous. Those guys are professionals. We could be killed. I don't think we should do it."

Lois frowned. "You're a part of Jeemoh now, and we do not vote about which missions we will take on."

"And what if I decide to skip this mission?" The look in Morrison's eyes was more challenging than curious.

"You could refuse to obey orders, but there will be consequences."

Morrison frowned. "Like what?"

"The ramifications vary. At minimum, it would mean a court-martial, and the repercussions become less pleasant from there." Lois shook her head. "I'm sorry if I've given you the impression Jeemoh's just a summer camp for spies. This is an important job. We take it seriously."

Erica recognized the combination of her mother's severe expression with her almost lackadaisical tone. In her house, Lois reserved it for the worst violations of rules. This wasn't good at all.

And a court-martial was the least punishment? They weren't even in the military, were they? Erica had no idea when she joined Jeemoh she was signing up for that. But maybe she should have. The organization clearly had a military focus, so perhaps military law was a natural extension. Even so, it still seemed wrong. She hadn't agreed to abide by military law.

From her limited understanding, a court-martial was pretty bad. So what did 'less pleasant consequences' mean? What would her mother do if someone with abilities went rogue? Perhaps the snipers they had seen back at her house when they were debating whether to join Jeemoh were the answer. She gnawed on her lower lip.

Morrison's eyes narrowed. "I never thought this was a vacation. I just want everything to be laid out on the table."

"Fair enough," Lois said, her tone still unnaturally pleasant. "So there it is, laid out like a Sunday buffet." She turned to the others. "We believe sending you in is our best chance of rescuing the hostages unharmed. You're early in your training, but you already show immense potential. We'd estimate that, without your involvement, there is a ninety-percent chance that one or more of the hostages will die."

"And the chance of one of us dying?" Eve said, arching an eyebrow. "Just so we know..."

"Less than twenty."

Erica didn't know what to think of that number. On one hand, the first squad had been gunned down so quickly that twenty percent seemed low. On the other, it was still a one in five chance.

But wasn't this what she'd signed up for? The school kids were innocent, and possibly some of the teachers were as well. She'd joined Jeemoh to make the world a better place, to do exactly this sort of thing. She never expected the job to be safe. Why would she back down now?

"I'm in," she said more confidently than she felt. "Let's go to work."

Ian stared at her for a few seconds and turned to Lois. "We're using Javelins?"

Lois nodded. "The other teams will have guns. Explosives run too big a risk of killing civilians, and tear gas isn't fast enough to incapacitate the enemy before they kill the hostages."

Ian considered it for a moment. "Okay. I'm in too."

Renee and Cam nodded.

"I'm in. Definitely," Eve said. "It'll be nice to get outside again."

Morrison looked like he might argue, but then sighed. "Yeah, all right."

"Good," Irenic said. "Life is not cowering in a hole, but boldly stepping forward."

Lois nodded. "While dressed as a librarian."

Irenic's spine became even more rigid. "That's a joke, right?"

Lois smiled. "Time to suit up."

CHAPTER TWENTY-ONE

A drop of sweat trickled down Erica's back as she crept along the paved pathway toward the school doors. She hunched down behind her ballistic shield, trying to roll it forward at the same pace as the others. Sergeant Irenic had assured them nothing short of a mounted assault weapon would penetrate the shield, and Erica knew that if someone fired on them, her visions would give her a few seconds' warning. Nevertheless, she felt exposed as she crossed the bare field, as if a sniper even now had his sights trained on her back.

"One small question," Ian said, his voice excessively casual. "I know these outfits and Erica's luck are supposed to result in the enemy making a mistake, targeting the others rather than us. But if this is an attack on Jeemoh, won't they realize that we're a bigger threat than the soldiers? That we're the ones who could have abilities?"

"Took you long enough to figure that out," Morrison replied bitterly, giving his shield an extra shove to bump its wheels over a rock. "We'll probably open those doors and find ten guns trained on us."

"Smart," Irenic said. "Plan for the worst." She scratched at her neck. Erica wasn't sure if the fabric itched, or if Irenic was just uncomfortable wearing the bulky turtleneck sweater on a hot day. Irenic's oversized, yellow-rimmed glasses and severe brushed-back hairstyle reminded Erica not so much of a librarian, but a great horned owl.

"That isn't really what I meant," Morrison muttered.

"Stop whining, Morrison," Eve said. "This is great. We finally get to do something real again and enjoy the first sunny day we've experienced in weeks. I feel like I've been in that dungeon for years." As if to emphasize her point, she stretched to her full height, raising her hands toward the sun.

Irenic, who was beside Eve, grasped her arm, pulling her back behind the shield. "Don't be stupid."

"Life isn't cowering behind a shield, but enjoying the open air," Eve said sarcastically, though she kept her head down for the rest of the journey.

"At the door," Irenic said into her microphone.

"Roger," crackled the headset in Erica's ear. "Us too."

Two of the teams were slower, so they had to wait. Erica was tempted to peer through the narrow window in the door, but she had been warned that doing so would be a good way to get shot.

"*Ready*," the headset said.

"Wait," Cam said.

Irenic frowned. "Why?"

Cam didn't even glance at her. He just stared at the door in front of him. "Just a sec."

Irenic's eyes bored into him. "I don't care if you're scared. We can't wait."

"Done," Cam said. "Each entrance has two hostiles sheltered behind desks. Hey, I can see us." Cam waved at the door. "The hostages and five remaining hostiles are in Mr. Ambrose's chemistry lab." His eyes widened. "Mr. Ambrose is shaking and screaming."

"What?" Irenic said. "How do you know that?"

"And it's gone," Cam said. "How on earth did they figure it out so fast?" He turned back to Irenic, saw her expression, and seemed to shrink. "I... I'm sorry. The cameras communicate wirelessly, and we've been in range for twelve minutes, forty-three seconds. I cracked the encryption and got in."

"You cracked the encryption in twelve minutes?" Renee said, tilting her head. "A smartphone can't do that. How many computers—"

"Discuss the details later," Irenic said. She looked at Cam. "You can see everything in there?"

"Not anymore," Cam said, looking at his feet. "They must have realized what I was doing, because they turned them off." He shook his head. "4.6 seconds. So fast. At least their surveillance is down."

Irenic took only a heartbeat to absorb the information. "Everyone hear that?" she said in a low voice. "Two hostiles at each entrance. Five hostiles and the hostages in the chemistry lab." There was a chorus of 'Rogers' over the headset. "We go three seconds from mark. Mark." Flipping the radio to a private channel to avoid confusion, Irenic held up three fingers in a silent countdown.

Erica's heart beat so fast she could almost hear it in her ears. Letting the anxiety course through her, she cast her mind ahead, willing herself to see what would happen five seconds in the future.

A door opening. An empty stairway up.

Though this was a different entrance, the vision confirmed the first team's intelligence. If there was anyone waiting, they were upstairs.

Irenic's countdown ended. She made a fist and punched the air in front of her. Erica reached out from behind the shield and pulled the door open. She awkwardly maneuvered the shield to the side to work the door around it before swinging it back in front.

The stairway loomed above. At the top was an archway that Erica had walked through hundreds of times, but never like this. Twelve steps until the excitement began.

The shields weighed as much as a grown man. Without the wheels, Erica would have struggled to move hers. There was no way to carry them upstairs, not without being totally exposed.

Irenic gestured them forward.

Eve moved toward the stairs, but Erica gripped her arm. "Luck," Erica murmured.

Eve frowned, but let Erica slide in front of her.

"You next, Morrison," Irenic ordered.

Morrison shot her a cold look, but Irenic just waved him forward with her chin. Gritting his teeth, he fell in behind Erica.

Eight steps up, visions started to cascade.

The top of the stairs. A shot in the forehead.

Poke her head out, and then immediately duck.

Shot in the leg.

Stutter step.

The visions and adjustments came almost faster than she could process them. Erica was so focused on survival that the transition from seeing the attack in her mind to the bullets flying was barely noteworthy.

As if in a dream, she stuck her head out from behind the archway, seeing for herself the desks in the hall with the two guns poking out.

Erica ducked. As she knew it would, she felt the bullet part her hair, tunneling through the air where her forehead had been an instant before.

She danced forward, bending, turning sideways, and dodging. Did everything that was needed exactly when was needed, moving ever closer to the desks. Bullets cut through the air beside her, never missing by much, but always missing. She pulled out her Javelin.

She was still fifteen feet from the desk when the hands holding the guns jerked and dropped to the floor. Half the upper torso of one of the hostage-takers fell into view. Morrison, behind her to her right, must have gotten close enough to eliminate the friction under his feet.

The hostiles didn't have a chance. Erica raised the Javelin and shot the exposed man in the neck. He twitched for a few seconds, and then lay motionless.

The visions continued to cascade. It was then Erica realized she had a huge problem.

She cast around for alternatives to what was about to happen. Ian was too far away. Morrison would be too slow to react to anything she said.

There was nothing else. No third possibility.

It was Morrison or her.

She kept evaluating minute variations, hoping to find a solution, knowing that her search was futile. Morrison should have made their enemies drop their weapons, not gone for their feet.

She was out of time.

No regrets.

Erica dove aside.

Though the hostile was on his back not even looking at his target, he could still aim his gun. The bullet intended for Erica flew past her leg, straight into Morrison's upper thigh. The sound as it hit bone reminded Erica of the crack of a bat at the baseball field. Morrison crumpled to the ground, groaning.

Erica had been in the lead, drawing fire. But now the desk was between her and the remaining hostile, so he refocused his attention on the others sprinting toward him. Ian was in front with Renee just behind.

Ian's head jerking. Blood spraying. A second bullet in the neck.

She cycled through alternatives. It was just like Morrison. Renee was behind Ian. If he moved, she'd be hit instead.

There was nothing to throw. No way to distract the enemy.

Would they lose both Ian and Morrison within seconds of each other?

She clambered to her feet, knowing she couldn't get there in time to make a difference, cycling through alternative scenarios.

Finally, she found it.

"Ian!" Erica screamed. "Your forehead. Then neck."

Ian used one of the two seconds he had left to live to turn his head toward Erica, trying to figure out what she was saying.

In the next second, he brought his right arm in front of his head. It was flesh that quickly turned to steel.

The bullet targeting his forehead ricocheted off his forearm.

The second bullet hit the steel on his left arm, raised in front of his neck.

And then, Renee was there. As Ian paused, she leaped from behind her brother. She kicked the attacker's hand, sending the gun sliding across the floor.

The man tried to stand, but Renee was faster. She pressed her javelin against the side of his neck and fired. The man shook and collapsed.

Their first job was to make sure the threat was nullified. Ignoring the gunfire that still echoed down the empty corridors of the school, Erica raced over to the man she'd stunned. She pulled his hands behind his back and secured them with handcuffs. Her goal accomplished, she looked over to Irenic for new orders.

Irenic crouched in a pool of Morrison's blood, gripping his right leg. Though she had cut open his pants and slapped an adhesive over the wound, the bandage was already soaking through.

"Aah!" shouted Morrison. "I'm shot." He gripped Irenic's shirt. "Do something."

"Shut up and let me work," Irenic said, removing his hands forcefully. She sliced a long strip from his pants, wrapped it around his thigh, and knotted it.

"It hurts," Morrison yelled.

Irenic ignored him. Grimacing, she yanked on the free ends of the tourniquet to tighten it. Morrison's shout cut off abruptly. His head fell back, his eyes closed.

"Renee, his femoral artery is severed," Irenic said. "Take care of it."

Renee ran to him and took over from Irenic, grabbing Morrison's leg. She looked at the bloody dressing, and then turned back to the sergeant, her face white. "I can't fix it. I don't have the equipment, the operating team."

"You're not a surgeon. You're a field medic."

Renee nodded. She tapped on her headset. "Morrison is RTC. Severed right femoral artery. Hostiles eliminated. Come and get him now."

"*The other doors are unsecured. Are you sure it's safe?*" crackled a man's voice on the earphone.

"Doesn't matter. Get him now or he dies," Renee said. Though her grip on his leg didn't loosen, her arms trembled. Eve knelt beside Renee, trying to help her keep the wound closed.

Erica wiped perspiration from her forehead. She didn't realize a simple leg wound could be so serious. Should she have taken the bullet herself? That was her only other option.

No regrets. She'd done what she needed to do.

"*Erica and Ian, help Renee. Cam, the hostile Erica restrained is wearing a thin backpack. Check what's inside.*" Lois' voice over the headset was easily recognizable.

Cam was still forty feet away on the stairs, but started forward, his eyes flicking from door to door as he advanced.

Irenic placed her hand upon Cam's chest, stopping him. "I'm commanding this field operation, Lois. If you try to give orders again, I'll turn you off." She waited five heartbeats. "Well?"

"*Acknowledged.*" Even over the earpiece, Lois sounded as if she'd swallowed some bad sushi.

Irenic nodded. "Cam, check out the backpack."

As Cam made his way toward her, Erica looked down at the man she'd incapacitated. Lois was right. The hostile's vest seemed unusually bulky in the back, much more than the bulletproof vest she was wearing. Running along the top was a black zipper and a hole with a thin wire sticking out.

Cam knelt down to stare at the vest.

A hand opening the zipper. An explosion. Cam, Erica, and

terrorist bits all over the hall.

"Wait," Erica said hastily. "It's booby trapped. I think."

Cam froze, his hand inches from the zipper. "How do you know?"

"That wire sticking out seems suspicious."

"It's an antenna."

"Maybe." Erica played through different scenarios in her mind. The bomb only seemed to detonate when she opened the compartment fully. She nudged Cam aside. "Here. Let me." She slid the zipper halfway, flipped a switch inside, and then safely opened it the rest of the way.

The compartment filled up the entire back of the vest. Inside, attached to the wire, was a metal box about the size of a thick magazine. On one side were USB and other ports.

Irenic came over to examine the box. "A computer. Processes the data from the sunglasses." Reaching into the backpack, she lifted out a small block of what looked like white modeling clay and held it under Erica's nose. "C-4. Plastic explosive. Don't open any more backpacks." She put her fingers to the hostage-taker's neck and then did the same to the other one. "Take back your handcuffs. They're dead."

"What?" Erica said, jerking her head around to stare at Irenic. "I thought the Javelins just incapacitated the targets?"

"There are different intensities. These are set to kill."

Erica was aghast. "Why? And why didn't you tell us?"

Irenic shrugged. "Lois' decision, not mine. Some people hesitate to kill."

"Damn right some people do," Erica said. Furious, she threw her Javelin against the wall with all her might, cracking the casing and sending the black button careening down the hall.

Truthfully, Erica had no problem with killing the hostiles. They hadn't hesitated to murder a full Jeemoh team. But to take that decision from her, to trick her into killing someone… that was reprehensible.

Irenic shrugged. "I imagine you'll regret that." Without an ounce of squeamishness, she wiped her bloody hands on the corpse's pants.

Ian placed his Javelin on the floor. "I'm not killing anyone."

Instantly, Erica's anger vanished. This wasn't what she intended. What the heck was Ian thinking, relinquishing his weapon when they were in a school full of terrorists?

But Ian's face was resolute. Erica swallowed.

"You're both stupid," Irenic said. She took the computer and sunglasses from the body and set them near Morrison, well away from the pool of blood. "How is he?" she asked Renee.

"I've staunched the bleeding as best I can," Renee said, sounding small and lost. "Ten minutes more and it won't matter."

Irenic nodded. "They'll come."

The door swung open. Four Jeemoh agents entered, carrying a stretcher. They glanced around, and, seeing Eve gesture, raced up the stairs. They took over Renee's hold on Morrison's leg, lifted him onto the stretcher, and rushed out the door.

Irenic turned her back as if Morrison didn't even exist. The gunfire had long since stopped. She flipped her headset back to the common channel. "Status?"

"*One team retreating, two teams down,*" came the response through the earpiece. "*You're the only friendlies inside.*"

"Hostiles?"

"*No confirmed casualties.*"

"Orders?"

"*Complete the mission.*"

Irenic nodded. "You sure you don't want that Javelin?" she said to Ian.

Ian shook his head, his jaw set.

"If this results in one of us dying, I'll thrash you when we get back to the dojo," Irenic said. "Never give up an advantage over the enemy."

Ian stuck out his chin. "I won't be tricked into killing someone."

Irenic nodded. Not, Erica thought, because she agreed, but rather because she recognized the futility of arguing. Erica wasn't sure she'd be as unflappable if she were in Irenic's position. Even now, she wanted to tell Ian to not be a fool, to just pick up the weapon.

"Don't stand near Erica," Irenic said. "Her good luck might become your bad luck."

Erica flinched. Never had she wanted to tell the truth about her ability more than that moment. It was so unfair, blaming Morrison's injuries on her. He was the one who ran right behind her. But she bit back her protest. At least if nobody was near her, what had happened with Morrison wouldn't happen again.

"Nearest hostiles, Cam?" Irenic said.

He pointed down a locker-lined hall that looked about a hundred yards long. "They set up there. At the end, just around the corner. But they might have moved."

Irenic nodded. "We go now before our intelligence grows stale." She began jogging silently down the hallway, ignoring her blood-covered slacks and blouse. Erica and the others followed.

"What about the chemistry lab?" Erica whispered. Their primary mission was saving the hostages, not killing the bad guys.

"Later," Irenic said. "Neutralize those outside first. Eliminate reinforcements and avoid crossfire."

Erica couldn't argue with the logic. As they neared the corner, they slowed to a cautious walk, their backs to the wall.

Irenic pointed to herself, Ian, and Erica, and then gestured at the corner. She made a fist, signaling that the three of them should lead the attack. Eve pointed to herself, but Irenic ignored her. Eve scowled.

As Irenic was about to turn, Cam clutched her shoulder.

"*Wait.*" The voice coming from the earphone sounded exactly like Cam, but Cam's mouth hadn't moved.

Irenic shook her head.

"*My way's better,*" Cam's voice said. He pushed by Irenic, touched his ear, and then stuck the tip of his finger beyond the wall. "*There are two of them. Cover your ears and don't look.*"

Cam reached down into his right leg and retrieved a small canister. He pulled a tab on it and tossed it around the corner.

Even with her hands over her ears, Erica found the bang as the grenade detonated painful. Nevertheless, with her foreknowledge of Cam's attack, Erica didn't hesitate. She was the first around the corner.

The overturned desks in the hallway were positioned to guard against an attack from the door, not the hallway, and had offered no protection against the stun grenade. One hostage taker still stood, but the other was sprawled on the floor. Both were shaking their heads and rubbing their eyes. They seemed to have no idea she was even there.

Erica focused on the one on his feet. Using her ability to make sure she didn't make any mistakes, she kicked the gun out of his hand, and then ducked to avoid his wild punch. He kept swinging, but the blows seemed random.

Erica evaluated the alternatives, finally settling on grabbing his arm, twisting her body, and throwing him over her hip to the ground. Then she put her arm under his chin in a chokehold. He struggled to escape, first trying to elbow her, and then reaching back to grab her hair. It didn't matter. She'd seen it before.

The other hostage-taker had climbed to his feet, but Ian was there before he could interfere. The enemy swung his gun toward Ian, but he was too slow. Ian slashed down with his hand, materializing a crude dagger an instant before he needed it. The knife sliced through the hostage taker's wrist, severing his gun hand.

The dagger vanished. Ian followed up with a left uppercut, metal rings girding his hand as he did. The blow landed perfectly, and the man crumpled to the ground, unconscious.

Irenic raced around the corner and fired her Javelin at the man Erica had subdued. A vision flashed through Erica's mind, showing her the unfortunate consequences if she was still holding the man when the Javelin discharged, so she released her grip an instant before the prong landed. The man shuddered and fell.

"I had him," Erica said. It came out as a whine. Trying to speak normally, she added, "He was almost out. You didn't need to shoot him." She understood killing in self-defense, but the fight had been all but over.

"Strategy," Irenic countered. "When life is at stake, choose the most certain path. There was a five-percent chance he could escape your choke. Now there's a zero-percent chance." She dragged Ian's foe over to the stairs and handcuffed him to the railing. Somewhat reluctantly, Erica thought, Irenic wrapped a bandage around the stub of his wrist.

Irenic saw Erica watching and muttered, "He's lost too much blood anyway. He'll be dead before medical gets here." She walked over to Cam. "Didn't you hear the orders? No explosives."

Blushing, Cam looked down, nudging the floor with his toe. "Well, it wasn't a *big* explosive. Just a flash bang."

Irenic frowned, considering Cam's response. "Got any more?"

"That was the only one."

She smiled. "Too bad."

Eve walked up to Irenic, her eyes steely. "I'm ready. I want to lead our next attack."

Irenic looked like she'd smelled something vile. "No. Prove your valor in the dojo. Here, we prize safety and efficiency above ego."

Eve's jaw dropped.

Irenic turned her back on her. "Where are the next ones, Cam?"

"Around the next corner."

They set up for another attack. But when Cam scouted the hallway using his finger camera, he discovered nobody, though the makeshift barriers and Jeemoh bodies gave testament to the skirmish that had occurred.

Irenic scanned the scene, her mouth a thin line, and then gave a business-like nod.

"If they know we're here, they will consolidate at the chemistry lab," she said. "We go there next."

CHAPTER TWENTY-TWO

Their soft footsteps seemed like a thundering herd in the heavy silence of the school halls. Erica couldn't remember a time when the building had seemed so empty. Even late after school, she'd see the janitor sweeping the halls or teachers preparing for the next day. Now there was nobody.

Renee tugged on her sleeve. "Are we going to class, Erica?" she whispered. "Where is everyone?"

Erica cringed. Renee had forgotten. "Some guys have taken hostages in the chemistry lab. We're here to save them."

"Oh," Renee said, pursing her lips. "Of course."

"The enemies are wearing sunglasses. Do whatever it takes to stop them."

Renee sucked in her breath. "Even kill them?"

Erica nodded. "They'll try to kill us."

When they were close to the final corner before the chemistry lab, Irenic turned. She pointed to her eyes and to Cam.

Once more, Cam stuck his finger around the corner.

"Four hostiles standing outside the door to the lab. No desks or cover. They're waiting for us," Cam said through the earpiece.

Irenic shook her head, and Erica knew what she was thinking. Without cover, getting anywhere near the chemistry lab would be hard. Even with her ability, Erica might have difficulty avoiding bullets from four guns firing at the same time.

Cam smiled as he pulled another grenade out of his leg. Irenic's expression was half-questioning and half I-want-to-punch-you-now.

"You asked about flash bangs. It's not a flash bang. It's a smoke grenade."

Erica had to hold back a giggle. It was a terrible time to laugh, but there was nothing funnier than Irenic's expression. She was a disgruntled sociopathic librarian, her conservative olive sweater splattered in blood, her owl-like glasses slightly askew.

As if reading Erica's mind, Irenic pulled off the glasses, placing them on the floor. "Ian, Erica, Renee, and I are the first wave. Eve and Cam, you follow and help as needed." Before anyone could say anything, Irenic did a silent countdown with her fingers. When her fist closed, Cam tossed the grenade around the corner.

"Wait a few seconds," Cam's voice said in Erica's ear, *"for the smoke to fill the corridor."*

"What's that?" a male voice said.

"Smoke grenade," another said. "Stay in position. They're coming."

Soon, red smoke billowed from around the corner.

"Now," Cam's voice said, though he didn't move himself.

Erica and Ian darted around the corner and were confronted with an opaque wall of red smoke.

"Can't see a thing," Ian murmured.

To Erica, that seemed like a good thing, considering they were charging an enemy that had guns.

She sprinted forward blindly through the smoke, aiming for where she knew the lab must be.

A massive man parting the smoke. A raised gun.

Why hadn't Cam warned them they were fighting Goliath? The person in her vision must have been at least six-foot eight and over four hundred pounds. He made Vince look like a child.

Her enemy loomed out of the smoke like a whale surfacing, swinging his weapon toward her. Erica ducked to avoid the shot and kicked the gun from his hand as she slid by him. Before he could turn, she leaped to her feet and onto his back. She wrapped her legs around his body and locked her forearm around his neck, knocking off his sunglasses as she did.

Perfect. Regardless of his size, if he couldn't breathe, it would be a short fight.

Spinning. Smashing the cinderblock wall.

The giant twisted. Erica barely released her grip and dropped to the floor before he slammed his back into the wall. She scampered away and turned.

While he was off-balance, Erica kicked his thigh, followed by a punch to the stomach. The man didn't even flinch. Visions cascaded through her mind as she considered a multitude of options to attack him. But nothing seemed effective. It was as bad as Irenic. He was just too big.

She was in trouble. She shouldn't have smashed her Javelin.

Then Renee was there, with her own barrage of blows to the giant's body. She was too short to land a solid head blow and didn't seem to be doing much damage to his torso either, but at least she distracted the monster.

"Use the Javelin," Erica said as she looked for an opening.

"What?" Renee said. She ducked beneath a punch.

"The Javelin."

Renee looked confused. She lashed out with her fist, catching her opponent in the stomach. He didn't react.

Erica winced. Renee had forgotten the Javelins.

Where were the other hostiles? Erica glanced around and saw Ian and Irenic engaging two men. They didn't have guns, so Ian and Irenic must have dealt with those during the initial rush, but they were both holding knives. The remaining enemy was prone on the floor, Irenic's Javelin embedded in his neck.

She saw Ian block the blade of the knife with an arm coated in steel, and then materialize his own weapon. She almost pitied his opponent. Erica had fought Ian in the dojo using a knife, and, even with her ability, had found it difficult to land a blow that didn't bounce harmlessly off spontaneously materialized steel.

Irenic was more decisive. Her attacker thrust his knife toward her. She moved forward, allowing the blow to pass harmlessly under her arm, and then trapped the limb between her bicep and her body. She slipped her right forearm under his elbow, then levered herself up. The man began howling an instant before his arm snapped at the elbow. He dropped his knife.

Irenic spun and crouched, catching the weapon in midair. Then, continuing her rotation, she surged upward, plunging the blade up under the enemy's ribs, deep into his chest.

No problems there, then.

No longer concerned about being cut down from behind, Erica focused on her own opponent. He seemed invulnerable. Neither teenager was strong enough to cause any real damage. So far, Renee had avoided most of his blows, but she would tire soon.

Erica continued to shift through attack strategies, looking for any vulnerability. Then she found it.

"Eyes," she murmured into her microphone.

Renee understood instantly. She leaped off the wall, thrusting her fingers into the giant's face. He tried to block, but Renee was too quick. He screamed, clutching his eyes.

Renee landed lightly in front of him in a crouch.

"Here," Irenic said. She thrust her knife into the back of the man that Ian was fighting before tossing it toward Renee.

In a single smooth motion, Renee caught the weapon in her left hand and slashed the giant's hamstrings.

As he fell, Renee brought the blade cleanly across his throat, and then embedded the blade in his stomach for good measure.

"Eyes. Neck. Gut," Erica murmured.

"What?" Renee said.

Renee wouldn't remember it anyway. Erica shook her head. "Nothing."

Red smoke swirling around Eve and Cam. Black forms.
Knives striking.

Erica turned to see Eve and Cam emerging from the mist. "Behind you," she shouted.

Perhaps fearing they would hit their friends hidden in the smoke, the two new attackers were wielding knives rather than guns. Erica's warning came barely in time. Eve and Cam deflected their enemies' thrusts as Irenic had taught them in class, but they couldn't avoid their bodies. They were both tackled to the floor, the knives going flying.

Irenic shook her head. "Don't grapple with Eve," she said, not even bothering to help.

The man on Eve seemed to be in full control. He had landed perfectly on top of her and must have outweighed her by half. He exploited that weight advantage mercilessly, pressing his forearm against her throat.

It didn't matter.

A bone spike shot up from Eve's collarbone, through the attacker's arm, and into his neck. Eve shoved him aside as he clutched at his throat.

Cam's fight lasted little longer. One moment, they were struggling on the ground, and the next, Cam had his mechanical hand on the attacker's neck. Erica knew from the dojo that normally it wasn't a big deal. Cam was underneath and shouldn't have enough leverage for the hand to be anything more than an irritation to his opponent.

But Cam had designed his gears and levers to be much stronger than flesh and bone. With the impersonal cruelty of a hydraulic jack, he crushed his opponent's throat, and then tossed the corpse aside.

Irenic surveyed the scene dispassionately and turned to Eve. "There's your action. Was it glorious?"

Eve struggled to her feet, looking down at the bone spike in her chest. Blood soaked her shirt. "I… I just wanted to do something."

"Mission accomplished," Irenic said blandly.

"Um," Cam said. "Should I remove that?" A circular bone saw emerged from his artificial hand and began to whirl, sounding like a dentist's drill. Erica shivered.

"No time," Irenic said crisply. "They know we're here. Any injuries?"

Renee held up her right hand. Two of her fingers were bent at unusual angles. "Broken fingers. I'll survive."

Irenic nodded. "Got any other tricks, Cam?"

He shook his head. "I can only fit two grenades."

Irenic turned to the others. "That's unfortunate, but we still outnumber them. So take them down and don't do anything stupid. Erica?"

"What?"

"You first. Open the door."

Erica sighed. It was getting old, always being the first around the corner, the first into the path of danger. She couldn't argue with the logic, considering her "luck". But was she condemned to be the sacrificial point person on every mission? It sounded like a job with a low life expectancy.

As in the Gauntlet, her visions allowed her to view the room before opening the door. Mr. Ambrose, Erica's chemistry instructor, three other teachers, and three students huddled in the near corner of the chemistry lab, their hands bound. In the far corner, beside the teacher's platform, another teacher was curled up on the floor, shuddering. Three hostiles stood over him, two men and a woman, none of them holding weapons.

Then the vision went to complete darkness. Someone had turned out the lights?

It didn't make sense, but Erica flung open the door, and rushed in. The scene was as she had envisioned it. She charged toward the enemy, avoiding tables as she accelerated.

And then, she was in a void. Not simply blackness, but a complete absence of anything. It wasn't warm or cold. She tried to move her hand in front of her face and realized that she had no hand. In fact, no body at all. Movement meant nothing. Was time even passing? Nothing existed except for her thoughts, and she thought she'd go mad.

Then she was back in the chemistry lab, lying prone on the floor next to the glass-doored cabinets where most of the chemicals were stored. Her knee was bloody, and her left arm throbbed. It had an unnatural bump. Broken. Again.

Then Ian fell hard beside her. His eyes were open, but his face was empty. He was dead.

Erica's world ended.

She hadn't told him how she felt. Not really. Now she never would.

Wait. CPR. Where was Renee? Where was Cam? They had brought Lizzy back.

She looked around wildly.

Renee had no sooner entered the room than she fell.

Ian's face firmed. He took in a deep breath. "Erica, are you all right?"

He wasn't dead. What was going on?

"Sergeant Irenic. Long time no see."

Erica looked up. The hostile was staring toward the door where Irenic was standing.

Slowly walking forward, Irenic dropped her Javelin. "What are you doing, Sam?"

"Returning home," Sam said, smiling. "You're actually a great person to run into."

Erica looked closer. The sunglasses made it difficult, but she recognized Sam from the pictures. Three years ago, he had been among the first of the students to disappear from Battlefield High.

Eve and Cam crowded through the doorway, but they had no more luck than the others. Eve fell first while Cam made it halfway to

Sam before he stumbled to the floor.

"You didn't tell them about me?" he asked Irenic. When she remained mute, he smiled and answered his own question. "Of course not. It's Jeemoh. It's all about the secrecy."

With her slow walk, Irenic had almost reached Erica.

"I think that's close enough. How about you sit?" Sam said, gesturing politely, like a host in a restaurant.

Quick as a viper, Irenic reached behind her back. But even she was too slow. She crumpled, her throwing knife ringing out as it hit the floor.

Sam sighed. "I guess she had to try."

Clearly, attacking directly wouldn't work. Erica needed more information.

"So what's your deal, then?" Erica said, hoping Sam would respond to the same sort of conversational tone he was using. "You have an ability?"

Sam nodded. "Yes."

"What do you do?"

Sam smiled. "I stop people from fighting."

Irenic said, "He controls nerve impulses—" but then began to shake. Her face contorted in agony, and she screamed.

Erica covered her ears. After about half a minute, Irenic fell silent, though her body continued to twitch.

Erica forced her eyes away from her sergeant, back to Sam. "Did you kill her?"

Sam shook his head. "She's just unconscious. No permanent damage."

Sweat dripped down Erica's temple, but she didn't wipe it away. Sam was chatty. She needed to ignore the nerves, ignore Irenic, and keep Sam talking. And maybe she could learn something. "You know about Jeemoh?"

"Oh, yes. Irenic and I are old friends." His tone implied the opposite.

"Was it you who tried to kill me with the tablet? And the elevator?"

Sam looked baffled. "What?" Then he shook his head. "Never mind." He looked at one of the other hostage takers. "Bind their hands, Dwyer."

As Dwyer approached each of them, they collapsed, allowing him to secure their hands with thick plastic cable ties.

Recognizing that resistance wouldn't help, Erica held up her wrists as Dwyer approached. But Sam didn't hesitate. Erica found herself once more bodiless in the void. When she returned to the real world, her hands, too, were tied.

"What do you want, Sam?" Erica said as Dwyer moved on to Eve.

"Funny you should ask that. Maybe you can help me. I'm here to find Jeemoh. To rescue—"

Cam, passive until then, raised his arms, pointing toward Sam. The Javelin's prong shot out of his forearm, but went wide, missing Sam and striking the woman in the hip. She shuddered and fell.

Cam twitched, stopped moving for a heartbeat, and then his legs began to shake. The bone saw popped out of his forearm and cut through the cable tie.

Sam stared at Cam. "How are you...?"

Cam's motions were jerky, like a marionette pulled in different directions by three mad puppeteers. The Javelin partially retracted, and then stopped. Three spring-loaded spikes shot out of his leg, embedding themselves in the ceiling.

During the whole encounter, Sam had only ever immobilized one person at a time. Was he incapable of targeting multiple people?

"Get Sam," Erica hissed. "While he's busy with Cam."

Eve reacted instantly. She snapped off the sharp bone fragment that was still protruding from her chest and threw it. Her aim was good, but the bone was too light. It bounced off Sam's shoulder, doing little damage.

Sam spared three seconds of attention for Eve. She screamed like he was shattering her skull and collapsed unconscious.

Cam took advantage of the moment of respite to smash the glass door on the chemical cabinet with his metal hand. He seized a jar and hurled it at Sam. For the second time, he missed. The jar smashed against the wall, and a fireball erupted. Then Cam was again struggling against Sam's grasp.

"How do you keep doing that?" Sam said through gritted teeth.

"Ian," whispered Erica. She held out her hands.

Dwyer turned back toward them, but was too slow. In a fraction of a second, Ian conjured a blade and severed the cable tie binding Erica's hands.

Though Dwyer was nearly upon them, Sam was the real threat.

But he was still ten yards away. Erica didn't need her visions to know that Sam would bring her down long before she got anywhere near him. She needed a weapon.

Erica cycled through the alternatives.

The throwing knife… Too close to Dwyer.

The shards of glass on the floor… Too light. They'd cut, but not enough to disable.

The cabinet of chemicals…

In her mind, Erica tried fifteen different compounds, covering Sam in all sorts of powders and liquids before she found one that would work. She glanced at the label as she grasped it.

Concentrated sulphuric acid.

Maybe she should have thought it through, rather than mentally trying every bottle.

Though it had been only seconds, the delay had been costly. Dwyer was only a couple steps away. If she targeted Sam now, she wouldn't have time to avoid his henchman.

Erica flinched as she foresaw the impact of Dwyer's punch. She'd already grown used to the idea that she'd have a chance to dodge any blow. Now she'd be as vulnerable as a child.

"Don't let him kill me, Ian," Erica murmured, not taking her eyes off her target.

She lifted the bottle and hurled it with all her strength. Her eyes tracked its trajectory, just long enough to see it shatter on Sam's chest and face.

Erica's last thought before Dwyer's punch hurled her into unconsciousness was that it was perhaps a blessing that she wouldn't be awake to hear Sam's screams.

CHAPTER TWENTY-THREE

The acrid smell almost burned. Erica opened her eyes.

Ian was waving something under her nose, but pulled it away as her eyelids fluttered. The concern etched on his face faded. "Just lie there for a second, Erica. There's no rush. Everything's fine."

Erica's chest filled with warmth. Ian was alive. He had seemed dead, but he was fine. Nothing to worry about.

Except he didn't love her. Except that. Her stomach roiled.

Erica rubbed her eyes and looked around. Where were they? Oh, right. The chemistry lab.

"Sam?" she said.

"He's dead. You got him. And the other guy is too."

Erica rolled over and pushed herself up onto her hands and knees. Ian hastily stood and pulled a chair over, helping her onto it. She surveyed the room.

Sam's body wasn't where he had been when she hit him with the acid. He'd made it about halfway to the emergency shower in the corner before he fell. She couldn't see the true extent of the damage—his head and body were mercifully covered by a lab coat. Morbidly, she wondered whether she had brought him down or one of the others had hit him while he was distracted.

The body of the woman remained where she had fallen. She was uncovered, but, from her staring, vacant eyes, she was clearly dead. Erica looked around for Dwyer. His legs poked out from under another lab coat that wasn't large enough to hide the pool of blood.

Ian saw where she was looking. "I didn't mean to kill him," he murmured. "I just reacted."

Erica gripped his hand. "I know. It was him or us."

"Was it?" Ian said, his shoulders slumping. "I'm not sure. He might have surrendered when he realized Sam was dead."

"When you're fighting for your life, you can't hold back." Erica's tone was sympathetic, but she was concerned. How on earth was Ian going to do this job if he constantly worried about killing the enemy?

"Yeah." Ian sighed.

Erica couldn't think of anything she could say to comfort Ian, so she just squeezed his hand. She looked around for the others. Irenic was talking with the hostages while Cam and Renee were tending to Eve's wounds.

"Everyone else is fine?" Erica said.

Ian nodded. "Eve's bleeding a bit. The usual."

Erica's old chemistry teacher, Mr. Ambrose, strolled up to them. "So you two work for Jeemoh now?"

Erica bit her lip and nodded. She didn't know how much she was allowed to reveal about Jeemoh to outsiders. But if Mr. Ambrose already knew, it must be fine.

"It was amazing seeing you guys in action. I'm glad I could help out," he said.

"Help out?"

"Yes, with the chemistry," he said smugly. "I don't want to take too much credit, but without our lessons, I doubt Cam would have known to throw the rubidium. Nor you the H_2SO_4." He smiled. "If you're anything like me, you'll find the things you learned in my class pop up constantly. Not just during terrorist attacks."

"Yeah," Erica replied, trying to sound sincere and not quite succeeding. At the sound of footsteps, she glanced at the door. A stream of Jeemoh soldiers ran in.

"So tell me, what's life like as a part of Jeemoh?" Mr. Ambrose said, his eyes alight. "What can you do? Cam seems—"

"We're going," Irenic said firmly. She grabbed Erica's wrist, hauling her to her feet.

"But I want to talk—" Erica began.

"Too bad. We hand it off now."

Reluctantly, Erica allowed herself to be pulled toward the door, gathering Eve, Cam, and Renee on the way.

"Bye," Mr. Ambrose said. Erica glanced back as he waved,

smiling. "Go save the world."

She blinked and nodded.

#

"Can you hear me, Sergeant Irenic?" Ian asked.

Irenic was driving the van back to headquarters, but her voice emanated from speakers embedded in the ceiling. "Roger."

"Why did we rush out of there?" Ian said. "We at least could have stopped to make sure none of the hostages were hurt."

"The hostages were fine. We accomplished the mission."

"But why did those guys attack the school in the first place?" Erica said. "Were they responsible for the gas in the elevator? Sam seemed confused when I asked about it."

Irenic's voice was devoid of curiosity. "They were trying to find Jeemoh's headquarters. If they wanted anything else, our people will discover it in our interviews with the survivors. Lois will tell us anything we need to know."

"But you knew Sam," Erica said.

"Yes."

They waited a few seconds, and, after it became clear that Irenic wasn't going to elaborate, Eve said, "Come on. You have to give us more than that. What's his story?"

There was a pause, and Erica thought Irenic might not even reply. But then she spoke, her voice as unemotional as ever.

"Sam was in the first cohort. He could control nerve impulses—block them, trigger them, magnify them. His standard attack was to block nerve impulses going into the brain, denying his victim all of their senses. But he could do much worse. He killed a couple of our guys in the Gauntlet when his ability manifested for the first time. He had the potential to become one of our most flexible operatives, able to knock out, black out, torture, or kill with just a thought. Like Morrison, he only learned the basics of hand-to-hand combat. No need for more."

"Cool," Eve said, her eyes shining. "If I had that ability, I'd have so much fun messing around. Making one ear deaf. Blocking nerve impulses from the bladder. Can you imagine?"

Erica grinned. She could imagine, and that image was ugly. She really didn't need to see what Eve would do with such an ability—Sam had been bad enough. He had completely incapacitated her, and Erica couldn't even think of how to resist it. They were lucky that

190

Cam had been able to fight back.

She glanced over at him. "Why did he have so many problems with you?"

Cam blushed, looking away. "You know I control electricity in my body? Whenever he blocked my nerve impulses, I routed around it."

"I didn't know you could do that," Erica said.

"I haven't done it much," Cam said, shrugging. "Just when tumors get in the way."

Erica rubbed her lips. Cam seemed to function so well she sometimes forgot about his illness.

She raised her voice, although she knew Irenic could probably hear a whisper from the backseat. "Sergeant, if Sam used to be part of Jeemoh, what happened?"

"He went on his first mission and vanished."

"What do you mean 'vanished'?"

"He didn't return, and we weren't able to track him down. And it isn't easy to hide from Jeemoh."

"What was the mission?"

"That's all I know. I didn't even realize he was involved in this until we saw him."

"If he used to be in Jeemoh, why was he asking about the bunker's location? Wouldn't he know?" Ian said.

"Do you?"

Erica shook her head. She suspected it was somewhere east of Battlefield, but beyond that, she had no idea.

"What about the other hostiles?" Erica said, keeping her voice casual. She'd never seen Irenic so talkative, and she didn't intend to squander the opportunity. "Do you know who they were? Were they ex-Jeemoh too?"

"No. We've run into them a couple of times before. We've been calling them Group S. But they're well equipped. We have standing orders to secure one copy of any of their technology we find."

"What does the 'S' stand for?" Ian asked.

"Nothing. Lois coined the name because they seemed to be an organized group, and we had to call them something."

Did that mean that there were also groups A to R? Erica almost asked, but then realized the question wasn't important and might make Irenic clam up. "Why didn't you warn us about them?"

"Didn't know it was them until I saw the computers. The

sunglasses are new."

"What do they want with Jeemoh?"

"No idea."

"They are unusual," Cam said, staring at the back of the seat in front of him. "Inconsistent. The guards shot at us, so they wanted us dead. But you claim Sam could kill us with a thought, yet he didn't. Why not? And they responded impossibly fast when I hacked into the video system. We're missing something."

"Not your problem, Cam," Irenic said, a hint of warning in her tone. "Our mission's over."

"Yeah," Cam said, though he was rubbing his temples as if doing so would stimulate his brain.

"Lois just called me on the radio. I need to talk to her." Irenic's tone made it clear she considered the conversation finished.

"Okay," Erica said. Was it just a coincidence Lois interrupted the second Cam started asking the interesting questions?

Maybe it was the adrenaline fading, but Erica suddenly felt exhausted. She looked at Ian on her right, and he smiled at her. Smiling back, she was about to lean into his shoulder to rest when she remembered that they were done.

She crossed her arms and stared down at her knees.

#

After a quick trip to medical, Lois debriefed them. She congratulated them on their first successful mission as a full squad and informed them that Morrison had survived, having made it back to the base in time to have his wounds healed by the medical printer. The other teams hadn't been so lucky. Of the eighteen soldiers that went in at the same time as Irenic's team, six had been killed outright and three more died on the way to medical. That brought the death toll to fifteen, the highest number of fatalities that had ever occurred on a Jeemoh mission.

Lois seemed to understand what had transpired based on their headset communications. But she nevertheless talked them through the entire rescue multiple times, questioning them about the enemy's technology and tactics.

Finally, Erica had had enough. "Why do you care so much about every detail of what happened?"

Lois looked perplexed. "This is a debriefing. We need to understand what worked and what didn't so we can optimize future operations." When Erica didn't respond, Lois added, as if it were obvious, "To save lives."

Erica blushed. She had thought it was a reasonable question.

"Who is this Group S? Why was Sam with them?" Ian's tone implied he was as frustrated with Lois' cross-examination as Erica.

"It's classified. If you needed to know, you'd know already."

"Don't give me that. We fought them. We killed them. We deserve to know."

Lois frowned. "You deserve nothing. And if you hadn't killed all of them, we'd have someone to interrogate to find out more."

Ian's face darkened. "You were the one who gave us those Javelins. You wanted us to kill them."

"I wanted you to have the most effective weapons for the mission."

"You didn't even tell us what the Javelins would do!"

"I'm in command. That's my right. And our fifty-percent fatality rate shows lethal force was justified. Discarding your Javelin was a senseless gesture that jeopardized your lives, the hostages' lives, and the mission."

Erica flinched. Smashing her Javelin was a huge mistake. They'd been lucky to win the fight against the giant. Still, it was wrong for Lois to trick them like that.

"How do you expect us to complete a mission when we don't even understand the capabilities of our own weapons?" Erica said loudly. "We need to know the equipment we're using."

Lois stared at her for a few seconds, and then her face relaxed. "Fair enough. In the future, I'll keep you informed about your weapons, and you don't make senseless gestures that risk the mission."

Erica bit back a retort. She had what she wanted. "Fine."

Lois nodded. "I think we're about done here. Two last things. First, Erica, your dad called."

"Is something wrong?" Erica said. It wasn't their prearranged time.

Lois shook her head. "He heard about the school." She turned to Morrison. "Second, I'm informing you that there will be a disciplinary action resulting from your disclosure of confidential information."

"What?" Morrison said. "What information?" He looked at her blankly.

"Discussing the details of your first mission with unauthorized individuals."

It took a few seconds for Morrison to process her words, and then his face reddened. "You designed the *Practical Persuasion* test. You can't punish me for something that happened in your own test."

"Yeah," Erica said. "That's totally unfair."

"We carefully evaluate what information should be classified and inform everyone involved. You knew that mission was classified, but discussed it anyway. It was a clear-cut violation." Lois held up her hands as if it would abort Morrison's protest. "I recognize the mitigating factors, and our discussion will take them into account. I expect we will have a decision in a week."

"But the whole thing is ridiculous," Morrison shouted. "It was your test!"

Irenic glared at him. "Morrison, shut up. You will be treated fairly. The mitigating factors matter a great deal, but you can invalidate all of them with your actions now. Close your mouth, stand up, and leave the room. If you want to yell, yell at me later."

"But..." Morrison stared at her for a few seconds, but Irenic was stone. He strode away, swearing under his breath.

"That's all," Lois said.

They shuffled out of the room in time to see the elevator door close behind Morrison.

"It's so unfair," Erica said to nobody in particular.

"It isn't," Irenic said, pushing the elevator call button. "There have been five major Jeemoh information leaks. Over fifty people died because of them."

"But it was your test," Ian said sharply, turning to face Irenic. "And we're all part of Jeemoh. There's no leak."

"Those are the mitigating factors," Irenic said. "His punishment will be uncomfortable, but bearable, and you will learn the importance of our confidentiality rules."

Erica's eyes widened. "That was the goal of the midterm. To have one of us share something classified."

"Maybe one of them. I didn't design it." Irenic shrugged. "Regardless, learning non-disclosure would be a positive outcome for everyone." The elevator bell rang. "Now, don't you have a call to make?"

Erica stared at Irenic. Finally, with an exasperated sigh, she entered the elevator with the others, frazzled enough not to even consider the possibility of another elevator attack. When they reached her floor, she retreated to the privacy of her room and dialed her father, still shaking her head at the injustice.

"Hello?"

"Hi, Dad. You called?"

"Erica, yes. I wanted to check in with you. Something happened at the school today."

"I know." Should she tell her dad about her involvement? Jeemoh would want to keep everything under wraps. But nobody said it was classified, so whatever.

"Some guys took hostages, and they sent us in to save them," Erica said, her tone blasé. She summarized their rescue attempt.

"You were nearly killed, yet you don't seem too upset." Philip sounded perplexed.

"My luck saved me. It wasn't a big deal." Her dad still didn't know the truth about her ability, but telling him anything over a Jeemoh phone was the same as telling Lois directly.

"I'm not sure about that. That guy knocked you unconscious."

"Yeah."

"He could have done some permanent damage."

She shrugged. It was too late to worry about that now. "Whatever happens, happens."

Her dad paused, and Erica could almost see his look of consternation. "Erica, you're too young to be so fatalistic."

"I'm growing up fast." Even to Erica, the words sounded sour, though she didn't know why.

"What's wrong? Was it the mission?"

"No."

It wasn't the mission. The mission, for all its horror, had been no worse than her life here. Sure, she could have died, but at least it would have been fast.

Now she was back in her room, alone. Based on what Sam said, it seemed unlikely that he orchestrated the attacks inside Jeemoh, so the paranoia would continue. Jeemoh would punish Morrison, and she'd probably catch the fallout. Her best friend barely remembered her. And Ian saw her as just another friend.

Everyone said that pain eased with time, but it was as bad as ever. Would her heart ever stop racing whenever she saw Ian? Would she ever be able to lie in bed at night and not think of him?

He was making her miserable, but she didn't understand how to let him go.

"Are you worried about being attacked?" Philip asked.

"No."

"Jeemoh?"

"No."

"Ian?"

Erica couldn't say a word, worried that everything would spill out.

"It's been weeks," Philip murmured. "And you said it was the right thing to do. To focus on your training."

"I know what I said. It doesn't matter. It hurts." Erica had to fight to keep her voice steady and ended up sounding petulant.

"I'm so sorry."

"It never gets any better. Actually, it's worse."

"Have you tried talking with Ian about it?"

"And say what?"

"Just tell him how you feel."

"What's the point?" Erica said bitterly. "He doesn't like me that way."

"Maybe he does, maybe he doesn't. He seemed like more than a friend when I saw you guys."

That had been when they were pretending. That didn't count. "Lois doesn't want us to."

"Forget your mom."

"She says it's dangerous. It leads to bad decisions. It's against Jeemoh's rules."

"Forget the rules."

"But—"

"Erica, it's okay to love. Give yourself a chance. Tell him."

The advice seemed insane. She already knew how Ian felt. Revealing her feelings would embarrass both of them and probably ruin their friendship. Why would she do that to herself?

But she thought he'd died today. And if he had, he never would have known that she loved him. The thought was appalling.

And maybe she was wrong. It had seemed so real, the time they had spent together in the Gauntlet, pretending to be in love. She had felt so connected to him, like she could tell what he was thinking before he said it. Was it possible that he cared and she didn't know?

Or was she just fooling herself, pretending she had a chance, because the truth hurt too much?

Maybe it would help even if he didn't like her. Since they split, every moment hurt. The pain was always there, a constant shadow darkening her life. If he would just look her in the eyes and tell her they'd never be together, maybe she could move on, start to heal. At least that would be progress.

"I… I'll think about it, Dad," she said.

"Good."

When the call ended, Erica was famished. She returned to the mess hall to find the others already there, halfway through their meal. Ian had retrieved her tray and saved her a place beside him at the table. Was that a sign that he liked her?

"Hey, Erica," he said. He patted her on the back, grinning. Was that just a friendly smile or did it mean something more? "Good job. I think it would have gone quite differently without you there today."

Erica felt her face grow warm. She knew it would have. She had saved Ian's life right at the start, and probably Renee's as well. If she hadn't been there, perhaps her whole team would have died.

"We worked well as a team," she said.

"Yeah, we are better together," Ian said.

Did that mean something? Was he dropping a hint?

Erica put her head down, focusing on her meal. She was going to drive herself crazy by parsing every word from Ian's mouth, every gesture he made.

This had to stop. She wasn't this needy girl, living and dying on every word dripping from a boy's lips.

Ian was amazing. He challenged her, amused her, and cared for her all at the same time. He made her feel like the world was bright and new, created just for the two of them. When she was with him, every day seemed too short, like sleep was stealing away time that they could be spending together.

But, in the end, he was only a boy.

This had to stop.

Before she could change her mind, she reached out and grasped Ian's hand.

"After dinner, can you come by my room?" Erica said. "I want to talk with you about something."

CHAPTER TWENTY-FOUR

As they walked to her room, Erica couldn't help but feel like she was marching toward her own execution. It wasn't that she regretted her decision to tell Ian how she felt. More the decision to tell him now. What was wrong with tomorrow? Or next week?

She felt nauseated.

But then, they were at her door… in her room… The door closed behind them.

She stood there, looked at Ian, and said nothing.

"You know that this room just seems private?" Ian said.

"Yeah, I know." She'd never forget the cameras.

"So what did you want to tell me in your completely public private room?"

Erica bit her lip. Now that she was in the moment, all the ways she'd imagined telling him vanished from her mind, like dandelion fluff floating away on the wind.

She needed to ignore her pounding heart, just ease into it.

"You know today when we were fighting Sam? He made you black out, and you fell beside me?"

"Yeah. That was the strangest thing. It was scary."

Erica nodded. "You fell beside me, and your eyes were open, but totally blank. You didn't move at all, not even blinking."

"His ability was amazing," Ian said, his eyes shining. "Trapping people in their own minds. Did it feel to you like you were floating in space, without any stars? Like in a completely empty universe?"

"Yeah, like being stuck in a prison with no walls. I found it terrifying."

"For me, it was like I was the only thing in existence. Everything else had been wiped away, and I was drifting in a void."

Erica shook her head. This conversation wasn't going the way she intended. "But the point is, I saw you there, unmoving, and I thought you were dead."

"Yeah, I can see that." Ian shrugged. "But I imagine my heart was still beating, if you'd taken my pulse."

"It probably was. But the point is, you seemed dead," Erica insisted.

Ian shrugged again. "I'm fine. Don't worry about it."

He didn't get it. Why was this so hard? "No, but you see, you were lying there, and it was just how I imagined you'd look if you were dead. Not that I think a lot about what you'd look like dead or anything, but you know."

"Yeah. But it's not a big deal. It might have seemed—"

"Ian, I love you," Erica blurted out. "I saw you on the ground, and you were dead, and it was horrible, and I knew that I'd never have the chance to tell you how I really felt. That I wake up in the morning thinking of you, and go to bed at night thinking of you, and think of you every moment in between, and I never told you that, and I'd never be able to tell you that, because you were dead, and I had missed my chance. And then you came back, and you were fine, and I couldn't just go on like it had never happened.

"I need you to know. And I know you don't like me that way, and this is all really embarrassing, and everything will be tremendously awkward from now on. I'm sure I'll cringe and feel like puking whenever I see you. But I needed to do it, needed to tell you. We have a dangerous job. We could be gassed tomorrow, and I can't risk you dying without saying it at least once. So there it is. I love you. That's all. I'm done. That's everything I had to say. You can go now."

Ian was staring at her, his mouth half open, his face frozen. She must look like a wreck, babbling, her emotions splayed across her face. This was mortifying. Why did she do this? Why wasn't he leaving? She said he could go.

Erica couldn't bear to face him. She turned her head and looked at a shirt she had tossed on the floor that morning, so long ago. A thread had unraveled from the hem, forming a blue swirl against the white floor.

"Erica..." Ian gently lifted her chin, turning her face toward him. "I... I thought I was the only one who felt that way. The truth is, I've been crazy about you for a while, since our time in the Gauntlet for sure, and maybe even before that, though I couldn't admit it to myself.

"You're brilliant, funny, and gorgeous. I love the way you talk, the way you move, the way you smile, and the way you see the world. I feel like you understand me better than anyone else in the universe—it's like you can read my mind. You wanted to break up, so I figured... well, that you realized I'd fallen for you and were trying to let me down easy.

"The last few weeks have been hell. I've been missing you like crazy, but hiding it because I didn't want to creep you out. I've been trying hard, but I can't get you out of my head. I've missed you so much."

He kissed her firmly, as if to punctuate his words. The warmth of his lips spread through Erica's whole body. She shivered. The kiss was glorious, like racing out of school on the final day before summer holidays.

Erica leaned in, put her arms around him, and felt like she belonged.

Finally, Ian broke the kiss. He hugged Erica, his lips nestled beside her ear. "Please tell me you aren't pretending this time," he whispered.

"Of course not." Erica giggled. "I meant every garbled word."

"Good," Ian said. Erica felt his muscles relax under her hands.

They kissed again, ending up on the bed. Ever conscious of the cameras, they did nothing they hadn't already done in the Gauntlet. But to Erica, it all seemed new. And maybe it was. Because this time, she knew it was real.

Eventually, they came up for air.

"You're a great kisser, Ms. Trestle," Ian said.

"Likewise, Mr. Nash."

"It comes from hours of rigorous study, all so I'd be skillful enough to meet your high standards in this exact moment."

"I see. Mine is natural ability."

"Ah, you're like the Bo Jackson or Michael Jordan of kissing."

"Yes. Only shorter and prettier in a dress."

"Now you're just being presumptuous," Ian said. "Clearly, you haven't seen Bo Jackson in a breezy summer frock."

"Maybe. But can Bo do this?" She kissed a path from his collarbone to his ear.

"Maybe if I asked him nicely," Ian replied, but then couldn't say anything for a while, as his lips became preoccupied.

A few minutes later, Ian asked, "So, what should we tell the others? I doubt your mom will approve any more than she did before, and Morrison still isn't your biggest fan. Not to mention Renee."

Erica shrugged. Once, it had seemed an important question. But now, lying in Ian's embrace, it felt barely worthy of discussion. "We'll tell them the truth. These are our lives. It's our decision."

"I agree." Ian stroked her arm. "They might find it difficult at first, but they'll get used to it. It's not like we're the first couple ever."

"Exactly."

There was a tentative knock on the door.

"It's probably Renee," Erica said, recognizing the knock.

"Hmm," Ian said. He glanced at the door, and then quickly rose from the bed. "Probably best not to surprise her. I need to go to the bathroom, so how about you introduce the idea, and I'll come out in a bit?"

Erica nodded. She waited until he went behind the curtain to answer the door. "Hi, Ren. What's up?"

"Oh, nothing really. Just came by to talk. You know."

Erica nodded. Nights were particularly bad for Renee. She dreaded going to sleep, never knowing what she'd forget by the morning. "Come in." Erica gestured toward a chair she had appropriated from the common area. Renee sat there while Erica chose the bed.

Renee glanced at Erica, and then shifted uncomfortably, patting her hair. "What? Do I have something in my teeth?" She tilted her head.

Erica grinned more broadly. "No, nothing like that. I'm sorry. I'm just… I've got news."

"Really? What?"

Erica took a deep breath. "Well, this might be weird, but Ian and I are going out again." She scanned Renee's face, looking for any sign that Renee was upset, but if anything, she seemed bemused. "Tonight, after dinner, we talked. One thing led to another, and now we're going out."

Renee smiled, and all of Erica's concerns dropped away.

"You seem happy," Renee said.

"Oh yes. I've wanted this for so long, and now it's finally happening." With a grin that felt as big as the universe, Erica grasped both of Renee's hands. "I feel like I'm in a dream. It's surreal, like I'm watching it all happen to someone else. But then, I realize it's not someone else. It's me! And it's so amazing."

"It sounds wonderful."

"It's the best feeling ever. But don't worry. You're still my best friend. This is a change, but it's a good one. It might be strange at first, but after some time, it will become normal."

"I'm not worried," Renee said, grinning as though Erica's elation were infectious. "I just want you to be happy."

"Happy doesn't even begin to describe how I feel." Erica stood and turned to the curtain that acted as the bathroom door. "Ian, come in here. Renee's okay with it all."

Renee stood as Ian pushed back the curtain and entered the room. She stuck out her hand, smiling. "Hi. I'm Renee. I have a few memory issues, so forgive me if we've already met. In any case, I'm sure we'll get to know each other better, now that you're dating my best friend."

Ian's jaw fell open. He took in one short breath, swallowed, and looked away.

Renee's hand dropped to her side. She turned back to Erica, confusion stark upon her face. "What?"

Erica rubbed her lips, unsure of how to cushion the blow. This must be how doctors felt telling patients they had terminal diseases. She grasped Renee's hand, squeezing it gently. "Renee, Ian's your brother. You've known him your entire life."

The blood drained from Renee's face. "No."

Erica nodded.

Renee stared at Ian for two long seconds before frantically shaking her head. "I'm sorry. I shouldn't have disturbed you. I have to go." She tugged her hand away.

"Wait, Renee." Erica reached out, but Renee pushed by her, almost running. Before Erica could figure out what to do or say, Renee was out the door.

Ian collapsed on the bed, his head in his hands. "She doesn't remember me." His voice was raw, exposed.

Erica put her arm around his shoulders. "Maybe it'll come back to her. Maybe she'll remember later." She didn't believe it, but perhaps Ian would.

"She won't," Ian said hollowly. "All the fun we had. All the jokes we shared. Everything. She doesn't remember any of it. Our entire relationship is gone. Like it never even happened." He sat for a few seconds, and then turned to Erica. "She must feel terrible." He stood. "I've got to go to her. Talk to her."

Erica hooked his arm. "Wait," she said. "I should go. You… You're a stranger to her now. She needs someone she knows, and I'm her best friend."

Ian looked dejected, but he nodded. "Yes. You go." He squeezed her hand.

At the door, Erica gave him one last glance. "Wait for me here. Please. I've missed you."

Ian nodded.

Erica pounded on Renee's door, but there was no answer. Eve was still in the mess hall watching TV, but she claimed she hadn't seen Renee since dinner. Erica finally found her in the chemistry lab.

"In here, again," Erica said as she entered.

Renee glanced up from the equipment briefly, barely acknowledging Erica's presence. "Yeah."

Erica pulled up a stool to sit near her friend. "It must be hard."

"It is." Renee stirred a beaker filled with liquid, bubbling on a hotplate. "I'd say it's the hardest thing I've ever gone through, but, really, how would I know?" Her bitterness stung.

"Eventually, you'll get used to it."

"That's what I'm afraid of."

They sat silently while Renee continued to stir the solution.

"You know," Renee said after several minutes, her tone now more wistful than sour, "you're the only one from before I remember at all now. We had some good times."

"We did."

"That's what I've been trying to hold on to. Going over memories in my mind every day. I don't know if that helps or not. I think maybe it doesn't." She sighed.

If Renee had forgotten Ian, Erica had her doubts. But she couldn't say that. "It's hard to know."

"Yeah." Renee fell silent for a few seconds, and then said, "Do you remember that time those boys wouldn't let us in their tree house? We must have been twelve or something. They used to yell at us, call us names, but whenever we came near, they'd pull up the rope ladder."

Erica nodded.

"And so you and I went to the dollar store and bought that huge bag of balloons. You slept over and we got up early the next day. We filled every one of those balloons with water and hauled them up the ladder. And then we hid up there, waiting.

"We must have crouched there out of sight for three hours. We talked about everything—what we'd say as we attacked, who we should target, whether we should use the biggest balloons first or save them for the end. We had everything planned out in exquisite detail.

"It seemed like they'd never come. And just when we were about to give up, the ladder twitched. We looked down to see several boys below, with the biggest starting to climb.

"Despite discussing it so much, I can't even remember what we shouted when we attacked. But the first balloon, the largest, hit that kid in the dead center of his head. He fell, but it wasn't high enough to get hurt. And then, we pelted them. We must have gone through fifty balloons in thirty seconds. We soaked them. It was the sweetest revenge ever."

Erica grinned. "Ian and Morrison were furious for days, but they totally deserved it."

Renee's slight smile faded. "That was Ian and Morrison?"

Erica nodded, mentally rebuking herself for not being more careful in choosing her words. "And a couple of other boys from the neighborhood."

Renee lapsed into silence for a few minutes. Her concoction continued to bubble, smelling like rubbing alcohol. Eventually, all the liquid evaporated, leaving behind a white powder.

"Erica, I'm scared." Renee's voice was like a lost five-year-old.

"I know. I'll be with you. I'll help."

"Soon, you'll be a stranger to me, too."

Erica rested her hand lightly on Renee's back. "You might not know me. But I'll know you. I'll make sure I'm not a stranger."

Renee nodded. She poured some distilled water into a beaker and dissolved the powder once more. Then she walked over to a cabinet, selected a large bottle filled with a transparent liquid, carefully measured out a few ounces, and dumped it in.

Idly, Erica read the label on the bottle. *Hydrochloric acid.*

"I don't know if it's enough," Renee said, staring at the beaker as she stirred the mixture.

"Enough acid?"

Renee straightened. "Enough of a life." Her words tumbled out, momentum building. "I'll wake up every day, not knowing who I am or how I got there. I'll have no friends, just strangers I meet anew every day. I'll decide something one day and forget it by the next. My life will slip by, one moment no different from the next. Everything always the same. Everything always new. There will be nothing else for me."

"We'll figure something out. We'll ask Cam. He's performed miracles on his cancer. Maybe he can help you."

"Yeah. Maybe he can." Renee's voice was empty.

Little white specks were floating in the liquid. Renee folded a circular piece of paper to make a cone. She placed the cone in a funnel, and then delicately poured the solution through the filter paper into another beaker.

"What are you making, anyway?" Erica said.

"$C_{11}H_{18}N_2O_3$. It's not the easiest thing to synthesize. I started it a while back, but didn't get around to finishing it until now."

White powder had coated the paper of the funnel. Renee dumped a beaker full of water into it and scraped the powder into a flask. She poured in more water, added a few drops of a black liquid from a small squeeze bottle, and mixed it all together using a glass stick. The liquid turned a brilliant shade of blue.

"Done for now," Renee said, raising the flask so Erica could inspect it.

"It's beautiful."

Renee nodded.

Together, they cleaned the equipment Renee had used, put everything away, and wiped the tables.

When they finished, Renee surveyed the room and nodded. She picked up the flask of blue liquid, turned to Erica, and squeezed her hand. "Will you stay with me tonight? Like when we had sleepovers as kids?"

Erica bit her lip. She really didn't want to. Ian was waiting for her. But Renee was her best friend and was having a hard time. She couldn't abandon her now. And it was only one night.

"Of course." Erica pointed to the flask Renee was holding. "You're taking that?"

"Yeah. If I leave it here, someone will throw it away, and there's still one more thing I need to do with it."

When Erica swung by her own room for clothes, she found Ian asleep in her bed. To avoid disturbing him, she changed in Renee's room, and then relaxed on the bed while Renee finished in the bathroom. Between the *Practical Persuasion* exam, the hostage taking, and the conversations with Ian and his sister, it had been the longest day ever. Erica was exhausted.

Renee pushed aside the curtain on the bathroom door. Her face was serene as she sat on the bed.

"Thanks for coming by," Renee said quietly. "I was upset, but I feel better now."

Erica hugged her friend. "I'm here whenever you need me."

"I know." Renee's words were slightly slurred and her eyelids droopy.

Erica smiled. Renee's day had been as rough as her own. "How about we get some sleep?"

Renee nodded.

They lay down together on the bed. Renee dozed off almost instantly. A few minutes later, Erica did as well.

When Erica awoke the next morning, Renee was dead.

CHAPTER TWENTY-FIVE

Erica felt Renee's neck for a pulse, but there was none. She tried her wrist. The upper side of Renee's arm was pale, but the lower half purple. No pulse there either.

Renee's body was cold.

Erica scrambled out of bed, leaving from the foot to avoid climbing over the body,

How could Renee be so cold?

She must have been dead for a while.

Erica felt her stomach churn and knew she was going vomit. She raced to the toilet.

Afterward, while splashing water across her mouth, she saw it on the counter. The flask that Renee had been working on the night before. No liquid remained.

Where was the alleged Jeemoh surveillance? Shouldn't they have three doctors in here by now? Were they not looking at *anything*?

Erica stumbled outside, tears streaming down her face. She needed help. She pounded on Ian's door before remembering he was in her room.

Erica opened her own door, but stopped just over the threshold, wiping her cheeks. How should she tell him?

"What's wrong?" Ian said, blanching.

There was no way to soften the blow.

"Renee's dead. I think she killed herself." Her voice sounded like it was emanating from the bottom of a well.

Ian leaped to his feet. "Where is she?"

"In her room."

Ian ran to Renee's door, swearing as he realized he couldn't open it.

Erica, trailing him, whispered, "I'm sorry. I should have propped it open."

"We need someone to let us in there." He looked around wildly. "There's no way to call your mother or Irenic though. Who designed this stupid place?"

"Cam might be able to reach them," Erica said. He had sent that message to Renee's tablet.

Ian nodded and raced to Cam's room. He rapped on the door, but nobody answered.

"The mess," Erica said.

Ian seized Erica's hand. Together, they ran there. Cam was eating breakfast with the others.

Erica's face was bathed in light. It was hot, unpleasantly so. Jen was scrutinizing her, confusion written across her features.

Why was Jen staring at her like that?

Oh, she was crying again.

"Cam, Renee is hurt," Ian said breathlessly, "and we need to get into her room. Can you contact Lois?"

Cam stared into the distance for a few seconds, and then focused on Ian. "Renee's dead."

"We need to help her," Ian said, his eyes boring into Cam. "Can you get Lois down here?"

Cam nodded. "Follow me."

They ran to Renee's door, Morrison and Eve in their wake. Cam touched the panel, and the door opened.

Renee was still on the bed.

"She's gone, Ian," Cam said.

Ian ignored him. After picking up his sister, he ran with her from the room to the elevator. He savagely punched the call button.

The ding as the elevator arrived echoed hollowly in the corridor. Ian and Erica entered while the others hung back.

"Cam, you come, too," Ian commanded.

Cam nodded. The instant he stepped inside, Ian pressed the button for medical on the ninth floor and hit the "close door" button.

The elevator stopped at eleven. A man in a white lab coat looked in. His eyes widened. "I'll wait for the next one," he said, backing up a step.

Ian stabbed the "close door" button repeatedly, but the door ignored him. Erica shuffled her feet and stared downward, trying to avoid looking at the man, the body, or Ian's eyes. Finally, the door decided it was ready to shut.

The elevator opened once more, this time on nine. Ian ran into the medical lab, still carrying Renee.

Dr. Rahal was there. She took one look at Renee, and her face fell. "She's gone," she murmured. "You can put her on the table."

Ian pushed by the doctor. He gently rested Renee's body on the medical printer's platform, and then pressed the red button to active the machine.

Renee's body was bathed in red light as the metallic throbbing sound began. The upper half of her limbs looked sunburned and the lower half seemed as if it were stained in blackberry juice.

The sound stopped, although the red glow continued. Ian waited, his face like a marble statue.

The doctor just stood there, her hands clasped in front of her.

A minute passed.

A second minute.

There was no change.

"She's been dead for six hours, Ian," Cam said quietly.

Cam's simple statement was enough to push Ian over the edge. Tears glistening on his cheeks, he put his back to the wall, sliding down it until he was sitting.

Erica walked over to Ian, shut off the medical printer, and sat beside him. She put her arm around his shoulder, not even noticing her own tears.

"What happened?" Ian said, turning his red eyes toward her. "Why didn't you stop her?"

"I didn't know. She was just making stuff in the lab, like she does all the time. I didn't know what she was doing. She said what she was making, but I didn't know what it was." The truth sounded hollow, even to her own ears.

Lois entered. Ian turned on her immediately. "Why didn't you see what was happening? Why didn't you prevent it?"

"There are thousands of cameras. We can't monitor everything," Lois said softly. "We only watch in real time if we think there's a high chance of something happening. Otherwise, we use the video for post-mortems." She winced and added, "I mean, we use the video later to piece together what happened."

Raising a tablet she had brought with her, Lois tapped the screen a few times. "Renee told you what she was making?" Lois asked without looking up.

"Yeah. Near the end. I think when she was filtering the liquid." Erica wiped her cheeks, but it didn't matter. The tears just returned. "Why do you care? It's too late."

"Just trying to understand," Lois said. She stared at the tablet, touching it occasionally.

The tablet's tinny speakers broadcast the conversation in the lab the night before. While Lois, Rahal, and Cam stared at the screen, Erica just sat on the floor with Ian and listened. She couldn't bear to watch.

As the replay went on, Erica felt worse and worse. Renee hadn't needed to leave a suicide note. She'd told Erica everything, but Erica had been too thick-witted to recognize what their conversation was really about.

How could she not see it? It was so obvious. Renee had done everything but wave a sign.

She'd killed another friend. This time, her best friend.

Erica buried her face in Ian's shoulder.

No regrets. That was how she was supposed to live now. No stupid, overwhelming, life-consuming regrets.

No regrets.

She had regrets.

Erica shuddered in Ian's arms.

Ian stroked Erica's hair. "It's not your fault," he whispered in her ear.

Even Ian knew it was her fault.

"What did she say? C_{11}—something?" Lois said to Dr. Rahal in response to Renee's recent statement from the audio track.

Dr. Rahal nodded. "Pentobarbital. It's a barbiturate used as a sedative or anesthetic."

"And for doctor-assisted suicides and death-row executions," Cam said as if he were once again playing the trivia game.

Lois, Rahal, and Cam continued to talk, but Erica ignored them.

She was so stupid, so naive.

These abilities seemed to give them almost limitless potential. In combination, they were almost invulnerable. She could foresee and avert any problem. Renee could do anything. Cam prospered, even fighting against the most persistent, deadly cancer. It had seemed impossible that any of them could die.

And yet, there Renee was, cold and empty. Erica would never again talk with her best friend. Ian would never again hug his sister.

She should have done more. Renee had been struggling so much, yet Erica had done nothing to help, not really. Just conversations filled with meaningless reassurances that everything would be fine. Now, Renee was gone.

After a few minutes, Ian stood and pulled Erica to her feet. They descended to Ian's room and lay on his bed.

She'd fantasized about this for weeks. Being alone with Ian, finally together, in a real way, without all the subterfuge.

It was hell.

In the Gauntlet, she'd promised Renee that she wouldn't let anything happen between her and Ian. After Renee had forgotten all about it, Erica thought she could pretend she hadn't promised. Renee wouldn't know the difference anyway.

But Erica knew the difference. One of the last things she told Renee was that she and Ian were going out. She had broken her promise so casually. She was a thief stealing change from a blind beggar's cup.

Erica got up. "I think I need to be alone for a bit."

Ian nodded. He turned toward the wall.

Erica returned to her room and lay down. Everything was wrong, and it was all because of her, because she hadn't taken care of her best friend. Jeemoh, the missions, the attacks. None of it seemed important when measured against the death of her friend.

With a flash of insight, she understood why Renee had decided to stop living. Sometimes, the pain was just too great.

#

Erica wasn't hungry, so she skipped lunch. When dinnertime approached, she still didn't feel like eating. She stayed in bed, reading a novel she'd picked up weeks ago. Though she read words for an hour, she didn't get beyond page eight.

There was a knock on her door that she recognized as Ian. Her bones creaked as she got out of bed to answer it.

Ian's eyes were red and his features haggard. Nevertheless, he smiled and held out his arms. Erica flinched but allowed him to wrap her in a hug.

"How are you doing?" Ian asked, his concern clear in his tone.

"About as well as you, I imagine."

"I missed you."

"Yeah." Erica pulled away from him. Ian's embrace was a betrayal after her promise to Renee. "What's up?"

Ian frowned, his uncertainty reflected in his eyes. "You weren't at lunch. So I thought I'd pick you up for dinner."

"I wasn't hungry. Still not."

"I understand. Come anyway. You don't have to eat."

Erica glanced back at her room—the twisted sheets on her bed, the discarded novel, and the dirty clothes. "Okay."

Gripping her hand, Ian pulled her lightly into the corridor. She took it back as she closed the door, and then crossed her arms.

"What's going on, Erica?"

She stared down the long, empty corridor. "Nothing. Let's go to the mess."

Ian pursed his lips and began walking. "You know, I think we can help each other through this."

Erica shook her head. "I need to figure this out on my own." She didn't look at him, fearful of the accusations she'd see in his eyes.

Ian fell silent.

Eve, Jen, Cam, and Morrison had already finished when Ian and Erica arrived, but they were still sitting at the table. They looked up, their conversation ceasing.

"Hi," Erica said, sitting down.

Ian sat beside her.

"You can get your tray," Erica said. "Just because I'm not hungry doesn't mean you have to skip dinner too."

"I already ate. I just wanted to check on you."

"Thanks," she said without looking at him.

"No problem." He swallowed, the sound audible.

"I already said this to Ian," Morrison said to Erica, "but I'm sorry for your loss. I know she was your best friend. And if it makes you feel any better, I don't think she was to blame."

Erica shrugged. She ran one finger along the wood grain in the tabletop. "I know. I agree."

"It's this place," Morrison said, gesturing at the room. "It does things to you. Living under the stone, far from the sun. Doing everything they say. Only seeing and hearing what they want us to."

Eve rolled her eyes. "Drama much? Renee died because she couldn't handle it. She was weak."

Ian looked at her, his eyes narrow. "What did you say?" Jen's light flickered to his face.

Eve stared right back at him. "I'm saying Renee had one of the best abilities in here. She could do anything she wanted. Almost all our abilities have downsides, but we deal with them. At least she didn't have to bleed. But she was too weak to handle it, and she took the easy way out."

Ian's eyes shot daggers. "Whatever. You don't know anything about her."

Morrison nodded, turning his body toward Eve. "She was losing her memory. I'd like to see you cope with that, Eve. It's Jeemoh's fault. Maybe if they'd had some professionals in to help her, she'd have stood a chance. But I don't think they cared about Renee at all. Not as a person.

"Think about it. How much would it be worth to a spy agency to have an agent who could speak any language—do almost anything, really—and then conveniently forget the mission the day after it was over? A lot, I think. I bet they didn't even bother trying to solve her memory problem."

Eve sneered at him. "I doubt they could have helped anyway. She just needed to deal. We all have challenges. But you don't see any of us offing ourselves…"

Erica let the words wash over her. Jen's glow flickered from Ian to Eve to Morrison and back, like a hypnotist's spinning watch.

It was all so pointless, arguing about it now. Like the discussion would make any difference at all to Renee. Why bother?

She sensed something out of the corner of her eye, and she turned her head. While the others were watching the argument, Cam was watching her. She gazed at him until he blushed and looked back at the others.

Erica rose and returned to her room, knowing it was too early to sleep, but intent on trying anyway. She had no idea if any of the others even saw her leave.

She lay there in bed, in the darkness, staring at the ceiling. Sleep didn't come, but she didn't have the energy to get up and do anything. And really, what was there to do anyway? It wasn't like she knew chemistry.

Despite herself, she eventually fell asleep. A persistent beeping from her tablet awoke her.

She picked it up, staring at the words on the screen.

Ian's in medical. Come quickly. He could die.

CHAPTER TWENTY-SIX

Erica arrived just in time to see the bone pierce Ian's throat.

He gurgled, jerked his torso to the side to snap the spike off, and pulled the fragment from his neck. "Seven-five," he said a moment after the wound healed. He coughed, spraying blood upon the wall, and the medical printer's low platform.

"What are you doing?" Erica shouted.

"Sparring," Ian replied, his shirt shredded and crimson, the light giving his skin a pink glow.

Erica barely recognized his opponent. The front of Eve's body was almost completely covered in rough bone plates, her face hidden behind a bony mask. Spikes—and broken-off stubs of spikes—stuck out in all directions. In several places on her torso, the bone was blackened. As Eve circled, Erica could see that the makeshift bone armor rested on top of Eve's clothes. They were torn so badly that Erica suspected the armor was the only thing holding them on.

Blood drenched the floor beneath the two combatants. Neither of them exhibited any obvious wounds. Although, it was hard to tell beneath the gore.

Ian kicked out his right foot, aiming for Eve's leg. Eve stepped back to avoid the blow, and then leaped forward, swinging her right hand at Ian's stomach. The bones springing from Eve's knuckles snapped as they hit the metal plate that materialized.

Ian followed up with a left punch to Eve's right cheek. She didn't even try to dodge, but let her bone mask take the brunt of the blow while extruding several jagged spikes to impale Ian's hand. The metal that materialized across Ian's knuckles snapped off several of the spikes. But, before Ian could pull back, bone hooks ripped in from the sides and pierced his hand, trapping it against Eve's cheek. She stretched her arm along his, spikes jutting out to perforate his bicep, her hand reaching once more for his throat.

Then Eve screamed, clawing at the bone mask. Steam rose from her face, and Erica caught a whiff of chlorine. Eve slapped her thigh over and over.

"And the chlorine makes it eight-five," Ian said nonchalantly. "Could you pass me the bone saw, Erica?"

"You've got to stop this," Erica pleaded, gagging at the smell. Nevertheless, she picked up the bone saw from where it was lying nearby on the floor, already plugged in.

"Why?" Ian said, not even looking at her. "It's just the natural continuation of Irenic's classes." He seemed disturbingly skillful at using the saw to extract his hand.

Erica reached out to pull him toward her, but recoiled as she realized she'd get blood all over herself. "Maybe, but it's horrible. What if you do something that can't be healed?"

Ian shrugged. "Hasn't happened yet."

"Kind of surprising, that," Eve said. "We've pushed it pretty hard." Erica couldn't make out Eve's mouth through the breathing hole in the bone mask, but she could hear Eve's lopsided smile.

"What the hell's going on here?" Lois' voice echoed through the room.

"Sparring," Ian said defiantly.

Lois' eyes darted around the room, taking in Eve's makeshift armor and the blood on the floor, walls, and even the ceiling. She blanched, collapsing into a chair near the door. Erica had never seen that exact expression of horror on her mother's face before. Maybe she had spotted Ian's severed hand on the floor.

"You can't do that. Erica, turn it off."

Erica pressed the button on the wall. The red glow faded.

"How long have you been fighting?" Lois asked.

"Not long. Maybe forty-five minutes," Ian said. "We were cautious at first, not doing anything too bad." His brow furrowed. "Well, nothing fatal, anyway. But after Eve stabbed my lung, we realized we could go all out."

Lois looked like she wanted to puke. "You must never do this again."

"Why not?" Ian said, a hint of obstinacy returning to his voice. "It's more painful than you could imagine, but it totally works." His mouth twisted. "We've already discovered four new ways to kill each other."

"The medical printer isn't a toy. It's... it's a sensitive, expensive piece of technology, intended for emergencies only. For what it costs to run it for thirty seconds, we could buy your parents' house. And what if you break it? It's never been on for forty-five minutes before. It could overheat or something." Lois put her fingers to her forehead, shaking her head. "Forty-five minutes."

Ian sighed. "Fine."

"I don't want to try it again anyway," Eve said, tossing her head. "Once was enough."

"Go shower, and then clean up this mess. I'll send Dr. Rahal down to help with Eve. I'm going back to bed," Lois said. She stood, affixing them with glare. "But if I ever catch you doing something like this again, I... I won't let you use the medical printer for anything. You can ask Cam how much fun Irenic's class is when you can't use the printer afterward."

Eve and Ian both nodded. Lois glowered at them for a few seconds more and strode out of the room, slamming the door behind her.

After washing, the lecture they got from Rahal—while similar in content to Lois' rant—lasted the two hours it took to carve off Eve's carapace with the bone saw. Mercifully, the doctor numbed her with local anesthetic before cutting.

It took almost as long to mop up the blood. Even when it was spotless, Dr. Rahal had them go over the entire area once more with a disinfectant rinse.

Finally, the doctor let Erica and Ian leave.

"Why did you do that?" Erica asked in the stairwell, not trying to keep the hurt from her voice. It made no sense, but she felt betrayed, as if Ian had been fighting her, not Eve.

Ian rubbed his lips. "I don't know. It didn't seem like such a bad idea at the time."

"Well, it was. I never imagined you'd do something so stupid. What were you thinking?"

"It just happened. Eve was shooting off her mouth all night. My sister is dead. You don't care about me or anything else anymore. Eve was into it, so I figured, why not?"

"Wait. Who said I don't care?" Suddenly furious, Erica stopped. "If anything, I care too much."

"Don't give me that," began Ian, opening the door to their floor. "I'm not having this discussion in the hallway." Snagging her hand, he pulled her along into his room.

"You care too much?" Ian said, turning to face Erica as the door closed behind them. "My sister dies and the first thing you do is vanish. I try to hug you, but you recoil like I'm some troglodyte. I can see it in your every movement. You want nothing to do with me." Ian's face contorted as if he were holding back tears.

"It's not like that at all," Erica said, her anger subsiding as quickly as it had flared.

"It is. It really is." Ian turned his back to her. "Renee's dead," he whispered. "She was your best friend, but she was my *sister*. My mother and father are fake. She was all I had left of my family." Ian's voice was raw. "But I thought you were with me. To care for me when stuff like this happens. And let me take care of you. But instead, you vanished. You won't even talk to me."

Erica hugged Ian from behind, resting her cheek against his neck. "I'm sorry. I didn't mean to hurt you. But it's more complicated than that. At least, it is for me."

"So tell me then. That's why I'm here. Don't leave me alone to wonder what's going on with you."

"I don't know if I can."

"Erica…"

"I know you blame me for Renee's death."

"What?" Ian turned around.

"You think I should have stopped it."

"No!"

"You heard the recording. It was obvious what she was about to do, but I did nothing to stop her. I should have done something."

Ian shook his head. "I had no clue either. I knew she was unhappy, but I wouldn't have figured out what she was planning from that conversation." He took her hands and stared into her face. "You're not to blame. She made the decision. Not you."

"It's more than that. I broke my promise to her."

"What promise?"

"In the Gauntlet. She said that she couldn't handle it if we started going out, and she made me promise to never let anything happen between us. I shouldn't have promised. But I did. Then yesterday, when we talked, I thought it didn't matter anymore. She'd forgotten, so why couldn't I just ignore it? But when I told her, she killed herself.

"Renee might not have remembered, but somewhere, deep inside, she knew I'd violated her trust. She didn't know you. She didn't know her parents. I was the only one in the entire world she remembered. And I betrayed her. No wonder she committed suicide."

Ian looked at her, his eyes narrow. "Erica. That's not even close to right. Listen to the conversation on the video. Renee didn't know about your broken promise. That wasn't a girl furious at her friend's betrayal. It was a girl who had just enough left of herself to decide to end it before she lost everything. She wasn't blaming you. She was grateful she had the chance to explain. And to say goodbye."

Erica's face crinkled up, and her lip quivered. She pressed her head into Ian's chest.

"And as for that promise, she never should have asked it of you." Ian shook his head. "It was just wrong. You don't get to decide who other people fall in love with. You don't get to extort your friends into giving up their happiness for the sake of yours. It's always wrong, whether your mother's doing it or your best friend.

"Erica, I love you. And I don't blame you for anything that happened. Not because I love you, but because you're not to blame. For any of it. Today has been horrible. I didn't just lose my sister. I lost you, as well. I don't care about any promises you made. I just want to be with you.

"Maybe Renee has changed everything between us. And if that's the case, I won't bother you anymore. But regardless, I'll love you. I have no choice anymore. You're the most amazing person I've ever met, and I can't force my heart to stop caring. But I also can't handle another day like this one. So tell me now, please. I love you. Will you love me, too?"

Erica could feel Ian's heart thumping in his chest. She leaned back and stared into his eyes. "Of course, silly. I told you that yesterday," she whispered.

Ian's smile made Erica's world seem shiny.

"Oh, but one condition," she added.

"What?"

"No more beating up helpless girls when you're pissed off."

"What, you get to have all these subtle shades of emotion, and all I get is that I fought with Eve because I was grumpy?"

"Yep."

"How is she even a 'helpless girl'? She killed me five times."

"I mean it. Lift weights or punch a bag instead if you must. Or talk to me."

Ian grew serious. "Yeah. I was messed up and didn't see it that way, but it was stupid. No more fights with Eve. I promise." He rubbed his lips together and murmured, "I'll take on Morrison instead."

"Nor him."

"Cam?"

"Nope."

"Irenic?"

"I'd like to see you try. But no. Are you not getting the underlying message?"

"Hmm, that doesn't leave too many worthy opponents. Maybe we should explore this 'talk to you' option. Is it just talking, or can it be other stuff as well?"

"Other stuff?"

"Allow me to demonstrate…"

It was only later, after they finished the kissing, hugging, and touching, when she was half-asleep, that the thought occurred to Erica.

"Troglodyte?" she said. "What does that even mean?"

Ian, his face inches away from hers as they lay on the bed, lazily kissed her. "I have no idea."

#

They didn't wake until well after breakfast and saw no reason to leave the room immediately. Instead, they reminisced about Renee. The pain was no less sharp from them suffering it together. But Erica felt less raw.

At noon, driven by hunger, they were forced to admit they couldn't stay in the room forever. As they walked to the mess, Ian reached for her hand and interlaced his fingers with hers. Erica couldn't help but smile.

Eve was already there, sitting with Cam, Morrison, and Jen.

"I guess I hurt you so bad you had to miss breakfast," Eve said. She stared at them for second, raised an eyebrow, and added, "Or maybe Erica did."

"We were up late. We were tired," Ian protested.

"I bet you were," Eve said, her eyes bright and her voice dripping with suggestion.

"Come on, it was like, three AM before we got out of medical. You were there."

"That's when you left, but the real question is when you went to sleep." She winked.

"It wasn't—"

Erica spun Ian around, put her arm around his neck, and kissed him soundly. She turned to Eve. "Stop needling my boyfriend, in mess or medical."

Eve smirked. "Okay, then. I like a girl who knows what she wants."

Jen's light flashed across Eve's face. "I want lunch," Jen said. "You like me."

Eve nodded. "I kind of do."

Erica and Ian picked up their food and sat with the others.

"So, what?" Morrison said to Ian. "You're regressing to deal with Renee's death? I thought you'd moved on from Erica."

Erica's mouth dropped open. "I'm right here."

Ian squeezed her hand, shaking his head as he turned to Morrison. "I'm progressing. This has nothing to do with Renee. We got back together before she even died. And frankly, saying something like that makes you sound like a total jerk."

"Whatever. I'm just trying to guard your back," Morrison said, his tone unapologetic.

"My back doesn't need guarding from Erica."

"Obviously, *you* think that. That's why it's called 'guarding your back'."

Ian snorted. "Fine. Guard my back. But do it without being a jerk."

"I can't believe you can't see it." Morrison turned to Erica, his eyes accusing. "Why don't you just confess? You're working for your mother, aren't you?"

"We all work for my mother." Erica's voice was cold.

"You know what I mean."

Erica sighed. "Morrison, I was as suspicious as anyone when we came here. Just ask Ian. But everything we've seen of Jeemoh shows they're the good guys. Their means are unconventional, but that's because Lois cares about results. Always has.

"But look at the missions. Even if you exclude everything we saw when we hacked into the computer systems—if you only take into account our own experiences—Jeemoh seems fine. Better than fine… Good. Rescuing hostages at a school. Stopping terrorists from blowing up a dam. Helping a girl deal with her dangerous ability when it manifests for the first time. We're helping people. Saving lives."

"That's exactly what your mother would say." Morrison made it sound like a sin.

Erica shrugged. "Maybe so. If it's true, it's true."

Morrison bit back a retort as Irenic entered the room.

She strode over to Erica and Ian. "You missed your morning classes. I'm just checking whether you were dead or severely injured."

"We needed a break," Ian said.

"Your break was yesterday. If you aren't in the dojo at thirteen hundred, we will do your training wherever I find you. The lesson will be on how to defend yourself against an armed opponent."

"What weapon?" Erica asked, perversely curious.

"Don't know. Maybe a stiletto. If you know anatomy, you can cause a lot of hurt with a stiletto before you have to worry about someone dying." Irenic turned and marched from the room.

Erica stared at Ian. "I reckon we should attend martial arts."

Ian gazed back with equally wide eyes. "That might be for the best."

"If you were a team player, you'd skip it," Eve said. "It would be educational for the rest of us."

"Some might find that admirable," Ian said. "That unquenchable thirst for knowledge."

"I'm just curious what Irenic can do with a stiletto." Eve's grin was wry.

"Some might find that depraved," Ian said.

"You're fickle," Eve said.

"Yes," Erica said. "Consistently so."

Ian looked from Eve to Erica, and then turned mournfully to Morrison. "Now they're ganging up on me. I can't win."

"It's good he's figured that out," Eve said to Erica, her eyes bright.

"Yes. Very good. We can move on to the final stage of our plan."

Ian held out his hands in a clear appeal to his friend. "See?"

Morrison just rolled his eyes and left the room.

Ian sighed.

#

Martial arts class felt totally different. Renee had been Irenic's partner for demonstrating new techniques, but, in her absence, Irenic needed to draft someone else. Ian, Cam, Morrison, and Eve's abilities affected their hand-to-hand combat tactics, leaving Erica and Jen as the most viable candidates. Since Jen had barely progressed beyond "curl up in a ball on the floor and cry", Erica was the natural choice.

Each demonstration made Erica feel more ungainly and inept than the last. Despite Irenic explaining the techniques beforehand and completing the motions at a far slower speed than she would in a real fight, only Erica's ability saved her from broken limbs.

As if that weren't enough, for the ten minutes of sparring at the end of class, she was paired with Irenic again. Though her instructor wasn't any more brutal than normal, Erica learned once again that Irenic's normal level of brutality was more than enough to leave her maimed.

"Do you feel like the pain lessens the more we get beat up?" Ian asked conversationally as he wheeled Erica's stretcher toward the elevators where Irenic was already waiting. The others followed a few steps behind them.

"No. It still feels like someone smashed both my knees with a sledgehammer," Erica said, trying to keep her tone equally conversational, but failing as the pain leaked into it. "I'd still trade three years of my life for ten minutes of morphine. I think the difference is that I've learned to exist with the pain, to think and act, even though I feel like dying. The pain's no longer crippling."

The elevator rang, and the door slid open. Ian nodded. "That's a good way—"

Irenic stepping. The door shutting on her almost instantly.
Irenic caught. Struggling, tipping, rising up the wall.

CHAPTER TWENTY-SEVEN

"Stop, Sergeant," Erica shrieked, the vision bouncing around her skull.

Irenic glanced back. "I'll hold it for you."

Erica turned to Ian, her eyes wild. "Stop her."

Ian moved instantly, but Irenic was already walking forward. As she did, the doors shut in a fraction of a second, trapping her half in and half out. She pushed against the doors, but they were relentless.

The elevator began to ascend. As her legs rose, Irenic's struggles made her tip horizontally, the elevator gripping her around the waist. "Argh!" she said, clawing against the doors, trying to find purchase.

Ian reached her as she floundered halfway up the wall, continuing to rise. He tugged at her torso, but the doors held her tightly. She shifted only a few inches.

Irenic was almost at the top of the doorway. Ian jumped, grabbing her body and raising his legs so his full weight yanked against her.

Irenic grunted as her torso ripped free. She dropped head first, almost to the floor, until her feet caught once more against the doors. Ian lost his grip and fell. Irenic barely had time to look up before the floor of the elevator reached the top of the doorway.

Irenic grunted once more as her feet were sliced off.

She landed heavily on her head and was still.

"Oh my God," Eve shrieked. Jen wailed and ran back to the dojo.

Cam froze, staring in disbelief as Irenic's blood sprayed out onto the elevator door, but Ian didn't pause. He twisted onto his knees, tore off his shirt, and pressed it against the stumps of her legs.

Morrison ran forward to help, pulling off his own shirt and pressing it over Ian's, already saturated with blood.

Why wasn't Cam helping? He should be an expert in handling amputations, but he was still standing behind her, rubbing his face and squirming as if he needed to go to the bathroom.

"Is she alive?" he said.

"Yes," Erica said, grabbing Cam's arm and spinning him toward her. "What should we do?"

"Um…" Cam swallowed. "I think stopping the bleeding. Hold your hand over the wound." Shaking off Erica, he crept forward to get a better view. "Yeah, like that. Using your shirts. That's a good idea."

"We need to get her to medical," Ian shouted.

"Yeah," Cam said as if it were a novel idea. "We can do that too."

"Use my stretcher." Erica dangled her upper body over the side until her hands almost touched the floor, twisting her lower body to follow it. She yelped as her broken knees smashed against the concrete, but then felt bad for distracting Ian with her cry.

Eve finally got moving. She ran the stretcher over to Irenic, lowering it the instant she reached her. The two boys released Irenic's legs, hauled her onto the stretcher, and then reapplied pressure to the wounds.

"Just a sec," Cam said. He shuffled over to Irenic, stared at her face for a few seconds, and then touched her neck to feel for a pulse. "She's alive." He squeezed his eyes shut and rubbed his temples. "There are three main things with amputations that are very important. What were they?" The others stared at him, ready to get moving, but also not wanting to make a mistake.

"First—and the importance of this shouldn't be underestimated— we should try to get her feet. Sometimes, they can reattach them. Can anyone think of a good way to get her feet?"

"It shouldn't matter," Ian said quickly. "The medical printer will take care of it."

"It might matter," Cam said slowly while rubbing his chin. "Maybe the printer can't do feet."

"It can. Eve sliced off my hand the other day, and it regrew."

"Neat. Maybe it's different with feet, though. Have you considered—"

"Cam! It doesn't matter. What are the other important things?"

"The other important things?" Cam looked confused for a few seconds, but then smiled. "Of course. This is perhaps even more important than getting her feet. Particularly in this case. You see, there are a bunch of ways she could die here. But the most likely is by bleeding out. So, we address that by trying to stop the bleeding." He stared at Ian expectantly. Then, blushing, he looked away. "Which we're already doing. But there's also the third thing. To get her to a hospital as fast as possible." As Ian and Morrison started to move, Cam held up a hand. "*However*, this is a special case, because we don't have a hospital. So I think we should take her to medical instead."

Ian stared at him in disbelief. "That's the final important thing? To take her to medical quickly? We decided that ten minutes ago."

"Well, yes." Ian heaved the stretcher, but Cam put his arm on Ian's, stopping him. "You shouldn't take the elevator though. You should use the stairs."

"I know." Ian tugged away his arm, looking like he was about ready to kill Cam.

Erica lay on the ground, watching as he and Morrison wheeled the stretcher to the stairwell.

Ian stuck his head back through the doorway. "Cam, help us. You're strong, remember?"

"Oh, yeah." He strolled to the door, disappearing through it.

Eve knelt beside Erica. "Do you want me to help you get to medical? You can lean on me."

Erica glanced down at her mangled knees. Her injuries were minor next to Irenic's, but walking seemed impossible. "No, I'll just wait. I don't think I can handle that many stairs. Let them deal with Irenic, and then they'll get me."

From the direction of the stairwell came the sound of boots. After a few seconds, there was a shout, followed by a heavy thud.

"Sorry, sorry," came Cam's muffled voice. "My fault. My balance can be off sometimes. The leg, you know."

"Just pick her up." The frustration in Ian's tone was clear. "Actually, no. Leave her. Let the other guys do it."

More bumping, footsteps, and cries echoed from the stairwell.

"I've never heard Cam babble so much," Erica said, her lip curling in disgust. "He's utterly worthless in a crisis."

Eve shook her head ruefully. "I swear I was about five seconds away from slapping him." She exposed her teeth in something between a smile and a grimace. "I still might."

Eve waited with Erica until Ian arrived with soldiers ten minutes later. He directed them to get the second stretcher from the dojo.

"Did she make it?" Eve said.

Ian nodded. "Barely. She lost tons of blood. We should've used tourniquets. Dr. Rahal said two minutes more and, well..."

"What about her feet?" Erica said.

Ian rolled his eyes. "The printer handles feet. Of course. Cam's such an idiot sometimes."

The soldiers hoisted Erica onto the stretcher and carried her up the stairs to medical. It was a frightening ride, with Irenic's blood splatters forcing Erica to consider just what could happen if she fell. But they made it without incident.

Afterward, Irenic insisted they attend their afternoon classes, saying they shouldn't be distracted by a "minor scrape". But Erica learned little. Her mind kept hopping from the attacks, to Renee's empty seat, to Ian, and then back again, focused on anything but the subject. The teachers seemed to understand her distraction and didn't push too hard.

Regardless, it was only over dinner that the group had a chance to discuss the latest "accident".

"I've never seen an elevator door close that fast," Ian said. "I didn't think it was possible."

"Jeemoh must have designed it to have that capability," Morrison said.

"Why would they do that?" Erica said. Chlorine gas already secured the elevators. Did they really need two different ways of killing someone with an elevator?

"To kill us, of course," Morrison said as if he were talking to a child. "After everything that's happened, do you still believe that Lois isn't behind these attacks? Heck, she was probably targeting you again. On the stretcher, you were the most vulnerable to that trap."

"There's no evidence it was her," Erica said crisply.

"Well, who do you think it was?"

"Those Group S guys. We already know they were attacking Jeemoh."

"How could they control the elevators from outside the building?" From his tone, it was unclear whether Morrison considered her naive or just stupid. "It's got to be someone inside."

Even Erica didn't find her own argument convincing. Nevertheless, she persisted, if only to contradict Morrison. "Maybe they have a mole."

"Now you're just stretching."

"It's irrelevant," Eve said, almost angry. "The question isn't who's doing the attacks. It's how do we protect ourselves."

Ian shook his head. "I think the elevator proved that we can't. Whoever is doing this will keep trying until they succeed. That's why we have to figure out who's responsible."

Eve grimaced. "Yeah, right. We'll look for fingerprints, interview everyone, and examine the elevator's software," she said sarcastically, rolling her eyes. "We need to consider another option."

"What?"

"Leaving."

At that point, the conversation devolved into a three-way argument between Morrison, Eve, and Ian about whether leaving would make things better or worse, or if it was even possible. But Erica saw no point in arguing. She'd already been through this with her dad countless times. She wasn't going to flee.

The problem was—Morrison had a point. If Group S was behind the attacks, that meant either they had hacked into Jeemoh's systems from outside or they had planted a mole within Jeemoh. Knowing Lois, either one of those possibilities seemed unlikely. Lois was obsessive about everything, security in particular. Erica couldn't imagine what sort of tests someone would have to pass to work at Jeemoh, but she was confident they would be far more stringent than even the CIA. And that was assuming Jeemoh had nobody with telepathic abilities. Infiltrating Jeemoh would be all but impossible.

So Group S was unlikely. But that left only Jeemoh operatives. It was probably a disaffected individual or small group. Not Lois. Erica was sure of that. Not because she trusted her mother, but because the attacks were too incompetent. Heck, the last elevator attack missed her by at least ten seconds.

That in itself was odd. The perpetrator was sophisticated enough to attack twice with an elevator and once with a tablet without being caught. Yet, they hadn't even been close to getting her this time. How could they be so skillful, yet so inept?

Unless they weren't targeting her.

Irenic had been in both elevator attacks. Heck, during the first attack, if Irenic hadn't held the door, the rest of them wouldn't have even been in the elevator. The tablet was similar. It exploded only seconds after leaving Lois' hands. Suppose the attacker wasn't targeting her with the tablet, but Lois?

That put the attacks in a whole new light. What if it were a Jeemoh employee, annoyed at their boss?

No, that didn't make sense. They were going after Lois and Irenic, but Irenic had no direct reports, other than them. So someone else. Someone who hated both Lois and Irenic. Someone in security or operations, good enough with electronics to hack both the elevator and the tablet and get away with it.

Jeemoh must have people capable of that. Though, with Renee gone, Erica herself didn't know anyone like that personally. Except…

Erica's eyes widened. She glanced at Cam. He raised his head, blushed, and looked back down at his mashed potatoes.

Erica gnawed on her lip. It couldn't be Cam. He was with Lois during the first elevator attack, and he had been standing beside her during the second.

He'd sent messages on the tablets when nobody else could. He'd opened Renee's locked door like it was nothing. He'd taken over the security cameras in the school, broken their encryption while walking through the schoolyard.

Erica raced through her meal, and then hauled Ian to his feet.

"Wait. I'm not done yet," he said.

"You'd really rather eat than hang out in your room with your adventurous new girlfriend?" Erica said with a mischievous grin.

Eve guffawed.

"Good point." Ian snatched a bun off his plate. Together, they raced to his bedroom.

The instant the door closed, Ian turned to Erica. "So, what sort of adventures did you have in mind?"

She smiled and pushed him onto the bed, straddling him. "How about I show you?" She kissed his lips, his neck, and then slowly kissed her way up to his ear. "I need to bounce a theory off you," she whispered.

"You do?" Ian's voice was weak. "Can it wait?"

"No," Erica said. "There is a time for work and a time for play, Mr. Nash, and this is clearly the former."

"Oh. That wasn't so clear to me."

"Let me assure you there will be ample time for the latter later." She kissed him soundly, slid off to lie beside him, and then returned her mouth to his ear. "I promise."

"Yeah. I guess so." Based on the placement of his hands, Ian still seemed preoccupied, but his choice of preoccupations had a certain appeal, so Erica didn't bother trying to stop him.

"I have a theory," Erica said. "Suppose that the attacks aren't targeting us, but rather Lois and Irenic."

"Then their aim is horrible."

"I know, but remember how Lois said when people come out of the Gauntlet, they sometimes want revenge?"

Ian's hands paused. He leaned back to examine her face, and then shifted closer to whisper in her ear. "You think it's one of us?"

"Maybe. I was just thinking. The elevators have electronic security—you have to scan your hand to use them. And the chlorine gas and the door are probably hooked into the same system. The tablet's also got to have a security system. And we hacked into Jeemoh so easily."

"Renee's dead." Ian managed to say it with only a slight quiver in his tone.

"Yes. But Cam isn't."

Ian shook his head. "There's no way Cam could do something like that."

"He hacked into the cameras in the school in minutes. Remember Renee was surprised at how fast he did it? He's been here for a month. To what extent could he have co-opted the surveillance and security systems here?

"Think about it. He opened Renee's door without a second thought. Heck, he was sending messages on the tablets, and nobody else can figure out how to do that. That's how he told me you and Eve were fighting in medical."

Ian's brow knitted. "He wasn't there, though. How would he have known?"

"That's my point. He saw you on the security cameras. It's the only thing that makes sense. Lois is paranoid. I can't believe she'd ever turn off the cameras in here, even if someone isn't monitoring them all the time. Yet, there's stuff she never recorded, like Cam sawing off his leg. That only makes sense if someone was messing with the cameras."

"Maybe someone forgot to hit record." Ian shook his head. "I still don't see how it's possible. This facility must have some of the most advanced systems anywhere. You're saying that Cam—a guy who was struggling to learn to tie his own shoes in grade four—subverted the security systems here to the extent that he could use them to launch three deadly attacks with no one knowing it was him?"

Erica nodded. "I'm saying the guy who designed a custom robotic limb to replace the leg he sawed off, beat Renee at trivia games, and brewed his own successful chemotherapy regime was also able to hack a computer system." She wasn't sure about her theory when she started the conversation, but the more she spoke, the more convinced she became.

"But how could that be? He's just Cam with a cell phone."

"Lois said she thought that the phone was like a missing piece of a puzzle that turned him into a genius. But I have another theory. When he hacked the cameras in the school, Renee said something about it being impossible to break the encryption with just a cell phone. But suppose that the cell phone is just a way for him to access a more powerful computer on the Internet. Or several computers."

"You can't crack encryption with a couple of computers," Ian said. "Or everyone would do it. It would take more. I don't know how many, but at least a hundred."

"Maybe he has that many. There are billions of computers on the Internet. If he can hack Jeemoh, it can't be that hard to crack a hundred of them."

"He couldn't have done it though. He was with Lois during the chlorine and us today."

"Cam speaks Wi-Fi. He doesn't need to be sitting at a computer."

Ian rubbed his forehead. "He's not that kind of guy. Cam's scared of his own shadow. When Vince was beating him up, he never even fought back. He doesn't have it in him. Heck, look at how much he panicked when Irenic was injured. He was babbling like an idiot and even dropped the stretcher."

"Maybe. Or maybe he was deliberately acting like that to delay long enough for Irenic to bleed out." Erica squeezed Ian's hand. "He isn't the same Cam he was a few months ago. He couldn't fight back then. But he was lethal against those Group S guys at the school."

"Yeah." Ian blinked. "So let's say it's true, that Cam's going after Lois and Irenic. What do you think we should do about it?"

Erica rolled onto her side, resting her head on her hand. She hadn't even considered that question yet. "Tell Lois?"

"We don't know for sure it's him. There's no evidence, just a theory. And he's a friend. We should at least talk to him first, to see if he can explain."

Erica frowned. "You sure that's a good idea? If he tried to kill already…"

"If he really attempted to commit murder, it's a terrible idea." Ian sighed. "But I still don't think he's the type. He's not like Vince. And I'm worried about what Jeemoh would do if they even suspected him of doing this stuff. It's not like they believe in 'innocent until proven guilty'."

"If it is him, he could get violent," Erica said.

"Yes, but you'll know before he does anything. You can keep us safe, and then we'll know for sure. And Jeemoh can handle it from there."

It was nice Ian had confidence in her, but frustrating that he couldn't see how unreliable her ability was. She'd almost killed Ian in the fight with Vince. She'd allowed Morrison to get shot while storming the school and had been knocked unconscious herself soon after in the chemistry lab. Out of all the times they'd sparred, she hadn't beaten Irenic even once. She wasn't even close to infallible.

Ian seemed to sense her shifting mood. "Don't worry, Erica. I trust you, and I know we can do this."

She nodded. "Yeah. I'm just paranoid." She gnawed on her lip. "I guess we do it after lights out, when we can talk to him alone in his room?"

"For sure. It's not a conversation we'd want to have in the mess."

They passed the time further discussing the evidence. Erica became even more certain, but Ian couldn't wrap his head around the idea that meek Cam had turned into a brutal murderer.

Eventually, Erica decided it would be more fun fulfilling her promise early in the conversation, and Ian agreed wholeheartedly. Then, the time flew by.

The lights dimmed. Erica hopped out of bed, adjusting her clothes. "Let's go."

"I don't mind waiting a bit longer." Ian sounded short of breath.

Erica grinned, tugging on his hand. "No, we have to talk before he goes to sleep."

Ian sighed dramatically as he climbed to his feet. "I don't know how you do it. I find you the most distracting thing on the planet."

"Oh, you mean this?" Erica said with a look of wide-eyed innocence. She distracted him thoroughly.

"And sometimes you're just cruel," Ian said.

Hand in hand, they crept to Cam's door. Erica tapped on it cautiously. When there was no reply, she knocked harder.

"Who is it?" Cam sounded exhausted.

"Erica and Ian. Can you let us in?" Erica asked. "We want to talk about something."

"I… I'm tired, Erica. Let's talk in the morning."

"It's important. I'd rather not wait."

"Sorry. I'm not up to it."

"Cam, it really is urgent. Please let us in."

"I have cancer, Erica. I'm doing my chemotherapy. Six tubes are sticking out of my body, pumping a mixture of nine different drugs into my veins. Hopefully, the sedative will knock me out quickly, because if it doesn't, I'm pretty sure I'm going to puke. And if that happens, I'll be up half the night, trying to empty a stomach that's already empty. I don't want to talk. Go away."

Erica looked at Ian. He shrugged helplessly.

"Sorry for bothering you," Erica said. "But we do need to chat. Can you come by Ian's room tomorrow before breakfast?"

"Yeah. Fine."

They returned to Ian's room.

"That wasn't how I envisioned it going," Ian said.

"No. He sounded tired. He seems so strong that I forget how sick he is."

"So I guess we have to wait."

"I guess. Do you feel like sleeping right away?"

"Heck, no."

"Me neither."

Two hours after they finally fell asleep, the door opened, and then the lights turned on. Erica sat up, squinting into the brightness.

Irenic strode into the room. Closing the door behind her, she turned toward the two on the bed. Her eyes were ablaze, and a vein on her forehead throbbed.

"Why were you talking to Cam in the middle of the night?" she hissed.

CHAPTER TWENTY-EIGHT

"What?" Ian said, shading his eyes against the glare.

"I saw you on surveillance. You wanted to talk to Cam. You said it was urgent. Why?" Irenic demanded.

"We needed to discuss homework we had for *Covert Ops* class," Ian said.

"What homework?"

"It's a secret," Erica said. "*Covert Ops*, you know."

"Tell me."

"It's just personal stuff," Erica said. "It doesn't matter."

"I'm not playing a game, Erica."

Erica squeezed her eyes shut. Her mind was still foggy. She couldn't think fast enough to come up with a plausible story, and Irenic looked ready to maim someone. Come to think of it, Irenic almost always looked ready to maim someone.

"Ian and I came up with this crazy idea," Erica said. She shared their theory about the attacks, half-expecting Irenic to scoff at the notion that Cam would be able manipulate Jeemoh's security system to the extent she was proposing. Instead, Irenic just nodded and let her speak uninterrupted. Irenic's face gradually relaxed.

"We have no evidence of any of it," Erica concluded. "So we thought we'd talk to him about it."

Irenic nodded. "I will." She moved toward the door, but then she looked back. "You come too."

"What?" Erica said. "Now? In the middle of the night? Why?"

"Because you're probably right."

"It's just a stupid theory."

Irenic pursed her lips. "We have evidence he's attacked our computer systems. Including surveillance."

"That was Renee," Ian said, looking abashed. "And us. We broke into your database. But we were just looking for information, and we haven't done it since you… talked with us about it."

A smile flashed across Irenic's face. "As you watch the shark glistening in the water, beware the stone fish hiding in the sand."

"What?" Ian said.

"Renee was easy to spot. Cam wasn't. Come on."

Irenic led them to Cam's room and pointed to Erica.

Erica knocked on the door. "Cam, it's Erica and Ian again. We need to talk now."

There was no response, so Erica knocked harder.

"Hello?" The voice from inside the room sounded even more exhausted and confused.

"It's Erica and Ian. Can you let us in? It's important."

"Go away, Erica."

"Please, Cam."

"Go away."

Irenic nudged Erica out of the way and placed her hand on the scanner beside the door. A light on it flashed red. She tried again, to the same effect. She frowned. "Cam, this is Sergeant Irenic. Let us in."

Cam took several seconds to answer. "I'm sick and can't move. I already told Erica. We can talk in the morning. Or just tell me what you want."

"Open the door, now."

"I can't. I'm sorry,"

"If you don't open it, I'll open it myself."

"That's fine."

Irenic stared at the steel door. She turned to Ian. "The door's biggest weakness is its hinges. Can you do anything?"

Ian examined the hinges. They were welded onto the steel doorframe.

Ian shook his head. "I don't think so. Maybe I could create a thermite or acetylene reaction to cut through them. But I doubt it would work, and my hands would be fried."

"Do it." Irenic's gaze on Ian was steady.

"No," Erica said, putting her arm across Ian's chest. "We don't need to talk to Cam that badly. He's not going anywhere. We can talk in the morning."

Irenic didn't acknowledge Erica at all. "Do it. We can heal you."

"No," Ian said. "I won't sacrifice my hands and go through all that pain just to open a stupid door."

"Life is—"

"No!" Ian said. "I don't care what life is."

Irenic contemplated Ian's face for a few seconds and then tapped the screen of her watch a few times. She swore.

"What?" Erica said.

"It's malfunctioning. Stay here. Don't let Cam leave. Lois is already on her way in, but I'll update her. Wake Eve and Morrison." Irenic strode down the corridor, disappearing behind the stairwell door.

Erica turned back to Ian. "Don't you think she's over-reacting?"

Ian shrugged. "Probably. I mean, even if Cam can access the surveillance system and jam the door lock, it doesn't seem that big a deal. What's he going to do? He can't stay in his room forever."

Erica grinned. "Jeemoh's so used to being the one spying on everyone. They're just panicking now that the tables are turned."

"There are the computer systems," Ian said thoughtfully. "They wouldn't want the information on those to be public."

"I suppose. But nothing there is too incriminating. I guess some of the missions are technically illegal. But it's no different than killing Americans with drones or torturing people in Guantanamo, and nobody cares about that."

"It might be more about the existence of Jeemoh. And us."

Erica nodded. "Good point." She squeezed Ian's hand. "You watch the door. I'll go get the others."

She woke up Eve and Morrison and explained to them what was happening. Both viewed Erica's theory about Cam being behind the attacks with skepticism and were more amused than concerned when she described how Cam had locked his door.

With twenty soldiers in her wake, Irenic returned, carrying an industrial-looking L-shaped metal tool. The bigger cylindrical arm was about two and half feet long, with flat rubber feet on both sides.

"He's still in there?" Irenic asked.

Erica nodded. She gestured to the device in Irenic's hands. "What is that?"

"Breaching tool." Irenic pounded on the door. "Last chance, Cam."

There was no response.

The soldiers gathered around, guns raised.

Irenic positioned the longer arm of her breaching tool to span the width of the doorway and pressed a button. With a low throbbing sound, the arm lengthened until it was jammed between the two sides of the doorway. The perpendicular shorter arm stuck out toward them.

She turned back to the others. "This is why we train. The five of us should be able to restrain him. If things go sideways, lethal force is authorized."

"What?" Morrison said, aghast. "There's no need to kill him."

"Yeah," Ian said emphatically. "The guy was just messing around and now is too sick to come to the door."

"If that's the case, things won't go sideways. But the order stands." Irenic turned back to the door, touching a second button on the tool. The throbbing sound returned. This time, the shorter bar pressed forward, pushing into the door a few inches above the handle.

Erica flinched as the vision coursed through her mind. Ian glanced toward her, his eyebrows raised. She shook her head minutely.

With a crack that echoed down the concrete corridor, the door gave in to the machine's assault.

Cam's room was littered with weapons and electronic devices in various stages of disassembly. Two clear pathways—one to the bed and one to the bathroom—seemed to be the only concessions Cam had made to organization. At the foot of the bed was a wastebasket overflowing with chocolate bar wrappers and soda cans. Four or five prosthetic limbs were heaped haphazardly in one corner, while another held an IV drip tube, a hanger, and several empty plastic bags. Erica could count fifteen mobile phone screens strewn around the room, a handful of computers, and thirty circuit boards.

But Cam wasn't there.

Irenic spun to face Erica and Ian. "You let him leave?"

Cam's face appeared on the tablet computer on the bed, a head and shoulders floating in the darkness. He looked down, blushing. "Not their fault. Don't beat them up over it."

"Where are you, Cam?" Irenic said, striding to the bed.

"Out. How much do you know about Jeemoh?"

Irenic's eyes narrowed. "I'm like everyone. Need to know. Where are you?"

Cam nodded. "I was just curious."

"Why did you attack us, Cam?" Ian said, unable to keep the hurt from his voice. "I thought we were friends."

On the screen, Cam was silent for a few seconds, rubbing his mouth. Finally, he shrugged. "I didn't mean to. I was going for them, but missed. It takes time to heat a tablet enough to make it explode. And when I activated the security protocols on the elevator, I didn't anticipate Sergeant Irenic holding the door for you guys. I'm, um, sorry."

Ian slumped, deflated. "I never really believed it was you. I didn't think you were... you know. Like that."

"Boys will be boys." Cam's voice was firmer, less hesitant.

"What?" Ian said.

"Whenever I got beat up at school, people told me one of three things. Often it was 'boys will be boys', which, loosely translated, seemed to mean, 'I don't care that they beat you up. That's your problem, not mine'. It wasn't helpful, but at least it was honest.

"Better than what the vice principal always said. She told me that the school had a zero tolerance policy for fighting. That meant that if someone hit me and a teacher saw it, I'd be punished. So I couldn't get help from teachers anymore. I learned to wipe up the blood myself, to walk without a limp, and the vice principal proclaimed that her zero tolerance policy had eliminated bullying.

"Then there was my parents. 'Escalate,' they said. 'If someone hits you, hit them back, twice as hard. Bullies are cowards at heart. If you fight back, they'll leave you alone.' I thought they were nuts, but I tried it once anyway. I found out that Vince was better at escalating than I was.

"But you know, now I think my parents were right. Now I can fight."

"You didn't fight. You tried to kill my mom, and, in the process, nearly killed me." Erica said, not trying to hide the bitterness in her voice.

"I escalated."

"It's not the same thing."

"You know, Erica, over the years, Vince did so much to me. He tormented me constantly, sent me home bleeding so often that my parents moved our first aid bin from our upstairs bathroom to the closet near the front door. And even then, nobody cared about him beating me up. Why should anyone care about me beating up Jeemoh now? Heck, you should support me. Your mom lied to you for years. Tortured you. Tortured all of us."

"That doesn't justify slicing off Irenic's feet. Or all the other stuff you did," Erica said.

Cam shrugged. "Boys will be boys."

"It's not right, Cam."

"It is right. It's the natural continuation of what they started. But I knew you wouldn't get it. I just needed to explain. To be understood. I'll go now."

"Wait," Irenic said, holding up a hand. "I understand. Come here and talk to us, Cam. I don't think what you did was so terrible."

"You wouldn't. You're the biggest bully of all."

Irenic stiffened. "I teach."

"You break our bones every day. When Erica and Ian hacked into your system, you didn't even bother trying to talk with them. You just thrashed them."

"He has a point," murmured Morrison. Irenic shot him a warning look, and Morrison flinched.

Erica could almost see Irenic consciously relax her body as she turned back to the tablet. When she spoke, her tone was casual, not in the least defensive. "I use the most effective methods. If you think it's unjust, let's talk about it. Come here and explain it to me."

"I'm not stupid, Sergeant. Not anymore." Cam glanced briefly to his left. "I'm in the middle of something. I have to go."

"Wait, Cam," Irenic said.

The tablet fell silent, its screen black, refusing to respond to Irenic's further exhortations.

Erica turned from the tablet. She looked for somewhere to sit, finally concluding that the bed was the only option amid all the clutter. She grimaced. "You let him take all this equipment from the electronics lab?"

"It didn't look like this on our cameras," Irenic said, looking up from the tablet. "Just a standard, empty room."

Eve shook her head in disbelief. "But there's so much here. It must have taken weeks to accumulate so much garbage."

Irenic glared at her. "Are you that stupid? He's in control of our video surveillance. We've only seen what he wants us to see. He's probably watching us right now." Eve swallowed and looked away.

Cam's voice emanated from the still-dark tablet. "Yeah. I am."

Morrison chucked.

Irenic turned to him, trembling with fury. "Tell me what's funny."

Morrison held his ground in the face of Irenic's wrath. "You've been spying on us for how many years? And now, it's happening to you. And it's not some all-mighty organization, but just one guy. One teenager took over all your cameras. How is that not funny?"

Irenic spoke through gritted teeth. "He controls Jeemoh's systems. He could kill everyone on this floor."

There was a brief hiss, just like in the elevators. Erica's eyes jerked upward to the holes in the ceiling. Though she couldn't see any signs of chlorine, she could smell it. Trembling, Erica looked toward Irenic.

"Not just this floor," Cam's voice said. "Their plan to confine the chlorine to certain areas makes no sense considering the bunker's ventilation system is computer controlled."

"You can send the gas elsewhere?" Irenic asked warily.

"Everywhere. It's a blunt weapon. My simulations show a two- to five-percent survival rate." From Cam's tone, it sounded more like a boast than a threat.

But Morrison didn't hear it that way. In seconds, his expression had shifted from amusement to fear. "We have to leave."

Irenic shook her head, crossing her arms.

Erica's jaw dropped. Were they really going to just stay there when Cam could kill them all at any moment? It seemed mad.

Trying to appear calm—though she was still trembling—Erica half raised her hand to get Irenic's attention. "Morrison's right. We should evacuate."

"We're not running." Irenic's face was stone. "If he wants to kill us, we'll be dead before we get outside."

Erica gnawed on her lower lip. Irenic wasn't wrong. It would take ten minutes for them to get outside using the stairs, but only seconds for Cam to bring them down with the gas. Fleeing wasn't an option.

"Good point." Despite her pounding heart, Erica kept her voice steady.

Irenic nodded almost unnoticeably, and Erica felt more grounded. Surely, Irenic's composure meant she had a plan.

Irenic turned back to the tablet. "You're bluffing. If you gas the whole bunker, you'll die too."

"Maybe. Maybe not."

Irenic's eyes narrowed.

That wasn't right. Cam sounded too confident. Maybe he had a gas mask? Erica scanned the room for signs of protective gear. Her eyes fell on the garbage can.

Wait a minute. Chocolate bar wrappers and soda cans?

"Are there vending machines somewhere in here?" she said.

As Ian followed Erica's gaze, his eyes widened. "I don't know of any."

"Then where did he get all that junk food?"

Irenic whirled toward Erica, and then the garbage can. She strode over to it, dumping it onto the floor. Buried beneath the candy wrappers were boxes for three smartphones.

"He's left the bunker before. He… might be outside right now." Erica nervously glanced at the ventilation holes in the ceiling, fear rising once again. If Cam wasn't in the building, what was stopping him from gassing them?

Irenic nodded crisply. "That complicates things." She straightened to her full height to address everyone in the room. "Our top priority now is finding Cam. He could be inside or outside the bunker. With our compromised security systems, we can't rely on what we see on the cameras. We need to do a full sweep."

She turned to one of the soldiers. "I'm putting you in charge of that, Clark. Station someone at every stairwell and elevator door and search every floor. Recruit anyone you need to help. Don't use the elevators. Don't use the internal communications systems. Only walkie-talkies. Deadly force is authorized, but capture is preferred. And remember, Javelins don't work on him. Got it?"

"Yes, sir," Clark said. "Should we sound the evacuation?"

Irenic shook her head. "No. At this hour, only essential personnel will be in the building, and an evacuation might be what Cam wants. Go."

The soldiers ran off to the stairway with Clark barking orders into his handset.

Irenic turned back to her students. "It's well past midnight, and he knows you were looking for him hours ago. If he were nearby, he would have returned to his room when you first tried talking to him. So, he's probably not in the bunker. Searching outside is our job."

Erica tried not to let her relief show, but she suspected Irenic knew anyway.

Morrison's eyes lit up. "Let's go, then. No need to delay."

Clark appeared at the door. Irenic stared at him as if he were a cockroach crawling its way through her salad.

"We need the hydraulic breach," Clark mumbled. "He's locked the stairwell."

Irenic helped him force open the door and began ascending the stairs with the teenagers following. Erica's pulse continued to pound. In only minutes, they'd be outside. Would Cam let them escape or would he deploy the gas before they were out of his reach?

To Erica's surprise, they stopped on a landing six floors up. Irenic tried to open the door with a palm print, but, once more, the electronic lock showed her as unauthorized. She lifted the breaching tool into position.

"I thought we were leaving?" Morrison said, almost whining. He glanced up the stairs.

"We're searching outside. Not going outside," Irenic said.

"What?" Erica exclaimed. "Where are we going then?"

"One of our operations rooms."

Erica's stomach clenched. "Oh." Ian reached out to squeeze her hand.

They walked down a corridor until they reached another metal door. Irenic tried half-heartedly to unlock it before setting up the breaching tool.

"I'm forcibly opening the door," Irenic shouted.

"Go ahead," a voice said from inside.

The door burst open.

A rectangular boardroom table with enough space for twelve people dominated the room. Built into the surface of the table were computer screens and keyboards, one at every seat. On one wall were four large television screens displaying a map, a satellite image, and two lists of names. The other walls had whiteboards. Five people sat around the table, all dressed in civilian clothes of varying degrees of formality, from a suit to jeans and a T-shirt.

As Irenic entered, the man in the suit stood. "The security system is malfunctioning. Every door is locked. Communications are down."

"Yeah," Irenic said dismissively. "Cam's gone rogue. He's cracked our security and can see everything we do. Don't worry about securing headquarters. Outside of life-and-death situations, our top priority now is finding Cam."

"Understood," the suit said.

"What about disabling the chlorine?" Morrison asked. "That should be our top priority."

"No."

"But—"

Irenic glared at Morrison. "Cam will know if we try. I don't want to force him to decide whether to use his weapon before he loses it. Now stop wasting everyone's time."

Morrison looked like he wanted to say something, but he kept his mouth shut.

"We think Cam's outside," Irenic said, turning back to the suited man. "He probably took a Jeemoh vehicle within the last five hours."

"Then we should be able to track him," said a woman wearing a white T-shirt with a pink unicorn on it. She stared down at the monitor embedded in the boardroom table in front of her as she typed. "We have eight vehicles checked out at the moment. Let's see, five have been away longer than five hours." She pursed her lips as her index finger hovered over the screen. "I know what that one was, and I know what that one was."

The woman looked up, smiling. "Here you go. Car 22 left the garage three hours and twenty-four minutes ago. It's on Highway 90, thirty miles west of Spokane, heading west toward Seattle. Right about there…"

The map on the wall shifted, and a red flashing dot appeared on it. The woman continued to type, and the satellite image zoomed in on a black car racing down a highway. The two remaining screens flashed to video, one showing Cam driving the vehicle and the other a view of the road ahead.

"Good work," Irenic said, her voice taking on a predatory note. "Can you shut off that car?"

The woman typed on the keyboard, and the vehicle rolled to a stop. Cam stared at the dashboard in consternation, turning the key several times to no effect. He slammed his hand against the steering wheel, hopped out of the car, and then started walking westward down the highway.

"Excellent," Irenic said. "Keep the satellite on him and send out four choppers. We'll be in the fifth." She looked toward Erica, smiling grimly. "This shouldn't take long."

Erica shook her head, sighing.

"What?" Irenic said.

"What was it you said to Eve? Something like, 'Are you that dumb?'"

Irenic stared at Erica for a few seconds, and then winced.

"Yeah, exactly," Erica said, feeling almost giddy from the combination of the adrenaline and finally being one step ahead of Irenic. The others in the room looked at her in confusion. "If he's had control over your security systems for weeks without you knowing, you can be certain he's broken into your other systems too. And he can create fake videos of himself in his room, so he can create fake videos of himself driving. And mess with your satellite. In fact, I'd bet Ian's life that Cam isn't anywhere near Spokane."

"What?" Ian said. "Bet my life?"

"It's just something I value a lot. I'm saying I'm confident I'm right."

"Oh. Because that's not how I heard it."

"Don't worry. I won't recklessly gamble you away like I did with my last boyf—" Erica broke off as the vision raced through her head. "Oh, dear."

Without any other warning, all the lights, TVs, and monitors shut off, leaving them in complete darkness.

"Damn," Sergeant Irenic said.

CHAPTER TWENTY-NINE

"This sucks," Eve said.

"At least Cam won't be able to see what we're doing now," Ian said.

"Infrared cameras," Irenic muttered. "He can see everything. Does anyone have a mobile phone?"

"Mine's dead," said a voice.

It was followed by a chorus of "Mine too".

"How incompetent are you people?" Irenic sounded disgusted. "Are you telling me Cam's taken over every phone in the bunker?"

"We don't know that." Erica was pretty sure the voice belonged to the woman in the unicorn shirt. "Technically, we only know that he's controlling the phones of everyone in this room."

"Shut up," Irenic said. "We have no time for that kind of smart."

"I'm just—"

"I said shut up."

"Oh."

After a few seconds of silence, Irenic said, "He's decided that throwing us off the trail won't work. So now he's trying to slow us down."

"That's good. It means we're making progress," the suited man said.

"I assume the regular phone doesn't work?" Irenic said.

After a thump and a scraping sound, a male voice said, "No dial tone."

"Of course," Irenic said. There was a quiet click. "Sergeant Irenic here. Lois, can you hear me? Over." The only response was static. "Lois, are you there? Over."

"The signal from those walkie-talkies can't propagate underground," unicorn woman said.

Irenic sighed, but when she spoke again, her tone was firm. "Erica, Ian, Morrison, and Eve. You're with me. We're going upstairs."

"What about us?" said a male voice.

"Figure out how he's doing all this and fix it." Erica couldn't see a thing, but could hear Irenic's glare. After a few footsteps and thuds, Irenic got the door open.

Unlike the operations room, the corridor had an emergency light near the elevator. Just enough of its light seeped through the doorway to allow the others to find their way out with no injuries. They assembled in front of the stairway door with Irenic still carrying the hydraulic breaching tool.

Dim emergency lights also lit each landing in the stairway. But despite that blessing, Erica despaired.

Cam was too smart. Even if they escaped the bunker without being gassed, he'd eventually figure out a way to get to them. The only way to be sure, to be truly safe, was to find him, and that would take a miracle. If Cam wasn't in his room the first time they checked, he had been gone for hours. Long enough to drive to Battlefield, certainly. But he could be anywhere. Even if Seattle was discounted, he could be at Boise, Salt Lake City, or a dozen smaller towns by now. And every minute that passed expanded the list of possible destinations. Without Jeemoh's surveillance equipment, finding him seemed impossible. They needed to narrow down the search radius.

"How did you first figure out that Cam had hacked the security systems?" Erica asked.

Irenic remained silent, not even glancing her way.

"You said he was harder to detect than Renee. If he was so good at covering his tracks, how did you figure it out?"

Irenic continued to ignore Erica.

Letting her frustration show wouldn't help. "I'm not asking because I'm curious. I'm asking because, if I knew how you found him last time, maybe he made the same mistake this time as well. Maybe it can help us figure out where he is."

Irenic stopped. She looked at Erica and shrugged. "If Cam was watching, I suppose he already knows. A year ago, your mom got worried about electronic attacks. She saw our digital security as a vulnerability, so started adding non-electronic security measures. Cam was able to erase all his electronic footprints, but in some places, we have cameras. Not digital cameras. Old, film-based cameras. Nothing but light and chemicals. We got a photo of him entering a secure room."

Erica sighed. "I guess that's no help in locating him now."

Irenic shook her head. "No. We have ways of finding people. Traffic cameras, GPS, cell phone triangulation. But it's all digital and the computers are down. And even if they weren't, we can't trust anything that goes through our systems." She began climbing the stairs once more.

"So what are we going to do then?"

"Use non-computerized resources. We have people and non-computerized technology. Figure out how to find him, Erica."

"What?"

"I need to get us a vehicle. You're lucky. Find him by the time we're ready to roll."

Erica exchanged glances with Ian, baffled about how to even approach the problem. "But—"

Irenic's tone was as uncompromising as ever. "Life isn't about excuses. It's about finding a way to do what's necessary. Even if it's impossible. So figure it out. Or throw a dart at a map on the wall. With your luck, you'll probably be right."

Erica nodded, internally cursing the lie she'd told about her ability being good luck.

Where would Cam go? Battlefield was the most likely destination, but there was no way to be sure.

They stopped at the second floor. Irenic didn't bother trying the lock, but deployed the hydraulic breach immediately. The door opened onto the familiar parking garage. Erica glanced at the ceiling. It had the same tiny ventilation holes that were on every other floor. Was there chlorine here as well?

Ian saw where she was looking and squeezed her hand. "It'll be fine."

Erica nodded.

A man in dirty coveralls ran toward them, but Irenic kept walking, heading toward the main exit. "Get me a van. An old one, without an onboard computer. Disable all its tracking, cameras, and remote control devices. Nothing computerized at all."

"That'll take an hour or two," the mechanic said, trotting beside Irenic to keep up.

"You have five minutes. Smash the computers with a wrench if you need to."

The man, looking like he was about to argue, saw the expression on Irenic's face and gave a quick nod. He turned away, vanishing behind a door in the corner.

With the rest of them still in her wake, Irenic entered the guardhouse beside the exit. It was big enough to fit a desk, several chairs, and a cabinet, and still leave room for all of them.

"Have any teenagers left tonight, Jenkins?" she demanded of the armed guard sitting there.

"Yeah," the guard said laconically. "The bald guy with the hand. He took car 22, a black four-door sedan."

"Why did you let him go?"

"He was authorized."

"By whom?"

"I don't know. I'd check, but the computer's down."

"How long ago?"

Jenkins glanced at a logbook and then his watch. "Three and a half hours."

"Open the door. We're leaving."

"The computer's down."

Irenic swore. "The garage door's computer controlled?"

Jenkins nodded.

Irenic stared at the breaching tool for a few seconds and then at the reinforced-steel garage door. It was a hopeless mismatch.

"Is there another way out?" Erica said, nervously running her tongue over her lips. No wonder Cam projected such a high fatality rate from the gas.

"Not for a vehicle. I'll take care of it. You find Cam." Irenic walked to the door and held up the hydraulic breech, flipping it as if trying to work out a way to secure it firmly enough to batter down the door.

"Do you know how many times Cam's left here? By himself, I mean," Erica said to the guard.

"I can check. He left and re-entered at least one other time when I was on duty."

"When?"

"Let me look." He paged through the logbook. "Three days ago."

"For how long?"

"Four hours, twenty minutes."

"Any other times?"

After a few seconds of staring at the paper, he said, "About two weeks ago. And three days before that. All about the same duration."

The man continued to page through his log until he reached the beginning. "That's it for this one. It only goes back to April."

"That's enough," Erica said. "Thanks." She turned to the others. "My theory is that he went out to get electronics to cannibalize for his prosthetics. And chocolate. Probably to Battlefield since it's got to be the closest town. Any other reasons he might have gone outside tonight?"

"He might be trying to escape," Morrison said, glancing through the window. "Now that Irenic's out for blood."

Ian shrugged. "Or maybe he went to see someone? Like his parents?"

"He sounded pretty frustrated at the vice principal for the zero-tolerance stuff. He might be going after her," Eve said.

Erica nodded. "We can call his parents and the vice principal." She turned to the guard. "Pass me your phone. And can you get me the phone numbers for all the Fletchers who live in Battlefield?" Erica glanced at the computer, grimacing. "Is there a phone book, by any chance?"

"Won't work," he said. "Phone went down with the computer."

Erica growled. "This is impossible."

"We could go to Battlefield and drive around," Eve said, a dubious expression on her face. "It'll be slow, though."

"If Irenic can even open the door," Erica said. She stuck her head out the door. "Sergeant, is there a way that our twelve billion dollars' worth of technology can communicate with even one of our agents in Battlefield?"

Irenic nodded. "Sure. Most of them have ham radios. They should still work."

"Ham radios?" Erica said.

"Like CB radios but with a longer range."

"And they don't use computers?"

"No. They're unhackable. They're used during natural disasters when the phones go down."

"Can we use one to talk to Cam's parents? And Vice Principal Taritha from Battlefield High?"

"Probably Cam's parents. Taritha isn't a Jeemoh agent as far as I know. Jenkins can help. I need to get this open." She stared at the steel door for a few more seconds, pounded her fist on it several times, tossed the hydraulic breaching tool to the side, and walked deeper into the garage.

Erica turned back to the guard. "Jenkins?"

He nodded, spun his chair, and opened the door of the cabinet behind him. Inside was a narrow shelf holding a radio and an attached handset. He pressed a button and adjusted several dials. The buzz of static filled the air.

"These don't work like phones," Jenkins said. "Everything is broadcast. So, everyone who has a radio with Jeemoh encryption can hear what you say. Our radios have been modified to beep when we want to talk. All agents within range will have their radios ring, and you'll be talking to everyone who picks up."

"Got it," Erica said.

Jenkins pushed an orange button on the radio and passed her the handset. "Hold the button when you want to speak. Release it when you want to listen. Wait for about thirty seconds. You're waking everyone up."

Erica nodded. "I wonder if Cam is listening," she said to Ian.

"Best to assume he is," Ian said.

"And even if he isn't, he's probably watching through the cameras," Eve added, glancing at the ceiling.

"Try it now," Jenkins said.

Erica lifted the microphone to her mouth. "Hello? Is anyone there? I'm looking for Cam's parents."

"*Who is this? Over.*"

"This is Erica. Erica Trestle."

"*Lois' daughter? Over.*"

"Yeah. Who am I talking to?"

It took almost five seconds before the speaker replied. "*This is Greg Fletcher, Cam's father. What do you want? Over.*"

"We're looking for Cam. He attacked some people and left unexpectedly. We're worried he might be a threat to you. Have you seen him?"

"*You must mean a different Cam. Over.*"

"No, it's the same guy. He's changed a lot in the last month."

There was another long pause. "*We haven't seen him. Over.*"

Erica's face fell. It had been a slim hope, but the best they had. She looked toward the others. "Any ideas?"

Eve's lip curled. "The car, maybe?"

Erica nodded, turning back to the radio. "We think he's driving a black sedan. Do you see anything like that on the street?"

"*Just a sec. Over.*"

Erica released the button on the microphone. "What's the license plate number on car 22?" she asked Jenkins.

Jenkins riffled through some papers. "KSRJ22"

"The license plate is KSRJ22," Erica said. She pulled a chair in front of the radio to wait.

A loud motor broke the silence. Erica instinctively covered her ears.

"That mechanic must have ripped out the muffler when he disabled the tracking stuff on our van," Ian yelled.

Erica nodded, not even trying to speak over the roar.

The shriek of metal against concrete was like a knife in Erica's brain. The ground began to vibrate.

"I don't think that's a car," Morrison said, barely comprehensible over the din.

"No, it's—" Jenkins began. His eyes widened. "She wouldn't."

"I don't know what you're thinking. But if you're talking about Irenic, let me assure you, she would," Ian shouted.

A tank rumbled out from behind one of the dividers in the garage. As it swung around the last corner before the door, it accelerated. The clatter the treads made upon the concrete made Erica's teeth vibrate.

"Take cover!" shouted Erica. Still covering her ears, she scrambled behind the desk.

The tank was still speeding up as it slammed into the steel door with a horrendous crash. The door proved almost as tough as the tank, bending only slightly. On the other hand, the concrete that was holding the door in place proved inadequate. The walls on either side of the door exploded, showering the garage with rubble. Several huge chunks of concrete smashed against the anti-ballistic glass window of the guardroom, leaving white marks.

The tank slowed, but continued moving, pushing the door a few feet before bumping over its slightly twisted remains.

Erica rose. The smell of diesel permeated the air. All the vehicles closest to the door had shattered windows and dents. One had a jagged boulder the size of a microwave embedded in its hood.

"*Erica, are you still there?* Over." The voice from the radio was insistent.

Erica went over to it and picked up the handset. "Yes, sorry. I was distracted. Go ahead."

"*Focus, Erica. I won't wait around while you browse Facebook or tweet pictures of your breakfast. Over.*"

Erica raised her eyebrows at Ian. He shrugged.

"Yeah. Sorry," Erica said into the microphone.

"*I said that the car isn't here. Over.*"

"*Break.*"

Erica looked at Jenkins.

"Someone else was listening in, and they want to speak," he said. "Say, 'Go ahead, break'."

"Go ahead, break."

"*Hello, Erica, how are you? Over.*"

Erica recognized the voice but couldn't place it. "I'm doing well," she said cautiously.

"*That's great. I haven't seen you in ages. Over.*"

"Sorry, who is this?"

"*Why, it's Rose.*" Rose had been Erica's neighbor for years. She'd been ancient when Erica was in preschool. "*Your mother updated me a few weeks ago about what you're doing. It sounds exciting. Over.*"

Erica rolled her eyes, shaking her head at Ian. "It is, but this really isn't a good time to catch up."

"*Oh, of course. I'm sorry, darling. I just broke in to say I've seen that car you're looking for. Over.*"

Erica jerked upright. "What? Where?"

"*It's here right now. Parked on the street outside your house.*"

CHAPTER THIRTY

Erica's heart was pounding, but she fought to stay calm. "How long has it been there?"

"*I don't know. I've been asleep, dear. Over.*"

"The driver is extremely dangerous. Stay inside. Don't let him see you. We'll handle it."

"*Roger.*"

Irenic walked back through the broken entranceway. Erica ran out to meet her.

"Got the door open," Irenic said blandly.

Erica barely registered the comment. "Where's Lois?"

"Probably in her office."

"You're sure she's not at home?"

"I called her in when Cam broke into our server room. She'd be here by now. Why?"

"Cam's car is parked in front of my house."

Irenic stared at Erica for a few seconds. "We're leaving now." She spun around and peered into the garage. "Where's my van?" she bellowed.

"'Fix the van. No, fix the tank. Now fix the van.' Calm down and give me a second," came a shout from deep in the recesses of the garage.

Irenic turned to the others. "Plan A is to convince Cam to surrender. If that fails, Plan B will be for you to immobilize him, Morrison. Use your ability to put him on the ground and keep him there. Plan C, if Morrison fails, is to subdue or—if necessary—kill

Cam. Erica and Ian will work as a sub-team, and Eve and me. The only person here who could have a hard time incapacitating Cam at close range is Erica. But her luck should help her accomplish that, or at least get Ian close enough to do what's needed."

"What about weapons?" Eve said.

"Cam's immune to Javelins, and you've barely begun your gun training. You can use your natural weapons."

"I'd rather have a gun." Eve's gaze was challenging. "We need to defend ourselves."

"Armor is defense. Jujitsu is defense. Guns are for killing," Irenic said, waving a hand dismissively. "Morrison should be able to immobilize Cam. A bunch of untrained people running around with guns only increases the chance of someone dying."

"I disagree," Eve said, thrusting her chin out.

"I'd feel safer with a gun too," Morrison said.

"Noted. Anything else?"

"My dad is probably there," Erica said softly.

Irenic nodded. "Try not to kill Erica's dad."

A van roared up from around the corner and skidded to a stop in front of the twisted ruins of the front gate. The mechanic hopped out. "Done. It's not the prettiest work and—"

"Let's go." Irenic didn't even make eye contact with the mechanic. She jumped into the driver's seat and the others piled into the back.

Though Erica was sure that Irenic was speeding, the drive to Battlefield seemed interminable. Without windows in the back, the only signs of progress were the centrifugal force as the vehicle turned a corner and the sound of the occasional car zooming by in the other direction. Erica's legs quivered like she needed to run. Ian put his hand on hers.

Finally, the van stopped, and the side door opened. "We're a block away," Irenic said. "Erica, you're our scout. We'll be twenty feet behind."

Erica nodded. She'd be in the lead again, but it was better than being entombed in the bunker death trap.

The sidewalk was too exposed, so Erica crept from yard to yard, keeping close to the houses and hiding behind the shrubbery. The neighborhood was deserted, but the streetlights still shone brightly enough to allow Erica to navigate over fences and through gardens with little difficulty.

She was two houses from her own when she realized that the car Rose had claimed was parked on the street wasn't there.

Had Cam tricked them again? Had he somehow imitated Rose's voice over the radio to lure them here? Rose's house, on the far side of Erica's, was dark, showing no sign of activity.

If Cam was behind Rose's messages, was this a diversion or a trap?

Erica looked back at the others, gestured toward where the car should have been, and held up her hands questioningly. Irenic nodded, waving Erica forward.

Her muscles tensing, ready to react in an instant, Erica kept moving. At least if Cam had set a trap, she'd know before she triggered it.

Passing the last two houses, Erica hugged the wall, knowing from countless childhood games that from inside her home, it was impossible to see someone on this side. Finally, she reached the last gap. Taking a deep breath, she sprinted to the base of her house.

She froze there, listening, but there was no sign that anyone had seen her. Erica turned around to face the wall, preparing to peer through a crack in the curtains into the living room.

Black on grey. A man in a chair, struggling.

Despite the vision, Erica popped her head up to look. She squinted, willing her eyes to pierce the darkness.

After a few seconds, she was certain. It was her dad. And he wasn't struggling. He was writhing.

Erica ducked back down and pressed her back to the wall. She gestured to the others, indicating one person.

This must be a trap. Cam expected that she'd see her dad suffering and mindlessly charge forward. Only an idiot would fall for such a transparent ruse.

On the other hand, she could see the future.

Erica mindlessly charged forward.

She leaped up the two steps of the front stoop, reaching for the door handle.

Crackling. Her body jerking sideways, slamming into the wall.

Cam had rigged an electrical booby trap on the door handle. No problem. Irenic had taught them front kicks.

She kicked the door, but misjudged the distance and didn't get full power. The door shuddered, but didn't open.

"What are you doing?" Irenic hissed from the bottom of the stairs. "We're supposed to be discreet."

"My dad's in there." Erica adjusted her stance, ready to try it again.

The door slamming open. Two buckets spraying. Liquid washing over the floor.

"On second thought, Cam's probably booby-trapped the door," Erica said. "Don't even touch the handle."

Irenic looked in the window while Erica lifted a football-sized rock from the garden. "Get out of my way."

"Wait, Erica," Irenic said.

"No. The door's got to be booby trapped, so I'm going in through the window. If Cam's in there, he already knows we're here." She hefted the rock in her hand. It was going through the window whether Irenic moved out of the way or not.

Irenic stepped back. "Only throw hard enough to break it. Don't hit your dad."

Erica nodded. Out of the corner of her eye, she glimpsed movement from Rose's house. Turning, she saw Rose peering at them from a side window. Erica waved her away impatiently, and the face vanished.

Erica took a few seconds to figure out the effects of throwing the rock at different speeds and contact points, and then hurled it. The window shattered as she expected. Without surveying the effects of her work, she used another rock to push aside the shards on the windowsill before boosting herself up and in.

She wanted to go directly to her dad, but she needed light. She flipped the switch in the entranceway, noting as she did two buckets filled with clear liquid on the floor against the door and a wire leading from a power outlet to the door handle.

The rest of the living room was tidy, everything in its place, as if her dad had just finished cleaning up. In the center of the room, between the TV and the couch, Philip was tied to a dining room chair, gagged with duct tape and writhing. Sweat dripped down his red face, but he appeared unharmed.

"Dad!" Erica ran over to him and tore off the tape.

"Erica," Philip gasped.

The pain in his voice hit Erica in the gut. She circled the chair, scrambling to release his hands, but the duct tape was solid. "Knife," she shouted at the others.

Irenic was climbing in through the window. Without pausing, she reached down to her ankle, produced a knife, and tossed it toward the wooden leg of the chair.

Erica caught the weapon and slashed through the tape. The instant she did, her dad slammed his hands down on his thighs and folded in half, still groaning.

"What's wrong? I can't see anything," Erica said.

"My legs." Philip was shaking. It was clearly all he could do to get the words out.

Erica moved to his right foot. She cut through the tape to release it. His socks felt wet.

She paused for an instant, gasping as the vision crashed through her brain. She sliced open the right leg of his pants, from ankle to knee.

Philip's leg was a mess of blackened skin, blood, blisters, and half-dissolved flesh.

Erica sat down heavily on the floor. "No! What is this?"

"Cam." Philip wheezed, trying to say more, but he was unable to.

Irenic glanced at the leg and turned back to the window. "Eve. A medical kit's under the passenger seat of the van. Run."

The sergeant took the knife from Erica's loose grip, freed Philip's other leg, and cut away the cloth there, too. It looked no better. She pulled up the hem of his shirt, and then replaced it.

Ian climbed through the broken window. He took one look at Philip and turned his head away, covering his eyes with one hand. He sat down on the floor beside Erica, hugging her head.

"Why did Cam do that?" Erica said, her voice breaking. "My dad didn't do anything."

"Information or punishment. That's what it's used for," Irenic said grimly.

"What?" Erica said. She pushed Ian away, standing up in front of Irenic. "You know what this is?"

Irenic nodded. "The Petite Gourmand."

"What's the antidote?"

"No antidote. It's an engineered version of necrotizing fasciitis. Accelerated flesh-eating bacteria. The treatment is a knife." Irenic's brusque tone seemed more forgiving than usual.

"A knife?"

"Removal of the infected flesh."

"We have to… cut it out? Amputate my dad's legs?"

Irenic shook her head. "No. It's in his torso."

"Then what?"

Irenic walked over to the window, fragments of glass crunching beneath her boots. She peered outside. "Everybody dies sometime, Erica."

"We have to save him! He's my dad." Erica clutched her father's hand.

Irenic had no response. She helped Morrison through the window. Eve was just stepping into the yard.

"We need to get him to the medical printer," Erica said, her voice shrill.

"Too far," Irenic said. She took a white box from Eve and placed it on the couch. She riffled through it, pulled out a syringe, and plunged it into Philip's hip.

"What's that?" Erica said.

"It'll take the edge off the pain." Irenic returned the empty syringe to the first aid kit

Erica grasped Irenic's arm. "We need to do something."

"We are doing something," Irenic said. She tugged her arm away from Erica and surveyed the room, her eyes coming to rest on Ian. He was looking anywhere but at Philip's legs, but still seemed like he was about to faint or vomit, or both. "Ian, dispose of those buckets. Don't mix the liquids. Don't touch the wire."

Ian struggled up to his feet and went over to the door. He peered into each of the buckets. "Ammonia and bleach, I think. If you mix them, they form a poisonous gas."

"So don't mix them," Irenic said. "Morrison, find pliers with insulated handles and disarm the electrical trap."

"We don't have time for that," Erica said, shaking Irenic's arm. Why was no one doing anything to help? "We have to save my dad."

Irenic just looked at her levelly. Ian picked up the buckets and headed out of the room with Morrison in his wake.

"I don't think I'll make it, honey," Philip said, his voice raspy.

"Jeemoh has healing technology. We can save you."

Philip looked at Irenic. She shook her head.

"How long have I got?" Philip asked.

"Twenty minutes to unconsciousness," Irenic said. "Thirty, thirty-five minutes to death, at the outside."

"We can save you, Daddy. Just hold on." Erica turned to Irenic. "We need to get him in the van." She tried to put her arms under her father's legs and lift him, but he was too heavy. Tears slid down Erica's face. "Help me, Sergeant. You can carry him."

Philip gripped Erica's hand, pulling it toward his chest. "It's not going to happen. I'm sorry."

"I can't lose you." Erica sobbed.

Philip wiped her cheek with his fingertips. "I'm sorry. I love you."

"I love you too."

Philip stared at her as if he were burning a snapshot of her upon his brain. Then he shook his head and winced.

"Does it hurt?" Erica said.

"Only a bit. Not as much as it did."

It sounded like a lie. Erica squeezed her eyes shut, holding her dad's hand.

Irenic knelt in front of Philip. "We don't have much time, and we need to talk. It could be important to your wife and daughter."

Philip nodded.

"Tell me what happened. What Cam wanted."

Philip squeezed his hand into a fist, hard enough that his fingernails drew blood. "Lois left in a rush. Fifteen minutes later, Cam broke in." He wiped away a drop of sweat that was about to fall into his eye. "A knife came out of his arm. He threatened me, so I let him tie me up. I figured I could talk him out of doing anything too bad.

"He wanted to know about Jeemoh. I said I didn't know much. So he poked each of my feet with a needle. It didn't seem like a big deal. Didn't hurt much at all. Until it did.

"Cam promised me the antidote if I cooperated. So I told him about Jeemoh. About Lois. Everything I knew. He wanted to find Lois, but all I knew was that she had left. But it wasn't enough for him. He kept demanding more answers, to understand every detail of Lois' life, everything about Jeemoh. He wouldn't accept that I wasn't part of it. And then, it hurt so much I couldn't talk, just beg. I think he finally believed me then, because at that point, he apologized and told me there was no antidote. And then, he left."

"So he was searching for Lois? Anything else?" Irenic said.

"Information about Lois and Jeemoh. That's all."

"Okay." Irenic rose. Morrison had returned with pliers. Irenic seized them from him and ripped out the wire connecting the power outlet to the door handle.

"It... still hurts," Philip said, his voice wavering. "Is there anything else you can do for me?"

Irenic walked back to where Philip sat. She crouched in front of him, her eyes fixed upon his face. "I have no other drugs."

Philip stared at her for a few seconds, and then bowed his head. "I understand."

Irenic nodded slowly. "I believe you do." She walked away from him, opening the front door. "Erica, I'm sorry, but we need to go now."

"No." She was going to lose her dad, but she certainly wouldn't let him die alone. She'd be with him to the end.

"Cam's going after your mother."

"Jeemoh can protect her." Erica put her arms around her father and pushed her face into his shoulder.

"Against him, it might not be enough."

Philip stroked his daughter's hair. "You have to go. Lois needs you."

Erica's face twisted. "I don't want to. Please don't make me," she begged.

"You must," Philip said. "Please, Erica."

Erica stood up. She wiped the tears from her eyes, although her chin still quivered. "Okay. I'm sorry. I want to stay."

"I know."

Ian came forward, put his arm around Erica's shoulders, and steered her to the door. As she reached it, Erica looked back.

"Goodbye, Daddy."

Ian led Erica down the stoop, past Eve, and onto the path going to the street.

"I can't save my dad, Ian. I want to so much, but I can't," Erica wailed, her palms over her face.

"I know."

"It's the abilities. If we didn't have them, if we'd never heard of Jeemoh, everyone would still be alive."

Ian nodded.

"We should just leave. Run away. Forget about Jeemoh, about

everything, and—"

A gunshot shattered the calm.

Erica turned back to the house. Irenic appeared at the door. She passed the first aid kit to Morrison, closed the door behind her, and continued down the path toward them.

Erica froze, her face blank with shock and agony. "You just killed my dad."

Irenic brushed by her. "Cam killed your dad."

Erica stared at Irenic's back for a few seconds. Then, her lip firmed. She nodded, rubbed her eyes, and strode after Irenic.

"Cam killed my dad."

CHAPTER THIRTY-ONE

"I'm sorry, Erica," Ian said, holding her hand as they followed Irenic along the sidewalk, halfway between a walk and a run.

Erica shook her head, her expression empty. "Cam killed my dad. Not you."

"I know, but... I'm sorry. That's all."

Erica frowned. "We don't have time for this." The rest of the block passed in silence.

Irenic reached the van and opened the side door. Morrison got in, followed by Ian. Erica looked back. Eve had been lagging and had stopped about thirty feet from the vehicle.

"Hurry up, Eve," Irenic said.

Eve shook her head somberly. "I'm not going back. Jeemoh's not for me."

Irenic glared at her. "Stop wasting time. Lois is in danger. Get in the van. Now."

"I've made up my mind, Sergeant." Eve's voice was quiet but firm.

"You need the medical printer. You'll bleed to death without it."

"Not if I avoid using my ability." Her lip curled. "Jeemoh's the only reason I've been using it at all."

"This is your job," Irenic said.

Eve shrugged, backing away. "Then I quit. The pay sucks anyway."

"You can't quit. It's your duty."

Eve smirked. "Duty. Yeah, right. Whatever." She glanced behind her, moving more quickly. "I think Lois is more important than me, so I shouldn't delay you. With your systems going haywire, I doubt you'll be able to find me, but please don't try. If I change my mind, I'll find you." She waved casually, turned, and vanished into the darkness.

Irenic peered in her direction for a few seconds. Finally, she shook her head and turned to Erica. "Get in."

Erica slid the side door shut. "This time, I'm driving."

"What? No."

"We're in a rush. My mom needs help, and we don't have time to argue." Erica's tone was flat, analytical.

"I'll drive fast. Get in the van."

"I'm driving." Erica sprinted to the driver's door, her ability helping her elude Irenic's grasp. She hopped into the driver's seat and locked the door.

"Are you crazy?" Irenic said.

In a distant part of her brain, Erica noted that, for once, she seemed to have thrown Irenic off balance. She gestured at the passenger seat. "Get in."

Irenic glared, but slid in beside her, nudging aside the broken fragments of a ham radio on the floor to make room for her feet. "You're slowing us down. I have a decade's experience in stunt driving and racing."

Erica nodded. "And I got my learner's permit four months ago. But I'm lucky." She pressed a button on the dashboard with an icon of a microphone. "Put your seatbelts on."

"They can't hear you. The electronics are disabled. Here." Irenic fiddled with a latch on the wall behind them, sliding open a small panel. "Put on your seatbelts," she said through the hole.

"Why are you in the passenger seat?" Ian said. "Who's...?" His eyes grew wide. He turned to Morrison. "You should hold on."

"Erica's not a good driver?" Morrison said.

"Well, I imagine she's the safest driver we have. But you should hold on anyway."

Erica took the keys from Irenic and started the van. She pressed down on the accelerator. The engine roared, but the van only crept forward. She pushed the pedal all the way to the floor, but the speedometer remained under fifteen. The noxious smell of burning oil permeated the cabin.

"Parking brake," Irenic said.

"Oh." Erica lifted her foot. She looked between the seats for the brake release, but it wasn't there.

Irenic sighed. "Pull the handle on the left, under the dash."

"Of course," Erica said.

"We're going to die, aren't we?" Morrison whimpered.

"No, no. We'll be fine. She's never killed anyone," Ian said. "I mean, never killed anyone accidentally." He paused. "Well, except at school, but that was an accident."

Erica stomped on the accelerator. The van surged forward. Morrison screamed.

"Head toward Alder Street," Irenic said. "Left up here." She gripped the handle above the door, but she didn't seem the least bit fazed.

Erica looked ahead, didn't see any problems, and so took the first turn at forty. She only eased up on the accelerator for a second.

By the next corner, they were going seventy.

The van slipping sideways. Hitting the curb. Tumbling.

Erica jammed her foot on the brake. Down to fifty-five.

Barely keeping the van vertical. Losing control at the end.

Hitting a car.

Erica braked even more. Forty-eight. That was safe. She accelerated coming out of the corner.

After about two minutes, they left the residential area and swung onto a boulevard. Her tires slipped as she hit the corner at fifty-eight, but she didn't run into anything, so didn't bother slowing down.

"Good driving," Irenic said.

The sounds of vomiting came from the back. Erica knew it was Morrison.

The major artery had the advantage of width, but also other vehicles and stoplights. Erica found that in the low-density night traffic, with a few adjustments to her speed, she could zoom through red lights untouched.

Erica glanced at Irenic. "What direction?"

"Head west." From Irenic's body language, they were only out for a quiet Sunday drive.

Before they reached the main highway out of town, Erica had avoided sixteen collisions with moving vehicles, seventy-two with various stationary objects including an inflatable gorilla, and one with an intoxicated pedestrian. Much of the time, her speedometer had been over a hundred.

On the highway, Erica was disappointed to find the van topped out at 125 mph. Even so, they reached the headquarters in a fraction of the time it had taken going the opposite direction.

Erica was half-expecting to see people waiting outside the bunker, but it was deserted. "They still haven't evacuated," she said. Either that, or Cam had gassed the place while they were away.

"A calculated risk," Irenic said blandly. "If he was planning to use the gas, he would have done so already."

Erica nodded, steeling herself as she drove over the broken door, careful to avoid the largest pieces of rubble. She felt her stomach clench as she passed the threshold into the danger zone, but at least she wasn't trembling anymore.

Just past the entrance was Cam's dark sedan.

"We should stay outside," Morrison said. "It's too risky going in."

Erica stopped behind Cam's car and turned to speak through the hole. "Cam's here. He won't discharge the gas when he's in the building."

Morrison snorted. "Says you."

"Says me too," Irenic said as she slid open the side door of the van. "We're going in."

Morrison scowled, but he undid his seatbelt. "Fine," he spat out. "You won't be happy until you kill us all, will you?"

Irenic just shrugged it off. "This is the job, Morrison."

Morrison gave Irenic a dark look, but she ignored it.

Erica clicked off the headlights. The garage was pitch dark, so she turned them on again.

"Cam probably smashed the emergency lights. Morrison, there should be a flashlight under the backseat. Erica, go ask Jenkins for his. I'll get that," Irenic said, gesturing toward the hydraulic breach she'd discarded earlier.

Erica nodded, setting off toward the guard station. She frowned as she realized what was bothering her. If Jenkins had a flashlight, wouldn't they be able to see its light already? Erica sped up.

She knew Jenkins was dead seconds before she saw the body. Just inside the doorway, he lay prone in a pool of his own blood, his hands clutching his neck.

"Jenkins is dead," she announced, surprising herself with how measured her voice was.

Irenic swore. "Did you check his pulse?"

Erica knelt beside Jenkins, tugging at his arm to get to his wrist. Moving his hand revealed a deep bloody slash across his neck.

"No, but I'm sure."

Ian came up behind Erica, took one look at the body, and spun around. "I'll help Morrison." He looked pale as he retraced his steps.

Remembering her original goal, Erica scanned the area. A few yards away was a flashlight, its bulb shattered.

"His light's broken," she said.

Irenic came up behind her, carrying the hydraulic breach. Avoiding the blood, she rested her hand against Jenkins' cheek. "It's only been ten minutes. We have to go."

"Where?" Erica said.

"Lois' office."

Morrison had located one flashlight in the van. Ian suggested searching the other vehicles for more, but Irenic preferred to leave immediately.

"Our top priority is to secure Lois," she said as they jogged toward the stairway. "Those incompetent geeks probably haven't regained control of our security system, so assume Cam can see us. Lethal force is authorized."

"You mean, we should kill him?" Ian said hesitatingly.

"If necessary."

Ian shook his head. "He'll talk to us. We don't need to kill him."

"Yes, we do," Erica said flatly. And she intended to be the one to do it.

Ian stopped and turned to her. "Erica, I know that—"

Irenic seized Ian's collar and pulled him around so that his face was inches from hers. "Cam's murdered two people already. If we lose any more because you're an idiot, I'm going to break your fingers and then watch you clean up everyone he's killed using nothing but a spatula and a soft-bristled toothbrush." She thrust him away.

Ian glanced at Erica, his expression like an injured puppy. But if he were looking for sympathy, he'd have to look elsewhere. Cam had tortured and murdered her dad, and Ian wanted to go easy on him?

Ian must have seen something on her face, because he sighed and turned away, following Irenic toward the stairs.

Erica nodded. Irenic might not have convinced Ian, but she had cowed him. And if that was what it took to make him do what they needed to do, well, that was good enough for Erica.

"Bloodthirsty psychos," muttered Morrison, so low Erica wasn't even sure she heard him correctly.

"What?" Erica's eyes were frigid.

"Nothing." Morrison took one last glance at the garage door before vanishing into the stairwell.

The stairwell was dark and stank of blood. When Cam amputated his leg, the odor had been distinctive but subtle. This time, in the closed confines of the stairwell, it was overwhelming, like a newly painted room.

"What's that smell?" Morrison said. "Is it gas?"

"Blood," Irenic, Ian, and Erica said in unison.

Irenic nudged Erica toward the stairs. "Erica."

Feeling queasy from the odor or maybe just nerves, Erica took the lead, stepping around the shards of glass from the broken emergency light. Irenic's flashlight was powerful, illuminating most of the stairway. Even so, Erica would have preferred to have her own light.

On the second landing down, they found the first bodies. Or rather, body parts. The beam swept over the area swiftly, but Erica thought that, even had the lights been on, it might be difficult counting how many Jeemoh soldiers had died here.

"He either acquired weaponry or replaced his smoke grenades with something heavier," Irenic observed.

As if to confirm her words, the stairwell lit up for an instant. Seconds after the flash, the sound of gunfire echoed. Erica crouched against the wall and covered her ears, but in the enclosed space, her hands barely softened the irregular percussion of the semiautomatic handguns.

The commotion trailed off after about thirty seconds. Irenic tugged on Erica's arm, pulling her to her feet and shoving her into the lead.

Though Erica's vision still hadn't readjusted after the flash, she continued down, guiding herself with the handrail. She felt something wet. Without thinking too hard about it, she wiped her hand on the wall.

The next landing was empty other than a few remnants from above. Erica kept her eyes firmly pointed down the stairs.

The next level had two bodies bearing contusions and knife

wounds. Did that mean that Cam had used up his grenades, or did he just not want to waste them against only two opponents?

"Lois' office is the next level," Irenic whispered.

For an instant, Erica stuck her head over the railing to try to glimpse what was below. The stairwell looked empty. Crouching against the wall, she crept down, ready to dive the instant her visions showed a threat.

Finally, she was close enough to bob her head out to look at the landing. The walls were pitted by bullet holes, but there was no sign of blood, and the landing was empty. She heard a gunshot, and then another.

Erica raced down to the landing and turned the handle of the door. Locked.

"Sergeant, we need this open," she said.

By now, Irenic was an expert. In seconds, she had positioned the breaching tool and forced open the door.

Erica counted five soldiers in the corridor beyond. Each had several thin, knifelike blades jutting from their bodies. Three looked dead, but two were still conscious.

"He's in here. Quickly," Lois called from inside her office. Another gunshot echoed.

Ian dashed to the closest soldier. He knelt down beside him, and then looked back to Irenic. "I don't know what to do. Should I take them to medical?"

"Ignore them," Irenic said without a second glance. "Come with me." Raising her gun, she darted down the corridor toward the open door of the room where Lois had briefed them several days ago. "We're coming, Lois," she hollered.

"Cam's fast. He been shooting knives out of his arms and legs," Lois said from inside the room. "He's wounded, but I don't know how badly."

"I'm fine," Cam said as another gunshot sounded.

"Does he have a gun?" Erica asked.

"The gun's mine," Lois said.

Irenic nodded. She shone the flashlight into the room. She pointed at Erica, made a fist, and began counting down from three using her fingers.

As Erica was about to charge into the room, a vision crashed through her head. She would be killed instantly. She made an adjustment and thought it through a second time. Again, she had a fatal outcome. With a few more changes, she was ready.

She turned the corner and immediately ducked. Cam's artificial arm hissed, and then a spike cut through the air where Erica's head had been an instant earlier. She didn't pause, but danced to the right to avoid the second projectile.

Cam had a wound on one shoulder. Blood dripped down his arm, but it didn't look too bad. The spikes embedded in the desk made it clear where Lois was hiding.

Cam fired two more projectiles from his left arm, both of which Erica dodged easily. She started making her way toward him.

"You're clairvoyant, right?" Cam asked, as if she were still his friend. "Not lucky."

Now he'd said it, denials seemed pointless. "Yeah."

"I, um, don't think it matters. I don't think you can stop me."

She wasn't going to stop him. She was going to kill him. She didn't know how, but she'd find a way.

"We really just want to talk," Erica said, continuing to advance.

Lois peering out, pointing her gun. Cam's Javelin shooting out.

"No! Mom!" shouted Erica.

Lois stuck her head out from behind the desk, but Cam's right arm was already raised in her direction. The prong of a Javelin shot out of Cam's forearm, embedding itself in her neck. Lois shook and fell back behind the desk. The flashlight she had been holding went out.

"We can talk after I'm done with Lois," Cam said. He retracted the Javelin's cable and crept toward the desk to finish the job.

"Erica," Irenic said, nothing but business.

Without taking her eyes off Cam, Erica raised her hand to catch the knife Irenic threw.

She positioned herself between Cam and the desk, holding up the weapon, finally confident enough in her position to let her anger show. "I can stop you, Cam. I can replay this scene a hundred times and choose the future where this knife ends up in your eye."

Cam stared at her, and then took a few steps back. He kept his right arm pointed at Erica, and his left arm at the door. "Um, yeah. I don't want that." He studied her face for a few seconds. "Erica, you should be on my side."

"You're trying to kill my mom," Erica said through gritted teeth.

"You massacred twenty guys just to get in here."

"Yeah, but they were all bad people."

"What?" Only the distance kept Erica from plunging the knife into his chest then and there. "You think you're the good guy in all this?"

"I am. I didn't use the gas. I didn't kill everyone. I just did what was necessary."

"You tortured and killed my dad!" Erica was trembling with rage.

The light was dim, but Erica could swear that Cam was blushing. He looked down at the floor. "I'm... um, sorry about that. I was just trying to find Lois, and... you know. She got the call and left, but your dad was still there, and I was almost at your house anyway. I figured he had to be involved somehow."

"You killed him, Cam. He died in agony!"

"I'm sorry." Cam shivered. "I... didn't make that bacteria. It seemed like poetic justice. Well, um, at least until I realized that he wasn't with Jeemoh."

"Torturing someone isn't poetic. What you did to him was way worse than anything Vince ever did to you. Way worse."

"I... Yeah. But... just let me explain. I know so much."

"Fine," she spat out. "Tell me." She'd use the time to get close enough to strike.

The second she said the words, Erica was hit by another vision. "Back off, Irenic," she growled.

Irenic ignored her. She swung out from behind the wall, raising her gun. Three metal spikes sprung from Cam's arm. The first missed. The second pierced Irenic's chest. The third went through her gun hand and into the flashlight.

Irenic fell, and the room was plunged into darkness.

"I wonder," Cam said.

Darkness. The hiss of Cam's weapon.

Erica threw herself to the side, but without the benefit of sight, her timing was off. The spike took her in her left shoulder. She ripped it out, not even feeling any pain.

Hiss. Hiss.

She desperately rolled and heard two spikes ricochet off the ground beside her.

It was too close to be luck. He must be able to see in the dark.

And that meant, Erica realized, she was completely vulnerable.

CHAPTER THIRTY-TWO

The killing spike didn't come.

Darkness. Thwack.

That wasn't a spike, but she'd heard that sound before. What was it?

Erica was dodging again almost before she figured it out. It was a Javelin hitting flesh. Her flesh.

The prong pinged as it struck the floor beside her leg, but Cam didn't pause. Almost immediately, Erica could hear the muffled whirring of the Javelin retracting.

Cam's artificial foot clicked against the concrete. Was he advancing on her or targeting Lois?

"Ian, I need light. Now," Erica shouted.

"Just a sec…" Ian's voice came from somewhere near the door.

Erica scooted back on her hands and knees, away from where she'd last seen Cam, knowing it was hopeless, but trying to gain an extra few seconds. "Now!"

A dim green light. A looming form. A spiked foot kicking.

And then, the room wasn't quite so dark and was getting brighter by the second. Cam was right there. Erica barely had enough time to deflect his kick with her forearm.

But now she could see… and she still had her knife.

On her sixth vision, she figured out how to stand up without being stabbed, kneed, punched, or otherwise maimed.

Cam backed away a few steps, giving her a chance to catch her breath. Erica glanced at Ian. His hands were glowing bright green.

"Thanks," she said. "Careful of the Javelin."

Cam raised his arm toward Ian and the Javelin shot out. The prong collided with the cement plate that suddenly appeared on Ian's chest. Before the weapon could retract, Ian's glowing hand slashed down. A blade materialized, severed the Javelin's wire, and disintegrated.

"No problem," Ian said.

"Darn." Cam retreated while Ian and Erica advanced.

Irenic lurched to her feet. She slammed her fist against the wall, driving the spike right through her hand. It clattered to the floor. Then, bleeding profusely, she pulled the second spike out of her chest. She rose to her feet, looked around for the gun, and, not seeing it, staggered toward Cam.

Erica put Irenic out of her mind. The sergeant didn't matter. She and Ian should be able to take out Cam before Irenic was even close. They needed to be cautious, but Cam was in trouble. It shouldn't matter how fast and strong he was. She was armed, and Irenic had taught her the key vulnerabilities of the human body. As long as Ian kept the light on, it would be over within seconds of her getting close enough to use her knife.

Erica crept forward slowly, not because she was scared, but because she knew the only way they could lose was if she rushed and made a mistake.

"I wasn't trying to kill you. I used the Javelin," Cam said, continuing to back away.

She shook her head. He'd shot three spikes at her. "You ran out of ammo."

"They really are bad people, Erica," Cam said. Erica had heard him use the same cajoling tone with Vince in the playground. It hadn't worked then, either.

The circular bone saw popped out of Cam's metallic arm, whirring.

Erica ignored it as she stalked her prey. She had no intention of allowing him to land a single blow before she cut his throat, so Cam's weapon was irrelevant. She focused on keeping light on her feet, just as Irenic had taught her.

"You're really going to destroy Jeemoh?"

Flinching, Erica glanced to the side. Morrison was standing in the doorway.

Cam nodded. "It has to end."

"I agree," Morrison said.

"No, Morrison!" shouted Erica as the vision coursed through her mind. She considered leaping forward to attack, throwing the knife at Cam or Morrison. But she was too far away, and they were prepared. In the end, she just lowered her body, bracing herself.

Her feet went out from under her as all friction disappeared. Ian fell heavily beside her. She couldn't turn to see Irenic, but Erica was pretty sure she was down too.

"Morrison," Ian shouted. He tried to climb up to his knees, or at least turn around, but he ended up just flopping like a stranded fish.

"Sorry, man." Morrison truly sounded regretful. "If I thought you'd see reason… But, with your girlfriend and everything, that won't happen."

"But why? Look at everything Cam's done…"

"Ian, you told me how Jeemoh tortured you." Morrison laughed without mirth. "Heck, we've watched the home videos of it. And they created those bacteria that killed Erica's dad. Cam's right. These are bad people. Jeemoh just wants to use us. They don't give a damn about our opinions. The only thing that matters to them is that we follow their orders. Irenic threatened to break your fingers just because you didn't want to murder Cam."

Erica tried to turn. She pushed Ian lightly. He spun one way, and she the other. For a few seconds, she was facing Morrison and Irenic. Once again, she considered throwing the knife. But it wasn't a throwing knife and without a way to brace herself, she couldn't see how to make a killing blow from her stomach. Even worse, if she flipped over to try to get more leverage, Morrison would see the knife and disarm her. She rotated 360 degrees, stopping herself when she came face to face with Ian again. Her shoulder wound left a perfect red circle on the floor.

"So let's figure out what's wrong with Jeemoh and fix it," Ian pleaded. "We don't need to fight."

"I already know what's wrong," Cam said. He gestured toward the desk where the unconscious Lois still lay. "Her. This is all her. Without Lois, Jeemoh crumbles."

Morrison nodded. "Then we eliminate Lois."

Cam took a wide berth around Ian, Erica, and Irenic as he walked toward the desk.

Erica's face twisted in anguish. For the second time today, she'd see one of her parents die. She and Ian were helpless. They couldn't stand, couldn't fight back. Without something to brace themselves against, they could do nothing but spin.

Something to brace themselves against.

Erica looked intently into Ian's eyes. "Drill," she hissed.

Ian looked at her for a second, and then he gave a barely perceptible nod. He touched his fingertips to the cement floor. A little cone of white powder grew around each finger. Erica blew the dust away. Now Ian's fingers were a quarter inch into the floor, now a half inch. The rate at which he ripped the molecules from the floor increased. His fingers sank into the cement as if it were sand.

"You use these," Ian whispered. He pulled his hands away and began excavating a second set of grips. Erica used the handholds to swing her body around beside Ian. She glanced warily at Cam and Morrison, but they were looking behind the desk.

"I don't think I can do it," Morrison said. His discomfort was clear on his face. "I've never even hit a woman before."

"She deserves it," Cam said, as if he were discussing what to have for lunch. "Think about the people she's hurt. Your old team. Everyone in the Gauntlet. Denise."

"I know. But still. I don't even know how I'd do it."

"I'll, um, do it. Okay?"

"Yeah. I guess so." Morrison stepped back.

Cam started moving around the desk.

Morrison was the bigger threat. Erica played out the scenarios in her mind and settled on one.

"I'm Morrison. You're Cam," she whispered to Ian. Without waiting for a response, she pulled back on the handholds that Ian had made, and then heaved her body forward.

The floor was slipperier than ice. With no friction, Erica slid silently. She considered slashing Morrison's Achilles tendons as she approached, but realized that she didn't need to.

Erica slammed into the back of Morrison's knees. His legs flew up, and he toppled over backward. The back of his head smashed into the concrete with a sickening crunch. Scrambling to her knees, Erica raised the knife to plunge it into Morrison's sternum.

Then she paused. Morrison was unconscious, and he was still Ian's best friend. Maybe.

She looked for her other foe.

Ian slid to a stop near Cam's feet as the friction returned. "Oh, no."

Cam turned. A spike clicked out from the toe of his prosthetic foot, and he kicked at Ian's head. Ian barely had time to create a steel helmet before the foot struck. The spike that had been aiming for his forehead skittered off the metal and embedded itself in Ian's left shoulder.

Ian screamed. He yanked on Cam's leg, pulling him down and ripping the spike from his own shoulder.

A knife popped out of Cam's arm into his hand. He swung it at Ian's face. Ian was once again able to create a metal plate to deflect the blow, but he underestimated Cam's strength. Though the knife didn't bite flesh, the impact knocked Ian to the side, stunning him.

Cam raised the weapon again.

But he had taken too long. Erica was there. As Cam's weapon descended, Erica touched it delicately with her own knife, just enough to deflect it. Cam's knife skidded off the concrete floor half an inch to the side of Ian's neck.

Before Cam could regain his balance, Erica followed up with a knee to the side of his head. Cam collapsed beside Ian, unconscious.

Erica looked down on Cam's limp form.

This wasn't Morrison. This was the boy who had tortured and killed her dad. Tried to kill her mother and her boyfriend. Heck, he had even tried to kill her.

He could release the gas the instant he woke. He was a threat to her friends as long as he lived. There was only one outcome here. And he deserved it.

Erica raised her knife.

The knife swinging toward Cam's temple. Ian's steel-coated arm deflecting the blade.

No. She couldn't let Ian stop her. Whatever Ian was thinking, he was wrong. Cam needed to die. She stared down at her foe and cycled through the alternatives.

Swing the blade as fast as possible.

Ian was there.

Slit his throat.

Ian grasped the blade itself.

Stab him in the eye.

Ian blocked that too.

Her jaw set, Erica ran through as many ways of killing Cam as she could think of. Every time, Ian foiled her.

She stared at her boyfriend, her eyes wild. What was he thinking?

"Let me kill him," she said.

"No."

"He killed my dad. He would've killed you."

"No."

"Please."

Ian shook his head. "No, Erica."

Irenic staggered toward them and leaned against the desk. "Ian's right." She was clutching her wound, the blood from her chest and her hand intermingling to drip down her side. "We only kill when necessary." She coughed, spitting blood upon the floor.

"It is necessary." Erica's voice was feral.

Sergeant Irenic shook her head. Erica glared at her, but Irenic didn't concede an inch.

"Damn you. He deserves to die." Erica finally wavered and broke. Tears running down her face, she turned back to Cam, bracing his head against the floor. She slowly lowered the knife toward the back of his head.

"Erica…" Ian said, raising his hand to only inches from her wrist.

"I promise. I'm not killing him." Erica eased the knife's edge against the bulge on the back of Cam's head.

Then, she sliced the phone from his skull.

Cam shrieked.

CHAPTER THIRTY-THREE

Renee's funeral was three days later. Irenic escorted Erica, Ian, and Jen to a conference room near Lois' office. A closed coffin rested on a table only slightly bigger than the casket itself. Lois and a soldier were already standing in the corner.

"You brought security?" Erica asked her mother.

Lois shook her head. "Howell wanted to be here."

Erica had never seen the man before in her life. "Why?"

The soldier stuck out his hand. "Private Jim Howell. Renee's primary monitor."

"Her primary monitor?"

"In the Gauntlet. I watched her. We aren't supposed to get attached, but you know how it is, right? I was cheering for her, all the way through. I was upset when I heard."

"Oh." Erica took a few steps away and turned toward the coffin. She had never thought about the people behind the cameras. What did her monitor think of her?

"They didn't come," Ian said, his face drooping.

"Who?"

"Mom and Dad. In the end, a security guard cared more about Renee than they did." Ian's voice was flat.

"Maybe they didn't know," Erica said. "Maybe nobody invited them."

"They knew," Ian said quietly. "They didn't care."

Erica pulled him into a hug.

Irenic stood at the front of the room. "I was Renee's commander, so my job is to speak for her." She cleared her throat. "Renee was one of the best fighters I ever knew. One of the best at everything, actually. But for her, that wasn't enough. Because character always matters, and that's what Renee lacked."

Erica stared at Irenic in shock.

"Renee didn't have the courage to face the future," Irenic continued. "So now, she won't. She squandered her potential, more than anyone else I've ever known. For that loss, I grieve." Irenic looked down for a few seconds before scanning the room. "Anyone else want to say anything?"

"I do." Erica released her grip on Ian and strode to the front of the room. She stared at Irenic as she spoke. "Renee isn't a case study in squandered potential, and she wasn't a woman afraid of the future. She was dying, and she knew it. Maybe not in the way that everyone else dies, but dying nevertheless."

Erica turned her gaze to the others in the room. "By the end, Renee had forgotten everything. Her family. Her friends. Everyone was gone, except me, and she knew I'd be gone soon too. Even early on, she knew what it would be like to lose her memory. She had the knowledge—the life experiences—of everyone. All the amnesiacs. All the patients with dementia. All their doctors. All their families. She knew how it was, from every perspective that mattered. She didn't want to wake up every day, alone, not knowing where she was. Not knowing *who* she was. Existing, but not living.

"So while she was still herself, still capable of making the choice, she decided not to exist that way. Decided to leave on her own terms."

Erica stared at the coffin on the table. "I just wish she'd chosen differently. I love her and hate that she's gone." Brushing aside a tear, she scanned the faces around her. "That's all I have to say."

Erica returned to Ian's waiting arms. Ian wasn't crying, but his eyes looked empty.

"Anyone else? Ian?" Irenic said.

Ian nodded. He disengaged from Erica to stand near Irenic. "Renee and I didn't always get along. We were brother and sister, so of course we fought. But even during our biggest squabbles, I never doubted Renee was a good person. That she'd have my back when I needed her. That she'd help anyone in need.

"I remember once when she was young, no older than four. It was the day after Christmas. I'd got a remote-controlled helicopter, and Renee had gotten this doll she'd seen in the store. To me, it didn't seem like anything special, but she loved it. Anyway, that afternoon, we got too rowdy, so our parents made us go outside. Renee took along this doll and started pushing it on the swing in the playground behind our house.

"This other girl, Sue, came by, and they started playing with the doll together. On the swings, the slides, even on the flying fox. Eventually, Renee asked Sue what she got for Christmas, and she showed her the winter boots she was wearing.

"Renee was baffled. For her, Christmas was about toys, and she couldn't figure out why Sue had gotten boots. So she asked her. Sue said her parents didn't have enough money for toys, but she needed boots, so that's what she got.

"After that, Renee was quiet. And that was unusual for her. I think it was the first time she realized that some people didn't have the things we did. She continued playing, but was distracted.

"Then after about half an hour, she ran back to the house. Morrison and some other kids had arrived, and we were playing grounders, so I stayed behind.

"By the time I noticed that Renee had returned, she'd already been talking with Sue for a while. Sue was holding a radio-controlled helicopter, her eyes shining.

"It turns out that Renee felt so bad that Sue had got nothing good for Christmas that Renee gave her the helicopter. My Christmas present.

"Sue looked so happy to get it, and the helicopter wasn't as fun as it seemed in the store. So I didn't say anything. I asked Renee later why she didn't give Sue her doll instead. Using the logic of a four-year-old, Renee said she would miss her doll if she gave it away, and that it would make me sad. And she didn't want to make me sad."

"It was selfish. No more than you'd expect from a preschooler. But her heart was in the right place. She saw someone hurting, and did her best to help, even if she messed it up a bit.

"I know everyone here is thinking about the way she died. And that's understandable. But I won't remember her for that. I'll remember her for what she was."

#

"So have you figured out how he did it?" Lois said.

Lois had invited Irenic, Erica, and Ian to something she called a post-mortem. After a few minutes of listening to the conversation, Erica decided that it was just a discussion of what had gone wrong on the night of Cam's attack.

Dara Marshall, IT Security Lead, and Martin Karth, Director of Operations—otherwise known as pink unicorn woman and suit man from the operations center—were also in attendance.

"Not everything," Dara responded. "But we will. Few of Cam's hacks are fully automated. Without him guiding the effort to thwart us, it's much easier for us to figure out what he was up to."

Erica rubbed her lower lip. "How was he doing it at all? Mom said his data usage had plateaued at a low level. How was he able to take over Jeemoh without even using the network?"

Dara looked questioningly at Lois.

Lois nodded, saying, "In this meeting, you may talk freely. Erica and Ian have proved themselves trustworthy, and it's impossible to do this post-mortem without open discussion."

Dara turned back to Erica. "He hacked every system in Jeemoh. The problem was that we could only detect his intrusions by looking for clues on a compromised machine. But whenever we looked, he wasn't showing us the true state of the system, but rather what he wanted us to see. So, even though he was transferring massive amounts of data, we couldn't see it. Nothing looked wrong."

Ian shook his head. "That explains why *you* didn't notice, but if he was transferring so much data, surely someone outside would."

"You're underestimating Cam's scope," Dara said, shaking her head. "He didn't restrict his attacks to Jeemoh. We estimate he corrupted something like forty-to-sixty percent of the backbone networks that make up the main links on the Internet. It enabled him to hide his outside activity."

"With just a cell phone?" Erica said, shaking her head in confusion.

"The phone was only a means of connecting to the Internet. That's where he did all the real processing. Computers on the Internet effectively became Cam's brain. That's how he got so much smarter—by doing massively paralleled computation across a network of millions of computers, all managed by a direct neural interface."

"So to summarize," Lois said, "Cam used all those computers on the Internet to crack our systems, and he compromised us to the extent that we didn't even realize there was a problem. Our electronic security failed completely. He could've killed us all."

"It's embarrassing to say, but yes, that's a fair assessment," Dara said. "If you want my resignation, you can have it."

Lois waved the suggestion away. "This sort of scenario was why we implemented non-computerized security measures. In a way, the experience was valuable in showing us how vulnerable we still are to such attacks."

"I agree," Dara said. "In fact, I already have some ideas—"

"This meeting isn't about finding solutions," Martin said, his tone firm, bordering on condescending. "Let's stick to the post-mortem." Dara's face turned pink and her lips thinned.

But, before she could say anything, Irenic said, "Yes. Our systems failed, but our tactics were equally horrible." She stared at Martin, not even blinking. "A single person reached Lois' office almost unscathed."

Martin's eyes darted toward Lois, and then back to Irenic. "Cam had extraordinary abilities. It's hard to predict every threat."

"If you, as director of operations, can't anticipate someone with abilities trying to invade Jeemoh, you probably lack the imagination needed for that role."

"But…" Martin glanced at Lois, who was watching the exchange coolly. "Well, your point is well taken. Henry—who was in charge of the tactics on the ground—would have some thoughts, but he passed away. I'll talk with Jenna about it. She's responsible for physical security, you know. She should really be in this meeting."

"You do that," Irenic said. "I'll be happy to review any plans you come up with."

"Oh. Yeah. It would be great having your help," Martin said. Keeping his head down, he scribbled in his notepad, clearly too busy recording his ideas to continue the discussion.

"The other big oversight was Morrison," Lois said. "His betrayal was surprising, considering his history. He didn't face the Gauntlet, and, after quitting following his first mission, he actually sought me out to rejoin Jeemoh. Morrison claims allying himself with Cam was a spur-of-the-moment decision. But we need to investigate whether he simply was misguided or was a mole planted by an enemy. You're on that too, Martin."

Lois turned to Ian. "Martin may need your help. Morrison might say things to you he wouldn't to us."

"No problem," Ian said. "But I'm pretty sure it's as he claims. That he was angry and confused. With his ability, he had plenty of opportunities to kill you, but he didn't."

"He might have been delaying because he had a larger goal than assassination," Lois said.

Ian shrugged. "Maybe. But I doubt it." He frowned. "What about Cam? Do we have any insight on why he went psycho? Could we convince him to discuss the holes in our security?"

"Cam had a persecution complex. He blamed us for his time in the Gauntlet and couldn't see beyond that," Lois said authoritatively. "That's why we allow people weeks to decompress after discovering their abilities in the Gauntlet. Some people have violent reactions. Cam was different only in that he hid his anger more effectively and longer than any other candidate." Lois glanced over at Martin. "We should review those processes too."

Martin nodded, but didn't look up, writing furiously.

"Getting his help is an interesting suggestion." Lois appeared to consider the idea for several seconds. "He could be useful, and I hate to waste any resource. The problem is he claims he has amnesia and that he doesn't want to talk. At least, not to anyone but Erica."

Erica had been half dozing, but was suddenly wide awake. "He wants to talk to me? Why?"

"He claims he wants to apologize. But it could be a trap. We've eliminated all his weaponry and X-rays show him as clean. But maybe he has one last trick up his sleeve."

"I'm not scared," Erica said darkly. "He can't surprise me."

Cam's revelation that Erica's ability was clairvoyance, not luck, had resulted in a long, uncomfortable conversation between Erica and her mother. Lois insisted that Erica should have no secrets from her. Erica maintained that the difference between luck and clairvoyance didn't matter, and that Lois had a hundred times more secrets than she did anyway. Lois shouldn't expect Erica to share every detail of her life.

Finally, they had agreed that, if Erica knew anything that could impact Jeemoh or a mission, she'd inform her mother. Or at least, Lois had decided they'd agreed to that. Erica reserved the right to use her own judgment.

Lois smiled. "Yes, I'm not worried. Only considering every alternative. He could have useful information, I suppose. How do you feel about trying out some *Practical Persuasion?*"

Erica didn't care to hear Cam's apology. There was nothing he could say to make her forgive him for torturing her dad to death. But Lois had a point. After everything he'd been through, everything he'd done, he might tell her something useful.

And, after she learned everything she could, she and Cam would be alone, with Ian and Irenic—Cam's protectors—far away.

Erica nodded. "I'm in, if you supply the chicken wings."

CHAPTER THIRTY-FOUR

"Do you have any electronics?" the soldier said.

Erica shook her head. He was the fourth person to ask. Her mother had gone over all the rules while the elevator descended the thirty floors to the prison below the Gauntlet.

No electronics. Don't touch him. Don't allow him to touch you. Focus on the goal. Promise anything to get the information you need. Always remember he's a cold-blooded murderer who hates you.

Like she'd forget that last one. If anything, the problem was getting the image of her writhing dad out of her head.

Other than the tape tugging against her skin, Erica could barely feel Hack's pen against her left forearm, hidden by her sleeve. She didn't have the poison that Hack recommended for assassinations, but Irenic had taught her how deadly a simple pen could be. And the pen's concealed needle should only make it bite deeper.

It would be bloody, but it wasn't like she needed to be subtle.

The soldier led them into a small room with two guards and four chairs, all facing a wall with a curtain and a door.

"We'll watch through the one-way glass," Lois said. "The door will be unlocked. If you have any problems—or are about to have problems—alert us or slap your leg. We will intervene immediately."

Erica nodded. She'd heard it before.

The guard unlocked the door with a key attached to his belt. He held it open for Erica to enter, and then shut it behind her.

The room was smaller than her bedroom at home. Cam lay on a bed pushed up against the far wall.

Cam looked wretched. Two IV bags hung beside him, dripping fluid into his veins through a needle embedded in his leg. Black stitches crisscrossed his face like a demented patchwork doll. Though he was shackled to the bed, similar stitches darkened his arm, marking other sites where Lois had forcibly removed embedded electronics. Cam's prosthetic arm and leg were gone, leaving stumps ending in bandages. Another bandage, going around Cam's head, hid the damage caused by Erica's knife. That bandage bulged out obscenely above his empty eye socket. Similar egg-sized lumps distended the skin on his forearm and collarbone.

Only Cam's secret drug cocktails had held his cancer at bay. Now that he didn't have them, how long would he last? From the look of him, days.

"Erica." Cam's voice was rough.

"Hi. My mom said you wanted to talk to me." Erica kept her tone engaged, but distant, an acquaintance exchanging pleasantries. She couldn't stomach sounding like a friend.

"Yes." Cam closed his eyes. "They say I killed your dad."

"You don't remember?"

"No. I think I regretted it though. I'm sorry. For doing that." Cam was trembling.

"But why? There was no reason to kill him." Erica's voice wavered slightly.

"I really don't remember."

"You killed my dad. You changed everything for me. How can you not even remember?" Despite her best efforts, anger seeped into Erica's tone.

Cam didn't seem to notice. He sniffed, but it wasn't enough to keep mucus from dripping out of his nose. He smeared it away with the back of his hand. "I've forgotten a lot. All that's left is numbers and letters."

"What?"

"172.24.193.43.4.EA62C847. That's all I remember of your dad. Almost anything I try to remember is like that, starting from a few days after Lizzy."

"Almost everything?"

"I remember the floor plan here. I remember—" Cam looked at the door. "We're alone now, right? Is anyone listening?"

"I don't think so. I asked for privacy," Erica lied. "And if you whisper, they probably can't hear you even if they are listening."

Cam swallowed, and then said, "Jeemoh's bad, Erica. They're like Vince, only worse." His voice was low, but still well above a whisper. "I hate your mom."

"What did she do? Why do you think Jeemoh's bad?" Erica asked gently. She wouldn't believe anything he said, but one of the first steps in any interrogation was getting the subject talking.

"I don't remember."

"Cam, I need details."

He struggled to sit up, awkwardly levering himself up with his one good arm, wincing as he did. "I don't have details. I did before. Everything I saw. But now, it's just numbers. Mission logs: 172.27.132.58.1.F38329AA. Raymond: 172.27.145.21.1.942BCB23. Politics: 10.94.83.234.2.662AF3FC2. Room 903: 172:16.4.68.1. F5A33681. Denise: 172:16.4.68.1.F5A3DA29. It's all like that. Every time I think of anything."

"That's meaningless gibberish, not evidence." Erica sighed, trying to look sympathetic. "I understand, Cam. You feel bad about what happened, and you're looking for an explanation. You blame Jeemoh for Denise's death in the Gauntlet. I did, too. But there was no other option. The Gauntlet was the only safe way to elicit people's abilities. Jeemoh's making tough choices for the greater good."

Cam fell back. "Maybe Denise wasn't their fault. But what about me? I'm your evidence. Lois did this to me. I used to understand everything. I remember that much. I was strong and smart. I was going to fix everything wrong with the world. But she chopped me up with her scalpel. She cut off my leg, my arm. Poked out my eye.

"Erica, she took everything. Even my brain. I can't calculate a square root. I don't even know what a square root is." Tears dribbled from Cam's eye. "Would a good person do that? Transform me into… this?"

"You did all that to yourself," Erica said, her voice harsh. "You've forgotten, but my mother wanted to treat you. Instead, you sawed off your own leg. Plucked out your own eye."

Cam's face collapsed even further.

Erica looked away for an instant, and then back at him, her mouth set. "And Lois didn't take your brain. I did. With my knife."

Cam stared at the wall, wiping his cheeks with his upper arm. "I'm sorry I hurt you, Erica. I never meant to," he murmured.

"Well, you did."

Cam sat silently, and then drew in several shuddering breaths. "I'm not sure if you know, but I'm sick. Like, enough to miss school for a week or even longer." Cam gestured to the lump on his temple. "This feels like needles sticking into my skull. And I think I inhaled thumbtacks. They jab me whenever I breathe. That doctor says the liquid in the bags is medicine, but it hasn't helped."

"I thought your ability could block the pain."

"I don't remember…"

"Oh."

"Could you do me a favor? Just because I'm sick?"

Erica almost snorted at his brazenness, asking for her help after what he'd done. But Lois said to agree to anything to get the information they wanted. "Maybe. What is it?"

"Talking to my mom always made me feel better. Can you get me a phone?"

Of course not.

Erica nodded gravely. "Lois said that I can fulfill any reasonable request, if you help us out."

"What do you want?" Cam asked, the first spark of hope in his eyes.

"Can you tell us about the holes in our computer security? To patch things up?"

Cam shook his head, his uncertainty clear. "I can try, but I don't know much about that stuff. Not anymore. Maybe you could use drywall?"

"Drywall?"

"My dad patched a hole that way."

"I don't think that's what they were looking for." Erica shrugged. "It's probably just as well. I doubt I could convince them to give you a phone again."

Cam's shoulders slumped. He put his arm over his eyes as his shoulders shook.

He knew nothing. She had all the information she would get.

Erica slid her right hand over to the pen taped to her arm. She held down the button until the needle popped out, scraping against her skin.

"Oh…" Cam sounded close to weeping. "One other thing. It's not much…"

"What?"

"Drugs. Can you get me a pill to stop the pain? Something better than what they're giving me now? It hurts so much. All the time."

Erica stared at him levelly.

"I wouldn't need much, if it's expensive. Even if it's just a few hours a day."

Erica nodded minutely.

"Or just at night. So I can sleep." Cam looked exhausted, like the conversation had sapped his last reserves of energy. Trembling, he rotated his shoulder, wincing as he did. Even the slightest movement seemed agonizing.

Cam was no threat to anyone anymore. A quivering mass of mangled flesh just waiting to die. Although, he wasn't smart enough to realize it.

The way he was suffering, killing Cam now would be a mercy.

"Please, Erica," Cam begged. "Can you do something?"

She contemplated Cam's one remaining eye for a few long seconds and made her decision.

She had no space left in her heart for mercy.

"No."

Erica turned and left the room.

#

"Huh. So he really had amnesia," Ian said, placing the tablet and a pad of paper on the floor beside their bed. As part of the ongoing post-mortem, he had just finished watching Erica interrogate Cam.

Erica nodded. "We got nothing from it. Except verifying Lois' theory that he has a persecution complex. He blames Jeemoh for everything that happened, even stuff he did himself, like cutting off his own leg. I think he just doesn't want to accept responsibility for his own actions."

"It does seem that way. I'm surprised we didn't see it though. To be angry enough to kill." Ian shook his head. "I feel like we let him down by not realizing how upset he was and talking him through it."

"We were here, ready to talk, every day. But he didn't want to talk to us. We couldn't have done anything."

"Maybe not. I still feel bad, though." Ian pursed his lips. "Why did you refuse his request for anesthetics?"

"I'm sure the pain is no worse than what my dad went through," Erica snapped.

Ian looked down, swallowing. "Yeah."

Erica's face softened. "Besides, I'm not a doctor. Lois is in charge of his medical care. She'll give him what he needs."

Ian brightened. "That's true." His eyes darted to the tablet. "The one thing I don't understand is the numbers and letters he mentioned. What do you make of them?"

"I talked about that with unicorn woman—Dara. Her guess was that they were the addresses of computers where Cam had stored his memories." Erica shrugged.

"Hmm." Ian picked up the tablet, rewound the video, and played it a few times, transcribing the words and numbers onto the pad. "Who's Raymond?"

"I don't know. But I don't think it matters," Erica said. "Even with those addresses, there's no way we'll be able to access that data. In the *Practical Persuasion* midterm, he said his encryption was unbreakable."

"Good point. I find it interesting, though, because those numbers are his explanation for what he did. Why he attacked Jeemoh."

"He also attacked my father, and he wasn't involved in Jeemoh at all. It's not like he required much of a reason to murder someone." Erica couldn't keep the bitterness out of her voice. "Heck, Denise is on that list of 'explanations,' and we know exactly how she died. Only a complete psycho would use her death as justification for torturing my dad. It's just Cam rationalizing murder."

Ian rested his hand on hers. "It's okay, Erica. I'm not defending what he did. I was just trying to understand why."

Erica nodded, took a deep breath, and smiled. "Sorry. I don't mean to overreact. But it's simple. Power corrupts. Cam was always the weakling, never able to fight back. Then, when he suddenly wasn't, he decided to act out his revenge fantasies on the people who had wronged him, my mom and Irenic. That's all it was."

Ian nodded. "I suppose you're right. Still, it makes me... I don't know. Sad." Seeing Erica's expression, he quickly added, "Not for him. But for us. Cam's in rough shape. If he dies, then of the six of us who entered the Gauntlet together, we're the only ones left."

"I never thought about it that way." After a pause, Erica sighed. "I miss Renee."

Ian hugged her. "Me too."

Three days later, Lois told them of Cam's death.

If you enjoyed this novel, please consider leaving a review on Amazon.

ABOUT THE AUTHOR

R.B. Gibbons has a tech background, founding several companies and creating an artificial personality that failed a Turing test. He loves investing, to the extent that he invented his own automated stock-trading algorithm and, for several years, wrote freelance articles for investment website *The Motley Fool*.

He lives in Vancouver with his wife, two children, and too few dogs.

Blog & Mailing List: http://rbgibbons.com